K.D. Richards is a native of the Washington, DC, area, who now lives outside Toronto with her husband and two sons. You can find her at kdrichardsbooks.com

New York Times and *USA Today* bestselling author **Bonnie Vanak** is passionate about romance novels and telling stories. A former newspaper reporter, she worked as a journalist for a large international charity for several years, travelling to countries such as Haiti to report on poor living conditions. Bonnie lives in Florida with her husband, Frank, and is a member of Romance Writers of America. She loves to hear from readers. She can be reached through her website, bonnievanak.com

Also by K.D. Richards

Guardians of Justice
Killer on the Potomac
Death by Data

West Investigations
Catching the Carling Lake Killer
Under the Cover of Darkness
A Stalker's Prey
Silenced Witness
Lakeside Secrets
Under Lock and Key
The Perfect Murder

Also by Bonnie Vanak

Rescue from Darkness
Reunion at Greystone Manor

Colton 911: Chicago
Colton 911: Under Suspicion

SOS Agency
Navy SEAL Seduction
Shielded by the Cowboy SEAL
Navy SEAL Protector
Her Secret Protector

Discover more at millsandboon.co.uk

OVERDUE JUSTICE

K.D. RICHARDS

COLTON'S FIRESTORM

BONNIE VANAK

MILLS & BOON

All rights reserved including the right of reproduction in whole or in part in any form. This edition is published by arrangement with Harlequin Enterprises ULC.

This is a work of fiction. Names, characters, places, locations and incidents are purely fictional and bear no relationship to any real life individuals, living or dead, or to any actual places, business establishments, locations, events or incidents. Any resemblance is entirely coincidental.

Without limiting the exclusive rights of any author, contributor or the publisher of this publication, any unauthorised use of this publication to train generative artificial intelligence (AI) technologies is expressly prohibited. HarperCollins also exercise their rights under Article 4(3) of the Digital Single Market Directive 2019/790 and expressly reserve this publication from the text and data mining exception.

® and ™ are trademarks owned and used by the trademark owner and/or its licensee. Trademarks marked with ® are registered with the United Kingdom Patent Office and/or the Office for Harmonisation in the Internal Market and in other countries.

First Published in Great Britain 2026
by Mills & Boon, an imprint of HarperCollins*Publishers* Ltd
1 London Bridge Street, London, SE1 9GF

www.harpercollins.co.uk

HarperCollins*Publishers*
Macken House, 39/40 Mayor Street Upper,
Dublin 1, D01 C9W8, Ireland

Cold Case Cover-Up © 2026 Kia Dennis
Colton's Firestorm © 2026 Harlequin Enterprises ULC

Special thanks and acknowledgment are given to Bonnie Vanak for her contribution to *The Coltons of Dark Canyon* series.

ISBN: 978-0-263-42029-6

0426

Printed and Bound in the UK using 100% Renewable Electricity at
CPI Group (UK) Ltd, Croydon, CR0 4YY

OVERDUE JUSTICE

K.D. RICHARDS

Chapter One

The lock turned with a satisfying click, and Nichol Bunin pushed open the back door of the library. It was only mid-October, but with the breeze, she'd paired a cap with her jacket to ward off the chill, letting the ends of her shoulder-length hair fall below the cap. She knew from the frequency with which she was carded whenever she dined out that she didn't look her thirty-six years. Frequent hikes through the woods near her house and a healthy diet, including the many vegetables grown in her own backyard garden and taste for lemon water, kept her body lithe and her dark brown skin flawless.

She strode toward the front of the library, her footsteps gliding over the stretched carpeting as she flicked on the lights. Row after row of bookshelves illuminated like dominoes. The familiar scent of books filled her lungs, instantly soothing the nerves that had arisen when she'd awoken hours earlier to find that her alarm hadn't gone off. The rainstorms the night before had knocked out the power at some point, which meant she had to rush through her morning routine in order to make it to work on time.

She made her way through the stacks—history, science fiction, romance, each section holding its own treasures—before skirting behind the circulation desk and making her way to her small office. Every surface was covered with books, files, or trinkets gifted by grateful patrons over the years. It was cluttered but familiar. Perfect.

She dropped her coat over the back of her chair and locked her purse in the bottom drawer of her desk. "Time to get this show on the road."

A late start meant she didn't have time to settle in before the library opened.

She stepped out of her office and headed for the sliding glass door entrance, then turned the lock on the doors with a practiced twist and waved a hand over the motion sensor to activate the doors. The mechanism clicked, and the glass doors opened with a gentle whoosh of air. A young man, vaguely familiar, nodded and stepped inside past her.

She headed back to the circulation desk, glancing at the clock on the wall as she did. She'd just made it behind the desk when Lynn Riceny rushed through the door of the library and hustled to the front desk.

"I'm so sorry for being late," she said, her face flushed.

"It's alright, Lynn. I barely made it in on time myself. What's got you so flustered?"

Lynn hung her jacket on the coat stand in a large room behind the front desk area that served as the private office space for all the staff except Nichol, who had her own small office, before stepping back out. "Oh, my goodness. You haven't heard then?"

Accustomed to Lynn's overly dramatic personality, Nichol shrugged. "I guess not. Heard what?"

Lynn glanced around the library, making sure no one would overhear them before speaking. "Some hikers found remains in Galesburg Forest last night."

Nichol jerked. "Remains? As in..."

Lynn nodded vigorously. "As in a dead body. From what I heard, one that has been dead for some time now."

"Wow, that's..."

"Gruesome," Lynn finished with a shiver.

"Are you sure it wasn't just an animal? I mean, if someone had gone missing in Galesburg, we'd have heard about it."

There was no doubt about it. In a sleepy bedroom town, a little more than an hour north of Washington, D.C., like Galesburg—where the residents were wealthy and rabid about keeping up their property values—a missing person would not have gone unnoticed.

Lynn nodded. "I'm sure. I drove past the site on my way into work." Her cheeks pinked. The woods were on the opposite side of town from Lynn's house, but Nichol wasn't surprised that her coworker and friend had taken the long way to work. Lynn was a fantastic children's librarian, but she would have made a dogged reporter or private investigator.

Lynn cleared her throat and lowered her voice a notch. "I took pictures. Want to see them?"

Nichol took an unconscious step away from her coworker. "Of a body?"

"Sssh!" Lynn's head snapped around, ensuring again that they couldn't be overheard. Their lone patron, the twenty-something man, was sitting at one of the long tables situated in front of the stacks with headphones on. He didn't look away from his computer screen. "No, not of the body. I couldn't get that close. And it's not a body. Not really. Like I said, it looks like whoever it was was out there for a while. Like years. It's just bones from what I heard."

Nichol's stomach lurched.

Lynn pulled her phone from her back pocket. Strictly speaking, they weren't allowed to have their phones on them during work hours, but as the head librarian, Nichol was fairly lenient in enforcing that rule. She, Lynn, and her assistant head librarian, Josh, were the only full-time employees of the small public library. There were three other part-timers, all women with children. There was no way Nichol was going to tell them they couldn't be with their phones.

Lynn tapped her phone's screen then moved to Nichol's side so they could view the photos together. As Lynn swiped, Nichol was relieved to see that the photos were from the road and didn't capture anything that might leave her with nightmares. Mostly just trees, the ambulance, and the state police officers assigned to keep the lookie-loos like Lynn back.

"Well, I know it isn't much but..." Lynn let the screen go dark and slid the phone back into her pocket. "Not much happens around here. I wonder who it is?"

Nichol's stomach lurched again, but Lynn seemed not to notice her anxiety as she booted up the circulation desk computer. Lynn was amazing with children, connecting with them in a way that many adults couldn't. But when it came to older humans, she was more than a little oblivious. Her tendency to fail to pick up on subtleties and changes in other people's tones and moods had led to more than one situation that Nichol had to smooth over. But Lynn had a good heart, and she was a good friend.

"Maybe someone from out of town," Nichol answered, even as a voice inside of her screamed otherwise. "You know how people love to come to the Galesburg Forest and hike its trail. A visitor who went out, overestimated their preparedness for the terrain, and unfortunately got lost."

Lynn shot her a look. "Wouldn't we have heard about that? I mean, someone would have noticed if a tourist had gone missing during the season."

Nichol shrugged half-heartedly. "Maybe. Maybe not. If they only came up for a day trip they might not have checked into a hotel or the resort. And if their family or friends didn't know where they'd gone..."

"Maybe," Lynn said, but she didn't look persuaded.

Nichol wasn't convinced either. Even if the poor soul had

only come up for a day of hiking in the woods, they would have had to get themselves here somehow. There was a bus station, but Galesburg was more of a pass-through from the buses, not a destination. At least not for most people. The memory of a teenage girl standing at the bus station fluttered through her mind.

"Nichol? Are you okay?" Lynn's voice jerked Nichol back into the here and now.

She forced a small smile. "Yes, of course. Just thinking about how sad it is for whoever is out there and their family. I wouldn't wish that on anyone."

Lynn shook her head sadly. "Me either."

The sliding glass doors of the library swooshed open, interrupting their conversation, and a gaggle of toddlers ran inside followed by their harried mothers.

"That's my cue," Lynn said, stepping away from the front desk and heading to the rear of the library where the children's section was located.

Tuesdays and Thursday mornings they held the Toddler Tales program, a project that Lynn had spearheaded that involved reading, role playing and other creative activities for toddlers. In the six months since they'd begun the program, the number of attendees had grown so much that they'd had to institute a registration system to keep the library from being overrun with screaming three-year-olds.

Nichol spent the next hour and half helping patrons check out books and find resources. Once Bethany, one of the part-timers, arrived to work the desk, she went back to her office to work on some of the always-present paperwork that needed to be completed. But thoughts of the body in the woods were never far from the front of her mind.

At eleven, she let Lynn know she was taking her break and grabbed her jacket and purse from her office. The library stayed busy thankfully, but that meant she wasn't always able to take the morning break that her employment contract allowed for. When she was able to get away, she usually headed for the café and bakery just a few blocks away.

Today though, instead of making the two-minute walk down the block, she headed for her blue Kia sedan.

I don't know why you're doing this.

But that wasn't true. She did know why. She had to see for herself if the remains could possibly be those of the girl she'd seen so long ago. A girl almost everyone had forgotten about, it seemed, but not Nichol.

It can't be.

But still she drove on through, then out of downtown. Lynn hadn't said exactly where the remains were found, but her photos had shown enough that Nichol had a pretty good idea where she was headed. Ten minutes after leaving the library, she pulled her car into the breakdown lane and got out. Apparently, she wasn't the only one who'd gotten a hankering to see the site for themselves. There were at least four other cars parked on either side of the highway along with several marked police cruisers.

She walked toward the spot that had been marked off with yellow police tape. Two officers in Galesburg uniforms blocked onlookers from going into the woods.

Snippets of conversation between the other onlookers drifted toward her as she approached the perimeter.

"…nothing but bones…" a tall man with thinning brown hair said.

The woman next to him responded, "My son's a first responder. He said they looked like they'd been there for years."

"The recent rash of rain probably washed away whatever dirt they were under. Poor thing," another female onlooker said, then tsked.

"Listen up!" A young officer working as crowd control

raised his voice as Nichol approached. "We've asked you nicely to move along—now we're going to start ticketing cars parked without cause." He narrowed his eyes and let his gaze sweep over the small crowd. "That means unless you are legitimately broken down, standing here watching the trees sway in the breeze is going to cost you a hundred bucks. Fair warning."

The woman who had just tsked turned on her heels and hustled back to a black minivan. Two men grumbled about public spaces and their right of assembly, but they too turned and moved away.

Nichol shot a glance at her car. She was parked farther away than the other vehicles. Maybe the cops wouldn't get to her right away. She hadn't driven all the way out there only to turn around without at least attempting to satisfy her curiosity. And be sure that this body couldn't be that of a teenage girl whose scared blue eyes still haunted her to this day.

Turning away from the police officers, she moved down the street away from her car and the scene and ducked into the trees while the officers were still threatening the straggling onlookers with fines. She'd only take a minute. Get just close enough to assure herself that she was overreacting, and then she'd hightail it back to town. She was already going to be late getting back from her break, but she knew Lynn would cover for her. The forest seemed to close in around her, branches snagging at her clothes.

This is insane, she thought, but she didn't turn back. She couldn't stop now. The truth she'd wondered about for years might lie just ahead, hidden in these dark woods all these years.

Her feet sank into the earth as she crept forward, each step calculated to avoid snapping twigs or rustling leaves. She'd lived in Galesburg all her life, stomped through these woods ever since she was a girl about the size of the children at the library earlier that morning. She knew how not to leave tracks.

Muffled voices drifted through the trees as she neared the spot where the bones must have been found. She dropped to a crouch behind a cluster of ferns, careful not to let the cuffs of her slacks drag on the ground.

Through gaps in the foliage, she caught her first glimpse of the scene. Police officers moved with grim purpose, their faces etched with concentration. The coroner, his brown-and-gray hair sticking out from under a baseball cap in tufts, and clad in a blue jacket with white lettering announcing his position, knelt beside a shallow depression in the ground.

"Crap," a balding white man in an ill-fitting suit swore, loud enough for her to hear. Galesburg had a small police force, but she didn't recognize the man, which probably meant he was from the state police. The residents of Galesburg thought of the forest as part of their town, but in reality, it was state-owned property.

"How long do you think they've been out here?" the man she suspected was a state police detective asked.

A second older, Asian man in a jacket with the word *Coroner* emblazoned in yellow across its back shook his head, carefully lifting a long, dirt-encrusted object. "Hard to say without lab work but given the state of decomposition, several years."

Her stomach churned as she realized what the man held. A human bone. Her need to know more warred with rising nausea.

The coroner bagged a smaller bone, his movements precise and respectful. "What happened to you out here?" His question was directed to the bones.

She didn't have an answer to that question, but she suspected she knew who it was out there. *You can't be sure. Don't jump to conclusions.*

A different voice cut through the trees. "Detective, you need to see this." A uniformed officer made his way to the suit-clad man standing at the coroner's back. The uniformed officer held something up and out in his glove covered hand for the detective to see.

She felt her eyes widen as she caught a glimpse of tarnished silver glinting in the streaks of sunlight that made it through the trees. A purse, caked with mud and weathered by time, but unmistakably familiar.

"Oh my God," she whispered, her heart thundering loud enough that she feared she'd be discovered any moment.

The world around her seemed to fade as memories flooded back, vivid and visceral.

SHE'D STOOD JUST inside the oak doors of Galesburg Public Library, nervously tapping her one foot as she waited. Outside, rain streaked the glass in thin, silver lines, and for a moment, she was seventeen again, standing in this very spot after her shift as a library page.

It was three minutes past closing time. Her backpack dug into her shoulders, heavy with her school textbooks, and she was annoyed. He's probably lost track of time again, thinking about her father.

She checked the time on her wristwatch, then glanced out through the glass door, expecting her father's beat-up old pickup to appear. But it wasn't his truck she saw. It was the local commuter bus, hissing to a stop across the street, just like it always did, twice a day, every weekday, shuttling Galesburg commuters to and from Washington, D.C.

Several familiar faces stepped off, heading for the adjacent parking lot. But one figure remained behind.

A girl, blonde, about her own age, stood alone in a pink wool coat, a silver purse dangling from her shoulder. Her hair fell in soft waves down her back, her makeup defining her eyes and lips with the kind of precision Nichol had only ever seen in magazines.

Definitely not a local. Nichol had been sure about that.

The girl had looked down the road toward Main Street, brows drawn, tapping one foot with visible impatience. The girl was waiting for someone who was late too, she'd thought to herself.

Just then a black luxury sedan had glided up to the curb, windows tinted too dark for her to see the driver. The girl hesitated, leaned down to peer through the passenger door window, which the driver must have rolled down. The girl said something to the person inside, her expression still reticent. After a moment, her body language softened. She smiled and opened the passenger door, then slid into the car.

A moment later, the sedan pulled away, disappearing down Main Street as the familiar growl of her father's engine broke the quiet.

Nichol likely would have forgotten all about the girl and the doubt she'd seen on her face if she hadn't seen the same girl several days later.

This time, she was on the nightly news. Addison Kober, fifteen, had gone missing that night, twenty-one years ago. And now Nichol knew she may have been one of the last people to see Addison alive.

Chapter Two

Landon Elkins grabbed a pair of broken-in jeans from the shelf in his closet and a warm sweater and folded them into the large duffle bag on his bed. He'd carried the bag all over the world in his travels as an investigative reporter for the *District Sun*. In the three months since the *Sun* had closed, a victim of the usual ravages facing print media, he'd found himself at loose ends. Not having a job had given him the time he'd needed to finish the renovations on the row house he'd inherited when his mother passed away. Now he had to decide if he should stick to the original plan of fixing up the house and selling it, which would yield a tidy sum. Money he could use, given his unemployed status. But he wasn't sure he wanted to part with the place he'd called home for most of his life. He'd never really thought of himself as the settling down type of guy, but even before the *Sun*'s downfall, he'd begun to question his future. He loved being an investigative reporter—emphasis on the investigation.

When he'd first started out, he couldn't fathom how he could do his job well and maintain a family life. His father, Samuel Elkins, had somehow made it work as an investigative reporter for the *Sun* for twenty-three years, but it had meant most of the scandal, illegality, and immorality he'd uncovered had been close to home. Not that there was a scarcity of scandal, illegality, and immorality in Washington, D.C., which some might say used to be the epicenter of such things.

But for once Landon wasn't packing to head out to some far-off place and investigate a corrupt dictatorship's ties to illegal organizations. This time, the case he was investigating was closer to home and far more personal. He was headed north to Galesburg, Delaware, to put a name to the remains of a recently discovered body and to hopefully find his father's killer.

He stepped into the bathroom adjoining his bedroom and tossed his toothbrush and half-empty toothpaste tube into his toiletry bag.

"Landon? Anybody home?"

The sound of his brother's voice carried up from the main floor of the house. He went to his open bedroom door, poked his head into the hall and yelled, "Upstairs."

The familiar sound of footsteps pounded up the stairs. Landon and his siblings had grown up in this house. When his mother passed away five years earlier, he'd bought out his siblings, who had their own homes, out of their shares of the property. He'd begun an extensive renovation, most of which he'd done himself.

Logan appeared in the doorway. All his life, Landon had been told how much he and Logan looked alike, but he never really saw it. They shared the same umber skin tone and dark brown eyes with honey-colored flecks, but Logan had been the brother who was into sports. Landon had been much more interested in writing and reading. He was, however, three inches taller than his younger brother, and he made sure to lord those inches over Logan whenever he got the chance.

"I got your message," Logan said, stepping into the bedroom. "What's in Delaware?"

"One-point-one-million people according to the last census," Landon griped, throwing his toiletry bag into his tote.

Logan made a face siblings around the world were familiar with. "You know what I mean. Why are you headed to Delaware in such an all-fire hurry?" Logan shot him a smile that let Landon know that he was about to say something smart-assed. "Have you finally got a girlfriend?"

He rolled his eyes at his brother. Even though he and his siblings were all in their forties. As the oldest, he still occasionally found himself annoyed by his siblings, especially Logan, his younger, cooler, more laid-back brother.

"No girlfriend."

Logan threw himself sideways on the bed next to Landon's duffel bag. "Then what the hell is in Delaware?"

Landon picked up a remote control from his bedside table and turned on the sleek black television mounted to the wall in front of the bed before answering. "Galesburg."

"Ooookay?" Logan answered, obviously still bewildered.

Landon hit a few more buttons and then the news report he'd watched, and then rewound and taped, from the night before began to play.

And out of Delaware, the police in Galesburg report finding remains in a nearby forest. Investigators are being tight-lipped, but it appears that the remains are those of a young woman and that they had been buried for several years. Locals speculated that the recent rains may have led to the soil around the makeshift grave being washed away. Dominica, back to you.

He hit Pause on the remote as the anchor moved on to the next story.

Logan sat up on the bed, rubbing his temples. "Listen, man, you know I love a good mystery, but I was up all night working on a case. I hadn't even had a chance to go home to kiss my beautiful wife good morning when I got your message that you're going to Delaware and you don't know when you'll be back, so cut me a break okay? Just lay it all out for me like I'm a five-year-old."

"Galesburg is where Morris Gillory lived with his wife and son, Will, in 2004."

Landon watched as the light dawned in Logan's eyes and his gaze swung back to the now-paused television. "And you think…"

"The remains that were just found belong to Addison Kober."

Logan shook his head. "Landon…"

"I know what you are going to say, so just save it, okay?"

Logan shot him a skeptical look. "Do you? Because it seems like you are grasping at straws here, man. You have no idea if those remains are Addison. And even if they are, do you know how long it takes for remains that have been buried for decades to be identified? Weeks, if you're lucky enough to have a good idea who the person is and dental records are still available. Without those things, it could take months, if ever, to identify the person."

Landon stepped back into the bathroom. He didn't need anything in there, but he did need a moment to bank the irritation with his brother swelling inside of him.

He knew the truth of what Logan was telling him. From a reasonable perspective, what he was doing was rash and likely to be a waste of time. But all he had was time and a burning desire to know the truth at the moment.

A truth he was becoming more and more convinced his father had died trying to get to.

He stepped back out of the bathroom. "I know this isn't rational, but I just have a feeling. I think this is Addison. Both her parents are gone now. They died without ever knowing what happened to their youngest daughter, but the last time I spoke with her father, he admitted that they'd given up hope of finding her alive a long time ago."

Logan's gaze dropped to the floor.

"The Kobers' oldest daughter, Kayleigh, lives in California now and she has held on to all of Addison's medical records just in case her body was ever found."

Logan raised his head, meeting Landon's gaze. "So, let her send the medical records to the coroner. If it's Addison, the police will have to open an investigation."

Landon didn't hold back the scoff and watched as Logan frowned. He respected Logan and the difficult job he did. He knew that it was dangerous and that without people like Logan doing the job, the world would be a worse place. But he'd also seen and investigated too many incidents where law enforcement either failed or flat-out didn't do their job. Hell, he'd broken more than one story about law enforcement who were no more than criminals themselves.

And he'd seen how power could corrupt. Only those with the strongest moral constitutions tended to avoid falling prey, usually by getting out before they crossed the line. Their father's murder had sat, unsolved, for twenty-one years, and even though it was still an open case, the last detective assigned to the case had bluntly told him that he wasn't going to do anything unless he received new evidence. Landon scowled at the memory of that conversation.

"You and I both know that twenty-one-year-old remains aren't going to take priority with the police."

"You don't know that's what's been found. That's my point."

Landon growled at his brother. "I'm going."

Logan sighed, slapped his hands against his thighs, and rose from the bed. "Okay, you do what you have to do."

"I always do," Landon said as he tracked his brother's footsteps.

Logan turned at the bedroom door. "Hey, how far is Galesburg, Delaware?"

"About an hour and forty minutes from here."

Logan tapped the doorframe twice. "At least it's not too far. You call me if you need backup."

Landon found a small smile. "Will do, little bro. Will do."

LANDON EASED HIS rented Subaru into a spot in the public lot. He stepped out, stretched his legs after the long drive, and took in the quaint yet surprisingly modern downtown of Galesburg, his journalist's eye taking in the details.

The streets were clean and the sidewalks well maintained, storefronts a mix of century-old brick buildings and newer facades. A Starbucks occupied the corner, its familiar green logo contrasting with the orange on the sign of the mom-and-pop hardware store next door. The golden arches of McDonald's peeked out from behind a row of pruned trees. The town gave off a small-town charm with big-city convenience. The kind of place that looked good on paper but harbored dark secrets just below the polished surface. Or maybe that was just his bias showing.

As he locked his car, a familiar name caught his eye. Gold lettering sparkled on a storefront window. Gillory Real Estate Investments.

His stomach tightened involuntarily with memories of his last encounter with Will Gillory. Two years ago, at a swanky D.C. event honoring Morris Gillory, he had made the mistake of approaching Will and requesting an interview with him. The conversation had not gone well. Once Will realized Landon wanted to speak to him about Addison Kober's disappearance, he'd spouted off several choice words and had Landon removed from the event.

He'd planned to head to the police station first and, hopefully, get an update on where they stood regarding the found remains. But now, staring at the Gillory Real Estate Investments office, he wondered if Will was inside.

He drummed his fingers absently against his thigh as he weighed his options. The memory of the man's hostility still stung, but the potential for valuable information was too tempting to ignore.

He glanced at his watch, then back at the Gillory Real Estate Investments sign gleaming in the afternoon sun.

"Screw it," he muttered under his breath. "I'm already here. In for a penny, in for a pound."

With a determined set to his jaw, he stepped off the curb and strode to the front door of the real estate investment firm. A blast of cool air hit him as he pushed open the glass door. The interior was modern and minimalist. Clean lines and monochrome colors. A young woman with auburn hair pulled back in a neat bun sat behind a curved glass reception desk.

She looked up as he approached, her smile brightening a touch as she met his gaze. "Welcome to Gillory Real Estate Investments. How can I help you today?"

Landon took in the way her gaze swept over him from head to toe and the flicker of interest that was evident in her warm brown eyes. He turned on the charm in return, hoping to leverage that interest to his advantage.

"Good morning," he said, flashing his most brilliant smile. "I was hoping to speak with Mr. Gillory, if he's available." He leaned casually against the desk.

The receptionist's smile widened. "Do you have an appointment, Mr...?"

"Elkins. Landon Elkins." He bumped up the charm another notch. "And no, I'm afraid I don't. It was a bit of a spur-of-the-moment decision. I'm in town on business from Washington, D.C., and thought I'd drop by."

The receptionist's fingers hovered over her keyboard.

"Well, Mr. Elkins, let me see if Mr. Gillory has any availability. Please, have a seat while I check with Mr. Gillory."

As Landon settled into one of the plush leather chairs in the waiting area, he took in his surroundings. The office was eerily quiet, save for the soft hum of the air-conditioning and the occasional click of the receptionist's mouse. He glanced at the empty chairs around him, then at the vacant hallway leading to what he assumed were other offices. He knew that most of the real estate investing the company did was for the Gillory family, friends, and close associates. A family business that Morris Gillory had set his son up with so that Will had a job. Guilt niggled at him for letting the receptionist believe he was a prospective client.

Minutes later, the sound of a door opening snapped him to attention. William Gillory emerged from his office, his tall frame filling the doorway. Landon rose, steeling himself for a potentially hostile encounter. To his surprise, Will's face showed no hint of recognition as he approached with an outstretched hand.

"Mr. Gillory," he said, shaking Will's hand. "Thank you for seeing me on such short notice."

"Of course," Will replied with a wide smile. "Please, step into my office."

Will led him down a hallway that was as quiet as the reception area was. As they entered Will's well-appointed office, Landon noted the large mahogany desk and the wall of windows overlooking the town square.

Will gestured to a chair. "Have a seat, Mr. Elkins?"

Will studied Landon intently. "You know, you look awfully familiar. Have we met before? It's been a while since I've made the trip to Washington, but…"

Landon saw his opening. "You used to live in D.C., right? When you were in high school, and your father worked as a lobbyist?"

Will's smile dimmed, his expression suspicious. "Yes, is that where I know you from? Did we go to school together?"

Landon shook his head, steeling himself for the hostility that was coming. "No, we didn't. I'm actually a freelance reporter. We met at a ceremony honoring your father a couple of years ago."

Will's eyes narrowed as recognition dawned. The easy charm evaporated, replaced by a guardedness that made the spacious office feel claustrophobic.

"I remember you now," Will said. He leaned forward, placing his elbows on the desk. "What are you doing here, Mr. Elkins?"

"I'm in town because of the remains that were found yesterday in the woods near here," Landon said.

Will's eyebrows shot up. "Remains?"

Landon's brow arched. "You hadn't heard?"

He watched the man sitting across from him, noting the slight tremor in Will's hand as he reached for the pen on his desk.

"Of course. I'd heard something about it, although I can't say I know the details. But I wouldn't have thought some old bones being found was newsworthy enough to make it all the way to D.C." Will tapped the pen against the blotter on his desk.

"Well, it did," Landon snapped, irked by the casualness with which Will spoke of another person's death.

"That still doesn't explain why you're here," Will pressed, his eyes boring into Landon's. "What's your interest in it?"

Landon hesitated, weighing his next words. How much should he reveal? The ticking of the wall clock seemed to grow louder in the charged silence. He'd already come this far.

He took a deep breath then said, "I think the remains are those of Addison Kober."

Chapter Three

Will had clammed up after Landon dropped the bombshell that Addison's remains may have been found and had all but frog-marched him out of the building.

Landon made a quick stop to check in at his hotel before getting back into the car and driving the short distance to the squat, redbrick structure that housed the Galesburg police station, figuring he might have better luck there.

The scent of stale coffee and industrial cleaner assaulted his nostrils as he pushed through the glass front doors. He approached the portly clerk with thinning hair at the front desk. The clerk made him wait several long moments before glancing up from his computer screen, eyebrows raised in silent inquiry.

"Good afternoon. My name is Landon Elkins. I'm an independent investigative reporter." He handed the clerk a business card. "I'd like to speak with the detective handling the remains found earlier this week."

The clerk took the card without looking at it, his lips pressing into a thin line. "That'd be Detective Simmons, but he's with the state police. You'll want to contact their office instead." The clerk held the business card back out to Landon.

A flare of irritation zipped through him, but he kept a hold of his temper and made himself smile even broader. "Actually, I've already spoken with the state police. They informed me Detective Simmons would be working out of your offices for the duration of this investigation."

"Is that so?" the clerk drawled, dropping the card onto the desk. He leaned back in his chair, his arms crossed over his chest. "Well, I haven't seen any state detectives around."

Landon's mind raced. Either the clerk really didn't know anything about the state detective's role in the case, or he was deliberately obstructing him. Either way, he needed to speak to Detective Simmons.

"Is it possible there has been a miscommunication?" Landon asked, fighting to keep the irritation out of his tone. "Would you mind checking with your supervisor? I've come a long way to follow up on this story, and I'd hate for there to be any unnecessary delays."

The clerk's eyes narrowed. The man clearly did not appreciate his persistence. "Listen, Mr. Elkins, we don't get many big-city reporters sniffing around here. If there's news to share, we'll put out a statement. Until then, I suggest you enjoy our local attractions. The peach cobbler at Mabel's Diner is particularly good."

Landon bit back a sharp retort, his smile now strained. This wasn't his first rodeo with uncooperative law enforcement, but it never got less frustrating. He opened his mouth to press further when the station's front door swung open, letting in a blast of cold air.

A tall, striking Black woman strode in. She had high cheekbones, full lips, and eyes that seemed to spark with intelligence and determination, despite her face being screwed up in a mask of irritation. She clutched a crumpled parking citation in one hand, and her purse strap in the other.

The woman stepped up behind Landon in line, her presence impossible to ignore. The faint scent of jasmine wafted past him.

Landon's attention snapped back to the clerk, who was now eyeing him with growing impatience.

"Look," the clerk said, "the detective ain't here. But I can take a message if you want."

Landon's jaw tightened. A message. Right. He'd been a reporter long enough to know how that game worked. Messages always had a funny way of disappearing.

"I appreciate the offer," Landon replied, "but I think I'll wait. Any idea when the detective might be back?"

The clerk shrugged. "Could be an hour, could be never. We don't keep tabs on state folk."

Landon contemplated his next move. An officer rose from his desk several feet behind the reception desk. The man's crisp authoritative tone suggested he wasn't just another beat cop. The officer walked to the far end of the reception desk and motioned Landon over.

"Hold on there. I couldn't help but overhear. I'm Officer Daniels, the media liaison for our department." He extended a hand and Landon shook it. "Perhaps I can assist you with your inquiries?"

"Landon Elkins. I appreciate any help you can give, Officer Daniels. I'm here about the remains found in the woods earlier this morning."

Landon reached into his jacket pocket and produced another crisp white business card. He handed it over, watching Daniels scrutinize every detail.

"What questions do you have?" Daniels asked.

"For starters, do you know how long the remains have been in the woods?"

Daniels hesitated. "The coroner estimates several years."

Several years. The words echoed in his mind. His heart raced, but he kept his voice calm.

"What about gender? Have you determined if the remains are male or female?"

Daniels shifted his weight, his gaze darting to the side to avoid meeting Landon's.

"Look," Landon pressed, "I understand the need for discretion, but any information could be crucial."

Daniels sighed. "Female. Young. The coroner's initial estimate puts her between fifteen and twenty years old."

The words hit him like a physical blow. He inhaled, his mind racing. Young female, fifteen to twenty years old, several years in the woods. It fit. God help him, the characteristics fit Addison Kober to a tee.

"Are you alright, Mr. Elkins?" Daniels asked, a note of concern creeping into his voice.

Landon nodded, reining in his temper. "Yes, fine. Thank you."

A mix of emotions coursed through him. Excitement and anticipation because this could be the break he'd been chasing for years. But alongside it, a cold dread had also settled in his stomach.

If this was Addison.... He'd spent so long hoping to uncover the truth of what happened to her and how it connected to his father's death. But now, faced with the possibility of getting answers, he was torn. Part of him desperately wanted it to be her, to finally know the truth about what had happened to her and possibly his father. Another part of him shuddered at the thought. He realized he'd been unconsciously clinging to the faint hope that Addison might still be out there, alive somewhere.

"Landon?" Daniels's voice cut through his thoughts. "Is there something specific you're looking for here?"

Landon blinked, realizing he'd been silent for too long. He forced a smile, pushing down the mix of emotions swirling inside him. "Just following up on a lead."

The officer's eyes narrowed, his posture stiffening. "A lead, huh? Seems like an awfully long way to come for a hunch. What's got a D.C. reporter so interested in our Jane Doe?"

Landon hesitated. He didn't want to reveal too much. The minute it got out that the remains could be those of Addison Kober, Galesburg would be swamped with reporters. Her disappearance had been big news twenty years earlier and he was sure finding her body would reignite that attention from the press.

Landon studied the officer in front of him. The man looked to be only a few years younger than him. "Have you heard of a girl named Addison Kober? She went missing from Washington, D.C., twenty-one years ago."

A sharp gasp was his answer, but it hadn't come from Officer Daniels.

Landon whirled around, startled by the sound. The woman who had been standing behind him in line stared at him, her eyes wide with shock.

"I'm... I'm sorry," she stammered. "I didn't mean to eavesdrop, it's just... I haven't heard that name in years."

Landon's pulse raced. He turned toward the woman, his reporter's instincts on high alert. "Did you know her?"

The woman shook her head, her gaze darting between Landon and the officer. "Know her? No. Of course not, but her disappearance was a big deal for several weeks when I was a teenager. I was just about the same age as her and my parents kept a tight rein on me for weeks after she disappeared."

Landon's eyes narrowed as he studied the woman's face. Her reaction was too visceral, too immediate to be mere recollection of an old news story. But she didn't give him a chance to ask her any further questions.

"I'm sorry. I'll come back to pay a parking citation. I've...

I've got to get back to work." The woman turned and all but ran from the station.

Landon turned back to Officer Daniels. "Thank you for your time," he said, already moving for the doors.

Maybe Detective Simmons wasn't the only person in town he should be talking to. Which begged the question: How many people in this town knew more than they were letting on?

NICHOL BURST INTO the library, her breath coming in quick pants.

Lynn's eyes met hers over the computer screen at the circulation desk, her fingers going still over the keyboard. "Nichol, are you okay?"

"I'm fine." Nichol tried to force a smile, and failed, based upon Lynn's reaction. She needed to steady herself and gather her thoughts. The reporter's sudden appearance and hearing Addison Kober's name again after all this time had thrown her. But whatever he was doing in Galesburg, it had nothing to do with her.

Right. Keep telling yourself that.

Lynn arched an eyebrow, her gaze unwavering. "You don't look fine."

"I just... I have a lot on my mind," Nichol said.

Lynn frowned.

There was no hiding the truth from her friend. Lynn knew her too well for that. Luckily, the sudden swoosh of the automatic entry doors of the library grabbed Lynn's attention.

The reporter from the police station strode in, his tailored navy blazer hugging his broad shoulders and his snug jeans emphasizing a well-carved physique. Something jolted in Nichol's chest as he approached the circulation desk.

Lynn spoke low so that only Nichol could hear her. "Well, hello good looking. I'd love to know what you've got cook'n."

Nichol elbowed her coworker lightly.

The man reached the desk and Lynn said loudly enough for him to hear, "Good morning. How can I help you?"

The man smiled brightly. "Hello, I'm Landon Elkins." His voice was rich and deep.

"Lynn Riceny, children's librarian."

Then he turned to her, his gaze locking on hers, and for a moment everything else around her disappeared, the distant whispers of library patrons and the rhythmic clicking of keyboards fading into nothingness.

"We didn't really meet at the police station just now. Landon Elkins," he said again, extending his hand toward her and giving her a dazzling smile.

"Nichol Bunin." Nichol took his hand, but the connection ignited a rush of heat through her, and she snatched it back quickly.

"How can we help you?" Lynn asked, her eyes darting between the two of them.

"I'd like to talk to Ms. Bunin alone, if she has a moment."

Nichol shifted, glancing at Lynn, whose interest in Landon seemed to have cooled into suspicion.

"Um, I'm not sure how I can be of any help," she stammered.

"I promise I won't take up much of your time. Please." The gentle insistence of his tone quelled some of her hesitance, leaving curiosity to fill the void. What did he know about Addison's disappearance?

"Alright," she said after a moment.

"Come with me." Without waiting to see if he would follow, she turned and headed for her office. He was several inches taller than her so by the time she pushed the office door open, he was right behind her. She stepped behind her desk and took a seat while he looked around, assessing the cluttered space. She got the feeling he did that a lot. Noticed things others didn't, which made sense given his profession, but still, it put her on edge. What had he noticed about her?

"Please have a seat," she said, waving a hand toward the single visitor's chair in the office.

He settled in the chair, his broad shoulders wider than the chair's back. "Thank you for speaking to me."

"How can I help you?" Nichol clasped her hand on her desk in front of her, then unclasped them. Why did he make her so nervous?

"At the station you seemed stunned when I mentioned the name Addison Kober."

"I was. I think anyone about our age would be," she said, attempting to project a casual tone.

"Maybe." Landon tapped one slender finger on the arm of his chair and studied her now. "But I don't think that was all there was to it, was it?"

"Why are you here?" she countered without answering his question.

"You didn't answer my question."

Her jaw tightened. "No, I didn't."

He sighed. "I feel like we're talking at cross-purposes."

"I don't trust you."

"You don't know me."

"Why do you think the remains that were found are Addison Kober's?"

"I didn't say I thought they were."

She cocked her head and shot him an incredulous look. "You show up, asking about the remains, and then drop the name of a girl who has been missing for two decades now. I don't have to be an investigative reporter to put two and two together."

His lips curled into a smile that sent a flutter through her. "Touché."

"It's not just another story for you, is it?"

The smile fell from his face. "No, it isn't."

"Why not?"

He leaned forward and sighed again, his expression taking on a slight look of defeat. "My father was an investigative reporter in D.C. too. A few years ago, I found an old notebook of his from twenty years ago. It looked like he was investigating Addison's disappearance."

Nichol shrugged. "Makes sense. I bet every reporter in the city was at some point or another."

"You may be right. But in his notes, he'd written Addison's name and Will Gillory's."

She gave a little jerk of surprise. "Will?"

"I assume so. They were about the same age, but I haven't found any real connection between them."

Her brows went up at the stress he'd put on the word *real*. "But you've found something."

"I told you I found my father's notes." Landon hesitated for a moment, then reached into his laptop bag and pulled out a small black notebook. He flipped to the end of the book and turned it toward her. He tapped the bottom of the page where the words *William Gillory. Suspect?* were written and circled multiple times. "I think my dad suspected Will was involved with Addison's disappearance, but he didn't say why in his notes."

Nichol chewed on her bottom lip. The Gillorys were easily the most prominent family in Galesburg. Morris Gillory had been a voice in state and federal politics for as long as she'd been alive. Will was a year or two older than her, but his parents had made sure he went to the best private schools, which meant he'd spent a lot of time with his father in Washington, D.C., traveling back to Delaware on weekends and holidays. If it was good enough for the state senator who would become president, it was exactly what Morris Gillory wanted for his son. But all the kowtowing hadn't worked. Will just didn't have the aptitude for politics.

"Can't you ask your father what his notes mean?" Nichol asked.

A familiar sadness clouded Landon's eyes. He shook his head. "He was killed in a hit-and-run not long after he wrote these notes in his journal."

She had the urge to reach out and offer him comfort, which was silly. She didn't know this man at all. Yet, something told her that he didn't share his emotions easily. "I'm sorry for your loss."

He cleared his throat. "Thank you."

An awkward moment sat between them before she spoke again. "I still don't understand why you're here. Or why you think the remains that were found could be those of Addison Kober."

Because he couldn't know that she'd seen Addison in Galesburg the night she'd gone missing, and she wasn't about to tell him until she had a better handle on his intentions.

He pushed up from the chair and began to pace the small space. "I don't think my father's hit-and-run was an accident. He was worried and anxious in the days—the weeks, really—before his death. He never said about what, but I knew it had something to do with work. With whatever story he was working on. And he was scared. We'd had a gun in the house for as long as I remember, but my father always kept it unloaded and securely locked away." He stopped pacing and pinned her with a meaningful look. "Until two weeks before his death. Then he started keeping it loaded and in his nightstand. He didn't know I knew, but I was at least as nosy as he was."

She let a small smile curve her lips. "So, reporting is in your blood."

He chuckled. "I guess so." He reclaimed his seat, his face

hardening once again. "I think whatever had my father so scared had to do with Addison Kober's death. And I think he'd made some connection between Will Gillory and Addison, and that making that connection got him killed."

Nichol blew out a breath. "That's a lot of supposition."

Landon blew out a breath. "It is. But that's all I've got. All I had until I saw a news report this morning about remains being found in the very city where the Gillorys lived at the time of Addison Kober's disappearance. Being the good investigative reporter that I am, I figured I should look into it."

Nichol's heart thundered. She was at a crossroads. Trust Landon Elkins and tell him what she'd seen twenty-one years ago or not? She gave him a long, appraising look. In general, she liked to rely upon research and reason to make decisions. She was a librarian after all. But she also knew that instinct wasn't a feeling to be casually ignored. And her instinct was telling her that she could trust the man sitting in front of her. That she *should* trust this man.

"I saw Addison Kober in town the day she went missing."

Landon's body tensed. "Are you sure it was her?"

She nodded. "Pretty sure. I didn't know who she was when I saw her, of course. I'd just gotten off my shift working as a library page. I was standing at the glass doors, waiting for my dad when I noticed her at the bus depot. I'd never seen her before, which was strange because it's a small town. It was pretty hard not to know people at least by sight. And this girl, Addison, she stood out."

"Why do you say that?"

Nichol picked up her favorite pen and tapped it nervously against the desktop. "She was wearing this gorgeous pink wool coat. Even from across the street I could tell it was expensive." She hesitated. "But what I remember most is the shiny, silver purse she carried. It was the only thing on her that wasn't designer." She focused back on Landon's face but couldn't read his expression. "What?"

"When Addison Kober was seen last, she was wearing a pink wool coat, black leather boots, and carrying a silver purse."

A sick feeling clenched Nichol's stomach. "It was really her."

"I think it was."

"When I saw her at the bus stop, she looked…upset. Then a black sedan pulled up and she got in. I never saw her again. Not in person."

Landon slid to the end of the chair. "But you did see her again."

Nichol nodded. "On television. After she disappeared, her photo was all over the television. Congressional page goes missing. You know how scandal-ridden the program was. It was news all over the country."

"That it was," he said. "Did you tell anyone that you'd seen her?"

Nichol nodded again. "I told my dad after I saw the news. He took me down to the station and I told an officer what I'd seen. He said he'd pass the information on to the D.C. police who were investigating the disappearance, and that's the last I ever heard about it."

Landon frowned. "No one from the D.C. Metropolitan Police ever contacted you?"

"Not me. I guess they could have reached out to my father and spoken to him since I was a minor, but if they did, he never mentioned it to me."

"Do you think we could ask him?"

"He passed away eleven years ago."

"Now it's my turn to say I'm sorry for your loss." Landon ran a hand over the stubble on his chin. "I've seen the police file on Addison's disappearance. There's nothing in it about her being seen in Galesburg on the night she disappeared."

A sudden chill went through Nichol despite there being no windows in her office. "How could that be? I know the officer said he'd pass on my contact information and what I saw."

"The information either never made it to D.C. or it got lost or overlooked somehow. It happens, but..."

Somehow, in the half hour they'd been talking she'd begun to learn how to read him. "But you can't help but wonder if it was a mere oversight or something more deliberate."

He shrugged, but she could see his mind working.

"I wouldn't be as good as I am at my job if I didn't entertain all possibilities."

She bowed her head in acknowledgement. "So, now what?"

He pushed to his feet but stayed still instead of pacing this time. "Now I investigate."

Not liking how small she felt looking up to him, Nichol got to her feet as well. There was still a significant height difference, which was an unusual feeling for her. At six feet tall, there were more men she looked down on than looked up to. But she liked the feeling more than she cared to admit at the moment. "You're sure that the remains found this morning were Addison Kober's?"

"As sure as I can be without a DNA test, but yes."

"Then I want to help you."

His left eyebrow arched.

She pointed to the master's degree in information science from the University of Delaware that hung on her wall. "I am an expert at research. If it exists, I can find it. And I owe Addison. I should have pressed the police more. Followed up to make sure my statement made it into the hands of the right people. Maybe if I had—"

"Hey," he reached across the desk and took one of her

hands. "One thing I've learned in this job is that you can't look backward, only forward. No one can change the past, but you can do your best to make sure the truth comes to light and that people who did wrong face the consequences."

"Does that mean you'll let me help you investigate?"

A crooked smile sprang over his face. And just like that, the flutter was back. "I have the distinct feeling I couldn't stop you if I tried."

Chapter Four

"So, what do we do first?" Nichol asked.

"Well, I'd like to see where the remains were found. Can you give me directions?" Landon asked.

Nichol hesitated for a moment. "I can do better than that. I'll take you there."

His brows arched. "Don't you have to work?"

She shrugged. "Lynn will cover for me." She stood. "Hang on a second."

He turned in the chair to watch her stride from the office, presumably to let Lynn know she'd be going out. He couldn't help but notice the gentle sway of her hips as she walked away. He quickly averted his gaze, reminding himself that he was there in a professional capacity.

Still, he wasn't sure that he should welcome Nichol's help investigating or discourage it, not the least of reasons being how attracted he was to her. Having her around would undoubtedly be a distraction he didn't need. And if the bones were Addison's, that meant someone in this town had killed her. Having Nichol at his side while he asked questions could put her in danger.

She may already be in danger.

Based on what she'd told him, she was a potential eyewitness to Addison's last known moments. If the person responsible for Addison's disappearance, and now likely murder, discovered that fact, they might think Nichol was a liability. Two minutes later, Nichol was back. She grabbed her purse from a low desk drawer and snapped up her jacket from the back of her chair.

"All set. Let's go out the back. My car is in the lot there."

He followed her to a dim back hallway that led to a large metal door.

Nichol leaned against the bar on the door until it gave. The door opened with a swoosh. She held it for him as he passed outside and into the sunlight.

She led him to a blue sedan, then slid behind the wheel while he climbed in on the passenger's side.

"Thanks for driving. I left my car in the municipal lot."

"Since we're working together, I guess I should tell you I stopped by Gillory Realty and spoke with Will when I arrived in town."

Nichol shot a look across the interior of the car at him. "You've been busy."

"It didn't go well." He summarized the meeting for her.

"I don't know Will well. Only to say hello in passing, but it's hard to imagine him involved in...." She let the rest of the sentence trail off.

"One thing my job has taught me is that we never really know people." Landon gazed out of the passenger's side window as he spoke. "Even the ones we think we are close to."

"That's a sad thought."

He could feel her eyes on him, but he kept his focus trained out of the window. Sad? Maybe, but no less true in his experience. A long silence stretched.

Nichol finally broke it. "I went to where they found the remains earlier today. That's how I got the parking citation. The police had the area cordoned off but...."

His gaze lingered on her. "But?"

"I grew up out here. I may have cut around the police barrier. I didn't get a good look at the spot," she hurried to add. "I didn't want to get too close."

"What did you see?"

"Honestly? More than I wanted to, in retrospect." She gave a little shiver. "The coroner was collecting the bones. I also saw one of the officers holding up a purse that matched the one I saw the girl I believe was Addison carrying the night she disappeared."

"If that's the case, the state police should have a preliminary identification on the remains." He needed to speak to Detective Simmons as soon as possible and find out what, if anything, they'd found inside that purse. He had to admire her fearlessness.

Nichol increased her speed as they got out of the main area of town and hit the two-lane highway. The restaurants, shops, and office buildings gave way to miles and miles of trees, nature, and endless roads.

He settled into his seat, stealing glances at her profile as she drove. "Have you always lived in Galesburg?"

She shot a quick glance at him across the car. "Yes. Well, with the exception of college. I never wanted to live anywhere else."

"Where did you go to undergraduate school?"

"A small university just over the Pennsylvania border. I'm sure you've never heard of it. Briarwood."

"You're right, I can't say that I've heard of it. I went to Howard, but for me that was staying at home since it's in my hometown of D.C."

"The big city."

"Yeah, it doesn't really feel that way. I grew up there. Both my siblings and their significant others live there now. It's actually feeling very cramped."

She laughed lightly, the sound warming the confines of

the sedan. "Being an only child myself, I can't say I know what you mean, but coming from a small town…"

"You have a pretty good idea."

She pointed at him then tapped her nose with a laugh. "Don't get me wrong. I love my younger siblings and would do anything for them. But with both of them paired off in happy relationships now, they seem to think that I need to settle down and get married."

"Trust me. I get it. As one of the few single, over thirty women in Galesburg, it sometimes feels like everyone in town is invested in when and if I'm going to get married and have kids."

"You don't want to?"

She glanced at him again, her cheeks pinkening. "Maybe. One day. If the right guy comes alone."

He turned to look out the side window, hiding his grin. It hadn't been the smoothest attempt to weed out whether she was married or involved with someone, but it had worked.

A few minutes later, she slowed and pulled the sedan off of the street. "This is it. Looks like the coroner and police have finished up for the moment."

Yellow tape still draped between trees, marking off an area that it was clear the authorities did not want crossed. But there were no marked vehicles, no officers standing guard. That was good for him because he had every intention of seeing as much of the scene as he could for himself, and he'd rather not end up in jail for doing so.

He studied the natural surroundings as he climbed out of the sedan and walked to the end of the paved street. A narrow, graveled area led down into a gully before becoming the wooded area. He glanced at Nichol. He shouldn't have let her come. She was in her work clothes, a nice pair of gray slacks and black flats that would be ruined by the rain-softened ground if she followed him.

"Maybe you should stay here? Your shoes and clothes will be wrecked if you traipse through this brush."

She narrowed her eyes at him. "Please. I'm not a delicate flower that can't stand a little dirt. I told you I was out here earlier today." She bent, rolling up the cuffs of her pants, which he could now see were speckled with mud already. Straightening, she marched forward and down the incline leading into the gully, leaving him to catch up with her.

"Okay then. We'll do this together."

She glanced over her shoulder. "Together. And don't you forget it. I have as much an interest in finding answers as you do."

He had to admire her tenacity. He grinned. "Yes, ma'am." His cheeky answer did what he'd hoped and pulled a small smile from her.

"The spot where they found the remains wasn't far from the road." Nichol pushed through the brush with practiced ease. She hadn't been exaggerating about her ease with trekking through the woods. A city boy himself, he was decidedly less comfortable but did his best not to slow her down.

"The news report I saw said the remains were found by hikers. What would hikers have been doing this far off the road or a trail?"

Nichol shot him a knowing look. "The hikers were probably teens looking for a private place to make out."

"In the woods?" he responded incredulously.

She laughed. "There are hunting blinds out here. You bring some candles, a soft blanket. It can be romantic if you're sixteen, seventeen with little place to go for privacy."

He cocked an eyebrow. "You sound like you are speaking from experience."

"No comment," she said with a chuckle.

A thread of jealousy weaved through him.

"Here." Nichol stopped in front of another piece of yellow

tape strung between trees. "This is where I saw the coroner working this morning."

Landon glanced at his watch. It was 2:45 p.m. and it looked like the cops had finished the retrieval of the remains and evidence collection. Figuring out what happened to a girl who wasn't even from Galesburg would be low priority, but he'd expected the police to have at least done a thorough canvass of the area. But it seemed clear to him that the authorities were already putting the case on the slow track. Could that be because they didn't want answers to how this person ended up dead in the Delaware woods? Or because they already knew the answers and just wanted to keep them under wraps?

He glanced around. There was nothing but trees and brush as far as the eye could see. "Do you know of any hunting blinds around here?"

"Not particularly. Those things are always popping up. Technically, you're supposed to get a permit, but the law never enforces that requirement around here."

He didn't doubt it. Small towns liked to do things their own way. Sometimes that was for the good, but other times...

"You said you saw Addison get into a car. So, it's possible the person who picked her up brought her out here, maybe to have a rendezvous in one of the blinds."

Nichol chewed her bottom lip. "It's possible."

He studied her. "But you don't think so."

"The car I saw was fancy. I didn't catch the exact make and model, but I remember it was sleek. Expensive for the time. Whoever owned it had money."

"And if they had money, they wouldn't need to rendezvous in a hunting blind."

"No."

"But if they wanted to keep the fact that Addison was in town a secret..."

"They might have chosen to anyway. Yeah, I suppose that does make some sense. But they'd have run the risk of their car being seen on the road. There's nowhere to park around here."

"True. But even if the car had been noticed by someone, they could have said they ran out of gas and hitched a ride back to town to get some. Since no one knew Addison was in Galesburg they wouldn't know to connect her disappearance to the car." He turned back toward the road, though he couldn't see through the dense foliage. "Where does the road we were on lead to?"

Nichol followed his gaze. "There's a new housing development just over the hill. That wasn't there twenty years ago though. It was part of a farm that went under about ten years back." She tilted her head back, looking at the sky, thinking. "There are a handful of houses along the lake back there. They are mostly used as vacation houses, but a few of the owners live there full-time."

"Vacation houses," Landon muttered. Second and third homes then. And on a lake. Homes that only people with money could afford. It was something to look into.

Nichol walked him to the trail, and he clocked the distance between the area where the remains had been found and the path at just under a quarter mile. Not far, but far enough that the shallow grave could be seen by passersby. There was always the risk that a hunter or a local traipsing through the woods would happen upon it, but the fact that the remains weren't discovered for twenty-one years proved the risk there had been small. The person who buried the body had to know this area intimately.

He and Nichol walked around for another thirty minutes but didn't find anything of note. It had been twenty-one years. Finding a smoking gun was unlikely, but Landon couldn't help but be a little disappointed. He'd waited a very long time to find something to jump-start the investigation, but it looked like there wouldn't be any easy answers.

He turned to Nichol. "There's nothing here. We should get back before your coworker sends out a search party for you."

"I'm sorry we didn't find anything."

"It's not like on television and in the movies. Usually, getting a story is a slow, tedious, even excruciating process of gathering information and putting it together to form the best possible picture of the past. Even then, I never have all the pieces, and I never get all the details."

Nichol looked at him with curiosity shimmering in her eyes. "Then why do you do it?"

He held her gaze. "Because knowing most of the story is better than not knowing at all. Because victims like Addison and her family deserve to have whatever answers can be found."

"Not just Addison. If you're right about your father, you and your siblings deserve the truth too."

He swallowed the lump in his throat. "Yes. We do."

They made it back to the car in silence. Nichol pulled a U-turn on the deserted highway, and they headed back into town.

"Do you think you could find out the names of the hikers that found the remains?" Landon asked, breaking the silence. "I'd like to speak to them. I'm sure the state police won't release those names, especially not if they are underage as you suspect. But it is a small town..."

Nichol shot him a look. "And you figure I'd know who the town crier is?"

Landon grimaced. "I'm sorry. I know it's a stereotype. If I've offended you..."

Her mouth turned up into a smile that made his breath catch. "No offense. I do happen to know where to go to get the most up-to-date information on the happenings around town."

"It can wait until the library closes."

Nichol laughed. "You're in luck. Mary and her merry band should be in the library's large meeting room as we speak. Brace yourself. You are about to meet the town's grand dames."

Chapter Five

Twice a week, the library's small conference room was transformed into a cozy haven where stories were shared in more ways than one. The Purls and Prose group, Nichol's first initiative as head librarian, had grown into more than just a book club slash knitting circle. Designed as a welcoming space for anyone interested in reading and learning to knit, a close-knit group of retirees kept it going. Though the group was open to all, a core group of women, everyone a grandmother except Nichol, had earned the group the unofficial name of the Knitting Nanas.

Nichol drove back to the library and led Landon to the small conference room where she could hear the clacking of knitting needles and the tittering of laughter. She reached for the door, then paused a moment, turning to Landon. "Prepare yourself." It was all the warning she gave him before flinging the door open.

"Good afternoon, ladies. I'm glad I caught you," Nichol said.

Mary Tennyson was the first to look up as the door opened and Nichol and Landon walked into the room. She smiled a quick smile at Nichol before her eyes swept over Landon slowly enough to bring a blush to Nichol's cheeks. "We are too. Who's your friend there?"

"Mary," Hazel May admonished in the same tone that had kept generations of Galesburg teens in line when they'd been in her chemistry class.

Nichol answered quickly before the women could get into one of their frequent rows. "This is Landon Elkins. He's a reporter from D.C. Landon, this is Mary Tennyson, Hazel May, Emma Shakoor, and Lucia Gutierrez." Nichol turned back to Landon. "This is the Purls and Prose literature and knitting club. Affectionately referred to as the Knitting Nanas. They meet here in the library twice a week."

Landon graced the group with a smile that had Nichol's knees going weak, and sketched a shallow bow in the nanas' direction. "Ladies, it is my pleasure to make your acquaintance."

Mary let out a coquettish giggle while Lucia fanned herself with one hand. Even Emma's lashes fluttered just a bit too fast. Only Hazel, grumpy by nature, seemed wholly unaffected by Landon's charms.

"Well now, it is nice to meet a young man with manners," Emma said.

Nichol grabbed a chair from a table that had been pushed to the side of the room. Landon took it from her and reached for a second chair, carrying them both to the circle that the nanas had formed with their own chairs.

"Ladies, Landon is here doing a story, and he'd like to ask you some questions if you don't mind." Nichol nodded at Landon, signaling that she was turning over the reins of the conversation to him.

"What kind of story?" Lucia asked. The *Galesburg Gazette* wasn't in the same league as the *Sun*, but Lucia had spent twenty-seven years as its star, and only full-time, reporter. Her nose for news undoubtedly matched Landon's.

"I'm sure you ladies have heard about the remains that were found in Galesburg Forest last night," Landon began.

A chorus of "So sad" and "God rest the poor soul" rang out.

"Well, I'm here to make sure that whoever that poor person was, they get the justice they deserve."

Another chorus chimed out, affirming that idea.

Hazel's eyes narrowed suspiciously. "Is that so? It seems more likely that you traveled all this way with designs to exploit that poor person out there for your own ends. I know you high-flying city reporters only care about your tagline and what a big story can do for your careers. Can't trust the mainstream media anymore."

"It's byline, Hazel," Lucia said, a bite in her tone.

"I wasn't referring to you, Lu. You were the kind of journalist that did the profession proud."

Lucia's chest puffed out an inch farther. "Well, thank you, Hazel."

Landon turned to look Hazel directly in the eye. "I assure you, I don't have any plans to exploit anyone. And I agree, many of my colleagues are more concerned with their careers than in finding the truth and making sure it reaches the public. I'm an independent journalist."

He reached into his laptop bag and pulled out a stack of business cards, handing one to each of the women. "I have reason to believe that the remains found today may be connected to an incident back in D.C. One that happened years ago. It was a story my father, who was also a reporter, was following, and that I picked up after his death."

"I can already tell, you're a good one," Mary said, batting her lashes.

Nichol couldn't help but be impressed by his sincerity and the fact that he hadn't shrunk under Hazel's withering criticisms and judgment of his profession. The flirty smile that Mary directed toward Landon sent a sudden pang of jealousy through Nichol. She tamped it down. Mary was seventy-one and devoted to her husband, even if she was a notorious flirt.

"What questions did you want to ask us?" Emma chimed in without a pause in her knitting.

Landon shot a look at Nichol, but she just gestured for him to continue. She'd made the introductions, but it was his show.

"Well, I wondered if any of you ladies had heard who found the remains last night?"

Four pairs of eyes darted amongst each other, telling Nichol that they had in fact heard and had already dissected the information amongst themselves.

Hazel harrumphed. "That's no state secret. Jimmy Page and Ashley Bernard. Sneaking out to do who-knows-what in the woods." She tsked and raised a scandalized hand to her bosom.

Mary shot a look at Hazel over the rim of her glasses. "Oh please, Hazel. You act all pious now, but we all went to high school with you."

"Yeah," Emma chimed in. "You did your fair share of sneaking out to those woods back in the day."

Hazel's knitting needles stilled, her face reddening. "I most certainly did not!"

Mary grin made clear she loved stoking the drama. "What about the time when you and Ben McCartney got caught skinny-dipping in Lake Galesburg?" Mary cackled. "I thought your father was going to have an aneurysm."

The other two ladies' gazes swung to Hazel, their faces a mix of surprise and glee. Obviously, this was a story that they hadn't heard before.

"Mary, you promised you would never speak a word of that. You no-good—"

"Ladies," Nichol interrupted before the conversation could get any more heated. "Ladies, please. I am sure you have all lived full and colorful lives, but it's getting late, and Mr. Elkins here is looking for specific information. If we could stay on track, please."

Hazel harrumphed again, but picked up her needles and resumed knitting furiously. Nichol sighed internally.

"I just had one more question actually," Landon said. "Are you ladies familiar with Morris Gillory?"

The question resulted in another round of glances among the ladies.

"'Course we're familiar with him. Everyone around Galesburg, at least everyone of a certain age, knows Morris Gillory."

Emma spoke without raising her eyes from her knitting. "He was a couple of years behind us in school, but he made sure that everyone knew him."

Emma was the quietest and most soft-spoken of the group. She had a way of blending into every situation so much so that she was easily overlooked. And that's why Nichol was sure she saw and heard more of the goings-on in town than anyone else. It was always the soft-spoken ones.

"Speak for yourself," Mary said. "Morris Gillory and I are the same age. We went straight through kindergarten to high school graduation together. Not that you'd know it." She scoffed. "He was always making sure everyone knew how much money his family had and how much better that made him than us. Until he decided to run for state senate. Then he was a down-home country boy. Going on and on about his roots."

Lucia tucked her knitting into a canvas tote with *Friends of the Library* written in red letters on the side before speaking. "No one was really surprised to see him palling around with the Washington elite. He was always very good with getting himself up next to the right people."

"Just goes to show you how far the apple can fall from

the tree," Hazel chimed back into the conversation. "Morris's father, Abner, was the salt of the earth. Ran the cannery one town over in Unionville. Provided jobs for both towns and lived every day of his life here in Galesburg." She shook her head solemnly. "Just couldn't seem to rein in his son."

"What about Will?" Landon asked.

Hazel grimaced. Emma still didn't look up from her knitting, but Nichol noticed her shoulders stiffen. Lucia frowned.

"That one," Mary answered. "Morris Gillory was a menace, but his son was a downright hellion. Luckily for the town, the Gillorys didn't spend much time in Galesburg by then."

"I'd heard that Morris moved the family to Washington, D.C., at some point," Landon said.

Mary nodded. "When he decided he wanted more than little old Galesburg was likely to get him. He kept the big house on the lake though. Had to since he was still a state senator and it wouldn't have looked good if his permanent residence was out of state, but we all knew the score."

"Can't say anyone was sad to see the back of him," Hazel said.

"Things did quiet down around town," Emma concurred.

Landon shared a look with Nichol before continuing. "At some point as I understand it, Morris's wife moved back into the house on the lake."

"Oh, yes." Mary rolled her eyes. "Miss High and Mighty. As if we all didn't know that Morris shipped her out here so he could move his little chippie into their house in Washington, D.C. I'd feel sorry for her if she was even a little bit nicer to folks."

"She doesn't come into town much anymore. Prefers to have her groceries and whatnot delivered to the house on the lake," Hazel added.

"So, she still lives in town?" Landon questioned.

"Oh, yes." Mary slid her knitting into a large oversize knitted bag.

Nichol glanced at the clock on the wall. The knitting club was supposed to have ended more than a half hour ago. Landon had better hurry if he wanted to get all his questions answered.

"Caroline still lives here in her fancy glass house. Will built a house for himself and his wife, June, right next door."

"June is a Galesburg girl, born and raised," Hazel said with some pride.

"Shocked us all when she managed to snag Will," Mary said.

"Now, Mary," Emma admonished.

"What? I'm just telling the truth. I'd have thought Morris would have gotten his boy set up with one of those political-type marriages."

Hazel nodded in agreement. "June has had her eye on Will almost since she came out of the womb. She cozied right up to Caroline. That's what got her her man."

"Mary!" Emma and Lucia said at the same time.

"What? I'm just telling—"

"The truth. We know," Hazel said sharply. "But must you always tell it so indelicately?"

"The truth isn't delicate or indelicate, Hazel. It just is," Mary said, gliding toward the doors. "I've got to go get my dinner on the table. See you girls Thursday."

A chorus of "Goodbye" and "I've got to get home" followed.

Landon thanked the women for speaking with him and assured them that he and Nichol could handle putting the room back in order.

When they were alone, Nichol turned to him. "So? What do you think?"

Landon smirked. "I think we came to the right place."

Chapter Six

Landon perched on the side of the unmade bed, the mattress dipping beneath him in the dark, cramped hotel room. His phone was pressed against his ear.

"What have you uncovered so far?" Logan's voice carried over the phone line.

Landon's gaze drifted to the steam rising from his coffee mug, curling into question marks before dissipating. "Nothing concrete." He pinched the bridge of his nose, where tension had been building since the day before.

He reached for his coffee, the ceramic warm against his palm, and took a sip, grimacing. "Yesterday afternoon, I went to the area where the remains were found with Nichol."

"Who's Nichol?"

"She's the head librarian at Galesburg Public Library. Local. She's lived here all her life." Landon stood, stretching his legs. The hotel room only allowed him to walk about fifteen steps in any direction before he hit a wall. "She thinks she saw Addison the night she disappeared."

"Thinks?"

"It was twenty-one years ago, Logan." Landon paused by the window, peering through a gap in the curtains at the parking lot. Morning fog hung in the air, turning the world below gray and indistinct. "She worked at the library back then after school shelving books. She remembers seeing a girl matching Addison's description waiting at the bus stop across from the library around nine p.m."

"And she's just mentioning this now? Twenty-one years later?" The skepticism in Logan's voice was sharp enough to draw blood.

"She told the police back then. It looks like they either dismissed it or her report got lost in the shuffle, because I've almost memorized the file and I've never seen it."

A noncommittal noise traveled through the phone, something between a hum and a grunt.

"What's that supposed to mean?" Landon asked, suddenly feeling irrationally defensive.

"Nothing. Just be careful."

The words landed between them, ambiguous in their warning.

He wasn't sure if Logan was referring to the investigation or something else. But before he could formulate a response, a knock sounded at the door.

"I have to go." He ended the call, slipped the phone into his pocket, and crossed to the door in three short steps.

When he opened it, Nichol stood in the hallway. She wore a navy-blue blazer over a white blouse and black slacks. He thought she was the most beautiful thing he'd ever seen.

"Morning," she said, her eyes scanning his face with the same careful attention she might give a rare book, noting details, assessing condition. "You look like you've been up for hours."

"More like never went to sleep," Landon said, stepping back to let her in.

Nichol moved into the room, her gaze sweeping over the unmade bed, the scattered papers, and the open laptop displaying a grainy satellite image of the area of the woods where Addison's remains had been discovered after twenty-one years of silence. She didn't comment on the disarray.

"Coffee?" he offered, gesturing toward the small machine on the dresser, next to an ice bucket he hadn't used. "It's terrible, but it's hot."

"No, thank you." Nichol straightened her blazer, a gesture that seemed more habit than necessity. Her clothes were always impeccable. "We should get going if we want to intercept the teens before school."

"Absolutely." Landon nodded, pocketing his hotel key, and together they left the hotel.

Moments later, the car hummed along the county road. Landon followed Nichol's directions to get to Galesburg High School. Outside, the blue sky tried to peek through the fog. Galesburg was a town that had embraced the nature around it, building itself up in a way that also left plenty of open space and mature trees, which were almost completely bare now, their branches stripped by October winds.

"It's kind of weird." Nichol broke the silence in the car. "I haven't been back to the high school since I graduated. I almost feel like I should be wearing a backpack and worrying about algebra."

Landon's mouth twitched. "Bet you never thought you'd voluntarily go back to high school."

"God, no." She laughed, the sound unexpected and genuine. "Once was more than enough."

A beat passed, filled only by the rhythmic thump of tires over asphalt seams.

"What were you like?" Landon asked, surprising himself with the question. "In high school, I mean."

Nichol shifted in her seat, her seat belt making a soft shushing sound against her jacket. "Me? Oh, standard-issue bookworm. The kind who always had a novel hidden behind her textbook." She played with the edge of her coat, a nervous habit he'd noticed before. "I was the girl who knew where every single book in the library belonged."

"Somehow I can picture that perfectly," Landon said, risking a glance her way. The morning light caught the natural highlights in her hair, turning the brown to something warmer.

"I wasn't totally hopeless," she said, chuckling. "I did drama club. Three years. I was Beatrice in *Much Ado About Nothing* senior year."

"'Lady Disdain,'" Landon quoted.

Nichol turned to him, surprise evident in the slight parting of her lips. "You know Shakespeare?"

"Oh, yeah," he said, focusing intently on a truck ahead of them. "My mom was an English teacher."

"What about you?" she said, turning in her seat to see him better. "I bet you were a jock. Let me guess? A football player."

Landon's eyebrows climbed toward his hairline. "What makes you think that?"

"I don't know. Just…you seem…" Her hands made vague, encompassing gestures in his direction.

"I seem what?" He couldn't hide the amusement in his voice. It only made her cheeks turn more violently pink.

"You know," she tried again, stammering. "You're tall. Athletic looking. You have that…physicality about you."

"Physicality," he repeated, noting how cute she was when she was flustered.

"I just meant you look like you could have played football. Your height and…shoulders and…" She trailed off, apparently deciding that any further description of his body would only dig the hole deeper.

He laughed, taking pity on her. "My brother Logan was the jock. State champion wrestler three years running. He had college scouts circling like hawks by sophomore year."

Nichol seemed grateful for the redirection. "And you weren't?"

"I was..." He paused, considering. "I was more like you, I think."

The confession sat between them.

"Really?" The skepticism in her tone was impossible to miss.

"Really," he confirmed. "I spent lunch breaks in the audiovisual department. Ran the school radio station, WOAK, 'The Mighty Oak,' sophomore through senior year." He smiled at the memory. "Did the morning announcements. Even had a Thursday night show called Landon's Late-Night Lowdown that exactly twelve people listened to, including my mom, who was legally obligated."

Nichol's laughter was soft but genuine. "No way."

"Way," he countered. "And that's not all. I was also the head of the yearbook committee. I had my own darkroom set up in my parents' basement for developing photos."

"A darkroom? That's...impressively analog."

"This was before digital cameras took over," he explained. "There's something about watching an image emerge in the developer tray. It's like..." He hesitated, searching for words that wouldn't sound pretentious.

"Magic," Nichol supplied.

Their eyes met in an unexpected moment of understanding that felt fragile enough to shatter if examined too closely. Landon returned his gaze to the road.

"Yeah," he said. "Magic."

The high school appeared ahead of them, a sprawling one-story brick building with an American flag hanging limply in the windless morning. The parking lot was half full, cars clustered near the main entrance. Landon pulled into a space marked VISITOR and cut the engine.

They exited the car in unison, their breath forming small

clouds in the chilly air, and stationed themselves on the edge of campus with a view of the entrance.

They didn't have to wait long. Less than five minutes after they parked, two buses pulled up and students hopped off, swarming toward the school. Several dozen more walked down the sidewalk.

Nichol scanned the crowd. "There. That's them," she said, pointing at two teens walking toward the front of the school.

They intercepted. "Hi, guys. I don't know if you remember me. I'm Nichol Bunin." Nichol smiled and nodded at each teen in turn.

"Yeah, the librarian. I sometimes go to the public library to study on the weekend," the girl said.

Jimmy shot her a look that said everything about what he thought of studying on the weekend.

"This is my friend, Landon Elkins. He's an independent reporter here in Galesburg writing a story about the remains you guys found yesterday. Landon, this is Ashley and Jimmy."

A grin broke out on Jimmy's face. "For real? That's so cool."

"I was hoping you two would be willing to answer a few questions for me," Landon said.

Ashley took a step back. "I don't know."

"I'm not going to use your names in any way. I'm just trying to get an idea of how you found the remains."

The teens looked at each other, communicating without speaking.

"Okay," Ashley said finally.

"What were you doing out in the woods?" Landon asked.

Jimmy narrowed his eyes, and the girl looked away awkwardly.

Remembering that he was dealing with adolescents who'd snuck out of the house to make out and had been busted in a grand fashion, he backtracked. "I'm not judging. I just meant was there a specific reason that you went to that particular area of the woods?"

Jimmy visibly relaxed. "Oh, yeah, well, my friend built a hunting blind out there. We used it when we were hunting rabbits last month." He glanced at Ashley. "I thought it would be romantic and all that, you know. To go out, see the moon, have a bit of wine."

Landon's brow rose at the last part of the statement, but he didn't comment on it. They wouldn't be the first teenagers to imbibe before the legally prescribed age.

"Would you mind describing what you saw when you found the remains."

Ashely turned a greenish hue. "It was gross. I've had nightmares ever since we found it."

"I'm sorry to hear that," Nichol said, sincerity ringing in her tone. "I'm sure they will pass with time."

Ashley nodded without conviction.

"Whatever you are comfortable telling us would be a big help," Landon said hopefully.

Jimmy scratched the back of his neck. "There's not a whole lot to tell. We were walking through the woods to the blind. I forgot that it starts to get dark a lot earlier now, so we had to use the flashlights on our phones. Anyway, we were walking and then the light hit on something like, kind of shiny, but not."

Ashley glanced at her boyfriend with a scowl. "Jimmy wanted to see what it was, but I said we should just get to the blind. It was creepy enough being in the woods in the dark."

Jimmy winced. "Yeah, well for once I wish I had listened to you. I went over to see what it was and…"

Ashley shuddered. "I'd never seen a real skeleton before. Jimmy hurled," she said with a hint of pleasure in her tone.

It was Jimmy's turn to scowl at her.

"What happened then?" Landon pressed.

Jimmy looked at Landon like he was an idiot. "We got out of there, man."

"After Jimmy dropped my mom's favorite bottle of wine," Ashley added pointedly.

"I wish I hadn't. I could have used something to calm my nerves after seeing that."

"Did you see anything else?" Nichol asked. "Anything around the body that stood out?"

Landon suspected she was referring to the silver purse.

Ashley's face scrunched. "Honestly, I just wanted to get as far away from there as possible. I didn't notice anything other than the bones."

Nichol's gaze swung to Jimmy. He shrugged. "Sorry, ma'am. I didn't see nothing else."

The school bell rang. Ashley started to move toward the front door.

"One more quick question." Landon stopped them. "How did you get to the woods?"

"I drove my dad's truck," Jimmy answered, also moving to go inside.

"And did you park it on the side of the highway and hike in from there?"

"Naw, man," Jimmy said, giving him a look that said what he thought of the question. "I parked in the lot at the bottom of the trail, and we walked in from there."

Landon thought about where the trail was in relation to where the bones had been found and where the road began. "But then you'd have been coming from the wrong direction to have stumbled on the remains."

Jimmy's face pinked. "I may have gotten a bit turned around trying to find the blind."

Ashley snorted. "Ya think?"

Landon nodded. That made some sense. A second bell

rang, and the teens turned away, hurrying toward the entrance.

"Thanks," Landon called out to their backs.

They both disappeared inside the school without acknowledging him again.

"What are you thinking?" Nichol asked as they walked back to his car.

"Everything they said tracks."

"Okay, but I can see the wheels in your brain moving."

He glanced at her as his lips turned up in a slow smile. "You can, can you?"

She rolled her eyes, but she smiled back at him. "Yes. We're working together, right? So, spill."

He let the smile slide from his face. "What stands out to me the most is that whoever buried the body definitely didn't think it would be found. The spot is isolated and not likely to have been stumbled upon from the trail and not able to be seen from the road. They couldn't have known someone would build a blind out there."

He and Nichol got back into his rental car.

"So, what does that mean?" Nichol said, putting on her seat belt.

Landon fastened his own seat belt before turning to her. "It means that the person that buried that body was someone who most likely lived in Galesburg."

Chapter Seven

Nichol watched the hotel materialize through the windshield as Landon guided his car into the parking lot. In the less than twenty-four hours since she'd first met him, everything had changed. Long-buried memories had resurfaced, bringing with them a flood of questions and emotions she'd been avoiding for twenty years. Yet here she sat, unable to make herself reach for the door handle even as Landon cut the engine.

Landon shifted in his seat beside her, unbuckling his seat belt with a click that seemed unnaturally loud in the quiet car. He turned toward her, one arm draped over the steering wheel.

"So," Nichol said. "What are you going to do now?"

"I'm not entirely sure. Maybe go over my father's files again. See if anything we've learned in the last day connects to what he gathered back then."

"You mentioned that you'd been over them before. Do you really think you're going to find something new there?"

A subtle tightness appeared around his mouth. "I don't know. Maybe what I've learned here in Galesburg will put something from the files in a different light. Dad died a little more than six months after Addison went missing so there wasn't a lot of time to do an investigation, but he has notes from a few interviews. A few sketchy theories. It's worth a look, I figure."

She took a moment, taking in what he said. It occurred to her that Landon's quest wasn't just about solving a mystery of Addison's disappearance or getting closure on his father's death. It was also about completing something his father had started. Maybe even proving that his father had been right all along.

"It might help if you took a look at the files too," he said, interrupting her thoughts. "A fresh pair of eyes and all that. Plus, you grew up here. You might recognize connections that I'd miss."

"I want to help," she said, surprising herself with how much she meant it. "But I need to get to the library. I've already been away too much lately."

Landon nodded, no hint of disappointment on his face. "I could grab the files from my room and meet you there. If that works?"

"That would be perfect. We could use one of the study rooms."

"I'll just go to my room and grab the files." His smile didn't quite reach his eyes.

She reached for the door handle, then hesitated. "Landon. Thank you. For believing me about what I saw that night."

He moved his hand over hers. "Of course. We're going to get to the bottom of this."

A spark of attraction sizzled between them. She didn't let herself dwell on it too long before she opened the door and stepped out of the car. As she walked toward her own car, parked two rows over, she felt a weight lift from her shoulders. She had carried the memory of Addison Kober alone for so long. Always wondering if she'd really seen what she thought. And now she was sure even if they didn't have the evidence to prove it yet. She'd seen the missing girl. Maybe been one of the last people to see the missing girl. That thought had pressed down on her for two decades.

She got into her car and watched in her rearview mirror as Landon headed into the hotel, moving with a sense of purpose. How strange that a man who had just arrived, a stranger chasing a story, had become the person with whom she could share her darkest secret. But somehow, for some reason, sharing with Landon was far easier than it had any right to be. But now wasn't the time to ponder why. If she didn't get moving, she was going to be late for work. Again.

Less than ten minutes later, she pushed through the oak doors of the Galesburg Public Library. It was Lynn's morning to open, and the space already hummed with quiet activity, a pair of elderly men huddled over a table in the corner, a young mother helping her toddler select picture books, a cluster of teenagers with laptops at the communal table. Nichol nodded greetings as she made her way to her office.

"Morning," Nichol called, veering toward her office. She dropped her bag and coat off and made her way back to the circulation desk.

"So," Lynn said, leaning forward on her elbows once the patron had shuffled away. Her voice dropped to the particular library whisper that wouldn't carry beyond their immediate vicinity. "How was your night?"

Nichol focused intently on logging on to the second computer at the circulation desk. "Fine."

"Fine?" Lynn echoed, a grin spreading across her face. Lynn had the kind of animated features that made her expressions impossible to miss or misinterpret. Great for toddler circle time. Not so great at the moment.

"What?" Nichol asked, looking up from the computer.

"Nothing," Lynn said, her grin still in place. "Just seems like you've been spending a lot of time with our visiting reporter." She adjusted her glasses, studying Nichol with undisguised interest. "You seem to be getting close to him awfully fast."

The observation hit uncomfortably close to home. Was it that obvious? Nichol had known Landon Elkins for all of a day, yet she'd already shared more with him than with people she'd known her entire life. "I'm helping him with his story."

She'd been aiming for a professional tone but from the look on Lynn's face she hadn't quite made it.

"If you say so," Lynn replied, still clearly skeptical.

Her secret pressed in her chest, suddenly unbearable. She and Lynn had been friends for a long time, but Lynn had moved to Millfield shortly after the Addison Kober disappearance. She knew about the girl's disappearance—everyone in town did. But Nichol had never told her friend about what she'd seen that night. Maybe it was time.

"There's something I've never told you," Nichol said, the words escaping before she could reconsider. She glanced around, ensuring no patrons were within earshot. "Something I've never told anyone except my parents." And a police officer, but that hardly seemed relevant since the officer hadn't even seen fit to pass on the information.

The amusement faded from Lynn's face, replaced by concern. She leaned closer. "What is it?"

Nichol's fingers found a paper clip on the desk, bending it open as she struggled to form the words. "Landon thinks the bones found in the woods might be Addison Kober's."

Lynn nodded, her expression growing more serious. "Word has gotten around. He mentioned that poor girl's name at the police station yesterday, and it wasn't hard for people to put two and two together. It's all anyone's been talking about."

"I saw her," Nichol said. "The night she disappeared. I was waiting for my dad to pick me up after my page shift and I saw her get into a car at the bus depot."

Lynn's mouth fell open, her eyes widening behind her glasses. "Oh, my word. Are you sure it was her?"

Nichol nodded, the memory crystal clear despite the passing years. "I didn't know it was Addison. I'd never met her, but after she disappeared and her picture was all over the news, I knew. The streetlight caught her face when she turned to get into the car."

"Nichol," Lynn said, reaching across the desk to grasp her friend's wrist. "Why didn't you ever tell anyone?"

She explained telling her father and that they went to the police to make a report. "I don't know how, but Landon says my report of seeing Addison never made it into the D.C. police's file."

"So, you've told Landon." For once, Nichol couldn't read her friend's expression.

"He believes me," Nichol said. "He thinks what I saw matters."

"Of course it matters," Lynn said, her voice rising before she caught herself and lowered it again. "It might be the last time anyone saw her..."

Lynn didn't finish the thought, but she didn't have to. It might have been the last time anyone saw Addison alive. Anyone other than the person who had killed her. Because that was the most likely outcome. A teenage girl didn't just drop off the face of the earth for more than twenty years. No. The most likely explanation was that Addison Kober had been killed the night Nichol saw her, or soon after.

Lynn's expression grew troubled. "Nichol, if what you are saying is true, if Addison didn't run away, if someone hurt her, then you could be putting yourself in danger by getting involved now."

The thought had occurred to her too, surfacing in the dark hours of the previous night. If Addison had been murdered, the killer had walked free for twenty-one years, secure in the knowledge that no one was looking for them. Now there were bones, a reporter asking questions, and a witness placing Addison in Galesburg the night she vanished.

"I'll be careful," Nichol promised, though the words sounded hollow. How did one be careful when investigating a murder?

Lynn looked like she wanted to say more, but the library's front doors swung open, and Landon strode in, a leather messenger bag slung over his shoulder. His eyes found Nichol.

Lynn shot Nichol a look.

"He's bringing his father's research files on the case for me to look over. Maybe I'll notice something he didn't."

Landon approached the desk, giving Lynn a sexy, lopsided smile. "Good morning, Lynn. I hope I'm not interrupting."

"Not at all," Lynn replied, her smile a shade less open than it had been the day before. "I was just about to process these returns."

Landon's brow arched, letting her know that he'd caught the chilliness in Lynn's voice as well.

Nichol turned to the computer terminal. "Let me just check which study rooms are available." She clicked through the reservation system, aware of Landon's presence beside her, solid and reassuring. "Study room B is open. We can use that one."

She could feel Lynn's eyes on her back, filled with the kind of concern only a true friend could feel.

Study room B was a glass box masquerading as a private space. Three of its four walls were semitransparent, allowing Nichol to see the main library floor beyond, and more importantly, allowing everyone else to see in. The fourth wall held a whiteboard scrawled with faded marker from a community college study group. A circular table dominated the center of the small room, its surface scarred by decades of pens pressed too hard, coffee cups set down without coasters, and the occasional carved initial. Nichol watched as Landon pulled his father's files from his bag. There wasn't much. Three notebooks and a couple of file folders. She recalled Landon mentioning that his father had been killed only six months after Addison's disappearance, and wondered whether something in these notebooks or files really could have led to his death.

There was only one way to find out.

"I thought that while I read through the files, you could scan the library's digital archives and journal databases for information. I know you've probably done that already, but we might have subscribed to databases you haven't had access to. We have regional papers going back to the 1800s."

"You're right. I have searched all the major national newspaper databases, but it's harder to access the smaller, regional papers' archives. There isn't one uniform database and many of the regional papers just repost the *Associated Press* or other wire services for national news so it's not always worth the effort, but I'll give it a shot."

Nichol completed setting up his account access and pushed the laptop toward him. "There you go. You can search anything in our system now." She couldn't help but glance through the glass walls as she spoke. A middle-aged woman she recognized as a member of the historical society was standing near the biography section, her eyes trained on their study room with undisguised interest.

Landon followed her gaze. "Friend of yours?"

"Hardly," Nichol said. "That's Elaine Covington. She comes in maybe twice a year for historical society research, but suddenly she's fascinated by the thriller section right outside our door."

"You think she's watching us?" Landon asked, his voice dropping even lower.

"I know she is." Nichol turned back to the files, trying to appear engrossed in her work.

They worked in silence for a half hour before Landon spoke again. "The Kobers were upper middle class, but they weren't from the same social circle as the Gillorys."

"Your dad's notes say Addison went to Sidwell Friends School. They had to have had some money if Addison went there. Isn't that where the former president sent his daughters? It's one of the best private schools in D.C.?"

"But no real *connections*—" Landon made air quotes "—to speak of, and for the Gillorys that might as well have been the same as having no money at all. Mr. Kober was a doctor. Mrs. Kober taught at a nearby community college. They weren't hurting for money, but they definitely didn't run with the D.C. jet set."

Jeff Hannigan, who owned the hardware store downtown, walked by, slowing conspicuously as he passed the study room. Nichol was sure she'd never seen him in the library before today. His gaze lingered on them for a moment too long before he moved on.

"We seem to be drawing an audience," Landon observed, his eyes sharpening with interest.

"Small towns. News travels fast. I'm sure everyone knows you're in town because you think the remains that were found are those of Addison Kober."

Landon frowned.

"You mentioned her name at the police station when you were talking to Officer Daniels, and we've talked to the nanas. And I can almost guarantee you the entirety of Galesburg High School now knows you're investigating. By this evening, so will all the teens' parents."

Nichol reached for one of the folders, needing something to occupy her hands. Inside were photographs, some official police images that his father must have obtained somehow, others clearly taken for the newspaper. Addison's school portrait stared up at her, the girl's smile not quite reaching her eyes. Nichol remembered Addison's smile on her television screen and in the articles written about her disappearance. It was a ghost that had always haunted her.

A light tap on the glass door interrupted them. Lynn stood there, her expression apologetic. She opened the door just enough to speak through the gap.

"Sorry to interrupt," she said, her eyes darting to the files spread across the table. "Nichol, Ted Roberts is in your office. He says he needs to speak with you immediately."

Nichol's stomach dropped. Ted was on the county council and was a consistent vote for cutting library funding. She was no fan of his under the best of situations, and the feeling was mutual. She had an inkling that he hadn't come to speak to her to discuss the need for new printers or the library's community outreach program.

"I'll be right there."

Lynn nodded and retreated from the room quickly.

She stood, smoothing the front of her slacks with sweaty hands.

"Are you going to be okay?" Landon asked quietly.

"Yes." She nodded, she hoped convincingly. "Ted is not my favorite person, but he is a council member so technically he is my boss. I won't be long."

She felt eyes following her as she stepped out of the study room—not just Landon's, but those of the strangers who had suddenly found reasons to visit her library. The sensation crawled across her skin like insects, leaving her feeling exposed and vulnerable in a space that had always been her sanctuary.

"Councilman Roberts," she said, stepping into her small office. "This is unexpected."

Ted turned, his smile practiced and politician perfect.

"Nichol," he said, without a hint of warmth in his tone. "Sorry to drop in unannounced. I was in the neighborhood for a meeting and thought I'd stop by."

She didn't offer her hand, and neither did he. Instead, she moved behind her desk, using it as a barrier between them. "What can I do for you?"

He remained standing, towering over her desk. Ted had already served two terms on the county council, but she doubted he'd go any further in politics. He wasn't particularly smart, and he had a personality that tended to grate on most sane people's nerves. She suspected he kept his seat on the county council only because no one else wanted the job.

"I heard we have a reporter in town," he said casually, but his eyes held something sharp. "Looking into those remains that were found in the woods."

"Landon—Mr. Elkins, yes. He's using the library for his research. We're happy to assist any member of the public with their information needs."

Ted's smile thinned. "Of course. That's what libraries are for. But Mr. Elkins isn't a taxpaying citizen of this county and I'm sure there are quite a few libraries in Washington, D.C., with better resources than our humble town can afford."

She stiffened but stayed quiet. Ted had obviously come there to say something, and she wished he would just spit it out and get out of her library.

As if he could read her thoughts, Ted spoke again. "I'm told you've been doing more than just pointing him to the reference section. That you've been actively helping him with his…investigation."

The emphasis he placed on the last word made it sound distasteful, almost dirty. So much so that she fought the urge to fidget under his scrutiny.

"I grew up here," she said evenly. "I have knowledge of

the area and of the residents that might be useful for his article."

"Article," Ted repeated, nodding slowly. "And what exactly is this article about, Nichol? Because from what I hear, he's dredging up a lot of painful history and slinging quite a bit of false information."

She met his gaze directly. "I believe his focus is on the recent discovery and identification of the remains."

"Those remains haven't been officially identified," Ted corrected her. "And stirring up speculation about who the poor soul might be doesn't serve anyone. We should all wait for the facts to come to light."

"From what I can tell, that's what Mr. Elkins is doing. Looking for the facts and bringing them to light," Nichol said. "Isn't that what we expect from journalists in this country? To dig out the truth?"

Ted laughed, a short, humorless sound. "The truth? After twenty years? What good does that do anyone?" He moved closer to the desk, hovering. "Look, Nichol, I'm not here to debate the ethics of yellow journalism. I'm here as your friend."

The word *friend* hung in the air, so out of place between them that she almost laughed.

"The library budget comes up for review next month," Ted continued. "As you know, we're facing some difficult decisions about municipal funding allocations."

The threat was clear, wrapped though it was in bureaucratic language. Anger displaced her earlier unease.

"Are you suggesting that my professional assistance to a journalist might affect the council's budgetary decisions?"

Ted's expression hardened, the polite veneer slipping for just a moment. "I'm suggesting that this town has its own way of handling things. We look after our own. This reporter is stirring up trouble, making insinuations about respected members of this community based on nothing but conjecture and hearsay."

"You seem very concerned about his work," Nichol said, unable to help herself. "Any particular reason?"

The question dangled between them, dangerous and electric. Ted's jaw tightened, a muscle twitching at his temple.

"We all have a stake in this community's reputation," he said. "The Gillory family has invested generations into making Galesburg what it is today. My father sat on half a dozen charitable boards with Morris Gillroy, and I consider Will a close personal friend."

"And I'm sure the town is grateful for the Gillorys' support and Will for yours. But surely that support isn't conditional on controlling what information the public has access to?"

Ted stared at her for a long moment, something calculating in his gaze. "You know, I thought you were smarter than this. Despite my reservations about you, I have had to admit that you've been good for the library. The children's reading program, the digital literacy initiative for seniors—the community is grateful. All that could expand with proper funding." He paused, letting the implications settle. "Or contract, depending on budget constraints."

Instead, she let the quiet linger between them until it became uncomfortable.

"I'll take your concerns under advisement," she said instead, her tone just barely on the right side of professional.

Ted straightened, adjusting his already-perfect tie. "See that you do." He moved toward the door, then paused, and turned back with a smile that didn't reach his eyes. "Give my regards to Mr. Elkins."

With that parting shot, he pulled the door open and strode out, his footsteps echoing down the hallway.

She stayed seated, her hands pressed flat against her

desk to stop them from shaking. Only after several minutes did she allow herself a deep, shuddering breath. She checked her watch. She'd been away from the study room for nearly fifteen minutes. Landon would be wondering what had happened to her. Rising from her chair, Nichol steeled herself and headed back, trying to compose her thoughts. She wouldn't let Ted Roberts intimidate her. But she also couldn't ignore the very real threat to the library's funding, which affected not just her job but the entire community's access to resources.

When she returned to study room B, Landon was absorbed in his laptop, fingers flying across the keyboard. He looked up as she entered, his expression shifting to concern when he saw her face.

"That bad?" he asked, closing his laptop.

Nichol sank into the chair beside him. "Ted Roberts just threatened to cut the library's funding if I continue to help you."

Landon's eyes narrowed. "He said that?"

"Men like Ted rarely say anything explicitly," Nichol replied. "But the message was clear. My stirring up trouble might result in difficult decisions about funding allocations."

Landon muttered a swear. "Did he say anything else?"

Nichol recounted the conversation, watching his expression darken as she spoke. He was silent for a moment, his fingers drumming a restless pattern on the table while he thought.

"I'm sorry I've put you in this position," he said. "Look, I understand if you need to back off. This is your home. Your job. I can continue on my own. I've got enough to work with now that—"

"No," Nichol interrupted, surprising herself with the firmness of her tone. "I'm not backing down because some overgrown bully thinks he can threaten my library."

Landon studied her face. "Are you sure?"

She thought of Addison looking over her shoulder as she got into the black car that would take her away from the safety of downtown. Of the bones in the woods that might have been waiting twenty-one years to be found.

"I'm sure," she said.

A ghost of a smile crossed Landon's face. "My father would have liked you." He began gathering his materials, returning them to the box. "I should get going. I'm going to try and catch Detective Simmons at the police station. No one will tell me when he'll be there so I'm pulling a stakeout."

Nichol nodded, standing to help him organize the scattered papers. "I need to relieve Lynn at the circulation desk anyway. She's been covering for me all morning."

Landon hefted his messenger bag. "I'll call you later and let you know what Simmons says. If I catch up with him."

"Be careful," Nichol replied anxiously.

Landon nodded, his expression serious. "You too. Don't go anywhere alone if you can help it."

They parted at the study room door, Landon heading toward the exit while she made her way to the circulation desk. Lynn looked up as she approached, eyebrows raised in question.

"I'll tell you later," Nichol muttered, taking her place behind the computer.

Lynn looked like she wanted to press for details, but a patron approached with a stack of books, and she turned her attention to checking them out. Nichol busied herself with reorganizing the desk, her mind still churning over the confrontation with Ted.

She was so lost in thought that she almost didn't notice when Landon returned, his face set in grim lines. He approached the desk quickly, leaning in to speak in a low voice.

"Someone slashed the tires on my car," he said without preamble.

She felt the blood drain from her face. "What?"

"All four tires," Landon said. "Clean cuts. Definitely deliberate."

Lynn, who had been pretending not to listen, abandoned all pretense. "Oh my God. Should we call the police?"

A bitter smile twisted Landon's mouth. "I already did. They said they'd send someone over, but I'm not holding my breath for a thorough investigation."

Nichol gripped the edge of the desk, her knuckles whitening.

"I called a tow truck," Landon said. "And I can walk to the police station. But it confirms one thing for me."

"What's that?" Nichol asked.

"We're on the right track."

Chapter Eight

Landon stared down at his slashed tires in annoyance. Beside him, Nichol frowned, her eyes wide with disbelief.

"I can't believe anyone in town would do something like this," she said.

Anger simmered beneath the surface of his skin. He'd faced worse than petty vandalism in his career, but the blatant intimidation tactic still rankled.

"I have my suspicions," he said evenly, meeting Nichol's anxious gaze. "Councilman Ted Roberts springs to mind."

Nichol's brow furrowed. "No. Ted is bullheaded, but I can't imagine he'd go this far."

He shrugged, his mind racing through the possibilities. From what Nichol had told him of her discussion with the councilman and from what he knew of men like that, Landon wouldn't put it past him. But he had no proof so he didn't have high hopes that his suspicions would yield much by way of action.

"He was here, he had motive, and he's clearly not above throwing his weight around," he reasoned aloud. "It fits."

As he spoke, he couldn't help but feel a twinge of guilt. He hadn't meant to drag Nichol or the library into his investigation. But now that they were involved, he felt responsible for protecting her.

"I'm so sorry about this, Nichol," he said. "I never meant for you to suffer because of my investigation."

Nichol squared her shoulders, a determined glint in her eye. "Don't apologize. I decided to help you, and I stand by that decision."

Her support was touching.

She shook her head. "I just... I can't believe Councilman Roberts would go this far. "Threatening funding is one thing, but damaging your car like this? That's crossing a line."

He watched her struggling to picture the respected public figure she knew committing an act of petty vandalism. He understood her difficulty. It was a big leap from veiled threats to slashed tires.

"Sometimes, people in power feel threatened when their secrets are at risk. They can lash out in unexpected ways."

Nichol bit her lower lip, a habit he had noticed she did when deep in thought. "You might be right. But I hope you're not."

Before he could respond, the crunch of gravel announced the arrival of a police cruiser. Officer Daniels stepped out, his big frame moving with surprising grace for his size. He sauntered over, an amused expression on his face.

"Well, well," Daniels drawled, crouching to inspect the slashed tires. "Looks like somebody's not too fond of out-of-town reporters poking around." He straightened up, a mischievous glint in his eye. "Making friends already, eh?"

Landon chuckled, despite the situation. "What can I say, Officer? I have a magnetic personality."

The library's glass front doors slid open, and Lynn emerged. She jogged the short distance to the parking lot, her arms crossed over her chest against the cold. Her eyes darted between Officer Daniels, Landon, and the damaged car before settling on Nichol.

"Nichol, I hate to interrupt, but we've got a bit of a situation with the self-checkout system. Could you lend a hand?"

Nichol hesitated, her gaze flicking between Lynn and Landon.

He placed a reassuring hand on her shoulder. "Go on," he said. "I've got to file the police report and wait for the tow truck anyway. It'll be a while."

"Are you sure?" Nichol asked, her voice laced with worry.

"Positive," he nodded. "I'll call you later this afternoon."

"Alright," she said. She relaxed and she offered them a small smile before turning and disappearing into the library with Lynn.

He watched her walk away and felt another pang of guilt for dragging her into this mess.

Officer Daniels cleared his throat, drawing his attention back to the situation at hand. His demeanor had shifted, his earlier playfulness replaced by a somber expression.

"Look," Daniels said. "Your investigation… It's causing quite a stir in town. I'm worried about the backlash you and Nichol might face."

Landon raised an eyebrow. "Backlash? What have you heard?"

Daniels sighed, running a hand through his thinning hair. "There are some…influential figures in this town who aren't too happy with outsiders digging into old secrets. The chief has fielded more than one call. I'm concerned."

A chill ran down his spine. He'd expected some resistance, which was usual whenever he was chasing a story, but the gravity in Daniels's tone suggested something more serious. "Are you saying I should back off?" he asked, studying the officer's face.

Daniels sighed again. "I'm saying be careful." The officer's light blue eyes darkened with alarm. "This town has layers, and not all of them are pretty."

"I appreciate your concern, Officer Daniels," he said. "But I'm not leaving Galesburg without answers. In fact, I have reason to believe Councilman Roberts might be behind this." He gestured to his slashed tires.

Daniels's eyebrows shot up. "The councilman? That's a serious accusation."

"I know," he replied, his mind racing. "But he was in the library earlier today. All but outright threatening the library's funding, according to Nichol, if she kept helping me. It's not a stretch to think he might have done this on his way out. Even I could see he was pretty upset."

As he spoke, the image of the councilman's angry expression as he crossed the library and exited sprang to his mind.

Daniels listened intently, his expression a mix of doubt and professional curiosity. He stroked his chin, weighing his words. "I hear you, but...the councilman? Slashing tires?" He shook his head slowly. "That's a big leap. And you don't have any evidence to back it up."

"I know how it sounds," Landon admitted, frustrated, "but think about it. He has the motive, the opportunity, and frankly, the arrogance to think he can get away with it."

Daniels sighed, his skepticism evident. "Look, I'm not saying you're wrong, but I can't just accuse a public official without solid evidence."

He knew Daniels was right, but that knowledge did nothing to stop the frustration bubbling in his gut, so he took the opportunity to shift the conversation to a different topic. "Have you identified the remains yet?"

Daniels let out a long-suffering sigh. He sounded weary when he responded. "No, we haven't."

Landon's stomach sank, disappointment and frustration coursing through him.

Officer Daniels's expression hardened in response. "We care about who this person was and what happened to them. But these things take time. You of all people should know that."

"I do. Sorry," Landon said. Memories of late nights poring over documents and chasing leads flashed through his thoughts. "You're right. It's just...this story, it's personal for me. I'm frustrated, but I shouldn't take it out on you or your department."

The tension in Officer Daniels's posture eased. His eyebrows raised, curiosity replacing irritation. "A personal connection, huh?" he said, a hint of a smile tugging at his lips. "Well, I might just let you tell me all about it over a beer one night."

"You know what, Officer? I might just take you up on that offer," Landon replied with a smile.

Officer Daniels pulled out a small notepad and pen, the picture of professionalism. "Now, let's get this report filed," he said, clicking his pen. "Can you describe what you found when you returned to your vehicle?"

Landon recounted the details, watching as Daniels's hand moved swiftly across the page, jotting down each point with practiced ease. The scratch of pen on paper was oddly comforting, a tangible step toward resolving this mess.

It only took a few minutes to lay the situation out for Daniels. When he finished, Daniels nodded and closed his notebook. "I'll look into it," he said without much conviction. "You can pick up a copy of the report at the station later today for your insurance claim."

The rumble of a large engine cut through the air as the tow truck he'd called turned into the library parking lot, its yellow lights flashing.

"Perfect timing," Daniels said, pocketing his notepad. "Listen, have them take your car to Galesburg Auto Body. Tell them Chuckie sent you. They'll treat you right."

Landon smirked at the nickname. "Chuckie, huh? That's quite a moniker."

Daniels rolled his eyes. "Yeah, yeah. I'm the baby of six,

and my oldest brother still can't see me as anything but little Chuckie. But hey, at least it'll save you some cash. Mention my name and they'll skip the out-of-towner markup."

He couldn't help but laugh. "I appreciate that, Officer Chuckie," he added with a grin as Daniels headed back to his patrol car.

Daniels rolled his eyes, but Landon caught the hint of a smile as he climbed into his cruiser. "Don't push it, hotshot."

"Seriously, though." His voice softened. "Thanks for everything. I know I'm making your job a lot more complicated right now."

Daniels met his gaze, a look of understanding passing between them. "Just doing my job, same as you," he replied with a small nod.

As the patrol car pulled away and the metallic groan of the tow truck's winch filled the air, he turned back to the library.

The tow truck driver, a burly man with weathered hands and a rust-colored beard, approached with a clipboard. "You the owner?" he asked, his voice gravelly from years of cigarettes—if the smell of tobacco emanating from him was any indication.

"Unfortunately," he replied, signing the paperwork with a resigned flourish. "Take it to Galesburg Auto Body, please. Chuckie sent me."

The driver's eyes crinkled at the corners. "Officer Daniels, eh? Good man. They'll take care of you."

As the driver worked to secure his car to the truck, he caught sight of Nichol's silhouette through the library's window. She was assisting a patron. His gaze lingered on her. He watched her move purposefully behind the circulation desk, helping patrons with that beautiful smile of hers. Warmth spread through his chest, a reminder of the unexpected alliance they'd formed.

He turned back to his damaged rental car, the events of

the day crashing down on him once again. The morning had begun with such promise. His slashed tires were more than just vandalism. They were a message. Someone wanted him gone, wanted him to stop asking questions, stop digging into the past. He couldn't shake the idea that Councilman Roberts's veiled threats in the library were connected, despite Daniels's skepticism.

He massaged the back of his neck with one hand, feeling the tension knotted at the base. He'd faced opposition before—angry calls, threatening emails, even the occasional door slammed in his face—but this felt different. More personal. More dangerous.

And yet, amid the chaos of the day, one bright spot remained. Nichol. He glanced toward the library again, where she still stood, her back to him, in the window. There was something about her that settled him. Her presence had transformed what should have been a slog of a day into something manageable at least.

"We'll do this together." Her words echoed in his mind, and a warmth spread through his chest.

He hadn't come to Galesburg looking for a connection, he'd come for a story and to hopefully get closure on a difficult part of his life. Yet somehow, in the span of just a few days, Nichol had become more than just a helpful librarian. She'd become a confidant, a partner in his increasingly messy investigation, and a friend. And if he was being honest with himself, he was beginning to wonder if she could be more than just his partner in writing this story.

A few minutes later, the tow truck driver slammed his door shut, signaling he was ready to go.

"Alright. Let's see what other secrets this town is hiding."

LANDON TRUDGED INTO the hotel lobby, his feet aching and his mood dark. Four flat tires. The mechanic's sympathetic whistle still rang in his ears, along with the unspoken *ka-ching* of an imaginary cash register he'd seen in the man's eyes.

As he approached the bank of elevators that would take him to the blessed comfort of his hotel bed, the manager emerged from a back office.

"Mr. Elkins?" the manager asked, his expression a mask of politeness. "I'm afraid there's a problem with your reservation."

Landon's brow furrowed. "A problem? What kind of problem?"

The manager's eyes darted around the lobby before settling over Landon's left shoulder. "Well, unfortunately, we had a mix-up regarding the number of days you reserved. We can't accommodate you for another night."

"But I have a reservation for three nights and I was assured that could be extended if I needed to."

The manager cleared his throat, his words coming out in a practiced rush. "I am so sorry. It was a mistake in the system. There's nothing I can do about it."

Landon's investigator instincts prickled. The man's vague explanations set off alarm bells. Councilman Roberts's threats. Slashed tires. And now a mistake with his hotel reservation. It couldn't be a coincidence. Someone in this town didn't want him here, and they had enough pull around town to draft others into the attempt to frustrate him into leaving.

"Listen," Landon said, trying to keep his voice level despite his rising frustration, "I've had a hell of a day. I just need my room. The room I reserved and paid for."

The manager's face paled, a sheen of sweat growing on his forehead. "I truly am sorry, Mr. Elkins. But I'm afraid that won't be possible. Your reservation has been canceled, and we have no available rooms."

He stared at the manager, suspicion and anger warring

within him. This small-town investigation was proving far more complicated than he'd anticipated.

Landon took a deep breath, his jaw clenching as he fought to maintain his temper. "Look, I understand you're in a difficult position. But surely there's something you can do. I'm not asking for special treatment, just the room I booked."

"I wish I could help, Mr. Elkins. Truly, I do. But my hands are tied in this matter."

As Landon studied the man's face, he noticed a slight twitch at the corner of his mouth, a sign of discomfort. Whatever was going on here, it was clear the manager was caught in the middle of it, although it looked like he really didn't want to be. It was hard to feel sorry for the man at the moment though.

"Is there someone else I can speak to?" Landon pressed. "The owner, perhaps?"

The manager shook his head. "I'm afraid not. The decision is final."

Defeated and seething, Landon turned away. "Fine. I'll get my things."

He made his way back to his room but didn't begin packing. He took out his phone and called the one person in town he was sure didn't have it out for him.

"Nichol? It's Landon. You're not going to believe this, but I've just been kicked out of my hotel."

He massaged his temples, his chest tight with anger and frustration as he explained what had just occurred in the hotel lobby.

Nichol's voice came through the phone. "That's ridiculous! Hang on. I'm on my way."

The anger in her tone caught Landon off guard. He'd expected sympathy, maybe some advice on where he could get another room. "You don't have to—"

"I absolutely do," Nichol cut him off. "This isn't right,

and I'm not about to let them push you around." She ended the call without another word.

He folded his belongings into his suitcase, checking to make sure he didn't leave anything behind. As he packed, he considered who in this town was powerful enough to orchestrate something like this? Councilman Roberts maybe? As soon as he found a room for the night, he'd start looking into the man. Something definitely felt off there.

And there was also the Gillory family. Any number of them had enough pull to have someone slash his tires. He doubted they'd get their own hands dirty, and "cancel" his hotel reservation. He'd wanted to wait until he knew for sure the remains that had been found belonged to Addison before confronting any of the Gillorys, but maybe it was time for a face-to-face meeting.

Bags in hand, he headed back to the lobby. As he stepped off the elevator, the sound of Nichol's voice, loud and indignant, carried over to him before his eyes landed on her.

"...totally unprofessional!"

Rounding the corner, Landon took in the scene. Nichol stood at the front desk, one hand planted on the front desk, leaning toward the manager who seemed to be shrinking back with each word.

Landon failed to suppress the smile that spread across his face.

The manager's eyes darted from Nichol to him, a bead of sweat forming on his brow. "As I explained to Mr. Elkins, there was a mistake with our computer system. We never had the three nights he requested available. I am terribly sorry for the inconvenience, but—"

"Give me a break, Brayden. You can't seriously think anyone believes this entire hotel is sold out tonight. In Galesburg?"

Landon stepped forward, placing a calming hand on Nichol's arm. "It's okay," he said calmly. Part of him was thrilled at her passionate defense, but it wasn't worth arguing over it. He knew that the hotel could refuse to rent a room to whomever they choose as long as they didn't discriminate.

He tugged at her elbow, and she walked with him toward the hotel's entrance.

Outside, the evening air hit Landon like a slap, reminding him of his exhaustion. He slid in Nichol's car beside her and sighed. "Would you mind dropping me at a hotel in the next town over?"

Nichol's knuckles whitened on the steering wheel. "This is wrong. There's no way this place is sold out." She shook her head, fury evident in every line of her body.

"I'm sure you're right, but there's nothing I can do about it and right now I just want to know where I'm sleeping tonight."

"No, I'm not letting them chase you out like this. We need to figure out what's really going on here."

Landon leaned back, closing his eyes. He could feel Nichol's gaze on him. He opened his eyes. "What?"

"I have a spare room. Why don't you stay with me?"

He blinked, caught off guard by the offer. After a moment he said, "That's...incredibly generous of you, but I couldn't possibly put you out like that. I don't want to impose."

She waved away his concern. "It's no imposition at all. Besides, it'll make things easier for our investigation. We can compare notes after I get off work and plan our next steps."

Hesitation still gnawed at him. He rubbed the back of his neck, considering how to voice his next concern without offending her. "I appreciate that, truly. But... Well, have you thought about how it might look? A man you barely know staying at your place. In a small town like this, people might talk. I'd hate for your reputation to suffer because of me."

Her mouth twisted in a smirk. "I'm becoming less concerned with my 'reputation' in this town by the minute." She cast a disdainful glance back at the hotel. "The more I learn about some of my fellow citizens, the less I care what they think of me."

Landon studied her profile. "Are you really sure?"

Nichol turned the key in the ignition, the engine rumbling to life. "You bet I am."

Chapter Nine

The gravel crunched under the tires as Nichol eased her car into her driveway. She glanced over at Landon, noting the admiration in his eyes as they got closer to the weathered farmhouse she called home.

"This is it," she said, a hint of pride in her voice. "My family's been here for generations. My great-great-grandfather built it with his own hands."

The smell of freshly cut grass filled the air as they stepped out of the car. She breathed it in, letting the feeling of being home wash over her. She watched as Landon circled around the car, his gaze roaming over the white clapboard siding and wraparound porch.

The late afternoon daylight caught the angles of his face, highlighting the strong line of his jaw, and she found herself staring a moment too long.

"It's very homey looking," he said, genuine appreciation in his tone.

"Wait till you see inside," she said.

She fished her keys from her purse. She led the way up the creaking porch steps, aware of the subtle scent of Landon's cologne and the warmth radiating from his body.

She held her breath, anticipating Landon's reaction as she pushed open the oak door. She wasn't disappointed. His sharp intake of breath echoed in the foyer as his gaze darted around the sleek, modern interior. His shoulder brushed against hers as he stepped inside, the brief contact sending a ripple of awareness through her body.

"Wow," Landon said, his eyes darting from the polished concrete floors to the minimalist light fixtures. "This is... unexpected."

Nichol chuckled, slipping off her shoes. "I get that a lot. The outside may be all history, but inside, it's pure me."

She watched as Landon absorbed the stark contrast between the farmhouse's quaint exterior and its contemporary innards. Part of her wondered if he approved, and she quickly chastised herself for caring about his opinion. "I inherited the place after my parents passed. It was paid off, thankfully, and they left me enough to really make it my own."

Landon nodded, running a hand along the smooth surface of a nearby wall. "It's impressive. You've got great taste."

Warmth spread through her at the compliment. His eyes met hers, holding her gaze a beat longer than necessary.

"Thanks," she said, then cleared her throat. "Come on, I'll give you the grand tour."

She felt oddly exposed as she led Landon deeper into the house. She'd chosen everything in this house, every throw pillow, every piece of art and furniture. Every choice revealed something about herself, and Landon was an investigative journalist. If anyone could interpret it, it would be him. She stole a glance at him, curious and a little anxious about what impressions he might form as he wandered through the rooms that contained her life.

Nichol paused at the entrance to the kitchen. "And this is my favorite room in the whole house."

She stepped aside, revealing a spacious kitchen that gleamed with modern appliances and clean lines. The last rays of daylight peeked through large windows, casting a warm glow on the marble countertops.

"Wow," he said.

Her pulse raced at his reaction. "I know, right? I splurged a bit here, but it was worth every penny." She ran her hand lovingly along the island. "Those are my babies." She gestured to the double ovens nestled in the far wall. "Perfect for when I'm in a baking frenzy."

Landon stepped farther into the kitchen, his gaze roaming over the high-end appliances. "You bake a lot?" His voice had dropped, taking on a rich, velvety quality that made her skin tingle.

"It's my therapy," Nichol admitted with a soft laugh, her hand stroking the sleek stainless steel handle of the refrigerator. She stopped when she noticed his eyes following the movement. "Nothing calms me down like kneading dough or whisking up a meringue."

A thought struck her as she watched Landon explore her culinary sanctuary. "You know," she said, leaning against the counter, "I was planning to whip up something for dinner, but..."

Landon turned to her, smiling, his eyes dropping to her lips before meeting her gaze again. "But?"

A pleasant tension coiled within her at the way he looked at her. "Well, if you're comfortable, I'd love to see what you could do with this kitchen."

There was a moment of silence. Had she overstepped? But then Landon's smile broadened, reaching his eyes.

"I'd be honored," he said, already rolling up his sleeves, revealing strong forearms dusted with dark hair. "Any preferences?"

Relief washed through her, followed quickly by a spark of excitement. "Surprise me."

Their eyes met, and for a heartbeat, the air seemed to

thicken. Nichol's pulse raced. She was caught off guard by the intensity of Landon's gaze. She cleared her throat, breaking the moment. "I should, um, show you to your room first so you can get settled."

She took a steadying breath as they walked together out of the kitchen. *What was that?* she wondered, feeling both exhilarated and unsettled by the brief connection they'd shared, her body humming with a subtle electricity she hadn't felt in years.

Nichol led Landon up the creaking wooden staircase, her hand trailing along the smooth banister. At the top, she gestured down a short hallway.

"This way. I hope you'll find everything to your liking."

She pushed open a door, revealing a spacious guest room. Golden rays slanted through the thin sheers, highlighting dust motes dancing in the air.

"It's beautiful," he said, running a hand along the antique dresser.

Pride swelled in her chest. "I'm glad you like it. The bathroom's through there." She pointed to a door on the far wall. "I actually converted a small bedroom to make it. Seemed more practical to have two full baths than an extra closet-sized room."

Landon nodded appreciatively. "Smart move. Must've been quite the renovation."

"It was," Nichol conceded, leaning against the doorframe. "But worth it. The door in the hallway leads to it too, so you don't have to worry about guests traipsing through your room to use the facilities."

"You've really thought of everything," Landon said, his voice warm with admiration.

Her cheeks heated at the compliment. She watched as he set his bag down, the muscles in his forearms flexing. His rolled-up sleeves revealed tanned skin and a dusting of dark hair that made her wonder what the rest of him looked like.

"I'll let you get settled," she said, pushing off the doorframe. "Take your time. I'll be downstairs when you're ready."

As she turned to leave, Landon called out, "Nichol?"

She paused, her pulse jumping at the sound of her name on his lips. "Yes?"

"Thank you," he said simply, his eyes conveying more than his words. "For everything."

The sincerity in his voice made something inside her soften and melt. She wanted to get to know this man better.

She smiled, a genuine warmth spreading through her chest. "You're welcome, Landon. I'm glad you're here."

She closed the door behind her, leaned against it for a moment, heart hammering and her breath coming faster than normal. The wood was cool on her back, a stark contrast to the warmth flooding her body. *What am I doing?* The unexpected connection with Landon both thrilled and terrified her. It had been so long since she'd felt a pull toward someone.

Shaking her head, she made her way back downstairs, determined to focus on being a good host and nothing more.

NICHOL TUGGED AT the hem of her soft gray sweater as she padded barefoot into the kitchen. She glanced up to see Landon already there, his sleeves rolled up as he rummaged through her pantry.

"Find everything okay?" she asked, leaning against the island.

Landon turned, a jar of artichoke hearts in hand. "Almost. You wouldn't happen to have any garlic, would you?"

"Bottom drawer of the fridge," Nichol replied, gesturing. "What are you making?"

"Thought I'd try my hand at an artichoke and garlic chicken pasta," Landon said, retrieving the garlic. "If that's alright with you?"

Her eyebrows rose. "Sounds delicious. You weren't joking about being able to cook."

"There's a lot you don't know about me," Landon said with a wink that made Nichol's heart skip.

She busied herself gathering ingredients for her pear tarts, trying to ignore the flutter in her stomach. "Well, while you work your magic, I'll get started on these tarts for tomorrow's knitting circle at the library."

"Knitting circle?" Landon asked, his knife pausing mid-chop.

She laughed. "Don't look so surprised. It's quite the social event around here."

They fell into an easy rhythm, working side by side in the kitchen. She stole glances at Landon as they cooked, admiring the confident way he moved around her space.

"So," Landon said, breaking a comfortable silence, "tell me more about this knitting circle. I'm having trouble picturing you wielding needles and yarn."

She snorted, rolling out pastry dough. "Oh, I'm terrible at it. But it's less about the knitting and more about the gossip, if I'm honest."

"Ah, now that I can picture," Landon teased.

As they continued to work, she relaxed, the tension of the day melting away. *This is nice*, she thought, surprised by how natural it felt to have Landon in her kitchen. But a voice in her head whispered a warning. *Don't get too comfortable. He won't be here forever.*

She shook off the intrusive thought and focused on Landon's animated storytelling as he stirred the pasta sauce.

"...and that's how I ended up cooking for an entire wedding party with nothing but a hot plate and a prayer," Landon finished with a chuckle.

"You're kidding!" she said, eyes widening.

"Let's just say I got very creative with aluminum foil and a lot of improvisation," Landon replied, a mischievous glint in his eye.

The kitchen filled with the enticing aroma of garlic and artichokes, mingling with the sweet scent of pears from Nichol's tarts. She inhaled deeply, savoring the blend of fragrances.

"It smells incredible in here." She moved to stand next to the stove. "Mind if I have a taste?"

Landon grinned, lifting the wooden spoon. "Be my guest. But I warn you, once you try it, you might never want to eat anything else."

She rolled her eyes playfully but leaned in to taste the sauce. The flavors exploded on her tongue, rich, tangy, with a perfect balance of herbs.

"Mmm," she hummed, closing her eyes. "It's good, but..." She paused dramatically.

Landon raised an eyebrow. "But?"

"It could use just a touch more salt," she said with a wink.

Landon's laughter filled the kitchen. "Oh, a critic! I'll have you know, madam, that my sodium levels are perfectly calibrated."

She couldn't help but join in his laughter, surprised by how much she was enjoying their banter. It had been a long time since she'd felt this...comfortable with someone.

"Well, Mr. Perfect Salt Levels," she teased, "while you finish up your masterpiece, let me tell you about the time I accidentally used salt instead of sugar in a batch of cookies for the library bake sale."

She launched into her story, marveling at how easily conversation flowed between them. It was almost enough to make her forget why Landon was really here. Almost.

She leaned against the counter, watching as Landon gave the pasta a final stir. She admired the way he moved with such confidence around her kitchen, like he'd always belonged there.

"So," she began, breaking the comfortable silence, "what's on the agenda for tomorrow?"

Landon wiped his hands on a dish towel, his expression turning thoughtful. "Once I get my car in a new set of tires, I thought I'd stake out the police station and see if I can finally speak with Detective Simmons. He won't return my calls."

"I'm sure remains found in a small town like Galesburg don't make it to the top of the state detectives' to-do list."

"No, it doesn't seem like it."

"Do you think you'll have time to take a break for lunch? I thought of someone we should talk to. Someone who may be able to provide information that could help us in the investigation."

"Yeah, of course. Who is it?"

"A childhood friend of Will's, Ethan Hsu. He owns a restaurant in town now and I figured we could drop in for lunch...."

"And possibly ask some questions to go with our meal," Landon said with a knowing look. "It's worth a try."

"Great." Nichol nodded, tucking a strand of hair behind her ear. "The library is hosting the Spring Festival committee meeting, which I somehow got roped into serving on. I'm in charge of the snacks. Hence the pear tarts, but we can go after it's over."

"Ah, so that's why you're subjecting innocent children to your baking," Landon teased, earning him a playful swat on the arm.

"I'll have you know that my baking skills are legendary in this town," she retorted, trying to keep a straight face.

Just then, the timer buzzed loudly, making them both jump. Nichol hurried to the oven, slipping on mitts and extracting the tray of golden-brown tarts.

"They look perfect," Landon commented, peering over her shoulder.

Her pulse sped up at his nearness but she quickly pushed the feeling aside. "Let's hope they taste as good as they look. Now, shall we eat?"

As Landon plated the pasta, she set the table.

They sat down to eat, and Nichol took her first bite of the pasta. "Oh wow," she said, impressed. "This is amazing, Landon."

He smiled, a hint of pride in his eyes. "Glad you approve. So, tell me more about this reading hour. Any particular stories on the agenda?"

They continued to eat and chat, and she relaxed more than she had in years. It was nice, she thought, to have someone to share a meal with, to talk about the day ahead. But a nagging voice in the back of her mind reminded her not to get too comfortable. After all, Landon was here to solve a mystery, not to be her friend. And some mysteries, Nichol knew all too well, were better left unsolved.

Nichol twirled her fork in the pasta, gathering her thoughts. "You know, I've been running that reading hour for years, but I still get nervous sometimes. Kids can be a tough audience."

Landon leaned forward. "Really? I wouldn't have pegged you as the nervous type."

She laughed. "Oh, there's a lot you don't know about me." The words slipped out before she could stop them. "I mean, I'm sure there's a lot we don't know about each other."

"Well, why don't we change that?" Landon suggested, his

voice light but his eyes searching. "What made you decide to become a librarian?"

Nichol hesitated, then decided to share a piece of her past. "My mother, actually. She loved books, had a whole room full of them. When I was little, she'd read to me every night. After she passed, the library became my sanctuary."

Landon's expression softened. "I'm sorry about your mother. That must have been tough."

"It was," she said, surprised by her own openness. "What about you? What drew you to detective work?"

As Landon spoke about his passion for solving puzzles and helping people, Nichol found herself drawn in by his enthusiasm. She realized with a start that she was enjoying his company, not just tolerating it.

After they finished eating, they fell into an easy rhythm cleaning up. Nichol washed while Landon dried, their movements synchronized like they'd done this a hundred times before.

"You know," Nichol said, handing him a plate, "I can't remember the last time I had someone over for dinner like this. It's…nice."

Landon smiled, a warmth in his eyes that made Nichol's heart skip a beat. "It is nice. Thank you for letting me crash in your guest room."

A feeling of safety and contentment washed over her as they finished cleaning up, but she also couldn't help feeling more than a little anxiety. She'd let her guard down tonight, had shared more than she had shared with anyone in a long time with a man who wouldn't be staying. Maybe that had made it easier to share, but she also knew that sharing was a sign that her feelings for Landon had moved beyond that of the professional. If she was being honest, her feelings were rapidly moving beyond that of mere friendship. Landon was seemingly unaware of her conflicted feelings, which only had her questioning whether he felt any of what she did. She'd enjoyed their evening but couldn't shake the feeling that she was playing with fire.

They finished cleaning and Nichol followed Landon to the base of the stairs.

"I hope you'll be comfortable up there. If you need anything, just...well, you know where to find me."

Landon paused on the third step, turning back to face her. "Nichol, I can't thank you enough for this. Your hospitality, the dinner, the conversation. It's been..."

"Unexpected?" Nichol said, a small smile playing on her lips.

He chuckled. "Exactly. In the best way possible."

Their gazes held, and a frisson of attraction spread through her. It was a feeling she hadn't experienced in years, one that both thrilled and terrified her.

"Good night, Landon," she said, breaking the silence.

"Good night, Nichol." His voice was warm with genuine affection.

She stayed at the bottom of the stairs, watching him go up. A big part of her wanted to call him back and continue their conversation into the night. Another part screamed at her to be careful, reminding her of past hurts and the risks of letting someone in, especially someone who had no intention of hanging around after he got his story.

She heard the guest room door close and let out a breath she didn't realize she'd been holding. Turning away from the stairs, she made her way to the living room, then sank into her favorite armchair.

"What are you doing, Nichol?" she muttered to herself. "He's here for a case, nothing more."

But even as she tried to convince herself, she couldn't deny how safe she felt knowing Landon was just upstairs. The house, usually so quiet and empty, had come alive with him in it. She closed her eyes, savoring the feeling of companionship, however fleeting it might be.

With a sigh, she headed upstairs, casting a glance toward the guest room door before heading to her own room. She smiled to herself as she prepared for bed, grateful for the unexpected turn this day had taken.

Chapter Ten

After breakfast, Nichol left Landon at the police station to begin his quest to track down Detective Simmons, and headed to the library. The scrape of chair legs against the worn linoleum floor echoed through the library's large meeting room as Nichol and Lynn maneuvered tables into place. Morning sunlight streamed through the tall windows.

"I can't believe the hotel just put Landon out on the street like that," Lynn said, her voice tinged with disbelief as she straightened a stack of folding chairs.

Nichol paused, her hand resting on the back of a chair. "It's pretty messed up."

Lynn shook her head, her curls bouncing with the movement. "I mean, who kicks someone out like that? So, did he end up going to Unionville or heading back to D.C.?"

Nichol took a deep breath, steeling herself. "No, actually. He's still in town."

Lynn's eyebrows shot up, her interest obviously piqued. "Oh? Where did he end up finding a room?"

Nichol's her cheeks grew warm as she avoided Lynn's gaze, focusing intently on smoothing out a nonexistent wrinkle in the tablecloth. "He's...staying in my guest room."

The silence that followed was deafening. She could feel

Lynn's eyes boring into her. She braced herself for the inevitable barrage of questions that were sure to follow.

She looked up to find that Lynn had broken out a sly smile. "Is that right?" she drawled, leaning in conspiratorially.

"It's strictly platonic," she said hurriedly, straightening the serving plate full of cookies unnecessarily. She'd known Lynn long enough to recognize that tone. "I'm just offering him a place to stay while he's in town." She paused, then added in a lower voice, "And I'd appreciate it if you didn't tell anyone about his living arrangements."

Lynn held up her hands in mock surrender. "Your secret's safe with me." She paused, tilting her head thoughtfully. "But why does your relationship with him have to be strictly platonic? You're both adults. I know you aren't dating anyone. Is he?"

"I don't know because I haven't asked him. It's none of my business."

"Please, it's clear as day there's some interest there on both sides."

Nichol's face flushed. "I barely know him."

"If I had a man that looked like him staying in my house, you can be sure I'd get to know him." Lynn wiggled her eyebrows suggestively and winked.

Nichol opened her mouth to respond, but no words came out. Lynn's laughter filled the room, only intensifying Nichol's embarrassment.

Lynn wiped tears of laughter from her eyes, "You should see your face right now." After a moment, Lynn's laughter subsided, and her expression turned more serious. She placed a gentle hand on Nichol's arm. "Look, all I'm saying is it's okay if you like him. And if you want to have a casual fling, who cares what the old busybodies in town will say?"

She'd be lying if she said the thought hadn't crossed her

mind last night. But the complications, the potential gossip....

"I appreciate the support, Lynn," Nichol said, offering a small smile. "I'll keep your suggestions about a fling in mind, but for now, Landon is just staying in my spare bedroom. Nothing more."

As the words left her mouth, a soft cough sounded behind them. Nichol's heart plummeted as she and Lynn turned to find June Gillory, Will Gillory's wife, standing in the doorway. June's eyes darted between them, and Nichol knew instantly that she'd overheard. Heat flooded her face again, this time from mortification.

June, looking timid and apologetic, stepped into the room. "I'm so sorry for being early. I just wanted to make sure everything was ready for the committee meeting."

Nichol's mind raced. How much had June heard? What would she think? What would she say to others? She forced herself to respond, hoping she sounded steadier than she felt. "No problem at all, June. Lynn and I were just setting out the coffee and pastries that were sent over. I didn't realize you were on the Spring Festival committee."

June fidgeted with the strap of her purse. "Oh, yes. It was rather last minute. Poor Elizabeth Clower's husband's bursitis has flared up again. She had to step down from chairing the committee to help him at home, so I volunteered to fill in."

"That's very kind of you," Nichol replied, genuinely impressed. June was known to be unusually shy, especially given the family she'd married into. She typically avoided the spotlight. "The Spring Festival is such an important kickoff for our tourist season. It's great you stepped up."

"Tourism," she said, her voice taking on a subtle edge that made Nichol's skin prickle, "really is crucial for our town, isn't it?"

Nichol nodded slowly, a knot forming in her stomach. "Of course. It's our lifeblood."

June's eyes darted to Lynn, then back to Nichol. "I couldn't help but hear about that reporter staying in town. Landon Elkins, was it?" She paused, her words hanging in the air. "I do hope his...investigation...won't have any negative impact on our reputation."

Nichol's jaw tightened. She wanted to defend Landon, to explain that his presence wasn't a threat. But June's meaning was clear, and it stung. She could have never guessed how quickly the town's welcoming facade would crumble when the residents began to feel threatened.

Defensiveness and indignation rose inside her. She took a steadying breath before responding. "I'm not sure what you're implying, June. Landon is a professional journalist, not some tabloid hack looking to stir up trouble."

June's lips thinned into a tight smile. "Oh, come now, Nichol. We're all aware of your...collaboration with him." She emphasized the word *collaboration*. "Word travels fast in a small town like ours."

Yep, June had definitely heard her conversation with Lynn. And it wouldn't be long before the rest of the town knew. But she had nothing to be embarrassed about. She straightened her back. "I'm simply helping him with local context for his story. Nothing more."

June nodded. "Of course, of course. It's just that we're all so concerned about the town's image, you understand. We wouldn't want anything to jeopardize our quaint charm, would we?"

The little mouse had at least a little bit of roar in her.

Before Nichol could muster a response, the library's double doors swung open with a creak. A flurry of voices and the click of heels on hardwood flooded the room as other committee members arrived, their chatter filling the tense silence.

"Oh, looks like we're about to start," June said with saccharine sweetness, her eyes never leaving Nichol's.

Nichol's jaw clenched as she watched June turn to greet the newcomers, her posture relaxed like their loaded exchange had never happened. Lynn appeared at Nichol's elbow, pulling her sleeve.

"Come on," Lynn whispered, "let's get out of here before you spontaneously combust."

They slipped out of the meeting room, Nichol's heart pounding in her ears. Once in the relative privacy of the main library, she let out a long, shaky breath.

"Well," Lynn said, leaning against a bookshelf, "that wasn't very subtle."

Nichol ran a hand through her hair, her frustration bubbling over. "No, but I don't think she was trying to be subtle."

Lynn's grimace told Nichol everything she needed to know before her friend even spoke. "Not at all and she definitely heard the last part of our conversation, if not more."

The bad feeling in Nichol's stomach intensified, twisting into knots. She could almost see the gossip spreading through town like wildfire, judgment and speculation following in its wake. "This is bad, Lynn. This is really, really bad."

NICHOL KEPT HER head down through the rest of the committee meeting and left the moment June declared the meeting adjourned. When she arrived at the police station, she could tell right away that Landon's morning hadn't gone any better than hers. And his expression only darkened when she told him about June overhearing her conversation with Lynn and that the whole town would likely soon know about their temporary living arrangements.

"I'm sorry," Landon said. "I'll find another place to stay tonight. I should have my car back by this afternoon and—"

"No," Nichol cut him off. "We aren't doing anything wrong. Not in investigating Addison's disappearance and not with where you lay your head at night. It's nobody's business."

He gave her a searching look. "Are you sure?"

"I'm sure." She was sure she was right, but she was also sure the people in town who didn't like her choices would continue to make it known.

Do what's right because it's right, her father's voice echoed in her head.

She smiled and changed the subject. "Are you ready for lunch?"

Landon hesitated for a moment before answering. "Yes, lead the way."

She led him to her car, and they began the short drive through the narrow streets of the older part of town. Landon sat in the passenger seat, his gaze trained out the window. She wondered if he was regretting even coming to Galesburg. The town hadn't exactly welcomed him, and now he was bound to be the subject of gossip.

"We're almost there," she said, breaking the silence that had stretched between them since leaving the police station. "It's not much to look at from the outside, but I've heard the food is amazing."

Landon turned to her. "I'm never one to turn down lunch, but I am curious about why you're taking me to this particular restaurant."

"Because if we're going to find anything useful about Will and his possible connection to Addison, we need to talk to people who actually knew him twenty-one years ago."

She pulled into a small parking lot beside a squat, brick building that looked as if it had been built sometime in the fifties. Ethan's Eatery. The restaurant's door was heavy wood with a small window, the glass clouded from decades of use. A bell jingled overhead as Nichol pushed it open, releasing a rush of warm air.

The interior was bathed in amber light from vintage fixtures hanging from the ceiling that cast a warm glow over the worn wooden bar that ran along one wall. Behind it, a large mirror reflected the room, bordered by shelves of liquor bottles.

A woman in all black stood behind the hostess stand. Nichol requested a table for two and the hostess led them past a wall where photographs of the town through the decades hung on the wall. The lunch rush had apparently already wound down, leaving one table and two of the booths occupied. The waitress led them to the table by the front window looking out onto the parking lot and street beyond.

"Can I start you two with some drinks?" the waitress asked, placing menus in front of them.

"Coffee, black," Landon said.

Nichol nodded. "Same for me, and I already know what I'm having. I'll have the garlic noodles."

Landon scanned the menu quickly. "I'll take the Korean chicken wings."

"Coming right up." The waitress collected the menus and headed toward the swinging doors that led into the kitchen.

Nichol watched Landon's eyes travel around the restaurant, taking in the details.

"So," Landon said, turning his attention back to her, "are you going to tell me why we're really here?"

Nichol leaned forward, lowering her voice. "The owner and head chef here, Ethan Hsu, grew up with Will. They used to be close friends. If anyone might know whether Will knew Addison, it's Ethan."

Landon's expression shifted from polite interest to focused attention. "And you think he'll talk to us?"

"Ethan's a good guy. Straightforward." She glanced toward the kitchen. "He and Will had some kind of falling-out a few years ago. I don't know what happened, but I heard they haven't spoken in ages."

"That could work in our favor," Landon said, reaching into his pocket for his phone, checking something before returning it to his pocket.

Nichol nodded. "Ethan's not the type to spread gossip, but I'm hoping he'll help us out."

"And you think he might know if Will had a connection to Addison?"

"I think if Will ever mentioned a girl from out of town, Ethan would have been the person he told."

The waitress returned with their coffees. "Your food will be up in about ten minutes."

Before the waitress could turn away, Nichol spoke up. "Excuse me, is Chef Ethan in the kitchen today?"

The woman chuckled. "I'm not sure he ever leaves. Would you like me to tell him you're asking for him?"

"Please. You can tell him Nichol Bunin is asking for him. We went to high school together. I was a couple of years behind him, but I hope he'll remember me."

"Sure thing." The waitress smiled and headed back toward the kitchen.

Through the small window to the kitchen, Nichol could see movement, someone looking out at them before disappearing again. She recognized Ethan's profile immediately.

She watched the kitchen door swing open. Ethan emerged, wiping his hands on a towel.

He hadn't changed much over the years. His dark hair was now streaked with premature gray at the temples, and faint lines around his eyes suggested years of laughter. His white chef's coat was pristine except for a splash of sauce near the pocket of his coat, and his hands, though clean, bore the calluses and minor burns of someone who had spent decades in a kitchen.

When his eyes met hers, his expression softened into genuine pleasure.

"Nichol Bunin," he said, his voice warm with affection. "It's been too long."

She rose from her seat, a smile spreading across her face. "Ethan. It's so good to see you. I've been meaning to stop by ever since I heard you opened this restaurant, but life has gotten in the way of coming down to check it out until now."

Nichol caught a whiff of rosemary and garlic clinging to his clothes when he folded her into a hug.

Ethan studied her face as they pulled apart. "You look great. Haven't aged a day."

"Well now, you may need to get your eyes checked, but I'll take the compliment." She laughed then gestured to Landon.

"Ethan, this is Landon Elkins. Landon, this is Ethan Hsu, owner and chef of the best Asian-American fusion restaurant in Galesburg."

"It's easy when you're the only Asian-American fusion restaurant in town," Ethan laughed, taking Landon's outstretched hand. "Good to meet you, though I kind of feel like I already know you somewhat."

Landon shook his hand. "I'm gathering that my arrival hasn't gone unnoticed."

"That's putting it mildly," Ethan said, sitting in one of the two unoccupied chairs at the table. "Reporter from D.C. asking questions and dropping the name of the most prominent family in the county. You might as well have ridden into town on a neon float during the harvest parade."

"Not exactly the low profile I was shooting for," Landon said. "But I suppose that was inevitable."

Ethan's gaze shifted between them. "We don't get many outsiders asking difficult questions around here. Especially right after human remains were discovered. That's a lot of excitement in a couple of days for our small town. It was inevitable that some people would get riled up over it."

Landon cleared his throat. "I'm interested in learning more about some of the people I believe may be connected to the story I'm looking into. Nichol thought you might have some insights."

"Did she now?" Ethan's eyes flicked to Nichol while he shook his head. "I'm not in the business of gossip."

"This isn't about gossip," Nichol assured him. "It's about finding the truth about what happened to a young girl who disappeared."

Ethan's gaze swung to Landon, studying him for a long moment. "I admire journalists, especially those that dig into the stories that need to be told even when people don't want to hear them."

"I appreciate that," Landon replied.

"I don't begrudge any man for doing what he believes is right, so long as he's not hurting innocent people in the process," Ethan said pointedly.

"I'm not interested in sensationalism or gotcha journalism," Landon said. "My only interest is in finding the truth for Addison Kober's family."

Nichol couldn't help but notice that Landon had failed to mention his own possible familial connection to the case.

"Truth," Ethan echoed. "That's a complicated thing."

"Not to me," Landon replied forcefully. "Our responses to it are often complicated, but the truth just is. At least, that's how I see it."

Ethan studied his hands for a long moment. The restaurant hummed around them with the clatter of silverware and murmur of conversations. "I've got about five minutes before my sous-chef sends out a search party. What do you want to know?"

Through the restaurant window, Nichol could see cars passing on the street, people going about their daily routines, unaware of the conversation happening just feet away that might start to bring answers to Addison's disappearance.

"You and Will used to be close as teens," Nichol said without preamble. "Do you remember if he ever mentioned meeting or hanging out with a girl about his age named Addison Kober?"

Ethan's eyes went wide. "The teenager that went missing all those years ago?"

"Yes." Landon nodded, his expression giving nothing away. "We have reason to believe Will might have known Addison before she disappeared."

"Sounds to me like you're on a fishing expedition, Mr. Elkins," he said, the warmth fading from his tone. "And I won't contribute to that. Will and I have had our differences, but speculation without evidence is just gossip with a press badge attached to it."

He began to rise from his chair, the legs scraping against the floor. "I should get back to work."

"I saw her," Nichol said, her voice cutting through the tension. "Addison Kober. Here in town, not long before she went missing."

Ethan paused, half standing, his hands flat on the table. For a moment, he seemed frozen in place, caught between leaving and staying. Then, slowly, he lowered himself back into the chair.

"I don't know anything about that," he said, studying Nichol's face in what she thought was in an attempt to assess whether she was telling the truth or not.

She kept her eyes on Ethan, letting him see the truth in them.

Ethan sighed. "Look, Will and I grew apart over the years, but I don't have anything against him, and I don't want to cause trouble for him," he said, his voice low enough that it wouldn't carry beyond their table.

"I know you're a stand-up guy, Ethan," Nichol said quickly, reaching across the table though stopping short of touching his hand. "That's why I know you'd do whatever you can to help find out what happened to a missing girl."

The compliment landed as she'd intended, softening something in Ethan's expression. He ran a hand through his hair, leaving it mussed, letting Nichol see some of the boy he'd been in the man sitting in front of her.

"I know Will was seeing someone during his internship in D.C. that his father didn't approve of. He and his dad had a couple of arguments. The one I was at their house for was pretty loud."

A surge of adrenaline rushed through Nichol at Ethan's words, but she didn't let it show. She didn't want to spook Ethan now that he was talking.

Landon appeared to have no such reservations. He leaned forward, his attention laser-focused on Ethan. "Will had an internship in Washington, D.C.?"

Ethan nodded. "Yes. The summer before our senior year in high school. I remember because it was also the first summer I had a job, and I didn't get to hang out with Will that much. Looking back, that was when we started growing apart." A faint smile crossed his face, nostalgia overtaking his caution. "I was a busboy at my uncle's pub. The short-order cook was a genius with food, and he took me under his wing. It's when I realized how much I loved cooking, and decided to make it my life's work. Will started hanging out with Derek."

"Do you know where Will worked?" Landon asked.

"Sure. He had an internship with one of the states' congressmen. I don't remember the name, but I'm pretty sure it was a Delaware congressman."

Landon's reaction was impossible to miss. His back straightened, his eyes widening. "Are you sure?"

"I'm sure. His father got him the job." Ethan's eye roll said what he thought about that. "But Will didn't last long. He got fired for coming in late, when he came in at all, after about two weeks if I'm remembering correctly."

The information seemed to electrify Landon, though he hid it better this time, merely nodding as he absorbed what Ethan had shared.

"Did you and Will hang out with anyone else that summer?" Someone who might know the name of the girl Will was seeing then?"

"Well, there was June, of course. She was always around. Even back then she only had eyes for Will. Derek Bondi hung out with us a lot back then, but I doubt Will would have told him anything he didn't tell me."

"Is Derek still managing the plastics plant in Unionville?" Nichol asked.

Ethan shrugged. "Last I heard. I haven't seen or spoken to him in years."

Before Landon could ask more, their waitress approached with their food. She sat their plates down in front of them as Ethan rose from his seat, smoothing down his apron. "I'll let you two eat. I really do need to get back to work, but lunch is on the house."

"Thank you for lunch and for taking the time to talk with us." Nichol said, understanding that they wouldn't get anything more from him.

"I appreciate your candor." Landon extended his hand. Ethan shook it before walking away, disappearing through the swinging kitchen doors again.

Nichol turned to her noodles and took a bite. "The information about Will's internship hit a nerve. Why?"

Landon leaned closer, his voice dropping so low it was almost a whisper. "Because Addison Kober was a congressional page the summer she disappeared."

A chill ran down her spine despite the warmth of the restaurant. "So, she and Will could have met in D.C."

"Exactly," Landon said, his eyes bright with the thrill of a lead. "It's a possible connection." Landon took a bite out of a chicken wing and chewed before continuing. "But here's the thing—I've seen a list of names of all the congressional pages for the year that Addison was a page and Will's name wasn't on it."

"How did you get a list of the pages from twenty-one years ago?" Nichol asked around another bite.

Landon grinned, wiggling his eyebrows as he did. "I have my ways."

She chuckled then sobered, considering the new information and how it fit into what they already knew. "Maybe Morris was embarrassed by his son getting fired and made the evidence that he'd ever had the job go away."

"That's possible," Landon said thoughtfully. "The Gillory family certainly had the connections. But if Will did work on the Hill, even in an unpaid position for a short time, there has to be some record of it."

"What are you planning to do with the rest of your afternoon?" Nichol asked.

Landon finished the last bite of his wings, wiping his hands on a napkin before answering. "I'll work my contacts in Capitol Hill to see if I can confirm Will's short stint as a federal employee. Someone there must remember him."

"And?" Nichol prompted, sensing there was more.

"Back to the police station," Landon said with determination. "I need to catch up with Detective Simmons. If Addison and Will did know each other, that changes the entire framework of the investigation. It establishes a direct connection that was either missed or deliberately overlooked twelve years ago."

Nichol nodded, understanding the significance. "A connection that would have made Will one of the first people of interest in her disappearance."

"Exactly."

"The Gillory name carries weight around here," Nichol reminded him, though she suspected he already understood that all too well.

"All the more reason to push for answers," Landon replied, taking a last sip of his water.

"What can I do to help?" she asked instead of answering directly.

Landon considered while Nichol finished her noodles. "Do you think you could get us a meeting with Mr. Gillory?"

Nichol couldn't help the grimace that crossed her face. "We don't really run in the same circles."

"But you are from Galesburg," Landon pressed. "And in a small town, that counts for something."

"I'll see what I can do," she said. "Mr. Gillory and Mary served on the hospital board together years ago. I can see if Mary still keeps in touch and would be willing to reach out on our behalf."

Landon shrugged. "It's worth a try."

They finished eating, and Landon made sure to send his thanks to Ethan one more time before they both stood to go. As they made their way toward the exit, Nichol began speaking. "I can drop you at the police station," she offered as they stepped outside into the crisp autumn air. "And pick you up when I'm finished with work if your car isn't ready, or to the mechanic if it is."

Landon hesitated, his brow furrowing. "I don't want to put you out. I can call an Uber."

The suggestion brought a laugh to Nichol's lips. "We don't have many Ubers around here. And it's not putting me out. I will pay my parking fine from the other day when I come to pick you up after I get off work."

Landon chuckled, the sound warm in the cool afternoon. "In that case, I accept your offer. Though I feel like I should be the one driving you around, not the other way around."

"Consider it professional courtesy, partner."

Chapter Eleven

It was after five, and Landon had been parked in the same uncomfortable plastic chair since his earlier conversation with Officer Daniels had yielded nothing but carefully worded deflections. And Detective Simmons still hadn't returned a single one of his messages or turned up at the Galesburg police station.

The station had emptied gradually, leaving him alone with a lone clerk and the persistent *tick-tick-tick* of an analog wall clock that seemed determined to remind him of passing time. He scrolled through his notes on his laptop, the names and dates blurring together after hours of review, searching for the thread that would unravel this whole mystery.

He'd spent some of the afternoon talking to contacts in D.C., calling in favors from former colleagues, and trying to piece together a timeline for Addison and Will that summer twenty-one years ago in D.C. He'd gotten his first lead an hour ago. A friend of a friend had put him in touch with a woman who worked at a liberal think tank now, but who had been a page for Delaware Congressman Norman Pike twenty-one years ago. She not only recalled Will working in the congressmen's offices for a short time during the summer, she'd been able to dig up an old photo of the welcome party the office had thrown for the pages which included a young, but easily recognizable, William Gillory.

The door to the station opened and Nichol stepped inside. She moved with purpose, cutting an impressive figure as she paused to scan the reception area.

She spotted him and headed his way. The clerk behind the glass counter barely glanced up as she approached, but Landon straightened in his chair, oddly pleased by her arrival despite his usual preference for working alone.

"How's your afternoon been?" Nichol slipped into the seat next to him.

He leaned back in his chair. "Pretty good actually. I was able to confirm that Will worked on Capitol Hill the same summer as Addison."

"That's great," Nichol said excitedly.

He matched her grin. "It puts them in close enough proximity to have met, but it doesn't mean they did meet. There's still a lot of work to do before I can be sure there's a story here." But his reporter's instincts were humming. He was on the right track. "Did you make any inroads with Mr. Gillory?"

Her nose scrunched. "Kind of. I got a phone number, but I didn't call because I wasn't sure how you wanted to approach her."

He had already learned that, despite his health issues, Morris Gillory wielded considerable influence. He'd have to tread carefully if he was able to get an interview with him.

"Good call," he said. "We need a strategy before we approach him. If Will did have a relationship with Addison that summer in D.C., his father might have been aware of it."

"Are you still up for dropping me off at the mechanic? I called and he said my car was ready."

"Of course," Nichol said, reaching into her purse and retrieving her crumpled parking ticket. "Let me just pay this before we head out."

Landon closed several tabs and shut down his laptop while she settled her parking citation.

Nichol finished her transaction and returned to him, tucking her wallet back into her purse with methodical precision. "All set."

They walked toward the glass doors, their footsteps echoing in the nearly empty reception area. The afternoon's gray light had deepened into early evening dusk, visible through the glass panels that flanked the exit.

Officer Daniels emerged as they reached the doorway, his face set in hard, uneven lines. Something had happened. Landon had been around enough law enforcement to be able to read the body language. The tight set of the man's shoulders and the controlled precision of his movements meant bad news.

Daniels raised his hand, an understated gesture that stopped them as effectively as a physical barrier. "Landon, Nichol, hold on there a minute."

There was a subtle shift in the atmosphere. Earlier, Daniels had been professionally evasive, offering empty reassurances wrapped in bureaucratic language. Now, there was purpose in his approach, his eyes scanning the waiting area. He exchanged a quick glance with Nichol, who had already pivoted to face Daniels.

Daniels stepped closer, lowering his voice despite them being the only three present. "We're putting out a press release within the hour, but I figured your persistence should get you a heads-up. We got confirmation through dental records on the identity of the remains."

Daniels's voice was steady, but Landon caught the subtle tension beneath the professional delivery. His pulse sped up.

"The bones have been positively identified through dental records as Addison Kober."

THE WANING WARMTH of the day did nothing to chase away the chill that had settled in Nichol's bones. She sat beside Landon on a bench in the park across from the police station. Landon's gaze had been focused on some point in the distance for more than ten minutes, though Nichol was sure that he wasn't seeing the freshly mowed lawn or the manicured flower beds at all.

Her heart ached for him. As much as he believed that the remains were Addison's, it was something else to know for sure that the teen was gone. It was a waste of a young life that she felt acutely as well. Maybe if she had spoken up sooner? Had pushed the police to follow up? She was sure the what-ifs would follow her for the rest of her life.

She stole a glance at Landon, noting the tightness in his jaw. The urge to reach out and comfort him was strong, but she hesitated, unsure if her touch would be welcome.

Her chest tightened as the silence stretched between them. The urge to say something, anything, to break the quiet was strong.

She placed her hand on the bench between them, close enough to offer comfort without intruding. "I know we anticipated this, but it still hurts more than I expected."

Landon's eyes met hers, frustration and anger swirling in their depths. "I know. From experience, I can tell you that all you can do is feel it and use it to get justice for the victim. We need to keep digging, to keep gathering the facts, until we find the killer. It's the only way to ensure justice for Addison."

"You're right," she said, taking strength from his words. "Are we still in this together?"

She reached a hand out, her fingers brushing his arm. She watched his expression soften at the touch, some of the lines of tension in his face easing. His gaze, moments before clouded with anger and grief, now held a glimmer of something else. Her breath caught as his fingers intertwined with hers.

"Together," Landon said. "I don't know how I'd get through this without you."

The air between them seemed to crackle with an energy she couldn't quite name.

"I'm sure you'd get through it just fine. You are the investigative reporter, after all," she said, acutely aware of how close they were sitting.

Landon smiled, almost shyly. "Yes, but I never had a partner before. I didn't know what I was missing."

His gaze stayed trained on her and the world around them faded away.

The park, the distant sounds of the townspeople going about their business, their investigation—everything receded, leaving only that moment and their connection.

"Nichol," Landon began huskily. "I—"

She could feel the warmth of his breath, see the flecks of gold in his hazel eyes. Her heart hammered in anticipation of what he might say. What might happen next between them.

Before she could overthink it, she leaned forward, closing the distance between them. Their lips met, tentative at first, then with growing intensity. The kiss was charged with months of unspoken tension, shared grief, and a connection that had been building since they first partnered on this case.

Her mind reeled as she leaned into the kiss, her hands moving to Landon's shoulders. His lips were warm and insistent against hers, and she could taste the faint bitterness of the coffee they'd shared earlier.

As suddenly as it began, the kiss ended. They pulled back, both breathing heavily. Her eyes fluttered open to meet Landon's gaze. His expression was a mixture of surprise and desire, an expression she suspected mirrored her own.

"I..." Nichol started, then faltered. Her heart was racing, and she struggled to find the right words.

"I have wanted to do that since the moment I saw you. I just wasn't sure if you..."

She smiled. "Me too. We're obviously attracted to each other and there's clearly something here." Her eyes met his, uncertainty and hope swirling in their depths. She bit her lower lip. "I'm not sure what it is, but I can feel it. Can't you?"

Her heart raced as she waited for his response.

Landon nodded slowly, grinning. "Yeah, I feel it too." He reached out, taking her hand in his. The warmth of his touch sent a shiver up her arm. "I don't know what this is either, Nichol, but there is something here and I'd like to see what it is. If you want to?"

A wave of relief washed over her. Thank God, she wasn't imagining his feelings for her.

"I do. I know we have a lot on our plates with this investigation—"

"We do," Landon said. "But I think we owe it to ourselves to explore this too. We can do both. Get justice for Addison and see if this feeling between us could become something real."

Real. His words made her feel giddy, but she reminded herself that they had a purpose that was bigger than chasing their passions.

She gave Landon's hand a squeeze. "Okay, I'm sure it won't be long before word gets out that the remains have been identified as Addison's. That means we might only have a little time before anyone who knows anything clams up tight. So, what do you think we should do next?"

The tension lines bloomed on Landon's forehead again. "Your friend Ethan mentioned that he and Will used to hang out with another teen. Derek Bondi. I say we pay him a visit ASAP."

Chapter Twelve

The smell of hot plastic assaulted Landon's nostrils as he and Nichol pushed through the glass doors of the factory. The chemical odor filled the air, making him suppress a cough. He'd spent the car ride to the factory reeling between thoughts of his kiss with Nichol and his guilt over the confirmation that the remains were in fact Addison's. He'd always known that would be the conclusion, but he wasn't prepared for how the certainty that Addison was dead would hit him. No matter how jaded and worldly he considered himself, there was still a tiny part of him that had held on to hope. And now that tiny part of him was gone forever.

He shook off his growing melancholy and focused on the task ahead. Getting justice for Addison.

Landon's gaze darted around the space. Empty. Faux leather chairs were worn at the edges. A potted plant in the corner that had seen better days and a clock on the wall that ticked loudly in the silence. But otherwise, there was no sign of life.

"Should we wait or…?" he asked Nichol.

"Better to ask for forgiveness than permission," she answered. "I say we find Derek's office while there's no one to try and stop us."

The corner of Landon's mouth twitched upward. Nichol's

boldness was one of the things he'd come to admire most about her.

They moved down the hall. Their footsteps echoed off the polished concrete floors as they strode through the factory's corridors. The air hummed with the distant whir of machinery and fluorescent lights buzzed overhead, casting everything in a harsh, unforgiving glow.

They rounded a corner and Landon caught sight of a single employee hunched over a workstation, totally absorbed in whatever was on his computer screen. The light from the monitor cast an eerie glow over the man's face, highlighting the deep shadows under his eyes. Lines on a spreadsheet reflected in his glasses.

They walked past the oblivious worker, who didn't even look away from the screen. The worker's fingers clacked against the keyboard, the sound fading behind them as they moved deeper into the building.

At the end of the hall, the door to the corner office was ajar. The plaque on its front read Derek Bondi, the gold lettering catching the light as they approached. Nichol stepped forward but Landon paused, his hand shooting out to stop her. His hand brushed against the fabric of her sleeve, his touch light but urgent.

"Wait," he whispered, tilting his head toward the door. "Do you hear that?"

A low, soothing voice drifted through the thin gap between the door and its frame, punctuated by soft, muffled sobs. The sound raised the hairs on the back of Landon's neck. He leaned forward, his brow furrowed as he strained to make out the words. The murmurs continued, too quiet to decipher but unmistakably intimate.

"Someone is crying," Nichol whispered, her breath warm against his ear as she leaned closer.

Landon nodded, his hand hovering near the door handle.

"Someone's clearly upset." His stomach knotted with apprehension.

Landon pushed the door open, the hinges giving a barely audible squeak.

A man, Derek Bondi he presumed, stood with his arms wrapped tightly around June Gillory. June's face was buried in Derek's chest, her body shaking with quiet sobs. She clutched at the fabric of his shirt, knuckles white with tension. Derek's hand moved in slow, soothing circles on her back, his head bent low over hers, lips moving in whispered comfort.

For a moment, time seemed to stand still. The air in the room was charged with a cocktail of emotions that Landon couldn't quite define. It was clear that Derek and June had some sort of relationship, and that the relationship was intimate. Before he could figure out what that might mean, Derek's head snapped up.

Their eyes met across the room, pinning Landon in place by the intensity of the other man's gaze.

Derek's eyes widened first in shock, pupils dilating in surprise, and then narrowed with unmistakable anger. A flush snaked up his neck. He took a quick step back from June, his body language shifting from comforting to defensive.

"What the hell do you think you're doing, bursting in my office?" Derek snarled in a low, dangerous voice, moving to stand protectively in front of June. His hands clenched into fists at his sides.

June peered around Derek's shoulder, wiping at her eyes with a tissue that she crumpled in her trembling hand. Her mascara had run, leaving faint black tracks down her cheeks. Her expression was a conflicted mix of embarrassment and defiance as she looked at Landon and Nichol. Recognition flashed across her features but was then quickly replaced by anger that transformed her tearstained face.

"He's the reporter from D.C.," she spat. "The one who started all this."

Landon's jaw clenched, his muscles tightening painfully as indignation rose in his chest.

"I'd say that the person who killed Addison Kober started it." His words came out sharper than he intended, slicing through the charged atmosphere in the office. "I just want to find out who that is and make sure they face justice for what they did."

Silence reigned for a heartbeat. Nichol's eyes bore into him, a silent warning.

Derek's nostrils flared. "I'm calling the police. The two of you are trespassing." He reached for the phone on his desk.

"I don't think you really want to do that?" Nichol asked, calmly, her gaze shifting meaningfully between him and June. She tilted her head, one eyebrow arched in challenge. "Then you'd have to explain to the police what Mrs. Gillory is doing here."

Landon watched as the full weight of Nichol's words sank in for Derek. The subtle shift in the air in the room was almost palpable. Derek's hand still hovered over his phone receiver, frozen in midair, but he made no move to pick it up. His eyes darted anxiously to June, a flash of panic replacing the anger for just an instant.

"Maybe you should just let them say their piece," June said, her voice rough from crying. She dabbed at her nose with the crumpled tissue, smudging more mascara across her cheek.

Landon studied June's face, noting the shift to resignation there. The fight seemed to drain from her. Her eyes, still red-rimmed and puffy, avoided direct contact with anyone in the room. It was clear the last thing June wanted was for her presence in Derek's office to become grist for the Galesburg gossip mill.

Derek reached out to June, his hand gliding over her shoulder in a gesture that was possessive yet gentle. The touch spoke volumes about the nature of their relationship.

"Don't worry," Derek said. "I'll take care of this."

June hesitated for a moment longer, her gaze sweeping over Nichol and Landon one last time, before she slipped out of the office.

The door clicked shut behind June, and Derek's expression hardened again. He turned his attention to Landon and Nichol. "What do you want?" He tapped an impatient rhythm on the polished surface of his desk.

"We want to ask you some questions about Addison Kober," Landon answered.

Derek gave a slight shake of his head, a gesture that set Landon's teeth on edge. "I don't know anything about her." His expression remained neutral, but he wouldn't maintain eye contact.

"Twenty years ago, Addison was dating Will. You were friends with him at the time, weren't you?" Landon pressed. He leaned forward, watching Derek's face intently for a hint of deception.

Derek waved a dismissive hand through the air. "Will's childhood infatuation, nothing more. Ancient history."

Landon's ire rose at the casual dismissal of Addison, of the tragedy that had been her short life, but he forced himself to remain calm. "I have it on good authority that Addison came to Galesburg the night she disappeared." He made sure not to look over at Nichol while he spoke the words. "Someone picked her up from the bus station."

Derek's eyes darted to the side for a split second before meeting Landon's intense gaze again. A muscle twitched in his jaw, the movement so slight it would have been easy to miss if Landon hadn't been watching so closely. "I said

I don't know anything about that girl's disappearance," he shot back, the words coming too quickly to be true.

"Did you ever speak with a reporter named Samuel Elkins?" Landon asked, changing his approach. He kept his gaze trained on Derek's face, looking for the slightest flicker of recognition. "He was investigating Addison's disappearance right after it happened."

Derek's brow furrowed. A thin sheen of sweat had formed on his upper lip. After a moment's pause, he shook his head. "No, I don't remember anyone by that name." He picked up a pen from his desk and twirled it.

"What about June Gillory?" Landon asked. "Do you remember how long you two have been having an affair?"

Derek's face flashed panic that was quickly replaced by cold, seething fury. The transformation was instantaneous and chilling. The pen in his hand snapped, the crack audible in the silence. Ink leaked onto his fingers, but he didn't seem to notice.

"Get out," he snarled. Spittle gathered on his lips, his face contorted with a rage that seemed disproportionate to the question. "Get out now, and don't ever come back."

Nichol's hand brushed reassuringly along his arm, her touch light but firm. A signal that he had pushed too far. They made their way to the office door.

But at the doorway, Landon turned back to meet Derek's steely gaze. The man hadn't moved, his body still rigid with anger.

"I will find out what happened to Addison. And if you, or your buddies, had anything to do with her death, I swear I will make sure you pay."

The threat hung between them. His gaze never wavered from Derek's face, watching as the man's expression shifted from anger to something more complex, something that, just for an instant, looked like fear.

Chapter Thirteen

The door of the plastics factory clanged shut behind them, the industrial noise fading as Nichol and Landon stepped into the outside. Gravel crunched under their feet as they walked across the parking lot. Nichol's mind whirred, trying to process what they'd just witnessed. She glanced at Landon. His brow was furrowed in concentration. They slid into the car and Nichol couldn't hold back any longer.

"What do you think?" she asked, leaning against the driver's side door.

Landon's jaw clenched. "I think he knows something, but he's not going to tell us."

Nichol nodded, unsurprised by Landon's assessment. "I was surprised to find June there."

Landon's eyebrows shot up. "Yeah, that was unexpected. Are they known to be close?"

Nichol shrugged. "I mean, I knew they'd been friends as teens like Ethan said, but that was a long time ago. June and Will have been married for over a decade, and as far as I knew, happily so."

She thought back to the town picnics and charity events she'd attended, where June and Will had seemed the picture of marital bliss. But now, doubt seeped in. Had that all just been for show?

"Well, it didn't look all that happy from what I just saw." Landon settled into the passenger seat, his brow furrowed in concentration. The engine hummed, but Nichol made no move to pull out of the parking space.

He tapped the fingers of his right hand against his right thigh, a sign, she'd learned, that he was thinking hard about something.

"Okay, what are you thinking now?" she asked after a moment.

"Just trying to make all the puzzle pieces fit into something that makes sense. But even if June and Derek are having an affair, I don't see how it figures into Addison's murder."

Nichol sighed, feeling the same frustration. The pieces were there, but they just weren't clicking into place. She stared out the windshield, watching a few leaves skitter across the parking lot.

"Maybe it doesn't figure. Maybe the affair, if there's an affair, has nothing to do with Addison's murder," she said. "But I know someone, or rather *someones*, we could talk to who might be able to give us more insight."

Landon's expression shifted, a slow, sexy smile spreading across his face. The sight of it made Nichol's heart do flip-flops, a reaction she was still getting used to after days of working together.

"Ah, my favorite knitting nanas," he said. His eyes twinkled with amusement.

She couldn't help but smile back, both at Landon's enthusiasm and at the prospect of visiting the town's most notorious gossips. If anyone knew the intricacies of Galesburg's personal relationships, it would be those ladies.

The library's small meeting room buzzed with energy when Nichol and Landon stepped inside. The four elderly women sat in a circle, their knitting needles clicking, colorful yarn spilling from their bags.

Mary spotted them first, her face lighting up like a child's on Christmas morning when her eyes landed on them. "Well, if it isn't our favorite investigative duo!" she exclaimed, her needles pausing mid-stitch.

The other ladies' heads snapped up, their gazes landing on Nichol then quickly swiveling to Landon.

"Ladies." Landon greeted them with a warm smile. "Always a pleasure." The ladies twittered, and even Hazel blushed.

Landon grabbed two chairs from the tables that had been pushed to the sides of the room and the ladies scooted over to make room for them. She and Landon squeezed in between Mary and Emma.

Nichol couldn't help but feel a twinge of amusement at their reaction to him. Even in their twilight years, these women weren't immune to his charm.

Nichol cleared her throat. "We actually wanted to ask you all a question, if you don't mind."

The knitting needles stilled now, all attention focused on Nichol. She could almost see the curiosity radiating off them in waves.

"Oh?" Mary leaned forward, her eyes sparkling. "Do tell, dear."

Nichol hesitated, feeling as if she was walking on delicate ground. "Have any of you heard…rumors about June and Derek? Perhaps…having an affair?"

The ladies glanced at each other, their looks loaded with unspoken communication.

Hazel, ever the picture of propriety, straightened in her chair. "I'm not in the habit of gossiping," she declared primly.

Mary snorted. "Since when? This morning?"

Hazel huffed indignantly, while Lucia and Emma stifled

laughs. Nichol caught sight of Landon from the corner of her eye, a small smile tugging at his lips. She fought back her own amusement, reminding herself of the gravity of their investigation.

Mary took up her knitting again, her needles clacking decisively. "June and Derek have had an on-again, off-again thing for years."

"Mary!" Hazel hissed, shooting a worried glance at the library door. "Keep your voice down!"

Mary waved her hand dismissively, undeterred.

Emma, the last person Nichol would have expected to speak up, chimed in. "Given Will's numerous affairs during their marriage, who could blame June? That poor woman's been through enough." Her round face was flushed with indignation.

Nichol's eyebrows shot up. Will's affairs were news to her. She glanced at Landon, who had his investigative reporter's face on.

Hazel huffed, her needles working furiously. "Derek and June should have just married each other. Anyone could see those kids were wild for each other from the beginning."

Landon leaned forward, his brow furrowed. "Why didn't they?"

Mary's eyes gleamed. "Money. Derek makes a good living running the plastics factory, but he doesn't come from money. He was never going to have the kind of wealth the Gillorys have."

A piece of the puzzle clicked into place in Nichol's mind. She hesitated before asking her next question, unsure if she wanted to know the answer. "Does Will know about his wife and friend's...arrangement?"

Mary shook her head vigorously, her silver curls bouncing. "No way. He'd lose his mind if he did."

Lucia's usually kind face twisted into a deeper scowl.

"That man's ego is so big, he can't see anything other than himself."

Nichol sat back, her mind reeling. The web of relationships in this town was far more tangled than she'd been aware of.

Landon's brow furrowed. He leaned forward, elbows on his knees, and summarized. "So, Will has had multiple affairs over the years. And June and Derek have been involved in a years-long ongoing relationship that Will most likely doesn't know about."

Mary tsked. "That's about the sum of it."

Nichol watched Landon process the information, his eyes narrowing as he pieced together the complex web of relationships. She could almost see the gears turning in his head as he tried to connect this new information to Addison's murder. She was just as confused, unsure of how this tangled mess of affairs fit into their investigation. Or if it did at all.

Her eyes landed on Landon's face, and she gave a small shrug, silently communicating her uncertainty.

Mary caught the look between them. "Why are you asking? What's the Gillorys' convoluted marriage got to do with that poor girl's remains being found?"

"We're not sure," he admitted.

"We do have another question. More of a favor," Nichol said. "If I remember correctly, Mary, you served on the board of the Business Council with Morris Gillory a few years back."

"That I did," Mary confirmed. "Why?"

"Do you think you could reach out to Morris and see if he'll meet with us?"

Mary tsked again. "Well, it has been quite a while since I've spoken to him, but for you, honey, I'll give it a shot."

"Thank you." Hopefully, Mary would be successful.

Nichol couldn't help but feel a twinge of frustration. They

had more information now, but it seemed to have only complicated matters further. She wondered if they were on a wild-goose chase. Following a gossip trail because they'd found few real clues to lead them to the person who was responsible for Addison's death.

Mary set her knitting in her lap and reached out to pat Landon's hands with a gentle, grandmotherly touch. "Well, I for one am glad you're looking into it. That poor girl's family deserves to know what happened to her and the person that did this to her ought to be locked up good and tight."

Mary punctuated her statement with a firm nod, her wispy white hair bobbing with the movement.

Around the room, the other ladies expressed their agreement with soft "Uh-huhs" and emphatic head nods.

"We'll do our best," she promised. "For Addison and her family."

THE STEADY HUM of tires on asphalt was the only sound inside the car as Nichol steered the car toward her house. Landon sat beside her, his presence a comforting constant after another long day at the library. Their diversion to speak with Derek and then the nanas meant the mechanic's shop was closed by the time they left the library. She and Landon hadn't had time to talk over the information that the knitting nanas had imparted. She'd had to jump on a video call with a vendor right after leaving the ladies and the library had stayed so busy, she hadn't been able to find a moment to speak to Landon since.

Now as she drove them to her house, her mind drifted back to the conversation with the older women. "I can't believe I never knew about June and Derek."

A week ago, she would have struggled to believe that June and Derek... But after seeing them together in Derek's office, well, the idea didn't seem all that impossible. She searched through her memories, wondering if there were other signs she'd missed over the years, but she could barely ever recall seeing Derek and June together without Will. Of course, if the two really were having an affair they would have had to be extremely discreet to have kept it under wraps for so long.

"Secrets have a way of surfacing eventually," Landon said, leaning back in his seat. "Even the ones we think are buried deep."

Nichol turned the car onto the highway, sighing. "I just feel like I don't know this town anymore. I've lived here my whole life. I thought I knew these people, my friends and neighbors. But now, it's like they're strangers."

The car's headlights cut through the growing darkness, illuminating the path ahead. But for her, it was almost like she was seeing everything about the town in a new, less favorable light. She blinked rapidly, fighting back the sudden sting of tears.

"Everyone has secrets, Nichol. It doesn't make them good or bad, just human." He paused, a wry smile on his lips.

"Lucky for us, we only need to focus on one secret for now. Does June and Derek's affair have anything to do with Addison's murder?"

"Well, the nanas said that June and Derek have been having an affair for years," Nichol answered.

"And we know Derek, Will, Addison, and June partied together the summer Addison died," Landon replied.

The pieces of information they'd uncovered swirled in Nichol's head, but nothing fit together. "Maybe the affair between Derek and June started when they were teens and Addison was going to tell Will so one, or both of them, killed her to stop her." But that didn't feel right.

Landon must have agreed because his head was already

shaking. "No. Why would Will care if Derek and June were together back then? He was dating Addison at the time."

Nichol's hands tightened on the steering wheel as she processed Landon's statement. He was right. Her theory didn't make sense. Nothing did. There seemed to be no reason for anyone to want Addison Kober dead.

The streetlights flashed by, casting alternating shadows across her face. She bit her lower lip, another question forming in her mind.

"Do you think Will knows his wife is having an affair with his best friend?" She glanced quickly at Landon before returning her eyes to the road.

"It's hard to say. Will didn't strike me as a man who would sit by and let his wife and friend embarrass him, but..." He trailed off, his gaze trained on the dark road ahead. "The thing is, we never truly know what's going on beneath the surface of someone's life. I mean, Will seems to have kept his own secret all these years. It's pretty clear he never got over his feelings for Addison."

She couldn't disagree. This whole investigation was so frustrating. It felt like they were further away from answers than ever. She didn't know how Landon did it.

She navigated a gentle curve in the road. The highway wound around the forest. The long street was unlit, the only illumination coming from the sedan's headlights. Suddenly, another pair of headlights flooded the rear window. She drew one hand to her brow, attempting to block the glare. A large truck roared up behind them, seeming to have materialized out of the darkness. The truck's engine rumbled loudly, the driver revving the engine. The sound was a growl that made the hair on the back of Nichol's neck stand up.

"Argh," Nichol said, her heart rate speeding up. "I hate these big trucks. Turn off your high beams, buddy!" A chill ran down her spine as the truck's headlights bore down on them, uncomfortably bright and aggressive.

The truck loomed closer. The truck's massive black grille bore down on her sedan. She edged over to allow the driver to pass, her hands gripping the steering wheel so tightly that her knuckles were turning white.

"It's awfully close," she said, pressing down on the accelerator and sending her sedan shooting forward. The leather on the steering wheel grew slick with a sheen of nervous perspiration as adrenaline coursed through her veins. Her eyes darted between the road ahead and the mirror, watching the vehicle behind them with growing unease. "Why is it following so closely?"

Landon's eyes narrowed as he glanced back at the truck. Tension radiated from his body as he assessed the threat behind them. "Speed up. Try to put some distance between us."

She pressed harder on the accelerator, her heart pounding. The car's engine whined in protest as she pushed the old Civic beyond its comfortable cruising speed. The speedometer moved upward, but the truck easily matched their pace, its engine growling louder the closer it got to her bumper. She could hear the truck downshifting, preparing for another surge of speed.

"It's still coming," she said frantically.

"Just keep driving," Landon said, his voice taut.

The truck's headlights flashed in the rearview mirror, bathing the interior of their car in harsh white light. The glare was so intense it seemed to light up the entire area. Nichol squinted, struggling to focus on the road ahead.

"Why won't he back off?" she said, more to herself than to Landon.

Before Landon could answer, the truck sped up and slammed into their rear bumper. The impact jolted them forward. The crunch of metal bounced around the interior of the Civic. Nichol's teeth rattled as her head snapped back against the headrest. Their car lurched, fishtailing on the road. She wrestled with the wheel, her arms straining as she fought to keep them on the road.

"Hold on!" she shouted. The smell of burning rubber filled the car's interior.

Landon twisted in his seat, craning his neck to peer through the rear window. Nichol could see his furrowed brow reflected in the glass, his jaw clenched tight with determination.

"Can you see who it is?" she asked, too afraid to turn and take a quick look herself. She had to stay focused on the road. Every muscle in her body was coiled tight, afraid of what the truck's driver was going to do next.

"No. The windows are tinted," Landon growled, frustration evident in his tone. "I can just make out a figure in the driver's seat, but they're wearing sunglasses, and a ball cap pulled low."

Which meant the person driving didn't want to be recognized. This wasn't an accident or a spur-of-the-moment decision. Whoever was driving that truck planned this. Which meant they were in real trouble.

"Can you reach your phone?" Nichol asked.

"It's in my computer bag," Landon said, reaching into the back seat. His seat belt strained against his chest as he stretched, fingers grasping for the bag.

Before he could get a hand on it, another jarring impact rocked the car. The steering wheel jerked out of Nichol's hands. For one terrifying moment, she had no control at all. The car slid sideways across the road. Time seemed to slow around them. Every sound was amplified. The squeal of tires. The groan of metal. Their own heavy breathing.

Landon braced his arms against the dashboard as another hit to the rear of the car sent them lurching forward then spinning again. The world outside the windows became a blur of darkness and flashes of light from the car's headlights as it spun multiple times. Then the world seemed to tilt, and the car's wheels left the ground. Time seemed to slow, each second stretching as they sailed through the air and down into the gully on the side of the road.

"Nichol!" Landon yelled. His voice sounded as if it was coming from very far away. She could barely hear him over the rush of blood in her ears.

She didn't respond. She couldn't manage to make a sound around the terror clogging her throat. Then there was another deafening crash and the screech of twisting metal. Her head snapped forward, then back against the headrest. And everything went black.

Chapter Fourteen

The antiseptic smell of the hospital waiting room was doing nothing to assuage his anxiety and concern. Landon had insisted on riding with her in the ambulance and had breathed a sigh of relief when she'd regained consciousness on the ride, but the EMTs had quickly whisked her into the emergency room, and he hadn't been allowed to see her since.

Now his leg bounced uncontrollably as he pressed his phone tighter against his ear. "It happened so fast, Logan," he said, remembering the fear he'd felt for both of them. "One minute we were driving to her house from the library, and the next..." He swallowed hard, the image of Nichol's limp form being pulled from the car's wreckage seared into his mind. "She was unconscious, Logan. For a few minutes, she wasn't responding at all."

On the other end of the line, Logan's steady voice cut through his spiraling thoughts. "But she has regained consciousness, right? That's a good sign, Landon. Head injuries can be scary, but if she regained consciousness quickly, that's really positive."

Landon nodded, forgetting that his brother couldn't see him. He tried to take comfort in Logan's words, but the gnawing worry in his gut refused to go away. What if there was internal bleeding they couldn't see? What if she slipped back into unconsciousness?

"Yeah, you're right," Landon managed, his voice unconvincing even to his own ears. He glanced toward the curtained-off area where the doctors and nurses had taken Nichol. What was taking so long for someone to come tell him something? Did that mean her condition had worsened?

"Listen, I can be there in a couple of hours if you need me," Logan said. "Just say the word, and I'll hit the road."

Gratitude for his brother's offer momentarily calmed him. Logan was the younger brother, but he had always been the steadiest of the three Elkins siblings.

"Thanks, Logan," Landon said. "I really appreciate that, but I think I've got this handled." He ran a hand over his head.

"You sure?" Logan asked, concern evident in his tone. "It's no trouble, really."

He opened his mouth to respond, but movement in his peripheral vision caught his attention. His heart leaped into his throat as he saw a doctor emerging from behind the curtain the EMTs had slipped Nichol behind. Finally.

"Logan, I've got to go," he said hurriedly. "I see the doctor. I'll call you back later."

He ended the call before his brother could reply and shoved the phone into his pocket as he stood.

The doctor's face revealed nothing as he approached, his footsteps echoing in the quiet waiting room. Landon's heart raced, but he forced himself to stand still, bracing for whatever news was coming.

"Mr. Elkins?" the doctor asked, his tone reassuring.

"Yes. How is she? Is Nichol okay?"

The doctor's lips curved into a small smile. "Ms. Bunin will be fine. She's awake and alert."

A wave of relief washed over him, so strong it nearly took him to his knees. He let out a breath. "Thank God."

"She did sustain a slight concussion. I'll be discharging her momentarily so she can go home and rest. I'll include warning signs to look for that would indicate she should be brought back to the hospital in her discharge orders, but she should have someone stay with her. Just to ensure there are no complications."

"Absolutely. She won't be able to get rid of me, doc. I can assure you that."

The doctor chuckled. "Okay then. It will take me a few minutes to get the discharge papers in order."

"Can I see her now?"

The doctor smiled again. "Of course. I can take you to her." He led the way to the curtained area.

Landon's breath caught in his throat as he saw Nichol lying in the hospital bed. Despite the doctor's reassurances, seeing her like this made his heart clench. He crossed the room in three quick strides, his arms already reaching for her.

"Nichol," he whispered, gathering her into his arms.

He closed his eyes, feeling the warmth of her body against his. Relief washed over him in waves, and he struggled to keep his emotions in check.

Nichol's voice, somewhat muffled against his chest, broke through his spiraling thoughts. "Landon, I'm okay. Really."

He pulled back just enough to look at her face, searching her eyes. "You gave me a scare." He managed a shaky smile.

Nichol sat up straighter, wincing a little. "I know, I'm sorry. But I'm fine. Just a little headache." She glanced around the room, her discomfort evident in the way she fidgeted with the blanket. "The doctor says I'll need someone to watch over me for tonight." She gave him an inquiring look.

"Don't you worry. I'm not going to leave your side." He

squeezed her hand, his heart swelling with a mixture of emotions. "God, Nichol, when I saw you unconscious..." He paused, swallowing hard. "I realized how much you've come to mean to me. It's terrible timing and I know we've only known each other for a short time—"

He was blowing it. Saying too much, too fast, but he couldn't seem to stop himself.

"Landon, I feel the same way," she interrupted, her fingers intertwining with his. "I've been feeling it too, for a while now. I was just too scared to admit it. I know it's fast, but we'll figure it out."

His heart swelled with emotion as he gazed into her eyes. The sterile hospital room faded away, and all he could see was her. Slowly, he leaned in, his hand cupping her cheek. Nichol's eyes fluttered closed as their lips met in a tender kiss.

The kiss was brief, but it felt like time stood still for those moments. He reveled in the softness of Nichol's lips. As they broke off the kiss, a sense of rightness settled over him.

He smiled, his thumb caressing her cheek. "Let's get those discharge papers and get you out of here."

Nichol's smile sent his pulse into a gallop. "I'd like that."

NICHOL WATCHED AS Landon wiped down the kitchen counter with methodical precision. Each careful movement of his muscled forearms made her heartbeat race—something about a man so attentive to detail stirred warmth low in her belly. He'd been doting on her for the last twenty-four hours and while she appreciated that he cared about her, it was becoming a little overwhelming. He'd only left her side to pick up his own rental car from the mechanic and to stop by the junkyard to get a look at her sedan. Unfortunately, it was going to be a total loss.

"You missed a spot," she teased.

Landon glanced over his shoulder, the dish towel pausing mid-swipe. "Where?" The concern in his expression made her want to cross the room and trace her finger along the worry lines on his forehead.

She laughed, feeling lighter than she had in a long time, despite the aches left by the car accident the day before. True to his word, Landon hadn't strayed from her side. He'd slept next to her all night, his arm wrapped around her shoulders, his steady breathing against her neck a constant reminder of his presence. The memory of waking to find his face mere inches from hers, his morning stubble catching the dawn light, made her cheeks flush.

"I'm kidding." She gave him a smile, letting her gaze linger on his lips longer than necessary. "The kitchen hasn't been this clean since I renovated it."

He turned toward her, leaning against the counter. The small bruise on his forehead that she hadn't noticed until they'd arrived home the day before had darkened overnight, but he assured that he was okay. That bruise, evidence of his protection, made her stomach flutter with an emotion too new to name.

"How are you feeling?" His gaze swept over her, thorough and caring.

"I feel fine." She reached for her coffee mug, deliberately letting her fingers brush against his when he moved closer. "I promise I will let you know if that changes."

Landon's expression softened. He tossed the dish towel onto the counter and crossed to the table where she sat. He pulled out the chair across from her, the scent of his cologne drifting over the table. "Nichol, I've been thinking."

Something in his tone gave her pause. "That sounds ominous." She traced the rim of her mug anxiously.

"I think maybe it would be best if you stepped away from

the investigation." The words came out in a rush, as though he'd been rehearsing in his head.

Her grip tightened around her mug. She fixed him with the look she'd perfected over years of dealing with difficult library patrons.

Landon raised his hands, palms out. "Just hear me out. I know you're invested in the investigation, but we've clearly gotten under someone's skin. Someone dangerous. I've dealt with people like this before, but you..." He trailed off and swallowed hard. The motion of his throat, the tiny muscle jumping in his jaw, all betrayed his fear. "If anything happened to you—"

She sat her mug down slowly and reached across the table for his hands. His skin was warm and rough with calluses that caught against her softer palms. The contact sent a jolt of awareness through her.

"Yesterday was scary, Landon. I won't pretend it wasn't. But you're right. We have gotten under someone's skin, and I am invested in this investigation." She leaned forward, close enough to count each of his dark lashes. "The person that ran us off the road, they already know I've been investigating with you. Backing off now won't ensure my safety. The only thing that will ensure my safety is finding the person that killed Addison Kober, and we are more likely to do that together than apart."

A weighted silence fell over them. His thumb brushed over her knuckles in slow, deliberate circles that made her breath catch.

Landon's mouth quirked up at one corner, that half smile that made her knees weaken. "I don't know why I even tried to convince you to stop."

"I've noticed you're pretty stubborn," Nichol said, matching his slight smile with one of her own. Their fingers remained intertwined, neither willing to be the first to pull away. "Luckily, so am I."

The simultaneous buzz of his phone and ring of hers shattered the moment. They exchanged startled glances, their fingers untangling.

"I'm almost afraid to answer," Landon said, jokingly as he pulled his phone from his pocket, the fingers of one hand lingering on top of hers a moment longer before he pulled away.

Nichol reached for her own cell phone, already missing his warmth. "Hello?"

"Ms. Nichol Bunin?" The voice on the other end was crisp and professionally detached.

"Speaking."

"This is Gerald Matthews, personal assistant to Mr. Morris Gillory. Mr. Gillory would like to meet with you and Mr. Elkins at one o'clock today, if you're available."

No pleasantries, no room for questions. More demand than question. The expectation got under Nichol's skin, but her curiosity was also piqued.

"Well, I guess we could do that."

"Fine. He will see you at his home at that time." The line went dead.

Nichol stared at the phone in her hand. Across the table, Landon frowned down at the screen of his own phone.

"You won't believe this," she said, looking at him. "That was Morris Gillory's personal assistant. Gillory wants to meet with us today at one."

Landon's eyebrows rose. "Morris Gillory? The big man himself. I guess Mary delivered."

"I guess. Morris's assistant wasn't forthcoming with details."

Landon frowned. "It's interesting that Gillory wants to meet with us now, right after we were run off the road."

The implication hung in the air. She felt a chill despite

the warm kitchen. "You don't think Morris Gillory had anything to do with the attack on us?"

The man was in his eighties. It was doubtful he'd been behind the wheel, but that didn't necessarily mean he hadn't been behind the attack.

Landon's expression was thoughtful. "The first thing I learned doing investigative journalism is to suspect everyone. Especially people with money and power. He or Will undoubtedly had their fingerprints all over my cancelled hotel reservation, Ted Roberts's attempted intimidation of you, and director or indirectly, the slashing of my tires."

Nichol wished she could argue with him, but she couldn't. It was clear to her now that she didn't know her neighbors as well as she'd thought.

"Who was your text from?" she asked, nodding toward the phone he still held in his hand.

"Addison's sister, Kayleigh. We've spoken a few times over the years." His expression turned solemn. "The police informed her about finding Addison's remains, and she's coming to town to make the arrangements for burial."

A pang of sympathy rang in Nichol. "I can't imagine what she's been going through all these years."

Landon nodded. "It's been rough on her. She lost both her parents not long after Addison's disappearance. If it's okay with you, I'd like to invite her over here. I think it would be best to speak with her in private."

"Of course," Nichol agreed, without hesitation.

Her house had become an unofficial headquarters for their investigation, its dining room table covered with newspaper clippings, timeline charts, and Landon's meticulous notes. It seemed only natural that Kayleigh should come here too.

She glanced at the clock on the microwave. It was already nearing noon. "I should get dressed. We don't want to be late to meet with Gillory."

Standing up took more effort than she wanted to admit, her muscles stiff.

Landon rose with her, slipping his arms around her waist when they were both on their feet.

"Are you sure you should go?" His voice dropped lower, concern evident in his voice as his face hovered inches from hers. He held up his free hand as her expression hardened, his fingers barely grazing her cheek. "I'm not trying to keep you out of the investigation. I just worry jumping right back in might be too much."

She set her hand on his chest, feeling his heartbeat quicken beneath her palm. "I doubt an eighty-something-year-old man is going to be too much for me to handle."

Her fingers curled into the fabric of his shirt, neither of them moving away.

"You haven't met the eighty-year-olds I have," Landon quipped as he tucked a strand of hair behind her ear, his fingertips lingering against her skin.

"Funny man." She stepped out of his arms, missing his warmth almost immediately, and made her way toward the stairs.

Each step sent a small jolt through her ribs, but she didn't let it show on her face. She wouldn't give Landon any more reason to worry.

"We leave in thirty minutes, then," he called after her.

She raised a hand in acknowledgment and continued up the stairs. A hot shower would help with the soreness. And maybe two more ibuprofen. She wasn't about to let physical discomfort, or someone's attempt to frighten them off, stop her from finding the truth because she was pretty sure of one thing. The person who killed Addison seemed to have no problem killing again.

Chapter Fifteen

Landon and Nichol stepped into the grand foyer of Morris Gillory's lake house, where opulence was literally etched into the walls in the form of gold flecks in the wallpaper. Sunlight spilled through high windows, casting glimmers across polished marble floors. A housekeeper gestured for them to follow her. She led them into a spacious sitting room with high ceilings, wood paneling, and soft, upholstered furnishings that seemed far too inviting given the atmosphere in the room.

Landon's gaze fell on a bald man in an expensive gray suit, the crisp fabric and tailored fit suggesting a level of authority. The man appeared to be in his late fifties or early sixties and stood stiffly next to another man who Landon recognized from newspaper photos as Morris Gillory.

"I'm Mitchell Albrecht, Mr. Gillory's attorney." The bald man introduced himself in a smooth, clipped tone.

He gestured toward the man sitting regally upon a sofa, his posture stiff and commanding, arms crossed over his chest. He didn't bother to introduce the only other person in the room, a younger blonde woman standing close to the French doors that led out onto the patio, but Nichol acknowledged the woman.

"Hello, June. I didn't expect to see you here."

June Gillory turned from the window and nodded but didn't speak. She fidgeted nervously with the hem of the blue wrap dress that hugged her figure and matched the striking blue of her eyes.

The maid gestured toward the white sofa across from Mr. Gillory, but the older man held up a hand before either Nichol or Landon had a chance to move. "There's no need for you to sit," he declared, his voice slicing through the air with the sharpness of a blade. "I only agreed to meet with you to warn you away from harassing me or my family any further with your wild theories."

Gillory's eyes bore into Landon with a mix of disdain and something he could not quite place. Was it fear or arrogance? Most likely both.

He caught Nichol glancing sideways at him.

"Continue this investigation—" Albrecht stepped forward and handed Landon a document he'd pulled from the leather billfold under his right arm "—and you'll find yourself in court. Defending yourself against charges of slander."

Landon scanned the letter quickly. It was a cease and desist letter. Legally, it wasn't worth the paper it was printed on, but Landon's stomach clenched anyway. It was a common tactic, and he had seen it plenty of times in his career when he'd been on staff for the *Sun*. It was designed more to intimidate than to act as any serious legal roadblock. But Mr. Gillory had enough money to be a major annoyance and cause him a lot of trouble.

Mr. Gillory's gaze swung abruptly to Nichol, his eyes narrowing. "I've never met you before, young lady, but as a native of Galesburg, I'm surprised you're helping a man who seems intent on destroying our town." His words dripped with contempt.

Nichol's response came quickly and sharp. "I don't believe Landon wants to destroy the town. I think he is trying to uncover the truth, and that's what I want. What we all should want."

An incredulous huff escaped the older man. "You're too old to be so naive."

Landon bristled at the insinuation, and he had to fight not to lose his temper. "I haven't shared any of my theories with you so I find it interesting that you assume any ideas I have would cast your family in a negative light."

He could see the color rise in Mr. Gillory's cheeks.

"The police have confirmed that the remains found in the woods are those of Addison Kober," Landon pressed further, wanting to gauge Gillory's reaction to the news.

A silence fell over the room.

Mr. Gillory tensed visibly, his posture straightening. "That has nothing to do with anyone in this family."

"If that's true, then your family has nothing to worry about," Landon replied. "Did Will and Addison meet when they were summer congressional pages in 2004?"

Landon watched Morris Gillory close for his reaction. The man was a consummate politician, but his skills were rusty. Shock flashed across his face for the briefest of moments before morphing back into anger.

"I know what you reporters do," Morris sputtered. "You target good, hardworking people just to boost your ratings and clicks. You don't care whose lives you destroy in the process. But I won't let you destroy my boy."

Before Landon could respond, June said, "Now, now, Father Gillory. Don't get yourself too worked up."

The elder man shot a glance of withering scorn toward his daughter-in-law. "Don't get too worked up? These people are attempting to sully our family name," he snapped.

Tension rippled through the room.

In an instant, June's fragile facade cracked, a brief flash of anger crossing her face before she quickly shrank back against the wall, retreating into the shadowed corner of the room.

Mr. Gillory pointed a bony finger at Landon and Nichol. "I will sue you for everything you're worth if you continue this investigation, Mr. Elkins. And I have very powerful friends, here and in Washington, D.C."

"I can see we aren't going to agree here." He took Nichol's hand now and stepped backward toward the entrance of the room. "Thank you for your time, Mr. Gillory."

The maid turned and walked with them back to the large double front doors.

They were greeted by a cool breeze as they stepped out of the house. The large door closed before they reached the top step of the porch.

"That went well," she said.

They made their way back to the car.

Landon stopped at the driver's side door, his eyebrows going up. "Actually, we learned a lot." His gaze drifted from the lovingly tended shrubs to the ominous line of trees that marked the boundary between civilization and the secrets lurking in the forest beyond. "I don't know what Morris Gillory knows about Addison's disappearance, maybe nothing, but he is certainly afraid of something."

"Afraid?" Nichol questioned skeptically, one eyebrow arched in curiosity.

"Oh, yeah," Landon said. "Rich people only bring in lawyers when they're terrified. Did you see Morris's face when I asked about Will working as a page? He was shocked. He thought he'd hidden that bit where it would never be found."

"Do you think he knew the remains were Addison's before you told him?" Nichol pressed, crossing her arms in thought.

"That's harder to say," he admitted, a sigh escaping his lips. "He tensed when he heard the news, but I couldn't tell you what that meant. Maybe nothing. It is shocking."

They stood together in a moment of silence, watching the flutter of birds flitting about in the treetops. Landon pointed to the woods. "I hadn't realized how close the lake was to the woods."

Nichol nodded. "That's one of the features local real estate agents use when selling these properties—the allure of being surrounded by nature, the lake, and the edge of the woods. You can go from swimming to hiking in minutes. Assuming you have the several million dollars to buy one of these behemoths." She gestured back toward the Gillory house.

"So, even if Will didn't live out here during the week as a child," Landon thought out loud, scanning the tree line, "he would still have known these woods pretty well."

"That seems like a reasonable deduction," Nichol replied, frowning.

Landon glanced at her, remembering the threats made moments ago inside. "We have to be careful."

"If you're going to suggest I back off because I might get sued with you or because the friends that Mr. Gillory mentioned might target me somehow, save it."

Landon didn't try to suppress a grin. Her determination was one of the sexiest things about her, in his opinion. "Consider it saved."

The house door banged open, drawing their attention back to the building. June stepped outside, her face flushed as she hurried toward them. Landon tensed, bracing himself for another confrontation.

June came to a stop in front of the car. "I'm so sorry about my father-in-law," she blurted. "He shouldn't have spoken to you like that. It's just…this whole situation has everyone on edge. Look, I'm sure you mean well, but stirring up the past…it's not going to do anyone any good. Some things are best left alone."

"We can't just pretend nothing happened." Frustration rose in Landon's chest. "Addison deserves—"

"Addison is gone," June said. "I'm not saying it's right or fair. But digging into old wounds won't bring her back. It'll only cause more pain."

"We just want to find out the truth, June. That's all we're after," Nichol said.

June's shoulders sagged. "That's the police's job, not yours. They've done all they can. Why can't you let it be?"

A silence fell over the trio. The impasse stretched on, each second feeling longer than the one before.

June broke the tense silence. "Addison was my friend too, you know. I wasn't happy when she disappeared, but we have to move on."

Disgust rose inside him. Before he could voice his outrage, Nichol said, "If Addison was your friend, then you should want to know what happened to her."

Landon watched as June's face contorted, her earlier composure giving way to anger. "The past is the past. Leave it there. For everyone's good."

June spun on her heel and marched back toward the house. Landon and Nichol stood rooted to the spot, watching her retreat, the slam of the front door echoing across the yard.

NICHOL SPENT THE rest of the morning and the early afternoon helping Landon go over every detail of his notes and all the information they'd gathered, trying to make all the pieces fit together in a way that made sense. Unfortunately, the effort hadn't borne fruit. While they'd discussed the case, Nichol had baked croissants both to have when Addison's sister, Kayleigh, arrived later that afternoon and because baking helped her to relax, although it too was only having limited success.

Her hands trembled as she arranged delicate pastries on a

serving plate, the flaky crusts crumbling under her unsteady fingers. The rich aroma of freshly brewed coffee filled the kitchen but did little to settle the knots in her stomach.

"I don't know if I can face her, Landon," Nichol confessed. "What if Kayleigh blames me for not doing more that night?" She reached for another pastry, desperate to keep her hands busy.

Landon stepped behind her, his strong hands kneading the tension from her shoulders and planting a soft kiss on her neck. "I'm anxious about this visit too. But you did what you could at the time. You have nothing to feel guilty about."

The warmth of his touch soothed her frayed nerves but couldn't banish the gnawing guilt. She turned to face him, opening her mouth to voice the doubts still swirling in her mind. "But what if—"

The shrill ring of the doorbell cut through the air, startling them both. Her heart leapt into her throat, her unfinished question dying on her lips.

Landon gave Nichol's shoulder one more reassuring squeeze before heading to the door.

Nichol took a deep, shaky breath, willing her racing heart to slow. She focused on arranging the pastries and coffee cups on the tray with care.

From her vantage point in the kitchen, she could see Landon open the front door.

"Kayleigh, it's nice to see you again." He engulfed the woman in a polite hug. "Please, come in."

Kayleigh stepped into the foyer and Nichol caught her first glimpse of Addison's younger sister. The woman's face was a canvas of conflicting emotions. Her blond hair was stringy and washed out, her top in desperate need of a good ironing. Grief was etched into the lines around her eyes, but there was also a strength that belied the grief.

"Thank you for having me," Kayleigh replied, her voice

filled with sorrow. She paused in the doorway, clutching her purse like a lifeline. "I... I wasn't sure if I could do this alone."

Nichol's heart clenched at the raw pain in Kayleigh's voice. She picked up the tray, the coffee cups clinking against their saucers, and headed into the living room where Landon had led Kayleigh.

Landon and Kayleigh were already seated on the sofa, a respectable distance between them. Kayleigh's eyes, rimmed with red, darted up as Nichol entered.

"Here we are," Nichol said as she set the tray on the coffee table.

"Kayleigh, I'd like you to meet Nichol Bunin. Nichol, this is Kayleigh Kober Rogers, Addison's sister."

"Kayleigh, I'm so sorry for your loss. I can't imagine what you're going through," Nichol said as she settled into the armchair across from the sofa.

Kayleigh's lips trembled into a sad smile. "Thank you. That's very kind of you." Her gaze fell to the tray. "And thank you for having me over. You didn't have to go to so much trouble."

"It's no trouble at all," Nichol insisted. She wanted to say more, but everything she came up with seemed inadequate.

Kayleigh reached for a coffee cup, her hands shaking. "It means a lot, truly. To have people who care, even..." She trailed off, swallowing hard. She turned to Landon. "I wanted to thank you again for coming with me to the police station. Dealing with all that paperwork...and the remains...."

Landon's eyes softened with compassion. "Of course, Kayleigh. I'm here for you in whatever way I can be."

"You always have been," Kayleigh said with a shaky smile. "You and your father...if it weren't for the two of you, I think the whole world would have forgotten about

Addison by now." She paused, taking a deep breath. "I just hope that now the police can figure out what happened to her. Who's responsible for her death."

Another surge of empathy rolled through her, coupled with a gnawing sense of guilt. "I hope so too." She hesitated, then continued, "Kayleigh, I didn't know Addison, but Landon might have mentioned that I saw her the night she disappeared." She twisted her hands in her lap, avoiding Kayleigh's gaze. "My father and I, we made a report to the police, but... I wish I had pushed harder, done more. And I want you to know that if I could go back—"

Kayleigh's hand shot up, silencing Nichol mid-sentence. Her eyes, though rimmed with red, held a fierce determination. "No. There's no one to blame for what happened to Addison except the person who killed her. That's who I'm saving all my anger for."

Some of the weight she'd been carrying for over two decades lifted from her chest. She exhaled slowly, not realizing she'd been holding her breath.

Kayleigh's gaze softened as she looked between Nichol and Landon. "Anyway, there are things we all wish we'd done differently." She paused, her finger tracing the rim of her untouched coffee cup. "Actually, there's something I've never told anyone." Kayleigh's voice dropped to a whisper. "Before she disappeared, Addison confided in me that she was pregnant."

Nichol's eyes widened, her hand involuntarily tightening on the arm of her chair. She glanced at Landon, whose face had gone pale.

"She wouldn't tell me who the father was," Kayleigh said. "I had no idea she was even dating anyone. She was so secretive about it. I should have pushed harder, should have made her tell me. Our parents were so religious, and when she went missing..." She trailed off, swallowing hard. "I didn't want to sully Addison's name. So, I said nothing."

The room fell silent. Nichol's mind raced, piecing together this new information with what she already knew. The implications of Addison's secret. Her heart hammered as she looked at Landon. She knew that they were both thinking the same thing.

"Did Addison ever tell the father of her child she was pregnant?"

Kayleigh's expression was tormented. "I don't know."

Nichol cleared her throat. "That must have been such a burden to carry all these years."

Landon nodded, his movement stiff and mechanical. "Thank you for sharing that with us. It sheds new light on some things."

They spoke with Kayleigh for a half hour more before she left to go back to her hotel. She had a trying few days ahead of her and it couldn't have been easy to relive the last moments of her sister's life.

"This investigation has more twists and turns than Route 43," Nichol said as Kayleigh's rental car disappeared around the corner. She began placing the leftover croissants and empty coffee cups back onto the serving tray.

"You never know where a case is going to take you," Landon answered, taking the tray from her and carrying it to the kitchen. He sat it down on the island and turned back to Nichol. "But I think this new information definitely warrants another talk with Will."

Chapter Sixteen

Nichol's heart raced as she pushed open the glass door of Gillory Real Estate Investments.

The receptionist looked up with a smile that quickly turned into a frown.

She pursed her lips. "I'm afraid Mr. Gillory does not want to speak with you. I'm going to have to ask you to leave."

"We just have a few questions about Addison Kober's pregnancy. But if he'd rather we discuss it out here or with the police…"

The receptionist's eyes widened. She glanced at the hallway behind her.

Nichol held her breath. The receptionist's fingers hovered over her phone, hesitating. She could almost see the wheels turning in the woman's head as she weighed her options. She leaned in and said softly, "I'm sure Mr. Gillory would rather we address this discreetly."

The woman's eyes darted between Nichol and Landon before she reached for the phone. She dialed an extension and spoke into the receiver. "Mr. Gillory? There are two people here…they're asking about Addison Kober."

Nichol's heart raced as she strained to hear the muffled response on the other end. After a moment, the receptionist replaced the phone's receiver on the cradle.

Her expression was a combination of reluctance and resignation as she turned back to them. "Mr. Gillory will see you now. Down the hall, last door on the right."

Will Gillory stood behind his desk when they entered his office.

His eyes blazed fury as they swept over her and Landon. "Close the door," he barked. "And don't bother sitting. You won't be staying long."

Nichol's heart hammered, but she forced herself to stay calm. She exchanged a quick glance with Landon as he shut the door behind them.

Will's voice was low and threatening when he spoke again. "If you two go around town spreading lies about Addison and me, I'll sue you for every penny you have."

Even after all this time, Will was still only concerned about himself. But his reaction had only confirmed for Nichol that she and Landon were on to something.

Landon waved one hand dismissively. "Yes, yes. We've heard it all from your father."

"A lawsuit would only be successful if what we're saying isn't true, Will," she replied.

Will's face drained of color. His bravado evaporated as a sickly green tinge crept into his complexion.

Nichol studied him. There was guilt written all over his face, but was it the guilt over having killed Addison, or something else?

"We just want the truth about what happened to Addison."

"It is true, isn't it? You met Addison as a congressional page and began dating," Landon demanded.

Will deflated. He fell back into his chair, suddenly looking much older than his thirty-eight years.

"Yes," Will whispered.

"Did you know she was pregnant with your child?"

Will froze, his eyes going wide. All the color drained from

his face and Nichol worried he was on the verge of passing out. Will was either a very good actor or he hadn't known about the pregnancy.

Landon, apparently, wasn't convinced though. "You knew and you killed her before she could tell anyone."

Will's cheeks turned purple. "I did not kill her!" he shouted, slamming his palm on the desk. Then, just as quickly as it had come, the fight fled out of him. "She never said. She never told me.... A baby." A small tear escaped, rolling down his cheek. "I loved her." His voice broke on the last three words.

Nichol's heart twisted. She believed him, despite everything. There was raw pain on his face. "Why would Addison be in town if not to see you?"

Will shrugged, looking lost. "I don't know. I mean, she did hang out with me, Ethan, Derek, and June a little that summer."

Nichol pressed on, her mind racing. "Would Addison have come to town to see any of them?"

"I don't think so," Will replied, shaking his head. "I mean, she really only knew them through me. I don't think Ethan ever met her. He worked all the time at his uncle's restaurant. Derek and June were dating that summer, but we did a few couples hangs."

Nichol's eyes flicked to Landon, catching his sharp gaze. A silent understanding passed between them. Will's casual mention of Derek and June suggested he didn't know about his wife's current dalliance.

"Why didn't you ever tell anyone any of this?" Landon said, frustrated.

Will's shoulders sagged as he exhaled deeply. "Because my father forbade me from saying anything. After Addison disappeared, the police questioned me. Discreetly." He gave them a pointed look. "I told them the truth, I didn't know anything. When the police left, Dad was irate. He said that she'd run away and that I was never to see or speak to her again."

Landon's jaw clenched. "And you did what he said."

Will nodded, his eyes trained on a point somewhere beyond them. "She never called or reached out. I didn't know what happened to her."

Pity for Will washed over Nichol. He'd lived trapped for years between loyalty to his father and his own conscience. She wondered how different things might have been if he'd found the courage to speak up sooner. The truth about Addison had been buried for so long, and now that it was coming to light, she couldn't shake the feeling that she and Landon were on the cusp of something bigger and far more sinister than they'd initially imagined.

Will's posture sagged like a deflated balloon. "What do I do now?"

"We're only trying to get justice for Addison," Nichol said. "If you loved her like you say you did, I'd think you'd want that."

Will's eyes fell to his desk. Nichol resisted the urge to prompt him further, knowing that the decision had to be his alone.

Will lifted his head, meeting their eyes. "I'm going to go to the police and tell them everything I know. Addison deserves at least that."

LANDON'S KNIFE SLID easily through the ripe tomato, its juice pooling on the wooden cutting board beneath his fingers. He was no professional chef, but there was something deeply satisfying about preparing a meal with his own hands. Especially since this meal was for Nichol. The thought of her filled him with an unexpected warmth that had nothing to do with the steam rising from the pot of boiling water on the hearth. He'd only known her for a short time, but he was as comfortable around her like they'd known each other for years.

Landon chopped the tomatoes into rough chunks and added them to the pot where onions already simmered. The rich aroma soon filled the small kitchen, mingling with the scent of the herbs he had discovered growing in her backyard garden. He had offered to prepare dinner that evening.

He'd been buoyed by a call from Officer Daniels confirming that Will had done as he'd promised and gone to the police to make an official statement about the circumstances surrounding Addison's death. It wasn't enough. It still didn't tell them who killed Addison, but it was something.

He stirred the sauce, then added a pinch of salt and some dried chilies as Nichol entered the kitchen.

"Something smells wonderful."

She had changed out of her daytime clothes into leggings and a short-sleeved top, the deep indigo fabric complementing her dark skin. Her hair, usually bound in a practical bun during the day, now fell loose in coils that caught the golden light of the setting sun through the window.

The sight of her stole his breath for a moment before he pulled himself together.

"I hope you like pasta. It's about the only thing I can make without risking poisoning us both."

She laughed, the sound genuine and warm. "After the day we had, I'm just happy I don't have to cook."

Moving closer, she peered into the pot. Her arm brushed against his, and he felt a tingle of electricity at the contact.

"In the last couple of days I've eaten better than I have in…well, ever."

The compliment sent a warmth blooming through his chest.

He swallowed hard and focused on stirring the sauce.

"The bread should be warm by now," he said, gesturing toward the oven where he had placed the loaf she'd kept in her pantry. "Not exactly garlic bread, but I rubbed it with some herbs and oil."

"A man of many talents," she teased, reaching past him to retrieve a potholder and take the bread from the oven.

He transferred the noodles into two clay bowls, ladling the rich sauce over them while Nichol carried the bread to the table.

He followed her with two bowls of spaghetti and settled at the small round table where he'd already placed a glass of wine for each of them.

Nichol twirled her fork in the noodles and took a bite. Her eyes widened, and she nodded in approval. "It's really good."

He quirked an eyebrow and said, "You sound surprised."

"Well," she replied, "when a man says he's not a very good cook, I've learned to brace myself." Taking another bite, she clearly enjoyed the dish. "But this is delicious." She took a sip of her wine then set the glass down deliberately. "I was thinking about what the knitting nanas told us—"

"Wait," he interrupted, reaching across the table to lightly touch her hand. "What do you say we don't talk about the investigation tonight? Just for one evening."

Her eyebrows rose in surprise before her body visibly relaxed as tension melted away. "That's...actually a wonderful idea." She smiled. "I could use a break from work and the investigation. Everything."

"Good. Tonight, it's just you and me."

Her smile grew wider. For the next several minutes they ate in a comfortable silence.

"You know, I am curious," Nichol began. "About your career. You're an investigative reporter, traveling from place to place and uncovering stories. What's that like? Do you enjoy it?"

He considered the question while twirling spaghetti around his fork. "I've enjoyed it for the most part. When I was younger, I loved the travel. Seeing new places and meeting different people." He took a bite and swallowed before continuing. "There's nothing quite like the satisfaction of bringing important stories to light, giving a voice to those who wouldn't otherwise be heard."

"I can imagine that must be rewarding."

"It was—is," he corrected himself. "But the profession has changed so much over the years." He sighed, unwilling to sound bitter yet unable to hide his frustration. "News travels differently now. Faster. With the internet and social media. And so many people don't even care about accuracy or, God forbid, nuance." He shook his head. "It's all about getting the most sensational stories that travel around the globe as quickly as possible. No one wants to invest in deeply researched investigations that might take months or years."

"It sounds challenging," she said, leaning forward.

"Sometimes I wonder if a dinosaur like me even has a place anymore." The words emerged more vulnerable than he intended, revealing an insecurity he seldom acknowledged, even to himself.

Nichol set down her fork and gave him a long, appraising look that made heat rise to his face. Her eyes wandered from his face down to his chest and back up again, a half smile playing on her lips.

"You don't look like a dinosaur to me," she said in a suggestive tone that made his mouth go dry.

Before he could overthink it, he reached for her hand across the table. Her skin was warm and soft as he lifted her hand to his lips and pressed a gentle kiss against her knuckles. He let his lips linger.

"There are some advantages to experience," he said, his voice rough with desire.

He watched a subtle tremor pass through her. Her reaction sent a surge of need through him, making his breath catch. He held her gaze, tracing small circles over her palm.

"Is that so?" she asked, a flush spreading across her cheeks. "And what might those advantages be?"

"Patience," he replied, continuing the gentle caress. "Knowing that some things shouldn't be rushed."

Her tongue darted out to wet her lips, a simple gesture that made his pulse race even faster. "And what about knowing when something shouldn't be delayed?" she countered.

The air between them was charged with expectation and desire.

"That's important too," he said. "Recognizing the right moment to act."

She glanced down at their joined hands, then back up into his eyes. "And what do you think about this moment?"

Rather than answer, Landon rose from his chair, still holding her hand, and stepped around the table. She turned her chair to face him, looking up at him with a gaze laden with desire. He reached out his free hand and touched her cheek.

"I think it's perfect." He pulled her to her feet, waiting only a moment before he closed the distance between them, pressing his lips to hers.

Her mouth was soft at first. Her hands came up to wind around his neck.

She deepened the kiss, her lips parting, inviting him to go further. He tasted the sweetness of the wine on her tongue and felt the softness of her body as she pressed against him. His hands slid down to her waist, pulling her even closer. The contact sent a jolt of pleasure through him, and he groaned against her lips.

Her body fit against his perfectly, curves meeting angles in a way that made his head swim. He was drowning in her, the taste, the scent, the feel, and he never wanted to surface.

When they broke apart, he rested his forehead against hers, reluctant to put much distance between them.

"I don't want you to feel...."

"Landon," she interrupted, pressing a finger to his lips. "I'm a grown woman who knows what she wants." Then she replaced her finger with her lips, giving him a quick, firm kiss before continuing. "And right now, I want you."

His body responded instantly to her words, desire flooding through him with an intensity that was almost painful.

She took his hand, interlacing her fingers with his. "Come with me."

He followed willingly as she led him upstairs to her bedroom.

Dominating the center of the room was a bed covered with a handwoven blanket in rich earth tones.

She released his hand and moved to the lamp on the bedside table, and turned it on. It cast the room in a warm, golden glow.

He closed the distance between them, taking her face between his hands.

"You're beautiful."

He kissed her again, more slowly this time, savoring the taste of her. His hands slid down her neck to her shoulders, then lower still, tracing the curve of her spine through the fabric of her dress. Her body arched against his in response, and he felt her hands pulling at his shirt.

They undressed each other slowly, each revealed inch of skin an exploration and a discovery. Their clothes fell away until she stood before him in nothing but moonlight and lamplight and he was left momentarily speechless. Her body was strong and supple, marked with small scars that spoke of a life well lived.

He reached out to trace one such mark on her hip. "What's this from?" he asked, his voice laden with desire.

"A childhood adventure involving a tree and poor judgment," she replied with a small laugh.

Her hand then found a scar on his shoulder. "And this?"

"A less pleasant adventure involving a knife and a very unhappy subject of an investigation."

Her eyes widened before she leaned forward and pressed her lips to the scar. The gentle touch sent shivers through him, and his hands tangled in her hair, guiding her back to his mouth.

They moved to the bed, falling onto it in a flurry of limbs and heated kisses. Her skin was like silk as he explored every curve and every hollow.

She arched her back against the mattress, her soft moans echoing as their lips met. His arousal pressing against her.

"Are you sure about this?" he whispered seductively in her ear.

"Yes," Nichol replied. "God, yes."

He trailed his fingers down to her hidden center. The sudden, exquisite contact made her gasp, her back arching.

"Is this what you like?" he queried, his thumb moving in a slow, deliberate circle.

"Yes, just like that," she answered, clutching at him.

"You are even more beautiful than I imagined," he said, drinking in the sight of her flushed cheeks and parted lips.

He lowered himself, enveloping her in a tender embrace. The sensation of their bodies meeting was overwhelming, drawing gasps and moans from them both as he steadied himself on his forearms while seeking her eyes.

Their bodies merged slowly, accompanied by soft sighs of delight. When they were fully united, he paused, resting his forehead against hers, giving her time to adjust to him.

"You feel like heaven," he murmured.

Nichol cradled his face in her hands. "Move, please."

He did, setting a gentle rhythm that gradually built into

something far more passionate and urgent. They moved faster, chasing something just beyond both their reach. It wasn't long before he felt Nichol tighten around him, and heard her breath catch as she trembled on the edge of release.

"I've got you. Let go, baby. I've got you," he reassured her.

She clung to him as waves of ecstasy washed over her. Her loss of control made his own slip, his pleasure peaking as he buried his face in her neck and shuddered with release.

For a long, lingering moment, they remained entwined, hearts pounding in unison. Then he rolled to one side, drawing Nichol against his chest as he did. She nestled into his side, her head fitting into the crook of his shoulder. He traced a finger along her back until their breaths slowed to a peaceful rhythm.

"That was..." he began, then chuckled, "I don't even have words."

"Well, it is certainly one way to avoid talking about the investigation."

He laughed, turning to look at her. In the lamplight, with her hair wild around her face and her lips still swollen from his kisses, she was the most beautiful thing he had ever seen.

He raised their joined hands and kissed her knuckles with a grin. "A highly effective method."

Chapter Seventeen

Warm, gooey cheese stretched between Landon's teeth as he spooned ice cream into his mouth. Sitting cross-legged on Nichol's bed, he savored the casual intimacy of the moment. Nichol's laughter filled the room as she recounted a story about the knitting group.

"...and then Hazel actually said, 'Well, I never!'".

Landon chuckled, shaking his head. "She sounds like a character."

Nichol leaned in and playfully bumped his shoulder. He marveled at how comfortable they'd become with each other in such a short time. The easy companionship that had grown between them was both exciting and familiar.

"You've got ice cream on your chin," Nichol said, reaching out to wipe it away with her thumb.

Landon caught her hand, pressing a soft kiss to her palm. Heat simmered in her eyes. He sat the now-empty bowl on the nightstand and began to crawl on his knees toward her. She smiled a slow, incredibly sexy, smile.

A loud whoosh tore through the quiet, followed by a brilliant flash of light that illuminated the bedroom.

"What the hell was that?" he exclaimed, already scrambling off the bed.

Nichol was right behind him. "I don't know, but it came from outside."

They rushed to the window, Landon's heart pounding as he tried to process what he was seeing. Flames. And far too close to the house for comfort.

"Oh my God," Nichol said. "My garage..."

He turned away from the window and grabbed his discarded clothes. He yanked on his jeans and T-shirt. Nichol, who was already wearing his button-down shirt, pulled on a pair of leggings and followed him downstairs. At the front door, they paused long enough to slip on their shoes before rushing outside.

The detached garage was already partially engulfed. Orange flames shot up toward the night sky, devouring the walls and roof of the garage. The stench of burning wood and asphalt roofing tiles assaulted his nose.

His protective instincts kicked into overdrive. He turned to Nichol. "Go back inside and call the fire department," he yelled.

Nichol's eyes were wide with fear, but she nodded. "What about you?"

His eyes darted to the garden hose coiled at the side of the house. It wasn't much, but it was all they had until the fire department arrived. "I'll make sure it doesn't spread to the house. Go, now!"

Nichol turned to run back into the house then stopped suddenly, her gaze focused on a point beyond the garage. She pointed to a spot just beyond the burning structure. "There's someone over there!"

Landon followed her line of sight. A dark figure sprawled on the ground a few yards away from the fiery garage, partially obscured by shadows.

"Go make that call," he said, already moving toward the person. "Hey! Are you alright?"

The man's head jerked up, apparently startled by Landon's voice. The man struggled to his feet, swaying unsteadily.

"Hey! Stop!" Landon yelled.

The man stumbled forward, trying to escape on shaky legs.

"Stop!" Landon shouted again, breaking into a sprint.

The man's movements were uncoordinated and unbalanced. Landon closed the gap quickly. He launched himself at the man, tackling the stranger to the ground. They hit the grass hard, and Landon used his body weight to pin the man down.

"Derek?" he gasped, his mind reeling with shock and disbelief. "What are you doing here?"

Derek's eyes were wide with panic, his breathing ragged and labored. The sharp smell of gasoline hit Landon's nostrils, the smell wafting up from Derek's clothes and skin.

Realization smacked Landon in the face. "You set the fire."

Derek's only response was a strangled groan as he bucked beneath Landon's weight.

Derek freed an arm and threw a punch that grazed Landon's jaw, sending a sharp sting across his face. He took the blow and pressed down on Derek's chest harder, trying to control his thrashing limbs. Derek responded by arching his back and twisting and scissoring his legs in an attempt to flip their positions.

He and Derek rolled across the ground in a tangle of limbs and fury. And up close, Landon could smell the scent of alcohol on Derek's breath.

Derek clawed at Landon's face, making Landon rear back to avoid the attack. Landon grabbed Derek's wrists, wrestling to control his hands as they continued to grapple in the dirt.

The light from the flames from the burning garage danced across the sky and caught the nearby grass.

Derek twisted his body sharply to the left, throwing Landon off balance. His knee came up hard, aiming for Landon's stomach, but Landon shifted just in time to take the blow on his hip instead. Caught off guard, Landon's grip on the man loosened.

Derek seized the opportunity and drove his fist upward toward Landon's throat. Landon blocked with his forearm, the impact sending a jolt of pain up his arm.

Landon grunted loudly as Derek elbowed him sharply in the ribs. Derek's legs kicked frantically, throwing Landon off of him completely.

Derek swung his other elbow in a wild arc, catching Landon in the shoulder blade. The pain shot down Landon's arm, but he reached for Derek again. The thought of the danger Derek had put Nichol in fueled his anger and determination not to let Derek get away.

"Stop fighting," Landon growled, struggling to pin Derek's arms to the ground. "It's over!"

Derek ignored him. As much as Landon wanted to hold Derek for the police, fear, desperation, and adrenaline had given the man a surge of strength he might not have ordinarily had. Derek snapped his head forward, his forehead colliding with Landon's nose. Pain exploded through his face, his vision blurring with tears as he instinctively recoiled. He rolled away from Derek, swearing and tasting blood from his split lip in his mouth.

Derek rolled to his side and scrambled to his feet. He ran toward the trees lining Nichol's house, disappearing into the dark woods without looking back.

Landon got to his feet and took two determined steps after Derek before pulling up short. Derek wouldn't get far in his intoxicated state, and he didn't want to leave Nichol alone and vulnerable.

He heard the faint wail of sirens as he made his way back

to the house. The garage was now fully engulfed, casting an eerie orange glow across the yard. Landon's eyes fell on the porch, his heart clenching at the sight of Nichol. Her arms were wrapped tightly around herself and her face was a mask of worry.

"Landon!" she called out, relief evident in her tone. "Are you okay? What happened?"

He took the porch steps two at a time, reaching for her. "I'm fine."

Nichol's eyes widened as she took in his bloodied nose and bruised jaw. "Oh my God, you're hurt." Her hand hovered near his face.

"It's nothing. Are you alright?"

"Yes. I'm fine." Nichol nodded, her gaze drifting back to the inferno that was once her garage. "Who was that?"

"It was Derek."

"Derek?" Nichol's eyes clouded with confusion. "Why would he...?"

Landon's jaw clenched, his anger simmering just beneath the surface of his skin. "I don't know, but I smelled gasoline on him. He must have set the fire."

Nichol let out a strangled gasp.

Landon pulled her into his arms, feeling her body tremble against his. He stroked her hair as the sirens grew louder.

"Why?" Nichol said, as the fire trucks rumbled up the driveway.

Landon's grip tightened protectively around her, his mind already working on that very question. "I don't know. But I promise you, I'm going to find out."

THE SCENT OF smoke was thick in the air as Landon and Nichol stood side by side on her porch, silently watching the firemen pack up their equipment. His jaw clenched as he surveyed the damage, his mind racing with questions and theories about Derek's involvement. The once-pristine white siding of Nichol's garage was now a blackened mess, a stark reminder of how easily the situation could have been so much worse.

He glanced at Nichol, noting the worry lines etched around her eyes. He wanted to reach out and comfort her, but hesitated, unsure if it would be welcome in the moment. Instead, he turned his attention back to the scene in front of them, watching as the firefighters coiled hoses and stowed their axes.

Across the yard, Officer Daniels stood in deep conversation with the fire chief, their voices inaudible over the clanking of equipment.

"I can't believe Derek would do this," Nichol said.

Landon did put his arm around her now. "The police will find him, I'm sure."

As if summoned by their exchange, Daniels headed toward the porch. Landon could see the stress in his body.

"Any word on Derek?" Landon asked as soon as the officer was within earshot, unable to contain his impatience.

Daniels shook his head, his expression grim. "We sent cars to his house and to the plastics factory. No sign of him at either location."

Frustration coursed through him, and he could feel the tension in Nichol's body.

"How is that possible?" he asked, struggling to keep his voice level. "Derek couldn't have just vanished into thin air."

"We're doing everything we can to locate him." Daniels's words did little to ease the knot of worry in Landon's stomach.

"That fire could have spread to my whole house," Nichol said with barely contained anger.

Landon's mind was already racing ahead to their next

moves. They couldn't just sit around waiting for the police to find Derek. He'd proven he was dangerous.

"We'll find Derek. He can't get far," Daniels said, mirroring the words Landon had spoken moments earlier. "Now, explain to me again why you think Derek set your garage on fire?"

"Derek may have been involved in Addison Kober's death," Nichol stated. "We think he was afraid we were getting close to proving it."

"Were you?" Daniels asked skeptically.

"Not at all," Landon admitted, "We know Derek met Addison a few times, according to Will, but beyond that we had no reason to suspect him of involvement in her disappearance. But I'd say this..." He gestured at the still-smoldering garage. "It goes a long way toward indicating that we're on the right track."

Daniels frowned, his brow furrowing as he processed the information. "What I don't understand is why Derek would stick around long enough for you to see him."

"I don't think he meant to," Landon replied, thoughtfully. "My guess is he didn't anticipate how quickly the garage would go up. He may have been momentarily dazed by the sudden intensity of the fire."

Officer Daniels nodded slowly and closed his notebook with a snap. "Well, whatever he was thinking, I'll get it out of him when I find him."

Daniels promised to keep them in the loop before he turned and strode away to his cruiser. Landon watched as the fire truck rumbled to life, its red lights no longer flashing as it pulled away from the curb. Daniels's cruiser followed behind.

The night seemed suddenly quiet.

Landon turned to Nichol, noting the weariness in her eyes. "Let's go inside."

In the living room, they sank onto the couch. Nichol leaned into him, as the reality of the night's events hit them. They sat like that, both of them quietly processing the events of the last several hours.

He cleared his throat. "Maybe we should consider going to a hotel for a while."

"No." She shook her head. "I won't let Derek or anyone else run me out of my own house."

Landon sighed, unsurprised by her response. "Okay, but I'm concerned Derek might come back. He's desperate now, and that makes him even more dangerous."

Chapter Eighteen

Landon dabbed at the gash above his left eyebrow, wincing at the sting of the antiseptic. A dull throb pulsed in the back of his head, the beginnings of a headache. The adrenaline that had kept him upright for the last hour was fading, leaving a slight tremble in his hand and unease in his gut.

He eyed his reflection in the mirror. The cut wasn't deep, but it was angry and red, and a reminder of how close they'd come to disaster. How easily he could have lost Nichol. That thought sent a cold chill through his body. He applied a bandage and splashed water on his face. The scent of smoke still clung to his clothes but there was little he could do about that at the moment, and he didn't want to leave Nichol alone for long.

Stepping out of the bathroom, he gazed at the front door, which was open. Nichol was back on the front porch, looking at the charred remains of her garage, her posture as rigid as a steel post. He stepped through the doorway and onto the porch, sliding his arms around her.

Nichol leaned back into him, sighing. "I guess we should be happy that your car was parked in the driveway. At least you don't have to replace it."

Landon placed a kiss on the side of her neck. "I'm just glad you weren't hurt. I can't replace you."

Nichol turned in his arms, pressing her cheek against his chest, and pulled him close. They stood on the porch for a moment, Landon thanking the universe that Derek hadn't targeted the house. It was likely the fire was meant to be another warning. A foolish, desperate, insanely dangerous warning.

Landon pulled away. "Come on. Let's get inside the house."

They turned together, their arms still around each other, and went inside. Landon made sure to lock the front door and checked all the windows on the main floor and the rear door, before rejoining Nichol in the living room.

Landon sank onto the sofa beside Nichol.

"I can't believe Derek would do this," Nichol said.

"It was definitely him," Landon replied. He threw an arm around Nichol's shoulder and pulled her in close to his side. "I wish I had held on to him after I tackled him, but I was so stunned when I saw it was him."

Nichol shifted beside him, her hair brushing against his cheek, her hand on his chest. "I'm just glad you didn't get hurt," she whispered.

Landon allowed himself to relax into her arms for a brief moment while his mind circled the consequences of all that had occurred that night.

"If Derek set the fire, that has to mean he's involved with Addison's disappearance somehow." He paused, working through the logic. "Why else would he try to destroy evidence or frighten us off?"

Nichol tapped her index finger against his thigh. "Do you think we've been investigating the wrong person all along? We've been so focused on Will, but maybe..."

"Maybe Derek is the one we should have been investigating." Landon completed her thought.

Silence stretched between them, frustration and anger building in Landon with every passing moment. The house creaked around them. Outside, headlights passed slowly down the street. Landon glanced out of the window and saw that it was a patrol car. The headlights momentarily flooded the room with light before continuing on its way.

"But why would Derek hurt Addison?" Nichol broke the silence. "We haven't found any connection between them. As far as we know, they barely knew each other. They only met through Will."

Landon rubbed his temple with his free hand, feeling the headache behind his eyes getting stronger. "What if Addison and Derek were dating back then?" he suggested, the theory taking form as he spoke. "Maybe they kept it secret. I mean, they were teens and teens do tend to like their secrets."

"Possible," Nichol said. "Or maybe, Derek wanted to date Addison, but she was only interested in Will. He might have killed her out of jealousy."

Landon nodded slowly, rolling the idea around in her head. "Rejection can be a powerful motivator. Either theory would give Derek a motive."

He could feel the stirring of excitement that came with a new lead, but it was tempered by exhaustion and the knowledge that they had no evidence.

"But that puts us back in the realm of speculation," he said, frustrated. "We don't have evidence to support either theory, or really any theory that involves Derek. There could be some totally unrelated reason for Derek setting your garage on fire."

Nichol shifted so that he could see that her expression was openly skeptical.

"I'm just suggesting we consider all possibilities."

Nichol arched an eyebrow. "Okay. Then we should consider that June might know where Derek is. If they're having an affair, he might seek her help to hide."

"You're right. I should have thought about that," he said, kicking himself.

"It's been a big night. You can be forgiven for forgetting. I didn't think of it either."

"We should let Officer Daniels know about June and Derek's probable affair before we go to bed. See if they've made any progress finding Derek."

The thought of action eased some of his tension and frustration. He rose and strode toward the kitchen where he had left his laptop bag with his cell phone inside earlier in the evening. Nichol followed him.

He dialed Officer Daniels's number from the business card Daniels had given him and put the call on speakerphone so Nichol could hear.

Officer Daniels answered on the fourth ring, sounding gruff and tired. "Daniels here."

"Daniels, it's Landon. I wanted to check if there has been any progress finding Derek."

A soft exhale came from the other end of the line, not quite a sigh but heavy with the weight of a long night. "We've made a little progress. Derek's car was found abandoned near the lake about thirty minutes ago. No sign of him yet, but we've got officers searching the area."

Landon's eyes snapped up to meet Nichol's. The lake, where June and Will Gillory lived.

"Officer Daniels, I think you should check with June Gillory. She lives on the lake, and Nichol and I have reason to believe she and Derek are having an affair."

A surprised grunt emanated from the speaker, followed by a moment of silence. "That's…interesting information," Officer Daniels said. "I'll have someone stop by her place."

"Thank you."

"I'll call and update you in the morning," Officer Daniels said. "And don't worry. I've already instructed patrol to do extra rounds on Nichol's street tonight. After what happened, we're not taking any chances."

"We appreciate that," Landon replied, recalling seeing the police cruiser through the window minutes earlier. He ended the call.

"Derek's car by the lake, near June's house," Nichol said. "That can't be a coincidence, can it?"

Landon shook his head slowly. "It's...curious, for sure. But why abandon his car when he needs to get away? Is he hiding at June's? Or did he leave it as a distraction?"

The questions multiplied in his mind, each one leading to other questions.

A yawn caught him by surprise, his body reminding him of the hour and the toll the evening had taken. He glanced at the microwave clock, its green digits glowing 12:14 p.m.

"The morning will be soon enough to work through everything that happened tonight," he said, rubbing his eyes with the heels of his hands. The gritty feeling reminded him of the smoke and ash that likely still clung to his skin. "Right now, we should both go to bed and get some rest."

Nichol nodded, pushing herself away from the counter where she had been leaning. "You're right. There's nothing we can do tonight anyway."

Landon followed Nichol out of the kitchen and upstairs to her bedroom. Exhaustion claimed Nichol quickly, but as tired as he was, it took him nearly an hour to fall asleep. He couldn't stop his mind from swirling through the events of the night and everything he knew about Will, Addison, June, and Derek, trying to make the pieces fit. Trying to find answers. Even as something told him that the danger to him and Nichol wasn't over yet.

NICHOL'S EYES SNAPPED open in the darkness, her heart pounding. Something had jolted her from sleep, but she couldn't pinpoint what. She lay motionless, straining her ears for any hint of sound. The old farmhouse creaked and settled around her, but underneath those familiar noises was something else. Something out of place.

There. A faint scraping from downstairs. It could have been the wind rattling a loose shutter, but her instincts screamed otherwise. This sound didn't belong.

She sat up. Beside her, Landon's steady breathing filled the room. Nichol placed a gentle hand on his shoulder.

"Landon," she whispered, leaning close to his ear. "Wake up. I think someone's in the house."

He stirred, but didn't wake. Nichol squeezed his shoulder harder.

"Landon, wake up. I think there's someone downstairs."

His eyes flickered open, sleepiness giving way to sharp focus as he registered her words. "Are you sure?" he whispered back.

She nodded, her throat tight. "I heard something."

As if on cue, another faint scrape drifted up from below. Landon's body tensed beside her.

"Okay. I'll check it out."

She sent him a sharp look. "We'll check it out."

Landon pulled on his discarded jeans and T-shirt. Nichol followed suit, fumbling as she buttoned her jeans. Her heart pounded, each beat seeming to echo in the quiet room.

"Should we call the police?" Nichol whispered.

Landon shook his head. "Not yet. Let's see what we're dealing with first. But bring your cell phone with you."

They padded quietly toward the bedroom door, Nichol's mind racing. They eased onto the landing, the old floorboards mercifully silent under their careful steps. Nichol's eyes strained in the darkness, picking out the familiar shapes of her home, suddenly ominous in the shadows.

Landon walked in front of her, his broad shoulders tense

as he led the way down the stairs. She followed close behind, one hand gripping the banister, the other pressed to Landon's back. Each step felt like an eternity, the silence punctuated only by their shallow breaths.

As they reached the bottom, another soft sound drifted from the kitchen. The clink of metal on ceramic, barely perceptible. Nichol's stomach clenched. Someone was definitely in there.

Landon paused at the kitchen doorway, his body coiled like a spring. Nichol pressed close and peered around him.

June stood at the far end of the kitchen, her posture rigid. A pistol gleamed menacingly in her hand.

"Good. I was wondering if I was going to have to go up and get you. Sit down," she commanded, gesturing with the gun toward the stools at the kitchen island. "Both of you. Now."

Nichol's gaze darted to the island, taking in the sight of the large canister of flour sat next to another container filled with sugar.

Landon's arm went protectively around her as they slowly moved to comply. The wooden stool legs scraped against the tile as they sat, the sound now sinister in the tense atmosphere.

"June, what are you doing?" Nichol finally managed. Her mind reeled, unable to reconcile the woman before her with the June she thought she knew.

June's laugh was bitter. "What am I doing? I'm putting an end to this mess before you two destroy my entire life."

Landon's brow furrowed but he did his best to keep calm, despite the gun pointed their way. "Destroy your life, how?"

"Don't act like you don't know," June scoffed, her eyes narrowing. The gun wavered in her grip.

Nichol was mesmerized by its movement, her heart pounding. She exchanged a loaded glance with Landon.

Nichol's mind whirred, pieces of the puzzle rapidly falling into place, yet gaping holes remained. She could feel the tension radiating from Landon beside her.

"You really haven't figured it out?" June asked, incredulously.

Landon shifted on the stool, his gaze never leaving June or the gun in her hand. "I'm beginning to. Let's start with, you killed Addison."

Nichol's breath caught in her throat as she watched June. June nodded, her expression coldly indifferent. "Yes."

Nichol felt the blood drain from her face as she struggled to process the confession. "Why?" she managed to choke out.

June sighed. "Because she was pregnant."

Nichol shook her head, unable to comprehend the casual cruelty in June's tone. "I still don't understand."

June's eyes narrowed, her lip curling in disdain as she looked at Nichol. "She was pregnant with Will's baby," she spat out. "It was bad enough that he thought he was in love with her. A baby would have connected them forever."

Nichol's stomach churned, bile rising in her throat as the full meaning of June's words sank in. How could someone be capable of such cold-blooded murder?

"And that would have meant the end of your dreams of marrying Will," Nichol shot back.

June nodded with a smug smile. The casual confirmation sent a chill down Nichol's spine.

"How did you find out Addison was pregnant?" Nichol asked. She dreaded the answer, but knew she had to hear it.

June's eyes glittered with a perverse pride. "She told me. I told you we were friends. Or at least I made Addison think we were. Keep your enemies close and all that."

Nichol's stomach lurched. The calculated deceit, the manipulation of a scared, pregnant teenager. It was all too much.

She stared at June, seeing her not as the polished socialite she pretended to be, but as something twisted and nasty.

She's sick.

June said, mockingly, "She called me, upset, scared, and desperate. She was sure her parents were going to kick her out and she wasn't sure what Will and his parents would do. She wanted to keep the child." Her face contorted with disgust and anger. "I convinced her to take a bus to Galesburg, and I snuck out with my father's car to pick her up. She thought we were just going to talk."

Nichol's hands clenched into fists under the countertop, her nails digging into her palms. The pain grounded her, keeping her from being swept away by the tide of revulsion and anger swelling in her gut.

Landon's voice cut through the tension, sharp with accusation. "But you already had plans to kill her."

"I didn't have a choice. I wasn't going to let some common guttersnipe steal my future." She spoke about murder the same way she might discuss a minor inconvenience, her tone devoid of remorse or humanity. It was chilling to think that June had been only sixteen, almost the same age as Addison, when she committed such a heinous act.

"How did you get Addison to go with you into the woods?" Nichol asked, still working to piece the entire story together in her mind.

June smirked. "That's where Derek came in. He went with me to pick Addison up from the bus stop." June shot a look of disgust Nichol's way. "We didn't see you spying on us."

And thank God for that, Nichol thought. Who knows what June would have done if she had.

"Addison was angry that I'd told him about the baby," June continued, "but I convinced her that he could help."

Derek, Nichol thought, piecing together the puzzle. Not only was he June's lover, but he was also her accomplice to murder. She couldn't help but wonder how much of June and Derek's ongoing relationship was due to real feelings on June's part and how much was "keeping your enemies close," as she'd mentioned moments earlier.

Landon leaned forward, his eyes trained on June's face. "And then what?"

"We told her we were going to go out to the Gillorys' hunting cabin and talk things through, make a plan," June replied.

"But that wasn't what happened," Nichol said quietly.

June's eyes glinted in the dim kitchen light. "When we were on the highway, Derek pulled the pistol I'd stolen from my father's gun collection. I pulled over and we forced Addison into the woods."

Nichol could almost see it. The dark road, the terror in Addison's eyes, the cold metal of the gun. The scene played out in her mind, vivid and horrifying.

Landon's face contorted with disgust. "Did Derek kill her?"

June scoffed, haughtily. "He couldn't do it. So, I did."

Nichol's stomach churned with revulsion. How could anyone, let alone a teenager, be so callous about taking a life?

"You were only sixteen," Nichol said in shock.

June's eyes flashed with defiance. "So? Even then I knew what I wanted out of life. More importantly, I knew you had to be willing to fight for it or unless you wanted other people to take what was yours."

Nichol's mind reeled. Fight for it? This wasn't a fight. It was manipulation, deceit, and cold-blooded murder. She struggled to comprehend the twisted logic behind June's actions.

"What you wanted out of life was to marry a man that doesn't love you, and that you don't love except for money," Nichol responded, her voice gaining strength as anger began to replace her shock.

"I wouldn't expect a librarian to understand." June sneered dismissively, waving her hand like she was swatting away an annoying fly.

Landon's jaw clenched, his eyes burning with fury and pain. "What about my father?" he demanded.

"He kept contacting Will, asking him about his relationship with Addison," June said. "I couldn't let him sully the Gillory name before I even got it."

The pieces clicked into place. The hit-and-run. The years of mystery surrounding Landon's father's death. It all led back to June.

Landon jumped up from his seat, the sudden movement making Nichol flinch. He yelled, his voice raw with emotion, "So, you ran him down in the street like he was nothing?"

Chapter Nineteen

"I didn't want to kill him. He left me no choice," June hissed, her eyes focused on Landon.

Landon's fists clenched at his sides. "No choice? You murdered my father to protect your sick fantasy of marrying into money!"

"Sit down," June spat.

"Landon," Nichol whispered, reaching for his hand. "Please, sit down."

Landon's knuckles turned white as he gripped the edge of the countertop, his heart pounding in his chest. The barrel of June's gun glinted in the harsh overhead light, trained steadily on him and Nichol. He forced himself to take slow, measured breaths despite the rage and fear churning inside him.

He glanced at Nichol beside him, seeing the terror in her wide eyes. He had to stay calm, for her sake. Had to find a way out of this nightmare.

He sat.

June flashed a cold smile. "Just like your father. If either of you had just minded his own business, everything would have been fine. But neither of you could leave well enough alone, could you?"

"Landon's father was killed in D.C.," Nichol said, her brow furrowed in confusion. "How did you do it?"

June shrugged, her nonchalance chilling in the face of their terror. "My parents worked all the time, trying to give me a better life than they had. They were never around to see what I did, and D.C. is only a few hours away." Her eyes took on a faraway look. "I called your dad and said I knew something about Addison's disappearance. Then I borrowed Derek's truck and waited for your father a block away from the café where we planned to meet. When I saw him crossing the street...." She trailed off, leaving the rest of the statement unspoken.

Landon's world tilted on its axis. His father's murder, the mystery that had haunted him for years, finally solved. He'd always believed that his father's death hadn't been an accidental hit-and-run but knowing that now for sure, it wasn't the relief that he'd thought it would be. Rage boiled inside him, threatening to explode. His fists clenched as he fought to maintain control.

"So, what now?" he spat, his own voice twisted with fury. "You kill us and there will be even more questions."

"Questions I've already arranged answers for."

"What does that mean?" Nichol wrapped her arms around herself.

"The police are looking for Derek for burning your garage down. I'm just going to add your murders to his tab."

The tension in the room ratcheted up another notch. Landon's heart pounded in his ears as the gravity of their situation sank in. They were out of time and out of options. He had to do something. He had to find a way to protect Nichol. But with June's finger on the trigger, one wrong move could mean death for both of them.

"And what will you do when Derek is found and tells the cops the truth?" Nichol said, buying them some time.

June's face transformed, her cold expression cracking to reveal a flicker of sadness. "They won't find Derek."

A chill ran down Landon's spine, his blood turning to ice. "What do you mean?" he asked, dreading the answer.

June's eyes were emotionless again. "Derek had become a liability. I didn't have any choice."

The meaning of June's words hit him like a physical blow. His mind reeled, trying to process the depths of her ruthlessness.

Nichol leaned forward. "June, what did you do to Derek?"

For a moment, genuine anguish flashed across June's face. "I told him to scare you two off your investigation, but he messed it up. As soon as he arrived at my door smelling like gasoline and vodka, I knew he had to go."

His pulse skittered, his palms growing slick with sweat as the full weight of their predicament crashed over him. If June could coldly eliminate Derek, someone she supposedly loved, what hope did he and Nichol have? His heart raced, fear and determination warring within him. He had to protect Nichol, at least give her the chance to get away from the disturbed woman standing in front of them.

His eyes darted around the kitchen, searching for anything that might give them an advantage. His gaze landed on the flour canister on the counter, just within reach. A desperate plan formed in his mind.

"June," Landon said, forcing his voice to remain steady, "you don't have to do this. We can figure something out."

As he spoke, his hand inched toward the canister. June's eyes narrowed, her attention momentarily divided between his words and his subtle movement.

In one fluid motion, Landon grabbed the canister and hurled its contents at June's face. The air filled with a billowing cloud of white powder, momentarily obscuring everything.

A deafening crack split the air as June's gun went off,

the bullet whizzing past his ear. He heard Nichol's startled scream, his heart lurching at the near miss.

"Nichol, run!" he shouted, lunging toward June, praying his gamble would buy her the seconds she needed to escape.

His body collided with June's, his momentum knocking them both to the floor. The gun clattered across the linoleum, out of reach. June snarled, her face ghostly white with flour, as she clawed at his eyes.

"You bastard!" she spat, struggling beneath him.

Landon grappled with her, his heart pounding. He could hear Nichol's footsteps, but they weren't retreating. She was still in the room.

"Nichol, get out of here!" he yelled, dodging June's wild swings.

June's fingers dragged down the side of his neck. He grunted in pain but maintained his grip on her wrists. They rolled across the floor, each of them fighting for dominance over the other.

He managed to pin June's arms above her head, but she bucked violently, nearly dislodging him, despite her smaller form. Adrenaline made her stronger than she should have been. His muscles strained with the effort of holding her down.

Nichol's voice rang out. "June, stop! Don't move or I will shoot."

Landon risked a glance up. Nichol stood a few feet away, June's gun clutched in her hands. Relief and pride surged through him.

He pushed to his feet, pulling June up with him, holding on to her tightly just in case she attempted to get away. "I need something to tie her up with."

"There's some electrical tape in the second drawer," Nichol said, the gun not wavering.

June tried to jerk free, a stream of curses falling from

her lips. He yanked her toward the drawer, opening it with one hand. Thankfully, the electrical tape was on top of the mess inside.

He wound the tape around June's wrists while Nichol kept the gun trained on the still-snarling woman.

"No one will believe you!" Jane shrieked, spittle flying from her lips. "I'll say you two kidnapped me."

Landon ignored her as he taped her hands then forced her to the kitchen floor so he could tape her ankles as well. He wasn't taking any chances.

Finally sure that June wasn't going anywhere, his adrenaline high began to wear off, leaving him shaky and exhausted.

"Are you okay?" he asked, coming to stand next to Nichol.

She'd let the gun fall to her side, but still held it in her hand. "I'm fine. You?"

"Yeah," Landon said, touching the scratches along the side of his neck. "I think so. Nothing a little first aid won't fix."

Nichol pulled her cell phone from her pocket and dialed 911. While she spoke to the operator, Landon studied the woman at his feet.

June continued to spew curses and obscenities at them. The woman who'd terrorized them, who'd killed his father and Derek, was now trussed up on Nichol's kitchen floor. She was finally going to be forced to face justice for her crimes. It felt surreal.

"The police are on their way," Nichol said. "It's over, Landon. We did it. We found Addison's killer."

A wave of relief washed over him, but it was tinged with a lingering sadness. Nothing would bring his father or Addison back. "Yeah, we did."

Chapter Twenty

The sun warmed the morning air as Nichol stood on her porch watching workmen clear away the charred remains of her garage. The scent of burned wood and melted plastic had thankfully dissipated since the night of the fire. She wrapped her hands around her coffee mug, drawing what warmth she could from it, turning over the events of the past weeks in her mind. Two weeks ago, her life had been ordinary, predictable. The burned garage was a testament to how quickly life could change.

At least Addison could rest now. For twenty-one years, her killer had walked free among them, smiling at community picnics, attending town meetings, playing the role of the dutiful, loving wife. June had fooled them all. Nichol gripped her mug tighter, her knuckles whitening under the strain.

The initial shock of June's arrest had sent ripples through Galesburg. June denied everything at first, but ultimately the combined weight of the evidence had been too much to fight. Nichol had heard that June's lawyers were working on a plea deal.

Nichol's throat tightened as she imagined Addison stepping off the bus, thinking she was meeting a friend, instead having to fight for her life and the life of her unborn child. June had refused to go into details about how she'd killed Addison, but she had admitted to driving Addison to the woods and there being a struggle that ended with June hitting Addison over the head with a rock. She'd buried Addison under leaves and twigs and there she'd lain for twenty-one years.

When Samuel Elkins had come to Galesburg poking around, June had become scared that her secret would be found out, or worse in her mind, Will might somehow become a suspect in Addison's disappearance. So, she'd arranged to meet Landon's father in D.C., saying she had information about Addison's disappearance, and had lain in wait for him at their prearranged meeting spot.

The police had found Derek's body in the basement of June and Will's lakeside home, hidden beneath an old tarp, a bullet wound in his chest.

June had enlisted her lover to scare Nichol and Landon away from their investigation. The garage fire was supposed to send that message, but when Derek had called June, frantic after Landon saw his face, June knew that Derek had become a liability. She'd decided she could take care of both of her problems by killing Landon and Nichol and pinning their murders on the missing Derek.

Will had already hired a divorce lawyer. She'd only seen him once since his wife's arrest, emerging from his real estate office, which was closed indefinitely according to the sign on the door. He looked as if he'd aged a decade in weeks, his shoulders stooped, his face lined with creases.

One of the workers called to another, pointing at something in the debris. Nichol squinted but couldn't make out what had caught their attention. She stepped back from the railing, her thoughts turning to the other body, the fresher one.

Three people killed all so June could have the life with Will that she believed she was entitled to. Such a waste.

Nichol's thoughts drifted away from June and the horrors of the past and settled on Landon. Landon, with his journalist's sharp eyes that softened when they looked at her. Landon, who had stayed in Galesburg for a few extra days and then they'd driven together to D.C. to attend Addison's memorial. Kayleigh had decided to lay her sister to rest next to their parents.

After the memorial, she'd stayed in D.C. for a long weekend. For those first several days, they had existed in a strange bubble, removed from June's arrest, the phone calls from friends checking on her, investigations, stories, everything. Landon had shown her his favorite corners of the city. A hidden bookstore with creaking wooden floors. A café where the owner knew him by name. The bench along the Potomac River that he swore cured writer's block. They had talked for hours, about everything except the investigation that had brought them together.

But reality had intruded when the weekend was over, and she had to go back to Galesburg.

Landon had accompanied her to the train station and their goodbye was bittersweet. She had boarded the train with a kiss still hot on her lips and unasked questions on her mind.

They'd spoken every night for the past two weeks, their conversations flowing easily, and usually lasting for hours sometimes. But last night's call had been different. Landon had mentioned a "new story" that would take him away from D.C. "indefinitely." Her heart had plummeted at his words, even as she forced brightness into her congratulations.

She sighed, running her hand along the porch railing. She could guess what *indefinitely* meant. With only her job at the library to worry about now, she'd time to do a deep dive into Landon's professional life. She'd read articles he'd written on issues that had taken him around the world. Baghdad to Bangladesh to Santiago. She'd been crazy to think that he'd be happy rooted in one spot, especially a sleepy town like Galesburg. A fleeting fantasy had crossed her mind during those days in D.C., of maybe moving there, but reality was more complicated. Her life was in Galesburg, for better or worse. And now it seemed Landon's life would be taking him…she wasn't sure. Away from the possibility of them. Landon hadn't explicitly said their relationship was ending. But *indefinitely* had the same ring as *goodbye*.

Nichol wrapped her arms around herself, suddenly chilled despite the morning sun. It was for the best. It was better to let him go now, before she fell any deeper and the distance and push-pull of their careers turned the relationship sour. At least they were parting on a high note.

Nichol let out a deep, sad sigh and turned toward her front door, ready to retreat into the quiet solitude of her house. The sound of tires on gravel caught her attention. A vehicle she didn't recognize was making its way up her driveway.

She paused, hand on the doorknob, squinting against the morning light. Her breath caught as the driver's side door swung open and Landon stepped out of the car, grinning.

Her body moved before her mind had completely processed the motion. One moment she stood on her porch, the next she was flying down the steps.

Landon met her halfway, his arms going around her.

"You're here," she whispered against his collar, her words half lost in the fabric of his shirt. "You're actually here."

In answer, Landon's hand came up to cup her face, tilting it toward his, and kissing her with an intensity that would have been embarrassing given they had an audience, but they were too lost in each other to care.

They broke apart, both of them a little breathless.

"What are you doing here?" Nichol asked, her hands still resting against his chest, feeling the steady rhythm of his heart beneath her palm.

Landon's eyes crinkled at the corners as his smile widened. "I told you I was starting a new story. The story of us. D.C. is too far away. I want to be with you every day."

"Landon—"

His hands moved to her shoulders, gentle but firm. "I'm not suggesting we move in together," he hurried on. "I don't want to rush you into anything. I'm going to get my own place in town and—"

Nichol silenced him with another kiss, rising on her toes to reach his lips. The kiss was brief but full of promise.

"Move in with me. I don't care if it's too fast or that people will talk." She glanced toward the workers, who had given up any pretense of not watching the scene unfolding before them. "Let 'em talk. Us shacking up isn't the worst thing that has happened in this town."

Landon laughed. "No, I guess not."

He kissed her again then, and in a move that made her gasp with surprised delight, he swept her into his arms and headed toward the house.

"So," he asked, his voice low and only for her ears, "you ready to get started on this story?"

Nichol wrapped her arms around his neck, her smile so wide it made her cheeks ache. "Absolutely."

* * * * *

COLTON'S FIRESTORM

BONNIE VANAK

For all firefighters who risk their lives to keep us safe.
Special thanks to Mike, Tony and Beth,
who know what it's like to save people. Thank you!

Chapter One

Darkness. So much darkness. Pain. Her leg ached with fierce throbbing, as if someone had battered it with a hammer.

Moaning, she thrashed back and forth. *Someone make it stop. Please!*

Heart racing, she fumbled for an exit, any way out. She had to find her way home, get out of here. Smoke, thick and acrid, filled her nostrils. Coughing, she tried to crawl away from the heat and flames, but something restricted her.

I'm going to die here.

Air, blessed air, whooshed into her lungs. Coughing, she blinked, her eyes watering...

"Fern. You okay?"

Ryan Colton stood in the doorway. Embarrassed to be caught in a nightmare, she blinked and forced a smile.

"Fine, fine. Stupid dream. That's all."

Struggling to get her bearings, she looked around. *Times like this I need a GPS for my life. Some kind of direction.*

Still in Baldwin Hospital in Dark Canyon. Fern Hensley reached past the covers and felt her bad leg. She closed her eyes, forcing herself to center. *You're okay. Safe. Your leg healed. Okay, got it, in the hospital, you'll go home soon to your safe space.*

Except she had no place to be safe. Only here, where they watched over her every minute.

Her home wasn't safe.

Fern opened her eyes to see Ryan cross the room and pull up a chair and sit. A warm palm covered hers.

"You were calling out in your sleep," he said in his deep, soothing voice.

He seemed kind. Concerned. Ryan, the firefighter who rescued her from the fire. She briefly remembered him lifting her up into his strong arms and telling her she had to live, had to fight, his commanding voice seeping into her mind as she fell unconscious.

He'd rescued her from the bad men who'd kidnapped her.

Kidnapped her, but didn't sexually assault her. A memory briefly flared. A cruel voice speaking aloud in the darkness.

"Gotta save her for the online auction. She'll sell better if she's untouched."

Then the brutal pain in her leg when she'd tried to run and they'd beaten her. Couldn't escape.

The fire...

She took a deep breath. At least her throat had healed from the smoke inhalation. The superficial burns on her arms were healed. Her leg, well, the doctors said she'd walk with a gimp, but her leg was perfectly functionable.

Even if inside I am not. Damn, I need a drink.

"Silly dream, nothing more. I'm fine," she lied again, wondering if the smile she forced looked like she was gritting her teeth.

Even sleeping with the light on failed to chase away the darkness inside her. So many times she'd wake up, gasping for air, struggling to breathe as she had back at the burning cabin.

Ava, her counselor and Ryan's sister, assured her the

trauma would fade. But with her memory as scattered as jigsaw pieces, Fern wasn't as confident.

She began folding the bed's blanket into triangle shapes. The patterns soothed her for some reason. Maybe because they provided consistency in a world no longer consistent.

Calling her sponsor was a good idea. For the past two years, Belle had talked her off the ledge. But she didn't want to call her in front of Ryan. Bad enough to lie here, helpless, a victim. Much as she liked Ryan, she didn't want him to know her past or her battle with alcohol, even though she had not touched a drop of liquor in seven years.

Ryan's deep blue gaze raked over her body. Professional, assessing, yet she sensed more than compassion. His commanding air and courage fed her hope.

With her kidnappers still roaming free, she felt terrified they might return to finish the job. Maybe this time bring a gun into the hospital to kill her instead of leaving her in the wood cabin to die in smoke and flames.

Jeans hugged Ryan's trim legs, and he wore a blue and white baseball shirt. The clothing fit his lanky body well. Maybe some would call him lean, but she knew the strength in those arms that had snatched her away from death.

"Are you supposed to be working?" she asked.

"I have two days off. I wanted to stop by, see how you're doing."

She played with the covers, smoothed them, glad her hands were no longer shaking. "Thanks. I'm okay."

So many times he'd visited. Ryan was one of the few she trusted.

A brusque knock sounded at the door. Instead of the nurse, Jacob Colton strode into the room. As the lead investigator into her kidnapping, he'd spent a lot of time with her. He nodded at Ryan, his cousin, and studied her.

Fern squirmed, feeling like a bug under the microscope.

"How are you feeling?"

"Okay," she lied.

Not that Jacob wasn't a good guy, but he was a cop and cops always asked questions, probed, wanted answers.

Answers she didn't have but wanted to give him.

Jacob came closer, big and intimidating. "Maybe we can try some more questions. Jog your memory. You were abducted walking home from work. Whoever took you made sure you wouldn't run by breaking your leg."

Ryan frowned and spoke in a no-nonsense tone. "Jacob, is this necessary?"

"It is if we're going to find who did this." Jacob studied her as if he could pry answers from her broken memories. "Remember who hurt you? Anything about your broken leg?"

A faint memory surged. An angry voice, a fist raised to strike. *No, please don't. Don't! Don't hurt me!*

Fern bit back a whimper. Jacob leaned forward, intense and too much in her space.

"Get a memory back?"

Fern's fingers curled into the blanket. *I can't tell him about this. I don't know what memory this is. I feel like it's my childhood, but...*

Too raw and exposed, she shook her head. "No. I'm trying..."

Jacob's expression remained level. He seemed too big, too intense. "Can you try harder? You're the best lead we have now."

"I want to help! I do! But I can't remember!"

Ryan edged closer to Jacob, his expression darkening. "I'm warning you, Jacob, take it easy on her. She's not the suspect."

Jacob glanced at his cousin. "I get it, Ryan. Fern's suffered a great deal of trauma. But we need to find out who did this so we can prevent other women from being kidnapped."

So much pressure. Fern's fists tightened. "I remembered one of them was called Billy. I already told you before, one was Billy. I wish I could remember!" she burst out. "Can't you see I'm trying?"

"Enough." Ryan jerked his head to the door. He looked as if he might drag Jacob out. A warm feeling of wonder filled her. The sheer command in his voice soothed her agitation.

Ryan was her advocate, and she needed one right now.

"Jacob, outside. Leave her alone."

But Jacob was only doing his job. "I do want to help," she said in a small voice. "I wish I could remember."

Jacob focused on her. "I wish you could as well. What about hypnosis? Would you be willing to speak to someone about that?"

Torn, she bit her lip. Undergoing hypnosis could help them catch her abductors, maybe even find the people who killed that poor woman in Dark Canyon. But ghosts of memories flitted about her mind, vague and threatening.

Ghosts she didn't want to see right now.

"Maybe."

"If you're willing, I'll set something up."

"I—I don't know."

Ryan stood up. "Now, Jacob. Leave her alone. Pushing her isn't going to force Fern into regaining her memory."

"I'm not pushing, Ryan. Fern says she's willing and the hypnosis could work. She's our best chance of catching these bad guys."

"Not if you're going to stress Fern," he snapped.

Cousin against cousin—this was all wrong and it was her fault for not remembering. Families fighting, shouts, screams of pain...

Shoulders shaking, Fern buried her head into her hands. It was too much. She felt like a thread unraveling from a tapestry everyone was trying to sew back together.

Ryan left the room, returning less than a minute with Cassidy, her nurse. Fern raised her head. Cassidy gave one stern look to Jacob.

"Out. Now," she told him.

Jacob looked at Fern. "When you're ready, maybe we can consider the hypnosis."

Cassidy followed Jacob out of her room. Suddenly the walls seemed to squeeze in on her. Suffocating her, pressing her from all sides. She knew she was safe here, but was she really?

Was she safe anywhere?

Ryan gestured to the door. "Sorry about that. Jacob is a good guy, but he can be single-minded."

"It's okay."

"You're not okay. You're shaking."

Damn. Fern blew out a breath, tried to center herself. "I don't know what's going to happen. I can't stay here forever and…"

"It doesn't help having Jacob burst into your room whenever he wants." Ryan glanced at the door again. "You can't go home again. Not until Jacob catches these…"

He bit his lip as if biting back a curse.

Fern offered another faint smile. "You can say it. I'd probably call them worse."

Ryan sat close to her again. "Listen, I'm sure the doctor will discharge you soon…and this hospital must feel like a prison. Would you want a room at my place?"

She stared.

He flushed, and it made him look even cuter. "Just a spare room. I can talk with the police and arrange to have a protective detail—an undercover police officer—watch over the house and make sure you're guarded when I have to work. No pressure. I can only imagine how confining this room is."

Much as she hated being a victim and having no place to

go, she felt grateful. The guy had saved her life and was giving her a place to live. A safe place. She placed her hand over his.

Trust. Damn hard to come by these days, but deep inside, she felt the beginnings of it return. Maybe staying in his house, without the constant antiseptic smell of the hospital, nurses coming and going, would help her relax and recall her memories.

It seemed a generous offer, but leaving the security of the hospital would be challenging. Could she trust him?

"I don't know. Where do you live? I mean, why do you think I'd be safe there? Others would know my location, Ryan."

"They won't. I live in a quiet neighborhood and everyone minds their own business. My backyard is fenced for privacy, so if you need fresh air and sunshine, you can sit on the patio."

His intense blue gaze met hers. "I mean it, Fern. You'll be safe there. I promise to do whatever I can to protect you."

Ryan had saved her life. He had been a source of quiet and calm in a dizzying array of frustration and terror over the past three months. While the nurses and doctors, and Ava, her therapist, had been professional, only Ryan made her feel safe. Even Jacob, though he was a professional police officer, made her wary.

Though she wasn't one to gamble, she went with her instincts.

"Thank you. For everything. Yes, that would be great. Are you sure I won't be an inconvenience?"

His hand lingered a moment longer before he pulled it away. "No trouble at all. It will give me a good reason to clean out all that clutter. I have off today and tomorrow, so I have time to get everything ready."

He glanced at the door. "If the doc will sign you out, you can come to my place tomorrow. I'll pick you up."

Fern nodded, but she couldn't erase the fear every present beneath the surface, like a snake waiting to strike. Logically? She was safe, had stayed here in the hospital under another name and no one knew her real identity. The security here was excellent. But moving to Ryan's house, especially because he had to work and she would be alone and vulnerable...

As if reading her mind, he pulled out his phone. "I've been meaning to ask my cousin Mark to install a new security system. And you have your personal backup Mark got you."

He gestured to the locket given to her, now lying on the bedside table. A panic button in case something went wrong. The pretty jewelry had a button on the back for her to press if she had an emergency and contained a GPS tracking chip.

Fern gave a crooked smile. "Help, I've fallen and I *can* get up."

He grinned, making him look even cuter. Ryan brushed a hand through his light brown hair. Then his smile vanished. "I mean it, Fern. You feel scared or threatened, you press that button."

He glanced around the hospital room. "I know it must feel scary leaving here with so many people around to guard you, but I promise, we'll do everything to ensure you're protected."

Though his words offered comfort, Fern hated feeling dependent. She looked around the private hospital room, her home for the past three months. Ironic how she'd probably coded medical records of people who may have been at this very same hospital after leaving the doctor's office where she'd worked...

Medical coding. The memory returned, making her catch her breath.

"What?" he asked.

"I used to work for a doctor as a medical coder." She

frowned, pressed two fingers against her head. "I was walking home from work and then something happened…"

No, don't think about that!

"That's terrific." He gave an encouraging smile. "Little by little, you'll recall everything."

Everything? She wanted to help. She wanted her attackers caught. They had left her in the shack to die a horrific death.

But the idea of remembering everything in her life seemed overwhelming. Fern had a deep suspicion she'd deliberately forgotten some aspects of her life to move on.

Once she remembered them, would she face even greater pain than the physical hurt inflicted on her?

Chapter Two

The car crash was a bad one. Guy T-boned a truck much bigger than his tiny car.

A stench of fuel and blood filled the air. Bystanders stood nearby, some recording with their cell phones. He scowled, then forced himself to ignore them.

Ryan focused on the job at hand. Make sure everyone was safe, then comfort the victim as they prepared to extract him.

The man's leg was trapped under the dashboard, blood seeping onto the seat. A real mess. But experience taught him the guy's leg could be saved, even though it would take lots of hospital care and physical therapy.

As they removed the man from the car and secured the scene, his thoughts drifted to Fern. Rushing into the cabin and dragging her out of the fire, silently praying she would be okay. The stench of smoke still lingered in his mind.

He felt shock at how shattered Fern's leg was, how much it must have hurt, and fury at who could have done this to her.

He couldn't stop thinking about her and how easily she could have slipped away had he not arrived on scene when he did. Hands and feet tied up, left to die in the fire.

Fern, with her long brown hair, pretty hazel eyes, grit and determination not to be a victim.

By the time the engine and rescue truck returned to the station, he felt worn out, and it was only the beginning of his shift. He was professional, knew his job, but this save had triggered him.

As they removed their turnout gear at the lockers, his buddy Bob Marks kept looking at him.

"What?" he finally asked, in no mood for games.

"Heard you have a lady friend named Fern moving in with you." Bob grinned.

Ryan whirled, narrowing his eyes. "Where did you hear that?"

"Social media."

As he stared at his friend, Bob sighed. "Joke, Rye. Overheard your convo with Ava."

"You overheard nothing, Bob. Keep it to yourself. I don't want people to know where she is."

"Sure, sure. You want to keep it on the DL because it's a big step to have a woman live with you."

The teasing not only irritated him, it made him furious. "Cut the crap, Bob. I have an extra room and she needs to get out of that hospital. She's not moving in with me. I'm giving her a safe place."

Bob blinked and held up his hands. "Whoa, whoa. Sorry, man. Didn't realize you were that sensitive about it."

He sat on a nearby bench and pulled off his boots, throwing them with force into the locker. Ryan heaved a breath and righted his boots, then draped his suspenders over them. He placed his helmet on the shelf in the same place he always did, visor up. Superstitious ritual each time he returned from a call.

Equipment stored, he turned to his friend. Why couldn't Bob get it?

"Sensitive has nothing to do with it. Fern suffered a severe trauma, and she's the best chance we have of catching the ones who did this to her. The bastards who are making our town dangerous for women, *all* women. Get it?"

"Ryan, I was teasing..."

Raw anger bubbled up. "Teasing? How would you like it if Maggie got snatched off the street and beaten? Tied up and left to burn alive in a fire? Had so much happen to her it's a damn miracle she's alive? Couldn't remember half of her life?"

Captain Tom Colburn popped his head into the room. "What's going on? I could hear you upstairs."

Ryan took a deep breath. Bob put a hand on his arm. "Look Rye, I'm sorry. I wasn't thinking."

He shrugged off his hand. "Problem with you, Bob, is you don't think."

Ryan had to get away, cool down, stop reacting, because every time someone mentioned something even slightly derisive about Fern, he went into a tailspin. When he thought of Fern, lying on the floor, flames sweeping over the weather-roughened wood, licking closer to her, it sent him into a rage. How dare someone treat her like that? Tied up and helpless to fight her way free?

There are good people in this world, he'd assured her.

You're one of them, she'd told him.

Always a professional, keeping his feelings stuffed inside, Ryan knew Fern shook him deeply. The exchange with Bob, one of his best buds, proved it.

He was invested in what happened to her.

Fern haunted him. If Noah hadn't been there and Dancer hadn't alerted to her location, she would have died. No rescue. No ambulance growling away to nurses and docs treating her injuries.

Only a body bag.

Steadying himself with a calming breath, he shuddered.

Years of saves under his belt and this one woman had turned him inside out.

Another face flickered in his mind. Kate McIntyre, her terrified screams echoing in his head as she twisted, escaping his frantic grip.

Cap followed him outside as Ryan paced in front of the firehouse.

"Rye, talk to me. You have to chill out."

With his shock of gray hair, keen brown eyes and no-nonsense manner, Captain Tom was the heartbeat of the firehouse. Always one to defuse conflict, take charge, Tom was like a big brother. Ryan respected him and never dismissed his advice.

Until today. He was too tightly wound, a coiled spring ready to snap. The crash victim they'd saved reminded him of Fern, pale and stricken by pain. But Fern had been worse.

Cap put a hand on his shoulder. "Rye, what's really going on? Ever since you rescued Fern, you've been involved. Maybe too much."

Oh no, not today. He took another deep breath to calm himself. "How can I *not* get involved? I'm not going to ignore what's going on in town, Cap. I see it everywhere I go. People are scared, and women, they're terrified, knowing a kidnapper and murderer is out there. Fern's alive. She saw her kidnappers. She's our best chance of finding them, but she's too traumatized to remember anything."

"Ryan, we've talked about this. Save the victim and your job ends there. You've already had one incident. I don't want you to have another."

As if he needed reminding. Ryan's insides tightened. Could hear all the talk.

Savior complex. Guilt complex. Hell, his sister, Ava, was a psychologist. No need to remind him what he'd done shortly after taking this job.

I couldn't save her. She slipped from my fingers. I was so close, so close...

Aware Cap's steady gaze was assessing him, ready to analyze him, he forced a nod and a smile, hiding his feelings.

"Okay, Rye. Go talk to Bob. I don't want my team fighting."

He returned inside to find Bob sitting before his locker. "Look, Rye, I'm sorry about this. I won't tell anyone."

"Good." He took a deep breath. "It's okay. Forget about it."

"But I do have to ask, because you are my friend. You certain Fern moving into your guest bedroom is the right thing?"

"Absolutely. She has nowhere else to go. Mark is already working on the security system."

He stated this with more confidence than he felt. Fact was, he had to work and leave her alone. Couldn't be there all the time to ensure she was okay.

What if something happened to her while he was gone?

THREE DAYS AFTER Ryan invited her to stay at his house, the doctor finally signed her out of the hospital.

Ryan came to take her back to his home.

Leaving was scary, but she'd faced tougher. Fern struggled to sit up and threw back the covers. She gestured to the bed railing.

"Can you put this down for me? I need to get up."

He obliged and stood back. "I'm here if you need help."

Fern slid her legs over the bedside.

At least Ryan didn't treat her like an invalid. He stood by, ready to assist, but letting her stand on her own. Using her good right leg for balance and leaning on the walker, she hoisted herself out of the bed.

Pain flared briefly as she put weight on her left leg. Fern inhaled a deep breath.

Still watching her, Ryan frowned. "I went to get your meds from the pharmacy to expedite the check-out process. No painkillers. Doc prescribed them, but you refused."

Taking a deep breath, she put her full weight on the bad leg, relieved it held, relieved the pain was nothing compared to...

When you first got injured.

Though Ava, her counselor, had worked with her in trying to get her to recall those horrific memories, now was not the time. Focusing on the goal before her—getting out of the hospital—was far more important.

Fern glanced at him. "No prescription painkillers. I manage fine with over the counter."

Ryan nodded. "If you find you need them, let me know. I can always go to the drugstore to fill them."

He didn't ask why she fought the pain on her own, refusing to rely on heavy medications. Another thing she liked about this guy—he wasn't nosy like some. Nor did he argue with her.

Setting aside the walker, she tested the weight on both legs again and then walked over toward the door. Barely any pain at all now, not if she went slow. Yeah, she wouldn't be racing anytime soon, but at least she was mobile. Fern felt a jubilant surge at knowing she could stand on her own two feet.

She made her way across the room. It felt great to walk and be free from the bed. Balancing her weight, she moved one foot in front of the other. Yeah, she was doing good. Air brushed against her body, now freed from the covers, and her backside felt, well...

Oops.

Suddenly she became aware of the hospital gown flapping open from the back and her butt was showing. Her big butt. Even hospital food for three months hadn't eliminated that problem. Heat suffused her face. Ryan cleared his throat and turned around.

She tried for humor. "Sorry for mooning you. This gown doesn't exactly fit."

"No problem. Nice view."

She turned and saw him blush. He looked even cuter.

"Give me a few minutes to get dressed. I would have been ready earlier, but I slept late because they kept waking me up last night to take my blood pressure. You know, to make sure I wasn't dead when I left here."

Ryan chuckled. "Yeah, I know how hospitals are. I'll be in the waiting room."

Fern grinned as he left. She liked his casual attitude. But being in a hospital had been all about survival for the past three months. Now, knowing she would be staying at Ryan's house, she became aware of her body. A shower would help. Fern felt her hair, dismayed at how scruffy it was. Bedhead. Suddenly it seemed critical to leave clean and refreshed, her hair washed. New start.

Even though problems still followed, attached by invisible strings jerking her downward into a pit of darkness.

I don't need a drink.

But she did need to call her sponsor. Fern walked over to the bedside table and picked up the new cell phone Ryan had bought her.

Belle answered on the first ring, as if anticipating her call. "Hi, Fern. How are you handling everything?"

"I'm okay."

"Don't lie. Talk to me."

She smiled. Belle, always direct, her usual feisty fifty-nine-year-old self, sober now for more than twenty-five years. Her lifeline at times over the past two years, ever since her first sponsor had moved to Europe.

"I'm managing. Scared. I'm leaving the hospital today."

Fern cleared her throat. Though many memories eluded her, she knew her voice had deepened from inhaling smoke in the fire.

"I know. Big step. Is your plan in place?"

Belle taught her that having a plan helped to keep a semblance of control, even when life spiraled out of control. Taking responsibility for things within her control was part of AA's twelve-step program. Focus on what the next thing she could do was. Move straight ahead, like taking a simple shower. A shower wasn't climbing Mount Everest.

Her compass was the people helping her along the way. Accepting help wasn't easy, but she needed it.

"Plan is in place," she told Belle. "Shower first, then packing, and leaving with Ryan to go to his house."

"How do you feel about staying with him?"

Ava had asked her this as well. Fern bit her lip. "It's weird. I'm relieved I have a place to live that's safe, but I hate depending on anyone. I don't want to be a big imposition. I feel a little helpless that I can't make it on my own."

"You're not helpless. Look at how far you've come, Fern. You're standing. You're walking. Damn, girl, you're alive. Thank the good Lord you are!"

Emotion clogged her throat. So much gratitude, another important part of the twelve steps. Focus on the gratitude.

"You can do this, Fern. You're one of the strongest people I know, girl."

"You're right. I can do this. Thanks, Belle. I'd better get moving. That shower is calling me."

"I'm here if you need me. Deal?"

"Deal. Bye, and thank you." Fern hung up.

She depressed the nurse call button to get assistance with showering. Not that she couldn't do it herself, but they wanted to stand by in case she needed help.

Belle was right. She was alive and had plenty to be grateful for right now. But in the back of her mind, she couldn't help worrying about what the future held.

Especially with the men who'd kidnapped her still running free.

Fern shivered.

Chapter Three

Knowing Fern was going to stay with him, Ryan had done his best to clean the house. Couldn't do anything about the fact the walls needed painting or the kitchen looked like the eighties wanted their cabinets back, but at least he lived on a nice street in a safe neighborhood.

His house had cathedral ceilings, and best of all, lots of windows letting in natural light. French doors in the living room opened to a big yard, surrounded by a white privacy fence.

Ryan wished he had better furnishings to offer Fern. The guest bedroom was adequate, but the bed was secondhand, picked up at a garage sale. Furniture had been purchased at a scratch-and-dent sale.

On his salary, he didn't have money for the kind of luxurious furniture in his parents' house.

Dad would blame the thrift-store look on Ryan not following in his footsteps and taking a job with the family real estate business. Dad took every opportunity to remind him, *Hey, you can do better.*

But being a firefighter was a dream come true. He wanted to save people, not real estate holdings.

Fern gazed around the guest bedroom. In blue jeans that hugged her legs and her apple-round bottom, a light pink sweater that accented her curves, she sure was pretty. But her trepidation concerned him. He wanted to make her feel comfortable and safe, not scared.

He held her suitcase, the one donated by the local charity who'd also given her clothing and basic toiletries. "Sorry it isn't much, but the bed's comfortable. The quilt is warm, but if you're cold I have extra blankets in the linen closet."

She looked around, nodded. Hard to tell what Fern thought. Her expression was neutral.

"It's lovely. Thank you again. I appreciate you taking me in."

"Where do you want your suitcase?"

Fern's gaze dropped down as she pointed to the bed. "There is fine until I can unpack. It isn't really mine. I mean, it was given to me to get me back on my feet until I can get home again. Everything in my life right now is a loan."

Setting down the suitcase, he knew where she was headed with this. He cut her off. Ava had warned him not to indulge her in a pity party. It wouldn't help Fern mentally heal or help trigger her memory.

"You're not a victim, Fern. Remember that."

She gave a humorless laugh. "Funny, when I went to Florida for a vacation I remember seeing a sign at the airport about reporting human trafficking. I never gave it a second thought and here I am. So, do I report myself?"

He liked her spirit. Probably had helped to keep her alive and fighting. How many times had he seen people in bad situations, people he'd saved from a horrible car crash or lost in the canyon, whom he'd pulled out alive and breathing?

People who fought to live instead of giving up. Fern was that kind of woman.

Jamming his hands into his pockets, he gazed around the room. "Listen, I hate to do this, but I have to work a twenty-four-hour shift that started at seven o'clock. I did get permission to show up to work at eleven, so I have to leave soon. I tried to rearrange my schedule to be here for your first night, but with your delayed release, I couldn't get anyone to switch with me."

"It's okay. I'll be fine. It's great you were able to pick me up."

The staccato sentences didn't reassure him. The way her gaze kept darting around the room, as if looking into every corner for threats, worried him.

"I'll call my sister, Ava, and ask her to spend the night. I don't want you to be alone."

Finally she looked at him. "I'll be fine, Ryan. I have to be alone sometime, right? And I'm not going to be alone. There's a cop outside, nearby, watching the house. Plus this." Reaching into her sweater, Fern pulled out the pretty silver locket from the long necklace dangling from her neck. "I have my emergency GPS finder. All I have to do is double click the hidden button in the back and I send out an SOS to Jacob to tell him my location."

The determination on her face told him she didn't want to impose. Be a burden. Ryan made a snap decision. He hefted her suitcase onto the bed.

"Here, go ahead and get settled. The least I can do is make you a decent lunch."

"I thought you had to work." She glanced at the bedside glass clock that featured a fire emblem. He'd bought it on a whim.

"The boss won't care if I'm a little late." He flashed her a smile. "I'm not much of a chef, but I do make a decent spaghetti and meatballs. Even if my mom says my meatballs are a little too big."

"No problem. I like big balls. The bigger the better."

He grinned wider at the double entendre as she flushed. "Uh, ah, thanks. I'll unpack."

In the kitchen, he set about making lunch after texting Bob and Cap he needed another hour. Bob, as an apology for his words the other day, offered to take his shift until Ryan could arrive at the station.

Both texted back all was fine.

Cap and the others had stopped talking about him giving Fern a temporary place to stay.

Ryan boiled the water and fished in his cabinet for the pasta. He'd been so busy lately, he'd forgotten to grocery shop. Some welcome he'd arranged for Fern.

He turned off the water and walked to her room, knocking on the door jamb.

No answer.

Worried, he poked his head through the door to find her sitting on the bed. Not unpacking, not doing anything except sitting.

"Hey, you okay, Fern?"

She glanced up, touched the bed. "Sorry. I was trying to get my bearings. This is the first time I've been inside a real home in months. Your place is great, it's just that...the last place I was in before the hospital was...not."

Hugging herself, she shivered. "I guess it will take a little adjusting."

Ryan cursed his thoughtlessness. Here he was, worried about food when she was worried about the ground constantly shifting beneath her.

He pointed to the bed. "Mind if I join you?"

Seeing her pale face, sensing sitting next to her would be too much right now, he shook his head. "No, never mind. I think better on my feet."

Her relieved expression was heartbreaking. Ryan took a deep breath, sensing he was treading through a minefield. He didn't want to scare or upset her, but his sister asked him to work with Fern to trigger her memory.

The faster Fern could recall more details of her abduction, the quicker the police could nail the kidnappers. Then not only Fern, but many women in Dark Canyon and nearby towns would be safe.

For now, it was best to stick to essentials.

"I forgot to grocery shop. What would you like for takeout? Italian? Mexican? I'm game for anything," he told her.

A little frown formed between her eyebrows. Made her look thoughtful and cute. "I can cook."

"I don't have much." He paused. "Listen, Fern, you're my guest. I didn't bring you here to cook. Don't feel like you have to earn your keep."

Waving a hand, she left the bed and headed for the kitchen. Fern began opening cabinets.

"I like to cook and I'm good at it. My mom was, well, I learned to make dinner from nothing."

She found a bottle of barbecue sauce and some spices. Next she dug into the freezer and found a package of chicken breasts he'd bought on sale and had forgotten about. Ryan found a container for defrosting the chicken and put it into the microwave.

Fern removed a package of cheddar cheese from the refrigerator.

"Here we go! Cheddar chicken with barbecue sauce. Oh, you have bacon as well. Bacon-wrapped chicken with cheese and barbecue sauce."

He grinned. "A guy's gotta have bacon."

She beamed. Such a little thing, making a meal, yet her enthusiasm told him Fern felt happy to be useful. Intrigued, he watched her set about making the recipe.

Meal preparation was a great icebreaker. It put them on even ground, and she seemed more relaxed.

"We make a good team," he said.

Her expression fell. "You save people and I needed saving."

No pity. "I was talking about the food. I can defrost chicken like a pro."

The smile on her face felt gratifying.

Ryan removed the chicken from the microwave. "I'm really not a bad cook. Everyone takes turns at the station making dinner. I haven't heard any complaints yet."

She mixed the sauce and poured it over the chicken breasts. "If you haven't had to transport them to the hospital because of your cooking, I'd say you were ahead of the game."

He grinned. "I didn't say that. Never claimed they weren't conscious enough to complain."

After fishing out plates and silverware, he set the kitchen table. Fern wanted plain water and he opted for the same.

Ryan dug into his food. The flavor burst on his tongue. "Wow, this is good, Fern. You can make something out of nothing."

She pinked slightly under the praise. "It's not a big deal. Only a matter of figuring out what ingredients you have on hand can be combined. I learned early in life to economize when doing meal planning. I've survived on less. At the cabin, they gave me a granola bar, and even then I threw it back in their faces...their faces..."

Her expression went blank.

Excitement raced through him. "You remembered?"

Fern glanced at him, looked away. "I guess."

"That's terrific! Remember what they look like? Anything on them? Anything Jacob can use?"

Too late he realized his mistake. He was pushing Fern the same way his cousin and others had done. Fern stiffened.

"I'm not really hungry. You can leave when you want and I'll clean up. Excuse me, I think I'll get unpacked now."

Watching her leave the table, he groaned. Idiot. He'd blown it.

I have to do a reset with her before she bolts. Have to make her feel relaxed, not like I'm applying pressure like everyone else.

He glanced at the kitchen clock. Running late. But Fern came first. She was a priority.

Barely had he started out of the kitchen toward the hallway when he heard the commotion. Heart pounding, he ran toward the guest bedroom.

"Ryan! Help!" Fern shouted. "Someone's trying to break into my room!"

She screamed.

Chapter Four

This was supposed to be a refuge. Fern shrank back against the wall, quivering as the menacing man at the window peered inside.

Fingers in her mouth, she whipped her head around to search for a weapon and seized the first thing she saw.

Ryan burst into the room, saw her. In his right hand he carried a baseball bat.

"The window," she managed to say.

He ran over as the man staring inside raised a hand. Oh dear heavens, was that a gun in his hand?

"Security," the man outside yelled. "Doing rounds. Can I come in?"

"Badge," Ryan shouted back. "Let me see your shield."

The stranger raised a gold shield. "Officer McCarty. I'm the plainclothes officer assigned to patrol the house."

Lowering the baseball bat, Ryan gestured to the front door. "Ring the doorbell and I'll be right there."

He turned, went to her. "Fern, you okay?"

Nodding, she bit her lip. "I—I—I'm sorry. I saw him at the window and I thought..."

"Not your fault. He should have rung the damn doorbell in the first place before walking around outside." Ryan's gaze dropped to her right hand.

Amusement flared in his eyes. "Were you going to use that on him?"

Fern glanced down at the bedside clock in her hand. Goodness, as if this could hurt someone. Feeling silly, she set it down.

"I've heard of people having time on their hands, but never using it to defend themselves."

His boyish grin eased the tension from her shoulders. Despite her nerves rubbed raw, Fern managed a slight smile.

"Sorry, bad joke." Twirling the baseball bat in his hands, he shrugged.

"I've heard worse." She considered. "Though not in a while."

His grin widened. "I have worse, if you're interested."

Interested? Maybe. She liked his sense of humor and how he used it to defuse a tense situation.

Fern pointed to the baseball bat. "At least you brought something that's useful for defense. Were you expecting to score a home run on the intruder?"

He chuckled. "Something like that. My friends would say it's more likely than me scoring a home run on our softball team."

Fern managed a bigger smile. "Something tells me you're being too modest."

As the doorbell rang, Ryan lowered the bat. "Modesty isn't one of my virtues, but honesty is. Let's go meet this Officer McCarty."

Tim McCarty was a tall, muscled man who wore jeans and a white linen shirt under a denim jacket. He had a serious look, which she supposed went with the job.

"Sorry for scaring you, miss. I was checking out the house. We're renting the house two doors down, and I'll keep an eye out here for you. Another officer will take over the night shift around six."

Tight-lipped, she nodded but couldn't bring herself to relax around the man. Maybe it was his air of authority or how he'd scared her. As long as he remained in the background, she'd be okay.

But this man was responsible for her welfare, so she should trust him. Maybe it would take a little time.

Time, something Fern kept feeling was slipping away. Every day she failed to recall all memory of The Incident, as she referred to her abduction, another woman remained in danger.

One already died. Baby Ella Grace had been left abandoned. Thankfully Ava was now caring for baby Ella Grace. *I'm the key to helping others, but damn, I feel like I'm walking over a minefield. A minefield that can blow up any minute now.*

When Ryan closed and locked the door, she breathed a sigh of relief. Despite the fact she'd barely been here a couple of hours, his home felt like a sanctuary away from a scary world outside. Maybe because it was his home, filled with his personality and calmness and fierce protectiveness.

He gave her a long, assessing look. "You okay? You're a bit pale."

She started with her usual "fine" response and stopped. "I guess I'm a little jumpy. You'd think by now I'd stop being scared of my own shadow."

Ryan shook his head. "After what you went through, Fern, you have a right to be scared. But you're safe here. I want you to know that. And if you need me, I'm a text or a phone call away. I think it's best for my sister to spend tonight with you."

She nodded.

"Sorry there's no food in the house. I have an account at the grocery store, so feel free to order whatever you want and get it delivered. Put it on my bill. They're used to me getting deliveries. Let me give you the grand tour. I know the doc wants you to keep up with rehab, and I have a gym downstairs so you can do the exercises you did at the hospital."

So considerate.

He briefly showed her his bedroom, the largest one. Ryan jammed his hands into the pockets of his trousers. "Sorry for the mess. I don't sleep well sometimes after a shift, but I need to get my z's, and as a result, well, the bedroom…"

Fern walked over to the windows and the blinds. "You don't have blackout shades? How can you sleep during the day without a room being totally dark?"

He scowled. "I do my best."

"I didn't mean to criticize. Only an observation. I used to work night shift a few years ago when I was in college and blackout shades helped."

He shrugged. "Been meaning to buy some, but it kept getting away from me, with all the other stuff around here. Having a house is a lot of work."

"I'd be happy to help you purchase some."

The long, thoughtful look he gave her wasn't as uncomfortable as others' had been. Not like Ava's when Fern said something during therapy sessions or Jacob's when he grilled her about any details of her abduction.

Rather, it was like seeing her in a new light, ironically, because she knew how important it was to have a dark bedroom.

"Sure, if you want, but it's really not a big deal."

Fern wished she had her own money and access to her bank account. Ava might help with that. Helping Ryan sleep would be a small way to repay him for all his kindness.

The third bedroom he'd converted into an office/library. Bookshelves were filled with medical and science textbooks and crime novels.

"Feel free to borrow anything. I have plenty of light reading available," he told her.

"Physics and medical journals? You call that light reading?"

He grinned. "I'm trying to expand my knowledge. Helps on the job. I'm the senior hazmat technician at the station. Plus it never hurts to know more about emergency medical care."

"I thought there were EMTs and paramedics for that."

"Yes, however, sometimes we're first on scene and have to secure the vic." He gave her a steady look. "Like when I rescued you."

Heat suffused her cheeks. "That's something I can never forget. Thank you again for saving me."

"Part of the job."

His casual comment defused the seriousness of what happened. It wasn't part of his job to give her a safe space to live, or to visit her frequently at the hospital.

Downstairs, she gave an appreciative look around at the equipment, from a treadmill to weights and a lifting machine that looked far too complicated for her.

Opposite the gym was a wooden bar with shelving on the wall holding an assortment of liquor. Fern's smile dropped.

"You like to entertain?" she asked.

He followed her gaze. "Oh that. My dad set it up for me. Not really. A beer once in a while after a tough shift. Some of those bottles haven't been touched in years. I think Dad gave them to me to get them out of his house because Mom was nagging him about them."

Somehow that made her like him more. Ryan wasn't a hardcore drinker like some she'd met, like that guy who asked her out at the doctor's office who came in smelling like vodka and orange juice...

"I used to drink. A lot. I don't drink anymore," she said more to herself than to him.

Whoa, she hadn't meant to admit that to him, but there it

was, out in the open. She watched him, ready for the usual uncomfortable reaction. Many people liked alcohol and felt uncomfortable around those who did not.

Ryan looked indifferent, as if she'd told him she disliked a certain color. "I'll have my cousin come over and remove the bottles later. Mark mentioned he liked the design."

"You don't have to do that for me. It's your home, and I don't want to disrupt your routine or anything else. I'm fine, Ryan. I don't drink anymore, but I still go out once in a while to a bar on a date…"

Her voice trailed off as a memory flickered. Fern rubbed a spot on the polished wood counter of the bar. "I was walking home, thinking about this guy who asked me out to this Irish bar…and then…everything went dark."

"Irish bar with a date. Sounds like fun. So who was the guy?"

Such a casual question, but she heard the undertone. Fern tilted her head at him. "That much I remember. A guy I met at the doctor's office. Some kind of salesman."

"Oh." Ryan traced a line along the bars of the treadmill. "Rich, good-looking, huh?"

Was that a little jealousy in his voice? She wasn't the type to encourage it. Fact was, she never had been that type of woman. Hurt feelings weren't her forte, or playing games.

"Not sure about the wealth. He was okay in looks. Average. A little balding. I do remember I agreed on a date because he was nice."

"Did you tell the police about him?"

"No."

"I'll do it. Every guy needs to be checked out, Fern. I'll notify Jacob, and the police may have additional questions. Irish food, huh? I'll have to remember that."

Interesting comment.

"He called me Colleen," she suddenly remembered. "Because he saw at my desk the book I was reading on break about Ireland and its history."

Ryan raised his eyebrows. "Family history?"

Not my family. "Deep dive into the culture. I was fascinated by the Celts. So fierce, like Queen Maeve. Maeve was a mythical warrior queen of ancient Ireland. Strong and brave."

"No wonder you like her. She's like you."

The unexpected praise made her blush. "I doubt it. Maeve slew the men of Ulster with a curse because of a bull."

"Sounds like bull to me," he teased.

She liked this side of him—fun and charming. Ryan tweaked a strand of her hair.

Warmth filled her. "You're like Brian Boru, the greatest and most courageous king of Ireland."

Ryan dropped his hand. "Sounds like a name to live up to. My bet is Brian wouldn't be late for his shift, though. I really have to go."

She followed him up the stairs, watching as he clicked off the basement light. Basements usually bothered her, but his was half finished, with part of it sectioned off into a workshop. Plenty of lighting made it seem less ominous.

After grabbing his go bag and donning his jacket, he frowned. "I really need to leave or I'll be in trouble. But I hate leaving you alone here."

"I'm not alone." Fern gestured to the door. "I have my police protection outside. Besides, the quiet will be good for me. You said the hospital was too noisy, too filled with people."

"Well, if you get worried, or scared…"

Fern gave him a gentle push. "Go to work. I'll be fine. Please."

He nodded. "Ava will be over later to spend the night. I'll be back tomorrow around noon."

For a wild minute she thought he would kiss her. Maybe he thought the same, for he leaned forward.

Ryan pulled away with a solemn look on his face. "Good night, fair Maeve. Remember, if you need anything, I'm a text away."

"Got it. Have a good shift."

Fern stood at the window, waving goodbye as his truck pulled out of the driveway.

For a moment she stayed there, then she dropped the curtain. Lace curtains, feminine and pretty. Not the kind found in a bachelor pad. Maybe his mother or an ex-girlfriend had made them for him.

The house seemed too big, too empty and silent. Well, she'd wanted quiet and now she had it.

For so many months, the hospital had been her routine. Blood pressure checks, physical and occupational therapy and other therapy. Her morning routine had been breakfast, medical checks, everything dictated by the nurses and doctors.

I have to set my own morning routine now.

The idea cheered her. Taking control, instead of having her life dictated by someone else. Maybe tomorrow while Ryan was at work she could make herself hot oatmeal with fruit, use the treadmill and exercise.

Enjoy some light reading to work her brain out as well.

I can do this. I can regain my life back.

Fern busied herself with unpacking, and then repacking what she had unpacked. Her fingers stroked the cheap wig and fake glasses she'd asked Ava to purchase for her.

A disguise to go out in public again. Not that she felt confident enough to try it.

It seemed wrong to place everything into the dresser in the bedroom. This wasn't her home, her refuge, but another temporary place. The sense of displacement depressed her all over again.

She did remove the wooden bear Sassy had given her at the hospital. The sight of it on the dresser cheered her and reminded her of Sassy's friendship. *The bear's name means strength,* Sassy told her.

I don't feel strong right now.

At the hospital they told her returning home was too dangerous. Even someone going to her apartment to retrieve her personal items and clothing presented a threat. Someone might be watching and waiting.

Better to dress in new clothing, live a borrowed life.

A hotel would have been better, but with her attackers out there, not a good idea. Fern sat on the bed, hugging herself.

Ordinary people would catch up on email, watch television or do something perfectly ordinary they enjoyed during downtime, like knitting. Or wood carving.

I had hobbies. I liked...

She pressed two fingers to her right temple. "What did I like?" she asked the empty room.

Surely anyone seeing her now would think she was a little mentally disturbed, talking to herself, trying to remember what she'd liked in the past. Ava would not. Ava was calm and collected and encouraged her to remember the good times.

Because that will help remember everything, including the bad.

She touched the side of her neck and the dollar sign tattoo there. Funny, she didn't remember getting it. And why put a dollar sign on her neck, as if she were a commodity to be sold?

It made her wonder if she hadn't put the ink there. Well, she couldn't worry about that now. Priorities. The tattoo or its origin was not one of them.

Fern got up and walked through the house. Cozy and simple, with big chunky furniture that looked comfortable. Definitely a bachelor home, with Ryan's individual stamp upon it. She paused before a painting of Dark Canyon and a figure climbing the rocks. Oil painting, not bad and with no signature, so most likely Ryan or someone he knew had painted it. Most artists signed their work.

I never signed mine, either.

A memory flickered. Painting. Yes, she preferred watercolors, not acrylics or oils. Light pastels to counter the dark themes in her work. Sassy had encouraged her on this.

Fern touched the painting, forcing herself to follow the memory as if it were a signpost on a road she hesitated to travel. Art therapy. Classes to help her with the trauma of her childhood and the bitterness still lurking deep inside over a mother who'd abandoned her.

It wasn't all that bad. Remember Fuzzy Bunny? You carried him everywhere, even the fire at that camp where you learned to toast marshmallows...

Her smile faded as the memory returned in full force. Fuzzy, who'd been tossed into the fire by her foster sister.

She glanced at her hands and rubbed a faint scar. Burn mark. So desperate to save Fuzzy, she'd tried to rescue him from the flames, but a counselor pulled her away.

Another one had been called in when Fern launched all her rage and pain at her foster sister, trying to beat her with angry fists.

Yeah, and that ended quickly. Fern had been shipped off to another home, the incident disquieting to the family who'd taken her into their house and were ready to adopt the sister who'd tossed Fuzzy into the fire. They couldn't handle two little girls and had grown fond of the other sister.

I went back into the system like a recycled part.

But there were others out there. People like Ryan, and

Ava, and Belle, and certainly Sassy. Cassidy, the friendly nurse at the hospital. Others as well.

The world is a big place, kiddo. You can't stay afraid forever.

She went into the kitchen and rooted through his junk drawer, finding the tape measure. Fern went into his bedroom and measured, precisely, all the windows. She noted the measurements on her phone, but no business could deliver custom-made blackout shades by the time he ended his shift.

No matter. She could make do with supplies.

For the next couple of hours she remained busy, ordering groceries, taking stock of what food Ryan did have—sadly, his pantry looked empty, as if he seldom ate at home or had time to cook—and unpacking.

Fern was about to venture downstairs to test out his exercise equipment when her cell phone dinged a message.

She grabbed the phone, relieved to hear from Ryan. It made being alone in his house less strange.

How are you settling in? he texted.

Fine. I'm ordering you a lot of food. Be prepared for gourmet meals. Do you like fried octopus? she asked.

Green emojis followed. Fern laughed and typed back. JK. Normal food that most guys enjoy—chicken and beef. I noticed you have an air fryer and there's recipes for fried chicken. Thought I'd test it out.

Feel free. I want you to feel comfortable, Fern.

I have a favor to ask.

Go on.

I wanted to start painting again. Thought it would help. Is it okay to set up a space in the basement?

Sure, go ahead. BTW, my cuz Mark is coming over soon. He's the guy who set you up with the GPS emergency locket. He installed security cameras around my house and he's bringing over a surprise for you.

A flutter of unease shot through her. She'd met Mark briefly, but having him here alone with her felt intimidating.

Ever perceptive, he followed with a concerned emoji. You okay with being alone with him?

Not really. She thought about it. Okay if I ask Sassy to come over while he's here?

Having another woman present would help, plus she wanted to ask Sassy to bring art supplies, help her set up an easel in the basement.

My cousin Sassy who owns the art gallery?

His cousin. Ryan had a lot of family in Dark Canyon.

After she texted yes, he texted back. Sure. LMK when she's there and I'll ask Mark to drop by at the same time. He has a surprise for you.

What's the surprise? A Chihuahua guard dog?

Laughing emojis followed. Never heard of a Chihuahua being a guard dog.

You've never dealt with them. They could scare away a German shepherd.

No dogs. I work too much to deal with them. Surprise is electronic. You'll see. I think you'll like it. Opps. Gotta run—have a call. Take care.

U2, she typed back, not expecting a response.

The texting cheered her, made her more confident. She felt connected, but still, the day was bright and sunny and the thought of exercising inside seemed stifling with the warmer weather. A jacket should suffice.

Maybe she could venture outside, get fresh air, go for a walk. Ryan hadn't said anything about staying in the house. *I'm not a prisoner.*

A short walk while waiting for his cousin Mark. Then she'd call Ryan's cousin Jacob, tell him to set up the hypnosis. Anything to help out with the investigation.

Fern lifted the curtain in the living room.

She looked out the window again and saw a man pedaling by on a bicycle. He stared at the house. Her throat went dry and her heart beat faster.

The guy looked shady, with a ball cap pulled low on his forehead. He stopped right before the house. Stared some more.

Checking it out? Had he heard rumors about the woman staying with Ryan? Maybe wanted to pass on the information to those who'd kidnapped her?

She pulled down the window shade and retreated to the guest bedroom. Stupid of her to think this place was safe.

Nowhere was until the men who'd taken her were caught and brought to justice.

Chapter Five

Sometimes a shift at the station meant the *Q* word, which no one dared to utter out loud because then all of a sudden they'd get call after call. Usually he enjoyed the downtime, using it to catch up on checking equipment, even reading medical textbooks. Ryan found them fascinating.

Today wasn't one of the down days. Nearly as soon as he walked into the station, the alarm rang. Call was for a working fire.

Not pausing, Ryan grabbed his gear, dressing in the truck as they roared off. They arrived at a house in a fairly affluent neighborhood. A man waved them down. Ryan's adrenaline kicked in. He couldn't see smoke, but maybe the fire was inside. Or someone was down, in dire need of medical care.

After the rig was parked, Ryan jumped out. "Sir?" he called out.

"It's too loud!" the man screamed.

"Sir, where's the fire? Are you hurt?" Ryan asked.

"My ears are ringing. Can't you hear that crap?"

Ryan looked around. "What?"

"You deaf as well?" the man yelled. "That music! It's ruining my life!"

Strains of heavy metal drifted from the house next door. Ryan almost laughed.

No working fire. No medical emergency. He glanced at his friend Nick Malone, who shook his head.

"Takes all kinds," Nick drawled.

"You've got to be kidding," he muttered, pushing back his helmet. "We rushed out here for a complaint about music?"

Nick shrugged. "We aim to serve. Saving lives and saving eardrums."

"What are you going to do about it? I have hearing loss thanks to them!" The man pointed at the house. "Damn kids!"

"Long live rock and roll," Ryan told him.

As they returned to the truck, Cap told them there was a new dispatcher on duty, thus the probability for the mistake.

He glared at his captain. "Tell that new dispatcher to look up the definition of 'working fire.'"

"Take it easy, Rye," Tom said. "Everyone makes mistakes, especially newbies. At least it wasn't a real disaster."

"Only a musical one," he muttered.

"Could have been worse," Nick called out as he stashed the paramedic gear. "Guy could have been playing your favorite music, which really sucks."

Ryan cuffed his friend.

Did Fern like music? Maybe he should have told her about his collection in the basement of classic vinyl and the vintage record player he'd bought.

They left the homeowner to the police officer who'd arrived on scene. Soon as he climbed back into the truck, they received another call.

It remained like that until around eight o'clock at night. As they finally sat down at the long table to eat the casserole Cap had cooked, Ryan thought about the impromptu meal Fern had tossed together.

He barely heard the talk around the table. Something about the Salt Lake Urban Search and Rescue Team training.

"Ryan, I'm changing your shift later this month. I want you out of the station in training."

Ryan paused in shoveling a forkful of pasta into his mouth. He set it down. "Why?"

"It's time."

"But..."

"It's spring, Rye. Hikers are already taking to the trails." Cap looked at him. "Utah Task Force One is conducting a rope rescue technician course with departments around the state, and you need the practice."

The food congealed in his stomach. "Cap, I have no desire to become a heavy rescue technician with special ops. Or a rescue specialist on the task forces. So why me? Why not Johnson? He's the one angling to join the task forces. He needs this course, not me."

He waved a fork in the other firefighter's direction. Mike Johnson suddenly looked uncomfortable.

"There was one slot open for our department. Mike offered to give it up this time around so you could train. You've been avoiding rope rescues for more than a year, Rye." Cap leaned back, his gaze level.

Suddenly the other guys at the table seemed fascinated in discussing cooking duties for the rest of the week. Ryan pushed back his plate. He knew why Cap did this. Knew it was logical—hell, he'd do the same if he were in charge.

You need the training because you've avoided rope rescues ever since...

Since Kate McIntyre slipped out of your grasp and fell to her death a year ago.

Never could he forget that moment. Apparently, no one else could, either.

"And if I refuse?" he grated out.

Tom glanced at the others. "In my office."

Fine. He had no appetite left, anyway. As he paced Cap's office, his boss sat behind the desk, steepling his fingers.

"Ryan I'll lay it out clear as I can. You undergo this training. It's mandatory, not voluntary. If you refuse, you'll be subject to disciplinary action, probably insubordination and possible termination."

Stunned, he stopped walking. "You'd do that to me after all my years of service?"

"Not that I want it, Rye. I need every man and woman to follow the rules and orders. Most of all, I need all my staff to be ready to respond to canyon rescues. You know the terrain. Hikers get lost in those canyons or stranded in a crevice, and we need every working firefighter in this station to have rope skills."

"I'm a good climber. I have rope skills."

"And you haven't used them since Kate McIntyre died. It's partly my fault." Cap sighed. "I've been too easy on you this last year. That ends today."

Of course it did. It ended just when Fern moved into his house and he was distracted with her presence.

He flexed his hands, remembering how he'd dangled on the rope. Kate was so close, screaming and screaming and then...

Far easier to run into burning buildings with the proper PPE and save people, like he'd saved Fern, than to face the canyons again and risk screwing up once more. Watching another life slip away.

"You're a damn good firefighter, Ryan. You're our senior hazmat technician and I rely heavily on you. Ever think of taking the lieutenant's exam?"

Talk about a one-eighty switch. Ryan braced his hands on the chair before the desk. "Thought about it."

"Think harder. You're terrific in the field, a bit of a hotshot, but you show real leadership potential." Cap pushed back from the desk. "So I'll put your name into the slot for April?"

Despite the trepidation congealing in his stomach, he managed a nod. "I'll be there."

"Good." Cap's expression turned concerned. "How's Fern settling in?"

"Settling in where?" The fewer people knew Fern was staying with him, the better.

"In your house."

Dammit to hell! "How did you hear? Did Bob say anything?"

"Police who set up the plainclothes officer to watch your house informed me as a safety measure in case something happens and we're needed. Relax. No one else at the station knows. It's a need-to-know basis."

Ryan nodded. "Good. The fewer people who know where she is, the better. With her kidnappers still out there, we can't take chances."

"It's a big responsibility. You sure you're okay with it?" Tom picked up a pencil, tapped it on the desk. "You have a lot of work here, Ryan, and your hours are intense."

"You have a better suggestion? Fern doesn't trust anyone, but she trusts me."

"Because you saved her life." Cap stood. "It's your house and your life, Ryan, but as your supervisor and your friend, I caution you to take a step back and not get so involved. Fern probably already has PTSD, anxiety and fear. She needs professional help."

"She's getting counseling, Cap. Right now she needs a friend as well, a place where she feels safe."

"You have to move on, Ryan. Focus on the job, and don't get involved with victims. It's not fair to you, or her. You don't want her getting a rescue crush on you."

Fern wasn't a victim. Calling her one demoralized her

and what happened. It wasn't a rescue crush, either, but a woman struggling to recover from a horrific trauma that could have killed her.

He clapped a lid on his rising temper and managed to speak evenly. "Anything else?"

As Tom shook his head, Ryan's phone buzzed. "Gotta take this. It's my sister."

He went outside, confirming with Ava she was going to stay the night with Fern. Ava was a lifesaver, a true help when it came to Fern. Everyone thought the world of her trying to get Fern to recall her memories.

When it came to Fern's welfare, Ryan wished others would have the same confidence in him.

FERN TEXTED SASSY, who agreed to round up art supplies. As Fern waited for her, Ryan texted, asking how she was doing.

Fern texted him back. Your home is comfortable. Do you paint? I saw the picture in the living room of Dark Canyon. Yours?

Naw. Ex-girlfriend painted it from a photo when I went rock climbing with her.

Girlfriend, rock climbing. So normal. Ordinary. Fern sighed. And you kept it?

It's the only thing that goes well with the colors in the living room and it covers a mark on the wall.

She laughed, more from relief than the idea of him being practical over hanging a painting by his ex-girlfriend.

Gotta run. Call coming in. Make sure to order whatever groceries you need. See yah.

She touched the phone, grateful he'd texted. It made her feel less alone.

Her plainclothes police officer knocked on the door, letting her know he still patrolled but would soon go off duty. He introduced her to his replacement. Officer Paul Jenkins was on duty for the next two weeks. He told Fern he'd taken the assignment because he had a special interest in protecting her, and the overtime would come in handy with his wife having a baby in three months.

Knowing Jenkins was close by made her feel safer.

A little while later, Sassy arrived, toting a sketch pad, easel and watercolor paints and black poster board and tape. Never one to easily make friends, or trust anyone, Fern felt pure relief to see her.

Slim and pretty, with dark brown eyes and long dark hair, Sassy was a talented woman who owned the Zephyr Gallery. Impulsively, Fern hugged her, almost making Sassy drop the supplies.

Her friend looked startled, then set down the supplies and hugged her back. Never demonstrative, Fern felt embarrassed. Maybe it was from all the months at the hospital, or simply realizing that after never having any friends or wanting any, people did care and she needed them.

"Where do you want these?"

"I'll take the poster board and tape. It's for a project. The rest I'll put in the basement. Ryan said I could have a space."

Sassy helped her cart the supplies down to the basement. Her friend gave an appreciative look around. "Forgot what this place looked like. Came over quite a while ago when he had a family gathering, but Ryan works so much I barely see him. Where do you want the easel?"

"The corner over there by the bar."

After they arranged the art supplies, Sassy gave her a speculative look. "How's it working out with Ryan?"

"I'll let you know. Not many people know I'm here, so I'd appreciate it..." Her voice trailed off. Remembering the trauma of her kidnapping erased the joy at being able to indulge in art once more.

"I'll be quiet. Glad I can help. When is Mark getting here?"

A notification on her phone indicated someone had rung the smart doorbell. These days everything was smarter than her. Fern glanced at the screen, recognizing Mark from photos. "He's here now. Great timing. Thanks."

Still, she was cautious opening the door, making sure he recited something only Ryan's relatives would know. Mark nodded at her as she let him in. He carried a large bag and looked surprised to see Sassy and hugged her.

"I'll wait in the living room while you both talk," Sassy told her.

Fern looked at Mark, big, strong, steady. She could see a slight family resemblance. Ryan's cousin didn't intend any harm. Like others, he was here to help.

"I know you have to get back to work. I'm fine. You can leave if you wish," she told her.

Sassy squeezed her hand. "I'll be around if you need me. See you, Mark."

Fern watched her leave, knowing Mark was behind her. But to her surprise, instead of watching her, he was checking out the house. He gestured to her.

"Wanted to let you know I have hidden cameras in the living room, kitchen and hallway and the basement."

He escorted her around the house, showing her cameras in picture frames, the hallway smoke detector, a wall clock in the kitchen and a fake book downstairs.

"They're all infrared, so they work in the dark as well," he told her.

"None in the bedroom?" Fern smiled.

He gave her a wry look. "Didn't want to invade your privacy. Or the bathroom."

So serious, unlike Ryan.

"The DVR monitor is hidden in a cabinet in Ryan's office." He took her there and opened the cabinet. "I set everything up but didn't have a chance to tell Ryan about all the details. You can turn off the cameras from the switches in the back if you feel they're too invasive. Also, I want to install a couple of other cameras, one outside the guest bedroom. Heard you had a scare earlier."

Rubbing her arms, Fern nodded. "Guess I'm a little nervous."

His sudden smile relaxed her. "If anyone deserves to be nervous, you do, after everything you went through. How you survived it is a miracle."

Yet another reminder she was a victim. Not that he wasn't nice, but suddenly Fern tired of it. *I'm a real miracle. Then why can't I remember and get my act together?*

"If you want to install those outside cameras, go ahead. If you're hungry, I can get together cheese and crackers, and there's plenty to drink."

"No prob. I'm fine."

She went into Ryan's office to watch the camera monitors. So many of them. Would a security camera have helped stop whoever kidnapped her? The police had investigated closed-circuit cameras and traffic cameras near her home and found nothing. Nada. Nothing to indicate a crime.

I'm the best source for getting any kind of information about the crime. If only my brain would cooperate.

Staying busy might help. She consulted the local grocery site Ryan used for deliveries and began an order.

By the time she finished, Mark came inside. "All set. Come out into the backyard. I need to show you something."

Mark led her outside to the backyard. A mature elm tree

sprawled its branches, just beginning to sprout leaves for the spring, over much of the yard. Appreciating the shade, she followed him to two bird feeders erected on a double shepherd's crook set out in dappled sunshine.

He turned one bird feeder toward her. "Smart bird feeders with cameras on 24-7. Low profile—anyone peeking over the fence wouldn't think much of them. Added protection for the outdoor cameras on the house. Solar panels keep the batteries charged and the system works through Wi-Fi. I added a Wi-Fi extender for the feeders and the outdoor cameras, filled the feeders with seeds local birds like. Give me your cell phone and I'll set up the app and all you need."

In no time, she was watching the bird feeders with delight. In the kitchen, she gave him a bottle of water for the road as the doorbell indicated the grocery order was out front.

Mark helped her carry everything inside and put away the groceries. Then he went into the living room, returning with a pink laptop bag.

"The bird feeders aren't the surprise. This is."

Her heart beat faster as she set the pretty pink bag on the kitchen table and unzipped, withdrawing a slim brand-new laptop. Fern stared at him with awe. "This is mine?"

"Yeah. Heard they wouldn't let you have one in the hospital due to security worries about you being tracked or hacked. I set it up with a top-notch antivirus, plus a great VPN, everything you need, and a medical coding software program. Not sure if it's the one you use, but…"

Fern set down the computer and threw her arms around him. "Thank you! This is terrific!"

Pink tinted his cheeks for a minute, then he nodded gravely. "You're quite welcome. I know what it feels like to be cut off."

He looked around the house. "Ryan is a great guy. He could have taken the easy road to money, well, easier, by working with his dad. Instead he chose to put his life on the line all the time as a first responder. We have more in common than some of my other cousins."

He was recently home from the military, Fern remembered. Like Ryan, Mark served others and had his own experiences and probable brushes with death. Her respect for him grew.

"Thank the good Lord you and Ryan do. Otherwise I might not be here."

Ducking her head to hide her emotions, she opened the laptop. "Can you walk me through it briefly?"

In no time, she had accessed the medical coding software. A memory flickered. "I think I know this program. At any rate, it will keep me busy learning, or relearning. Thank you so much!"

Mark nodded, distant once more. "Thanks for the water. Tell Ryan I said hi and I'll call him."

She locked the door behind him and leaned against it with a happy sigh.

A new laptop, security cameras, plenty of food and her art supplies. Tension slid off her shoulders. Life was looking up.

First, her project. She found scissors—Ryan's junk drawer was surprisingly organized, a fact she appreciated, being an organized person herself—and began to cut the poster board to the correct measurements.

In no time, his bedroom was shrouded in darkness. Only the lamp on his desk cut through the blackness.

Pleased with the results, she put away the supplies and went outside with a pencil and her sketch pad.

Fern sat on the patio, staring at the phone bird app. A notification showed a video of a pretty yellow bird with a black head stopped at a feeder, pecking at the seeds. She pressed the identify button.

American goldfinch.

So soothing, watching a bird go about its business of finding food. Normal. A good reminder life went on. It was cool enough, but not too cold. Perfect for sitting outside and sketching. She took the pad Sassy brought over and moved a chair close enough to the feeders to watch but not scare off birds. Lots of action at the feeders this time of day.

Smiling, she began to draw. This was a good routine to begin reclaiming her life.

A few more goldfinches arrived at the feeder. The colors were amazing, the birds energetic as they fed. Almost absently, she filled in details.

Absorbed in her work, she barely noticed the setting sun. Fern glanced up at the lavender and rose gold streaking the sky behind the mountains near Dark Canyon. Gorgeous colors. Ryan was lucky to have a view of such a magnificent landscape from his backyard.

She went inside to get water and returned with the glass, setting it on the table next to her chair.

As darkness began to shroud the yard, she sat back with a happy sigh. Drawing made her lose track of time and place. Fern clicked on the light app on her phone to view the sketch pad and results.

Birds flying into the sunset, distant mountains that would look terrific with purple shadows. Something else as well. Odd. Small in the right corner.

Fern sipped more water and leaned closer to inspect what she'd drawn. A face, tight and drawn, the mouth in a sneer.

Only her death grip on the cell phone kept her from dropping it. The glass dropped to the concrete patio, shattering the silence. Leaving the canvas outside, Fern jumped up, ran into the house and locked the door. She ran around to all the windows, pulling the shades and making sure everything was locked up.

Sliding down the wall, she hugged her knees.

For a long time, she remained there, her breath coming in a terrified whoosh, her heart racing.
She couldn't be certain, but deep inside she knew.
What she'd drawn was a face recalled from memory.
It could be one of the men who'd kidnapped her.

Chapter Six

After years of fighting fires, Ryan was used to the rush of adrenaline, the clear-eyed focus on the job. Not this call.

It came as darkness fell and set him on instant alert. Riding in the truck, he controlled his breathing, relying on his training.

Residential fire, which meant possible victims inside. Maybe children. Pets.

People often ran back into a burning house to rescue loved ones and pets. These kind of calls, especially at night with limited visibility, were harrowing.

Automatically they went over the information given by the dispatcher. Hydrant close by, good news. Bad news was the house was approaching fully engulfed.

When Engine 69 pulled up to the curb of the scene, he jumped out to hear screams. As Cap began giving orders, a woman ran up to Ryan.

"Please, please hurry! My little girl Carolyn's inside. She insisted on finding Wobbles!"

"Wobbles?" he asked.

"Our dog!"

Damn. Ryan looked at Cap for orders.

Cap nodded. "Ryan, Bob. Primary search."

As the other firefighters got a line on the house and began

hosing down the flames, Ryan and Bob donned their self-contained breathing apparatuses, hoods and then their helmets. Sounds of his own breaths filled his eardrums as Ryan and Bob went into the burning house. Flames shot out the back rooms. Pitch-black inside—even the light on his helmet barely cut the inky darkness, making it hard to see. He heard the guys on the roof, cutting holes in the attic to vent the smoke and heat from the house.

If they didn't find Carolyn soon, the whole ceiling could collapse, trapping them and the girl and her pet. Through the acrid smoke and darkness cut by orange flames, he could see barely anything.

The memory flickered of running into the cabin, finding Fern unconscious on the floor, barely alive. A feeling of panic, erased by automatic professionalism kicking in, as he hauled her over his shoulder to rush outside.

Praying she would be okay.

Carolyn would not die here today. He couldn't let that happen. Not an innocent child who only wanted to rescue her pet.

"Fire department, call out," he yelled. "Carolyn! Fire department!"

"Carolyn! Fire department, call out!" Bob screamed. "Carolyn, where are you?"

Through the roar of the fire, he heard faint sobbing. Holding the portable heat camera, he found a heat sig through the smoke. Carolyn. They ran forward to find her coughing and sitting on the floor of the living room. The fire advanced, getting closer.

Ryan motioned to Bob. But the girl screamed and struggled. "My dog!"

He pushed Bob. "I'll find him. Go!"

Bob grabbed the girl and hauled her outside as Ryan combed the room for the missing dog. Using the camera, he searched through the smoke and saw something on the floor emit a heat signature.

Something with four legs.

He grabbed the animal as the guys trained water on the flames through a broken window in the living room.

Carrying the limp dog, he made it outside. Face blackened, her anxious mother hovering, Carolyn tore off her oxygen mask administered by the paramedics.

"Wobbles!" she sobbed. "Is he alive?"

Ryan grabbed the special pet oxygen mask. The conical shape fit over the dog's snout. Nick ran over to see what he needed.

"Portable O2," he told Nick.

Nick brought over a bottle, and Ryan began administering oxygen to Wobbles.

"I'll take care of Wobbles if you promise to get back to the paramedics and let them help you."

Cap pushed back his helmet and gave him a long look, but the girl stopped sobbing and hovered.

"Is Wobbles gonna be okay?"

He watched the dog's chest rise and fall and nodded.

Regular oxygen masks could deliver less than 20 percent of much-needed oxygen to dogs and cats suffering smoke inhalation. This special mask, which his rig carried, was designed to save the lives of much-loved pets.

At budget time, he'd lobbied to get one per engine, with Cap's backing.

The dog began breathing, and Ryan kept the mask on as the other guys trained water on the flames.

"Thank you," Carolyn whispered. She coughed.

"I've got Wobbles. Now you have to get back to let the paramedics help you, okay?" he told her.

As he kept helping the dog, watching the pet begin to

struggle against the unfamiliar mask, Carolyn returned to the rig. Her mother rushed over, tears streaming down her face.

"Thank you. I don't... I don't know how I could live with myself if my daughter died."

"Part of the job." Ryan nodded at the dog. "Wobbles should be on oxygen for at least a few hours due to smoke inhalation. There's an emergency pet hospital not far from here. You need to transport him."

"I have to look after Carolyn."

Ryan looked down at the dog on the ground. "Can a friend or neighbor take him?"

Another woman stepped forward, introducing herself as a neighbor and offered to take the dog. Carrying Wobbles over to her car, he waited for her to open the sedan's back door.

"I'm Carrie Armstrong," the woman told him. "I'll make sure he gets to the hospital."

"Keep the mask on him, and I'll drop by the hospital later to retrieve it," he advised.

He felt good about saving the dog. Yeah, some people might say that it was only an animal, but he did not. Carolyn would recover quicker, and the loss of her home was bad enough without compounding it with the loss of a beloved pet.

The neighbor took a long look at him. "I know you. You're that firefighter who was on duty when they brought in Kate McIntyre from Dark Canyon. I saw you at the hospital when they brought her in and tried to revive her."

His stomach gave a sickening lurch. "You knew her?"

"She was my student at the climbing school," Carrie told him. "Horrible what happened."

Gone was any sense of feel-good emotions, replaced by a swarm of fresh guilt. Ryan placed the dog in the back of the woman's car. "Remember, keep the mask on him."

He slammed the back door and walked off.

"Good save, Rye," Cap told him.

"It was okay. Bob got the girl."

Shrugging, he watched the car drive away, feeling like a total loser.

Cap noticed and pointed to the engine. "Rye, fire's almost out. Why don't you stand by and help with the overhaul?"

Simply because a blaze was extinguished didn't mean they finished. The overhaul was tough labor, tearing down walls and sifting through debris to make sure everything was extinguished. Last thing they wanted was for the fire to rekindle.

"Sure. Guess I'm good for that." He glanced at his captain. "That woman taking the dog to the hospital? She was there when Kate McIntyre was brought in."

Cap issued an order into his shoulder mic and turned to him.

"How many times do we have to tell you, Ryan? Kate's death wasn't your fault," Cap said gently. "Nothing could have saved her. This is why you never get involved with a victim, Rye."

A reminder he should not be involved with Fern as well. Ryan's mind reeled.

He saved a dog. Why the hell couldn't he have saved Kate that day in Dark Canyon? Was he also making a mistake by getting involved with Fern and trying to help her, and in the end, he would hurt her as well?

FERN COULDN'T MOVE. All she could do was grip her legs, huddled into a corner of the living room. Flashes of memory zinged by, a man with a baseball bat hovering above her, his face twisted in rage...

Gonna get you, bitch, for doing that. You'll regret it. No one messes with me.

Pain exploding in her leg, her cries turning into screams...

Darkness shrouded the entire house. When the doorbell rang, she still couldn't move, or talk, only listen to the sounds of her breath coming in and out in little whispering pants. Helpless.

If someone broke inside, she was toast. Fern tried to move and could not budge.

She'd left her phone outside with the smart doorbell notifications. Anyone could be at the door. A delivery person, Ava or a serial killer. But she couldn't move. Fern managed to pull her arms away from her legs. Nothing more.

The doorknob rattled and she heard the door creak open.

"Fern? It's Ava. I'm coming in. Are you okay? I have a key to the house and I'm coming inside. Can you call out?"

Somehow she managed to find her voice. "Here."

A light snapped on. More lights. Ava's sweet, wonderful face came into view as her counselor squatted down in front of her.

"Hi, honey. I'm here. Would you like a cup of chamomile tea?"

Tea. So normal and ordinary. Something a friend would offer upon coming over, a friend who would find the house's guest greeting her with a smile, not cowering in a corner, terrified of her own shadow.

Fern shook her head and flexed her fingers. Slightly numb, but working.

"May I help you to stand?" Ava asked.

Fern managed to lift her hand. Ava gently helped her get upright, letting her lean against the wall.

Ava went into the living room and patted the sofa. "Come, sit by me. Ryan's couch is much more comfortable than his floor."

Fern swallowed hard and got to her feet, her legs feeling like cooked noodles. She made it to the sofa, sitting at the far end. This drill was familiar. Ava was trying to establish a safe space. Glancing at the clock on the fireplace mantle made her startle. It was well after seven at night.

How long had she been sitting in the dark, too terrified to move?

Some progress.

"How do you like my brother's house? He may be a bachelor, but he did a great job decorating."

Hard to breathe. Think.

Ava looked at her. "Remember your exercises, Fern. Breathe. In. Out. Remember your mantras."

Fern took a deep breath and did what she asked. *You're safe now. This is a safe space. You are in control. No one is going to hurt you or make you do anything you don't want to do.*

A few minutes later, she felt well enough to talk. "It—it's a nice house. I like it."

"I remember when he bought it. Our dad was appalled he spent money on such a fixer-upper. But Ryan's done a great job restoring it."

Seems like your brother enjoys restoring things, and maybe I'm one of them? Fern took another deep breath.

"I know I locked the door. I'm glad you have a key, Ava."

Ava pulled out a key fob. "Ryan gave me a house key back in the days when I helped him with a furniture delivery when he was on shift. I kept it."

Her impish grin helped Fern relax a little more.

"Can you go outside? I left my cell phone there and my sketch pad. You need to see what I drew."

Ava glanced at her. "You okay with me leaving you alone right now?"

Nodding, Fern pushed a hank of hair behind her ear, her hand less shaky now. She focused her attention on a photo of Ryan and his family on the fireplace mantle. Normal and ordinary.

Ordinary was good. Could she ever feel ordinary again? Have a home of her own and a job, without fearing her own shadow?

When Ava brought it back, Fern felt enough in control of her body and her mental state. She took the sketch pad from Ava.

"I like it here. Your brother is kind, and I deeply appreciate what he's doing for me. So is your cousin—he brought me a laptop. I feel safe here."

"That's terrific, Fern. What did you want to show me?"

Grateful her hands no longer shook, Fern set the pad down on the coffee table and pointed to it. "This. I was drawing the birds outside and before I realized it, I drew this face. It—it scared me so much I ran inside and I couldn't move. Why did I do this?"

Ava studied the drawing. "You feel safe and you're more in control of your emotions. By relaxing, your traumatic memories are returning. It's rather like getting ideas when you're in the shower."

Fern shuddered. "Some idea. Should we call the police?"

Ava nodded. "I'm proud of you for thinking like this, Fern. You're getting stronger."

Stronger, when all she could do was huddle in the corner? She didn't feel stronger, but right now, she'd take all the encouragement she could receive.

"Have you been keeping up with making your lists of things you're looking forward to once you regain your memory?" Ava asked.

"No." Words stuck in her throat. She found it hard to think of something so ordinary as making a list when a cruel face stared at her from the confines of the sketch pad.

"How about we put the kettle on and make a cup of hot chocolate and then call the police? I know how much you enjoy hot chocolate."

Fern gave her a wry look. "You're trying to talk me off the ledge."

"You're already off the ledge. I'm merely giving you fortification for when you talk to Jacob, since he's lead on the case. Speaking of which, do you have any food? I came straight from work and I'm starved. Make something you like and we can eat together."

Minutes later, Ava had called Jacob and Fern had made a charcuterie board with cheddar cheese, Brie, prosciutto, grapes and whole wheat crackers. They sat in the kitchen, drinking hot chocolate and grazing.

"Is the drawing a good indication my memory is returning?" Fern asked after eating a bite of Brie. She turned over the sketch pad, not wanting to see that face unless absolutely necessary.

"Could be. It's important, but we can't be sure what kind of memory is returning until we discover who you drew."

Toying with a grape, she shook her head. "I feel bad for Ryan. He was nice enough to offer me a place to stay and get back to normal, but looks like my normal is far from normal."

"Stop it. You are normal, Fern. You're strong, remember?"

"You sound like your brother."

Ava smiled. "He's one of a kind. Hero complex."

"I don't think so. I think he's terrific, and thank God he is a hero or I wouldn't be alive today," she burst out.

Blinking, Ava gave a little smile. Fern's suspicions flowered. "You baited me into revealing how I feel about staying here."

"Perhaps. Do you feel safe staying here or would you rather return to the hospital?"

Fern knew regaining her independence remained a priority in her recovery. Independence meant regaining her memory as well, and in the hospital with everyone hovering, she couldn't focus on anything except the trauma and fear.

"I like it here for now," she said with caution. "Ryan has been a most generous host. Do you want to know my feelings about that?"

The last sentence she uttered with a little sarcasm, because much as she liked Ava, everything was subject to analysis. Ava knew she was being baited, judging from her expression.

"Right now we need to focus on you and this drawing. It could be a major clue to your memory returning."

Some memories she might not want to return. Though she didn't recall every detail, Fern knew her past was shady. She drank heavily as a teen and finally got herself straightened out, thanks to understanding foster parents and Alcoholics Anonymous. At least with Belle, her sponsor at AA, she'd learned to forgive herself.

But forgiving herself didn't mean she wanted those memories back any more than she wanted to be the old drunk Fern again, drowning her sorrows in a bottle of cheap vodka.

"If it's a memory from my questionable past, I'd rather not have that one back. I do want to help find the jerks who did this to me and stop them from hurting another woman."

Ava sipped her hot chocolate and set it down. "Those memories, good and bad, are part of you, Fern. You can't simply put them away in a locker and pretend they don't exist. You can help heal from them, but you have to acknowledge them first."

Fern sighed. "You make sense, but that doesn't make it easy."

"It never is. It's hard work putting your life back together. But it's worth it, Fern. You're worth it. Never forget that."

One reason she liked and trusted Ava was the woman had been frank and upfront with her from the beginning. Ava told her about the types of therapy she wanted to try to help Fern.

"What's the next step in my therapy?" she asked. "You mentioned a desensitization approach, getting me to return to the place where I was held. Must we?"

"One step at a time. The fact that you feel strong enough to live outside the hospital is an important first step to your recovery of your memory."

Ava gave another of her million-dollar reassuring smiles. "Now, while we wait for Jacob, why don't you show me the new laptop Mark gave you?"

Food had fortified her, and by the time she showed Ava the laptop, Jacob rang the doorbell. Confidence filled her. Maybe the face she'd drawn was an important clue to her kidnapping.

While Ava made coffee for Jacob, who asked for the caffeine, Fern talked with him. Odd how now she felt more comfortable with him at Ryan's house than at the hospital.

"I was sketching the birds and sunset and didn't realize I drew this face." Fern handed Jacob the pad. "I'm sure it's a guy from my past, only I don't know who he is. But the image was so scary it immobilized me for quite a while with fear, so whoever it is, he sure isn't Santa Claus."

Jacob flashed a rare smile. "Some kids are terrified of Santa." He studied the sketch. "Great detail. You couldn't remember anything about him, anything else such as hair color, or identifying marks?"

"I wish I knew." Fern rubbed her head. "I think it was one of the guys who hurt me, but I can't be certain. My memory is still fuzzy."

Jacob nodded. "May I take this? I can make a copy, run it through the national database to see what pops up."

What if it were a face from her past and not the man who'd abducted her? "One thing really bothers me. I lived in Oso. How did the kidnappers know where to find me? I mean, I don't live around here or near the place I was found, so…"

Jacob exchanged glances with Ava. "It wasn't by chance, Fern. Whoever took you had been observing you for some time and waited for the right moment."

A chill raced down her spine. Any semblance of feeling safe and confident fled. "Someone was stalking me, you mean. I'm no one special."

Jacob sipped his coffee before answering slowly. "That's what we're trying to determine. But you fit the profile. You don't have family or many friends. You're a loner."

Her lower lip wobbled, and she fought her emotions. "You mean because I like being alone I was a target for these monsters?"

"We can't tell for certain. It's an ongoing investigation."

Cop talk. They all talked like that, in circles. She pressed a finger to her temple, suddenly wishing Ryan were there to help her find her center. Ava was great, and she trusted her, but Ava's motive was to help her recall her memory.

If drawing a face from memory wrung out all the terror stuffed deep inside her, why would she want to regain those memories?

"Maybe you're both wrong. What if this guy I drew wasn't the kidnapper, but someone I liked?"

Ava shook her head. "Fern do you think you would have had such a violent reaction if it was someone you liked? Let Jacob do his job. We have to determine if this is one of the men who kidnapped you."

She didn't like the speculative look Ava gave her. "Or what? Who else could it be?"

"Someone from your past, perhaps. Someone you don't want to recall, but on a subconscious level, you did. We need to do some tests to make sure," Ava told her.

Somehow she knew what this meant. "You mean hypnosis."

At Ava's nod, she sighed. "I want to undergo hypnosis. I

want to help. Can't you understand that I want to do anything I can to find these guys so no other woman will get hurt?"

"Then we can set up the session as soon as possible. Day after tomorrow okay?" Ava asked. "I promise I'll be there the entire time."

"Can Ryan be there as well?"

Blinking, Ava glanced at Jacob. "If you want and he agrees and isn't working."

Ryan's presence would give her a sense of balance, of backup. Right now she needed stability in this upside-down world.

A few minutes later Jacob left with Ava promising to call him with a time for the hypnosis. Ava helped her clear the table.

"I need to get my overnight case from the car," Ava told her.

Fern took a deep breath. "I don't need you to spend the night with me, Ava. I'll be fine."

Ava frowned. "Fern, you've had a scare…"

"I'll have more of them in the future. I need to start being on my own. There's plenty of security cameras, and I have a phone, plus Officer Jenkins two doors down from here."

"Are you sure? It's not a problem for me to remain here until Ryan gets home."

"I'm positive. Besides, I need the space. If I need you I can call you. You know I have your number."

Ava nodded. "I'm proud of you, Fern. You've made a lot of progress, and the hypnosis may seem intimidating, but it's a huge step forward in your recovery."

When Ava left, Fern finished doing the dishes and tidied up. Though it wasn't even ten o'clock, she felt exhausted. After making sure the house was locked up, checking the DVR to see the cameras functioning, she got ready for bed.

Control was important to her therapy, so Ava had helped her pick out a cute pair of pink and yellow floral pajamas.

Yet an hour later, she still lay in bed, unable to sleep.

Try as she might, she couldn't relax. The unfamiliar surroundings unnerved her. But she wasn't going to capitulate and call Ava.

On impulse she went into Ryan's bedroom and grabbed his pillow. Fern brought it back to her bed, hugging it, breathing in his scent, and felt herself finally begin to relax.

She wasn't crushing on Ryan. Nope. Not at all.

The hypnosis session hovered in the future like a mandatory root canal. What would happen when her memory returned and she found out about all her past?

Fern dreaded knowing.

Chapter Seven

Because he needed to work a full twenty-four-hour shift, Ryan didn't get home the following day until noon. His stomach grumbled, reminding him he hadn't eaten since the previous night. Breakfast had been abandoned for a car crash, and by the time they returned to the station, he had no desire for whatever congealed mess was left on his plate.

He rang the doorbell and spoke into it to alert Fern he was home because she certainly didn't need any more frights.

"Ryan! Please, can you use your key? I'm in the kitchen."

Dare he hope she might have ordered food, something simple he could use to whip up a quick meal? Smells of something delicious wafted from the kitchen. After locking the door, he followed his nose.

Fern stood at the oven, beaming. She wore a red-and-white-polka-dot dress that looked faded and worn, and had tied around her waist the apron his sister had given him as a gag gift one birthday.

It read If Something is Burning, Call the Fire Department. Wait, That's Only Me Grilling.

It was such a domestic scene that he had to blink to make sure it wasn't a dream, because lately, he'd thought about what life would be like to have someone waiting for him at home after a tiring twenty-four hours.

"I figured you'd be hungry after your shift and made a chicken, potato and vegetable casserole. It's been warming in the oven."

Would it look impolite if he salivated all over the floor? Ryan's stomach gave an appreciative grumble. He felt embarrassed, but she nodded.

"As I thought. I've been monitoring your police radio, and I know how busy you've been. Sit down. Would you like decaf tea or sparkling water? I saw you had some water in the fridge."

"I can get it."

"No, sit, relax, please."

Soon they were both sitting at the kitchen table, Ryan with a sparkling water and Fern with tea as they dug into her casserole. He moaned as he tasted it.

"Whoa, this is amazing. Thank you so much, but you didn't have to do it. Honestly, Fern, I don't expect you to do anything for me."

"I was hungry as well, and it's a waste of good food to make a casserole for one." Her cute, pert nose wrinkled. "Or make one of those frozen meals you have, that are probably petrified by now."

All he'd had time for lately was cooking a frozen dinner. "Fern, cooking for me is not…"

"Please, Ryan."

The soft plea in her voice made him glance at her. "What's wrong?"

"I need to do this. Establish some kind of routine. I've felt so lost for months, and this feels good. Normal. I enjoy cooking. Please don't tell me not to do it."

Never had he thought about a simple task helping her. Ryan nodded. "As long as you let me clean up."

She smiled. "Deal."

He asked about her day and how it went with Mark. Fern toyed with her casserole. Finally she glanced up.

"I heard you saved a life again in a fire," she told him.

Ryan shrugged. "Bob was the hero, saving the little girl, Carolyn."

"You're the hero. I'm sure Carolyn would have been devastated without her pet. You helped her as much as your co-worker did."

"Guess so." He shook his head. "Then there are the ones I can't save, as much as I try. Those are the ones who haunt me, the ones I can never forget. Is it worth it?"

Fern's gaze remained steady. "Every shift you're out there, Ryan, fighting the good fight. Sometimes the end result isn't what you want, or hope or pray for. You did your best, and you have to leave it behind so you can fight another day."

Seeing him stare at her, she flushed and added, "At least that's what I had always believed when I was getting my act together. There were days when I didn't think it was worth it to get up the next day. Good people convinced me to never give up."

"I'm glad they were there for you," he said, meaning it.

"I don't mean to be a conversational downer, but I need to tell you about the sketch I did."

He ate while listening, letting her talk in halting sentences, not pushing her, knowing it had to be tough to talk about it.

She finished and added, "I told your sister I'll do the hypnosis tomorrow afternoon, but only if you're there. I—I am sorry to involve you, but I'd feel safer."

"Hey, no problem." Ryan drank some water. "Be happy to help. I don't have plans. I work a 24/72 shift, so I'm off for the next three days. I have some stuff lined up, but those appointments are flexible."

Instead of looking relieved, lines etched her forehead. "You need to know…it's not going to be pretty, Ryan. Because as I understand, from what I researched on hypnosis on my new laptop your cousin was kind enough to give me, the memories recalled may not be cut-and-dried, but stuff from my…ah, murky past."

"I understand."

"I wasn't a Girl Scout. Not even close. Much as I wanted to be one, it wasn't my destiny." She gave a grudging laugh that nearly broke his heart because he sensed the pain the laugh hid.

"So it could get ugly, and if you feel uncomfortable being there, please, let me know. I'll do fine with Ava. I trust her. Even your cousin Jacob, well, he's starting to grow on me." She laughed again. "Not like a fungus, either."

Such a great sense of humor, considering what she'd been through. Yet another display of Fern's courage.

After they ate, he insisted on helping her clean up. Soon as the dishwasher was loaded, he felt the crash coming on him.

"I need some sleep." He yawned. "Sorry to ditch you."

She nudged him toward his bedroom. "I have a surprise for you."

What kind of surprise? Normally a woman indicating a surprise in the bedroom turned him on. Not with Fern and what she'd endured. He liked her, and part of him wanted to know her better, but an intimate relationship was a bad idea.

For now.

When he walked into his bedroom, Ryan's jaw dropped. Blackout shades, sort of. He wanted to jump up and down with pleasure, except he was too damn exhausted.

He walked around the bedroom. Not only had she put up blackout shades, but she'd changed the sheets. Fresh sheets! A sense of happiness swept over him, along with vague unease. Did she think he expected this of her?

"Thank you." He turned and saw her hanging by the door, a little hesitant as if she disliked intruding.

"Fern, you don't have to do this. You're not the housekeeper, and I don't want you feeling like you have to cook or clean or do things for me."

Her eyes looked solemn. "I know. But that's what friends do for each other, right? I mean, it's been a long time since anyone cared about my welfare, and I wanted to help you out however I could. It's not a big deal, Ryan. Not compared to you sharing your home with me, which is something I can never repay you for."

She gave a pretty little sigh. "Let's not even mention how you saved my life, in more ways than one."

He would have liked to continue the convo, but suddenly the meal and the drop in his adrenaline nudged aside all desire to talk.

"We'll talk about this later." He yawned.

"Sleep as long as you like. I'll be downstairs in the basement. Night."

When she closed the door behind her, he undressed to his boxers, snapped off the lamp and crept between the freshly washed sheets. She'd even used fabric softener so they smelled a little like the outdoors he loved.

Fern smelled like that, he realized as he closed his eyes. Flowers and sunshine.

Ryan fell asleep, drifting into a dream of a field of flowers, Fern scampering through them and laughing, erasing the dark shadows from her pretty eyes.

By the time he woke, it was well after six. Ryan yawned, stretched and dressed in sweats and a T-shirt, hoping Fern was okay. He felt bad for abandoning her, but damn, he had been tired.

Thanks to her efforts, he slept the best he had in weeks.

He found her downstairs, painting. Fern looked absorbed in her work. Much as he hated to disturb her, he needed to exercise.

"Thanks to you, I slept great. Sorry to bother you, but I need to work out."

Fern wiped her hands with a rag. "No bother. I need to get my PT done as well. Mind if I use the treadmill?"

"Go ahead. Today's my weight day." He looked at the weights. "Let's get down to business."

As an incentive, he put a vinyl record on the vintage player. The eighties music made her laugh, and she began walking faster to the beat.

The music accompanied the weights going up and down on his machine and the treadmill's hum. Having a pretty woman work out alongside him pushed him a little further.

One reason he'd never worked out with past girlfriends. Ryan knew how easy it was to overdo it by showing off.

He took it down a notch, focusing on his breathing and reps, only to glance up and realize Fern did the same. Ignoring him, centering her concentration on her own cardio.

Finally she climbed off, panting. "Wow, I'm really out of shape. Need a break."

Though he could keep going, Ryan decided it was a good idea to stop. He chugged the water he'd brought downstairs while Fern drank the sports drink she had by the easel.

He should really push himself today, though. Knowing he had rope training presented him with a good incentive. Ryan returned to the weights as Fern began painting again.

By the time he finished with his reps, Fern was absorbed in her work. Curious, he set the weights down, wiped off the sweat and went over to her.

"Mind if I see?" he asked.

Fern shrugged. "It's not good. More therapeutic than pretty."

She'd painted the orange twists and turns of Dark Canyon, with a burning yellow sun overhead.

"I remember this much," she said slowly. "It was cold, oh

so cold. I could see the canyons rising above me, like prison walls. I remember I always enjoyed hiking there and now…"

Setting down her paintbrush, she took a deep breath. "Talk to me about something else. Are you always this dedicated with weightlifting?"

"Part of the job and training. I have to keep up with my workouts." He returned to the bench and sat. "My gear, just the turnout stuff like the helmet, coat, pants, gloves, weighs about fifty pounds, and the SCBA…"

At her puzzled look, he explained. "Self-contained breathing apparatus, which I use to breathe in a fire. That weighs around thirty pounds. Then you add in the equipment to get people out, like an axe…"

When he finished, Fern's eyes widened. "Wow. You gain about seventy-five pounds by fighting fires. No wonder you have to keep in shape."

With a rueful look, she glanced down. "Especially when you have to carry someone as heavy as me out of a burning building."

"Hey. Stop that. You're beautiful."

The skepticism on her face angered him. Why did women who weren't model thin think they were fat? Fern had gorgeous curves.

"I need to lose weight."

He walked over to her and touched her cheek. "You need to focus on yourself, regaining your memory and not losing weight. You're perfect the way you are."

Silence. Fern kept staring at him as if he were an alien dropped down from outer space. Ryan dropped his hand and backed away. Maybe this physical proximity proved too much for her.

"Please don't call me perfect. It's not a good word. Perfect to everybody means there is nothing wrong. It's a high standard to maintain."

"I never thought about that."

"I have, only because I've tried being perfect. It's exhausting. Being perfect in foster care with the first two families who took me in. Tried to be as little trouble as possible. Made my own meals, helped with the laundry, never complained, tried to do well in school, even picked up after my foster brothers and sisters. Well, perfect didn't cut it."

Ryan listened. Much as he wanted to provide comfort, he could not.

"If I helped with laundry, I used the wrong fabric softener. If I made meals, I wasted food and got yelled at for disrupting their plans. Perfect is a huge responsibility. No matter how hard you try, you can't be perfect because something always goes wrong and you get punished for it. I learned to settle for average and hopeful."

With all the family problems he thought plagued him, it was nothing compared to Fern's past. His father nagging him to find a better career, make more money, join the business was little compared to getting punished for trying your best.

"Thank you," he said quietly. "Thank you for sharing that. I've always tried to be the perfect firefighter. You're right. It is a hard standard to maintain, almost impossible."

Her expression brightened. "You are a great firefighter. You have courage and an amazing skill set. I'd say if anyone was close to perfect, you were."

Tension filled the air, a sweet tension he didn't mind. The impish light returned to her eyes.

"Of course, since you're a man you can't be perfect because you don't ask for directions. Men never do."

"I have a good GPS." He puffed out his chest in pretend outrage. "Men *are* perfect."

At her eye roll, he laughed. "Back to work."

Glad things were right between them again, he returned to the bench press. He didn't want to make her uncomfortable, but weight issues with women upset him. Too many of them judged themselves by impossible standards.

Fern went to the treadmill and sighed. "You're very sweet. And you are right about my weight. It's the least of my troubles for now."

Time to change the subject. "How's the leg? You okay on that setting?"

"Slow and steady. My PT gave recommendations, which I plan to follow." Fern glanced at him, and he saw grit and determination on her face. "Eventually I'll be strong enough to run if those bastards try taking me again. I don't ever plan on being a victim again."

You're not a victim. Words stuck in his throat. No matter how many times he told her, Fern wouldn't believe it.

She had to make herself believe it first.

Chapter Eight

Hypnosis wasn't a cure to recovering all her memories, Ava told her. They sat in an office with the hypnotherapist the following day. Neutral colors and a comfortable cream-colored sofa and armchair soothed her, in addition to the presence of Ryan. Jacob and Ava sat in chairs at the edge of the room.

Usually, an audience would unnerve her. Not now, with her on the fringe of recovering what her mind refused to remember.

Brenda, the hypnotherapist, had a kind face and professional air. "My job is to help you recall memories your mind buried, Fern, but there are no guarantees. Memories are tricky things. You may recall false memories or even change existing ones. It's not foolproof, but I'm going to work with you to avoid any false memories your mind conjures to protect yourself.

"Think of hypnosis as adjunctive therapy to what you're undergoing with Ava. I want you to relax. I can't make you do anything against your will. Only help you. You're in a safe place."

A wry smile touched her mouth. "You can't make me bark like a dog? Or you can only make me bark like a big dog and not a yapper?"

A chuckle from Ryan, a censuring look at him from Ava.

Brenda smiled. "No barking. Now I want you to sit back and get comfortable."

Fern settled on the armchair, leaning back against the scatter pillows. She propped her feet up on the ottoman.

"I'm going to do progressive relaxation induction, Fern. It's a method of helping you completely relax. Take three deep breaths and close your eyes," Brenda told her.

Though her heart raced and her palms felt clammy, she did so.

"Now I want you to think of someplace calm and serene that brings you joy…"

Brenda's soothing voice washed over her like a gentle rain. Gradually Fern felt the relaxation spread from her toes, up to her head. On and on Brenda's voice droned like the hum of rain on a tin roof.

She heard suggestions. Brenda nudging her to return to the place where she'd been held captive, reassuring her she was safe and nothing and no one could hurt her…

Fern stepped back into time and memory.

A face, sneering and ugly, looming over her. Had to protect herself because no one else was there for her. Bill. Going to hurt her, stifle her screams. Fight back! But immobilized with terror, she couldn't move, her body wouldn't cooperate. Legs that kicked and ran were useless.

Something hard and cruel descending. Pain exploded in her legs.

She tried to scream, nothing came out. Felt like someone wrapped her in chains.

I'm going to die.

Fern opened her mouth to scream. A voice called out as if from a distance, commanding her to wake up.

Wake up, Fern!

Her eyes flew open. Ryan staring at her. Ava concerned. Jacob grim. Brenda composed, but worried.

Judging from their expressions, she'd stunned them.

Stunned herself as well. Fern studied her hands, unable to lift her gaze.

"It wasn't one of the guys who kidnapped me. The man I remembered was one of my mother's boyfriends. The guy in the sketch I did. Bill. He—he...wanted to hurt me when I was ten. Same name as the kidnapper I remembered. Guess I got confused."

She gave a little laugh. Laughter was a good self-defense. "You'd think the guy who kidnapped me would have the courtesy of having a different name so I could keep them straight."

"Fern, it's going to be okay." Ryan's voice was gentle.

Shame crept over her. "I... I'm sorry it didn't work."

Then words failed her once more. The memories she recalled were dark and grim, but of little use to the case.

For she had recalled parts of a childhood she had desperately tried to forget.

AVA ASKED TO speak to him in private before they left.

He had a bad feeling about this. Ryan followed his sister into the hallway and closed the door, leaving Fern alone with Jacob and the hypnotherapist. Much as he loved his sister, she tended to worry too much about him. Like their mother and father did.

Maybe if I chose a career selling pre-owned vehicles, they'd be happier.

"What's going on? You weren't expecting this to be magic and suddenly Fern would recall everything and everyone would live happily ever after."

Ava gave him a level look. "Please stop the sarcasm. You're insulting her profession, and mine."

"Sorry," he muttered.

"I had a talk with Mom and Dad. They're worried about

Fern living with you, and after what happened, I tend to agree with them. Dad has offered to pay money to put Fern in a rental house with round-the-clock security. They've already leased the home."

What? His parents, especially his dad, had sometimes interfered in his life, but never to this extent. "You agreed with them? Since when did you start taking their side against me?"

Ava assumed what he thought of as her "counselor face," the smooth look she gave clients. He'd seen her give it to Fern. No trace of what she was feeling, enabling the patient to express their own emotions without being influenced by Ava's.

"Ryan, it's not a matter of taking sides. They're worried about Fern staying with you because of the trauma she suffered."

First his captain at the fire station, now his family. Was everyone against Fern being around him?

The woman *had* suffered tremendous stress. It deeply bothered him that people in his circle were more concerned with his welfare and not hers.

"Listen, Ava, I'm not the one who was held captive in a wood shack and left to starve and then burn to death. Show a little sympathy for Fern, will you?"

"Ryan, I have a great deal of sympathy, and compassion, for Fern. If I didn't, I wouldn't be working so hard to help her."

Sensing the frustration in her higher-pitched voice, he sighed. "I know."

"Fern has a dark past and psychological issues, ones you may not be able to handle with her in the house when you're alone."

"You make her sound like a serial killer."

A withering look from Ava had him regret the words. "It's

for her sake as well, Ryan. Have you ever heard of bonds formed over trauma?"

Now it was his turn to scowl. "I'm a firefighter, sis. It happens. People I rescue form attachments. Romantic ones. Common with first responders. We're seen as their saviors. Usually it's women who eye me as a romantic partner. Since I've rescued their lives, I'll automatically make them feel better about everything else. It never lasts, and I know how to handle it."

"You can handle it professionally through your work. But now you're living with the woman you rescued. It's altogether different, Ryan."

Couldn't argue with that. He knew it as well, had known it from the moment he'd considered asking Fern to occupy his guest room.

Yet Fern was different. Not clingy or starry-eyed because he'd risked his life to save hers, even though that was his job. Quiet and self-effacing, and strong, she didn't cling, as Mom put it, "like a kitten climbing the drapes."

Something about the woman pulled at him. Though he couldn't be certain it wasn't his desire to set her life right after such a devastating experience, he also knew it went much deeper.

Ava scrutinized him. He hastened to reassure her. "Look, I appreciate your concern…"

"No, you don't. You want me to butt out." She shook her head. "You have that same stubborn look you had when we were much younger, and you insisted you were firstborn and Mom and Dad found me in a bin in a secondhand store because no way we were related."

He had to grin at the memory. "Yeah. I do want you to butt out. In a nice way. In return, I promise if I feel like Fern staying with me is detrimental to either of us, I'll make safe, alternative arrangements for her."

"Not in a secondhand store, I hope."

Ah, there was his sister's good humor. He put an affectionate arm around her shoulder. "Nope. Fern and I are friends. Nothing more."

"Are you off next Saturday night or do you work?"

"Off." He mentally went over his schedule. "For now, unless an emergency arises, like a hazmat fire."

"Good. Then come to dinner at Mom and Dad's next Saturday night. It will set their minds at ease."

He wondered about that. "As long as they can keep it quiet that Fern's staying with me. I won't risk anyone finding out, not with her kidnappers still roaming free."

"They will. Mom said it's only family. Chay and Ella Grace will be there, of course."

This was a good opportunity to show his parents his relationship with Fern was merely friendship, as well as set their minds at rest. Once they got to know Fern, with her quiet strength and humility, he was certain they'd like her.

"Okay. We'll be there. Can't wait to see Ella Grace again. Now, will you quit worrying about me and focus all your concerns on your fiancé? He's the man in your life who deserves the attention."

The radiant glow on Ava's face assured him love was real. For a fleeting moment he envied his sister. His relationships were always brief and shallow. He longed for deeper.

"How *is* Ella Grace?" Ryan felt a tinge of guilt he hadn't spent much time with Ava's soon-to-be adopted daughter, his only niece. At least this family dinner would resolve that issue.

For a few moments Ava raved about the little girl, who'd been found abandoned at the fire station. Then she glanced at the closed door.

"Fern must wonder what we're doing out here. Take her

home, keep an eye on her. Even though her memories haven't returned, a few may, now that hypnosis has occurred."

Like shaking loose rocks and setting off an eventual avalanche? He hoped not. "I can handle it."

Ryan dropped a quick kiss on Ava's cheek. "Thanks for caring," he said, meaning it.

She gave him a look far wiser than her years. "Odd. I was about to tell you the same thing regarding Fern."

DURING THE ENTIRE drive home, Fern had been quiet. The hypnosis had shaken her up, and Ryan knew what she needed. Fern could use a dose of normal and ordinary. Not being poked and prodded and examined like a bug under a microscope.

He enlisted her help chopping vegetables for dinner, teasing her about how she liked cutting the tomatoes into quarters instead of halves. He liked the becoming blush tinting her cheeks, and when she teased him back about the lack of greens, Ryan felt relief she finally relaxed.

"My parents invited us over to dinner next Saturday. Ava, Chay and their baby will be there. You game?" he asked.

Fern looked doubtful. "Are you sure they want me there? You don't have to bring me, Ryan. It's your family, and you probably want alone time with them."

Always considerate. He gently gripped her shoulders. "I'm certain. Come to dinner. My mom is a terrific cook and you'll get to meet baby Ella Grace. She's a sweetheart."

She bit her lower lip. "If you're certain..."

"I am." He gave her an encouraging smile. "It will be fine."

Fern gave a little nod, though doubt remained on her face.

After a healthy dinner of grilled chicken, spices, corn and roasted tomatoes, Ryan asked her about watching a movie with him. Fern looked delighted.

"I'd love it."

"I'll make the popcorn. You choose the movie," he told her.

"If your popcorn skills are as good as dinner, you've got a deal."

Soon they were in the living room, and Fern picked up the remote to turn on the television.

"There's a rom-com on the DVR. Can't go wrong with that."

"Chick flick."

"Oh yeah? What's your preference? I didn't see any NASCAR or monster truck smash shows on. Or do you prefer some chest-pounding guy reality show where they run through the woods naked and try to make dinner from squishy bugs?"

At her teasing tone, he grinned. "How about the fishing channel?"

Her expression fell and he laughed.

Her eyes sparkled. "Besides this one is about an unwanted houseguest so you can identify with the main character."

"You're not unwanted," he protested, reaching for a handful of popcorn.

"And you don't have a house in the Hamptons. Lucky you. If you lived there, I'd probably never leave."

She laughed as he tossed a piece of popcorn at her. Fern put the kernel on the table and flicked on the remote. She scrolled through the channel guide.

"Hey, here's something on live television. A special on Ireland. You game?"

At his nod, they settled in to watch. Ryan felt a sense of peace. Hell, he hadn't been this comfortable with a woman in a long time. Dates, yeah, he'd dated plenty. But relationships were not easy, mainly because when the women realized he was a dedicated firefighter who sometimes went into burning buildings and faced a risk of not returning, well, they said their goodbyes.

Not that he blamed them. Except for Kim, his last girlfriend, he'd settled for having fun, casual dates and breaking it off when he sensed the women grew distant. Better for everyone.

With Fern he didn't feel the need to excuse his job. She understood what it was like at the end of a tiring shift, when all he needed was his bed and sleep, not dancing all night or being someone's arm candy at a party. Forget modesty. He knew he was good-looking, which attracted women.

Fern didn't seem to care about his looks. She did seem to care about his welfare, and it was refreshing.

Much as he knew his captain and his family were right about not getting involved, he might as well enjoy her company. Sooner or later she'd recall her memory and the house would fall silent once more.

Besides, this wasn't a date. It was watching a movie with his house companion.

Yeah, right. If that were the case, why did he feel tempted to slide his arm around her shoulders?

Fern pointed to the lush landscape shown on the wide screen. "So beautiful. I promised myself when I was younger, I'd go there someday. It was my little secret, my reward for making it from one day to the next."

Ryan glanced at her. "Making it from day to day? You said you were in foster care. What kind of childhood did you have?"

She rubbed her temple, a move he recognized her making when things troubled her or she tried to recall a memory. "Not a good one. Let's just leave it at that. I've had enough today of trying to remember things. What about you?"

Ava mentioned Fern had a lot of issues, so he didn't want to pressure her. "The usual. Dad said I wasn't doing as much as I could, achieving grades to his standards. I was more into hiking, rock climbing, sports, the stuff Dad couldn't understand. One reason I became a firefighter. I like the physical aspect of it."

"Did you want to be a hero?"

A hero? He watched the screen, trying to lose himself in the fascinating Brian Boru establishing himself as the last true high king of Ireland. "I'm no hero. I only do my job. Real heroes don't get paid to save people."

"Hey."

Firm pressure on his arm. Fern gave him a look he'd never seen before from her. "Stop denigrating yourself. Job or not, you are a hero. You put your life at risk every time you ride on the truck. You tackle life-threatening situations most people would run away from."

High praise. He'd heard it before, shrugged it off. Yet coming from Fern it sounded more sincere.

"Okay, I'll stop it and we'll bask in our mutual admiration society."

Damn, her smile could make a man's heart race, make him think he could be a warrior king like old Boru. Ryan munched on more popcorn, glad a boring commercial showed on the television.

One would be hard-pressed to find hemorrhoid supplies sexy or heroic. Though he might admit to having ex-bosses who were like hemorrhoids.

He grinned.

"What's so funny?" she asked.

"Ever work for someone who is a pain in the butt and you wish you could dunk them in hemorrhoid cream?"

Fern sputtered out her drink. "You're bad."

"The worst. Just ask around the station. They'll agree."

"Such a high honor. Ever get a trophy?"

"They didn't have one large enough to fit through the door. Like my head."

Laughing at her eye roll, he tossed a piece of popcorn at her.

"Hey, keep doing that and I'll make you clean up. After all your hard work popping..."

Fern went quiet, staring at the screen.

He looked at the television. A family gathered around a blue van, loading vacation supplies. The father was talking about how roomy it was inside.

Fern's breath caught. In a flash, she went from relaxed to deer-in-the-headlights scared.

Instantly he pressed Pause on the remote. "You recognize that person?"

Her hands shook and her breathing became rapid and shallow. "I..."

Closing her eyes, she seemed to struggle to control herself.

"Easy," he soothed. Ryan remembered what Brenda the hypnotherapist had said during Fern's session. "Deep breaths. You're in a safe space. I'm here with you right now. No one is going to hurt you."

Her eyes opened and she stared at the screen. Ragged breathing filled the room and a pulse jumped in her neck, but a little color finally suffused her face.

"I recognize the van. Not the guy. That van... I remember the van. Dark blue. Back windows tinted so you couldn't see inside. It pulled up as I was walking and the door slid open, exactly like on the television. Two men's voices, and one was tall and he grabbed me. His hand was rough... I looked down and I saw black leather boots, like biker boots."

Depressing the pause button, he let the commercial play. Such an innocent advertisement for a family vehicle. Not so innocent for Fern, who'd become an unwanted passenger.

Reaching for his cell, he depressed the camera button and snapped a photo of the television screen. Ryan texted it to Ava.

"We need to tell Jacob and Ava. This is critical, Fern. You're remembering!"

"I'm scared."

He paused in texting his sister. Fern's lower lip wobbled. Here he was, all excited about this clue, and she was scared out of her mind.

"Ryan, can you hold me, please, before you tell Ava? I feel like the ground is slipping out from under me."

He set down his cell and wrapped his arms around her, feeling her body shake. Much as he knew this was a bad idea, it felt good to hold her. Provide some slim comfort.

Warning bells sounded in his mind. He heard his sister's voice and the voices of Cap and friends urging caution.

Heard his own conscience scream at him.

Saving Fern won't bring Kate back. She's dead and it's your fault.

You're getting too close. Can't cure her of everything she's endured. Get in too deep and you can do more harm than good.

As if Fern needed more harm.

Chapter Nine

Going to be a late night. Why couldn't she have a normal life like other women? Watch a program with a cute guy, relax and have some fun, instead of ending up a shaky mess...

Over a stupid television commercial.

You have an obligation to other women to remember what happened to you. That's more important than feeling normal. Don't be selfish.

While Ryan phoned his sister and cousin, she excused herself to the guest bedroom—she still couldn't think of it as hers, her bedroom was back in an apartment she wasn't certain she'd ever call home again.

Fern stared at her cell phone, wanting to call her sponsor. Not that she longed for a drink, no, she needed to talk to someone who understood her past and never condemned her for it. Normally she'd go to a meeting, but meetings were prohibited while she was in hiding.

The closer she got to remembering the past, the more scared she became. Bad enough she knew she had a murky, troubled childhood. Worse were the looks of pity or disgust. That much she did remember—people distancing themselves from her because Fern Hensley was a problem child. The kind of kid who grew up and ended up pregnant, or homeless, or in jail, or passed out in some dark alley, an empty bottle of vodka clutched in one dirty hand.

Her shaking fingers dialed Belle's number. Her friend immediately answered. "Hey, kid, you okay?"

"No." Fern relayed to Belle what happened.

"Do you want to have a drink?"

"No." She squeezed the cell phone so hard her knuckles whitened. "I want my life back. But I'm scared, Belle. I'm scared once I fully regain my memory, people will look at me like a pariah because I know there's bad stuff in my past."

Fern gave a little laugh. "Not that people wouldn't stare at me in pity now anyway, knowing I got kidnapped in a sex trafficking ring."

"Who are you afraid of pitying you? Ryan?"

Silence gave them both the answer. "Has he indicated in any way he feels sorry for you?"

"No." Fern thought about the enjoyable time they'd spent together today. "Far from it. When I'm with him I feel normal. He treats me like any other person. It's refreshing and I like it."

"He gets you."

Hearing it from her friend and sponsor clicked on a light. How had she missed this? Ryan understood her and spoke her language. Not like a victim, or like fragile glass, but like an ordinary woman.

"He's becoming my person. You once told me everyone needs a person. I don't want to burden him."

"Seems to me Ryan doesn't regard you as a burden. He could have easily passed along the responsibility to someone else and washed his hands of you. He likes you, Fern. He's one of the good ones."

Ryan was a good guy. What happened if he found out she had not been a sterling member of society? Would he lose all respect for her?

"He is. I don't know if I deserve him. I—I never told you my history."

That much she did remember.

"Fern, you know me by now. I don't need to know, Fern, to know you're a good person as well. I never judge people by their past, only their present, and I bet Ryan is the same."

Belle's voice gentled. "You deserve to be happy, Fern. Lean on Ryan for support. People can be jerks, but they can also be wonderful."

So true. She released a deep breath. "Thanks, Belle. I have to go now. I'll be in touch."

By the time she went into the living room, Jacob and Ava had arrived. Ava was in the kitchen, making tea.

No amount of chamomile tea could decrease her nervousness. Sure did help having Ryan sit next to her on the sofa, his big, strong presence a rock of comfort.

Life was about choices. She faced a few now. Going forward and facing her fears with courage, or hiding from them.

Women in Dark Canyon and other nearby towns depended on her recovering her memory. Every bit of information helped, painful as it might be for her.

Ava brought out a tray and handed a mug to Jacob, curls of steam rising into the air. "Coffee for you, and tea for the rest of us."

Fern shook her head. "I'm fine. I'd rather get on with this."

Jacob hesitated. Ryan gripped Fern's hand. "Whoever it is, you'll be okay."

Her heart sounded too loud, and everyone looked at her. Fern pulled her hand away from Ryan.

"I was walking home from work. Usually I drove, but my car had a flat and I'd left it back at the apartment. It wasn't a long walk. Silly me, my head was elsewhere." She gave a bitter laugh. "Living alone, I was aware of my surroundings at all times and how vulnerable I could be as a woman, but this night all I could think about was my upcoming date."

Frowning, she tried to remember. There was something else, something critical, but it slipped through her mind like sand through her fingers.

She pressed fingers to her temples. "I remember he was cute. Funny. I was so looking forward to going to this Irish bar to meet him, listen to this terrific Celtic band playing there.

"It was cold, so cold, and I walked fast, and I didn't even think about anyone following me." She spoke faster now, trying to purge the fear. "It wasn't until this van pulled up to the curb... The streetlights showed it was dark blue, and I heard a door open and turned.

"Two men jumped out... I can't remember their faces but one grabbed me. Like someone zapped my brain into waking up, I tried to run, but the tall one grabbed me, and I heard him call a name. Billy, remember I told you I recalled his name? I kicked and screamed and looked down. He had on..."

Fern closed her eyes, willing to see the black biker boots.

"These leather boots with square toes. They were like biker boots, with a chain, and then I felt this prick on my arm, and I screamed but no sound came out. Th-that's all I remember."

Tears slid down her cheeks. Fear and absolute panic—oh, she remembered them as well. The feeling that she was being sucked into a vortex of danger, and she could try clawing and fighting her way out, but it was useless.

Her life was no longer her own. No control.

Barely registering the feel of Ryan's warm palm covering hers once more, she took a calming breath.

Jacob looked intense, but his voice softened. "I know this is tough, Fern, but any details help the investigation. Do you remember anything else about the van? Sounds, like was the motor running rough? Was it a panel van without windows? Scratched or dented? New? Anything about the man who grabbed you? Was he short, tall, skinny or muscled? When he grabbed you, did it feel like his arms went down or were they level to your height? That gives us an idea of how tall he was."

Fern took another breath and closed her eyes, willing to recall the horrid moments.

"I—I remember thinking before everything went dark that I needed to recall everything…in case someone rescued me. The van had windows, dark windows. That's why the commercial we saw tonight reminded me of it. Like a family van you'd see on vacation with a bunch of kids in it, or going to soccer practice. Except this van had a dent in the passenger's side like someone hammered it.

"The guy, the guy…" Fear gripped her in a tight vise, making it hard to breathe.

"It's okay, Fern. You're safe."

Words Ava used all the time, yet this time Ryan said them. Ryan, who had been there when the fire roared and despair had seized her as she thought no one would find her and she'd die there all alone.

Another deep breath, smelling Ryan's citrus aftershave. Not overpowering or cloying, only refreshing…

"He smelled!" Her eyes flew open. "His coat… He had on a coat, and it smelled like skunk, and I couldn't understand why he'd use aftershave like that…"

Jacob glanced at Ryan and a smile touched his mouth. "That's great, Fern. Good detail. High-potency cannabis contains a bigger amount of THC and smells like skunk."

A flutter of hope beat inside her, tiny butterfly wings. Encouraged, she nodded. "Yes! I've smelled it before, and I had this crazy wild thought that maybe he was too stoned to do much, but then I felt this pinprick on my neck and everything went dark."

Judging from the excitement on Jacob's face, this was a very good thing. "Can you track someone if they smoke pot?" she asked.

"We can access the businesses that sell it and ask for their video footage and send out a description of the suspects, along with any details you provide. Are you up to sitting with a sketch artist now to have her draw any details you can remember?"

Fern balked, shaking her head. Too much. "I told you, I don't remember details!"

"Okay, I understand. You've given us something. Thanks," Jacob said.

Ryan's hand slid over hers. "What about her drawing, Jacob? Did you find out anything?"

He nodded. Fern's stomach tightened. "What did you find out?"

She was proud her voice remained level. Calm.

Ryan's cousin nodded, set his mug down on the coffee table. "We got a hit on the face you drew. But it's not one of the men who took you. Guy's been dead for five years."

Was it possible to feel relief and disappointment at the same time? "So he's not one of the men who kidnapped me. But he must have a criminal record if you discovered his name. Or at least be in the system."

As Jacob stared at her, she added, "I know about this from a friend of my foster parents. He was a prosecutor. That much I do remember."

I wish I could remember more important things.

"Yeah." Jacob exchanged glances with Ava. "He's probably from your past, which is why you drew him. Those memories are surfacing."

All the bad memories. Were there any good ones? She

had vague recollections of some, but her life had hardly been ideal. Far from the childhood Ryan experienced. His parents, strict as his father might be, sounded loving. Judging from Ryan's interactions with Ava, his sister, the entire family was close.

"I need to know who he is. Every single memory I recall helps piece together my life," she said evenly.

Jacob nodded.

"Like I said, we ran the portrait through facial recognition, which only works if a person is in the system. Fortunately, the object of your sketch was, the man you remembered during hypnosis. His name is Bill. William F. Conners. He was arrested for petty theft and larceny in Salt Lake, died about five years ago in a botched robbery attempt on a convenience store. He listed as his next of kin a woman named Olivia Hensley. Your mother."

Ryan, Ava and Jacob all looked at her expectantly.

"He's dead. You're certain of this?" she asked.

At Jacob's nod, Fern rubbed her temple, the memory sharp and uncomfortable. But she could deal with this—she had support, and the face no longer terrified her.

Bill, her mother's old boyfriend, was in his grave and could no longer hurt her. Fern swallowed hard and gathered her courage. Admitting this to these people, who had ordinary, normal lives, was tough. But these were good people and they would not judge her.

"William, no, he went by Bill. He was my mother's boyfriend. He's the guy I recalled in Brenda's office. He...tried to hurt me."

She gave a bitter laugh. "Did more than try. Slapped me around a few times, especially when he got drunk."

Despite the air conditioning in the living room, she felt soaked with perspiration.

Silence hovered in the room for a moment. Fern couldn't

bear it. She looked directly at Ryan. "My life was pretty screwed up from childhood, Ryan. Knowing my background, you sure you want me to stay in your house?"

Ryan scowled and gripped her shoulders. "Hey, hey, stop it. You are not your mother. We all have problems with our families. My dad thinks I'm a loser for not joining the family business and making a million dollars by my thirtieth birthday. The important thing is you're starting to remember, Fern. And in remembering, you know you got past that lousy upbringing and became the woman you are today. Strong and independent, not taking crap from anyone."

Embarrassed at the curtain of her past pulled back, she felt naked and exposed. Ryan could reassure her all he wanted, but facts were facts.

She didn't look at him. Or anyone else. "I'm really tired. I'd like to go to sleep now, if you don't mind."

Grabbing her bag, Ava was the first to stand. "It is getting late. Fern, we have an appointment tomorrow in the morning, but because it's so late, I'll push it back a couple of hours. I'll be here at ten."

Her therapist hugged Ryan. "If you need me, I'm a phone call away."

An almost cryptic warning. Was Ava afraid she might have a breakdown and her brother couldn't handle it?

Fern blocked the doorway with her body. She had to show these people she wasn't a hot mess, but could handle her own problems. "Ava, I'm fine. I'm not going to fall apart. Or hurt myself or anyone else."

Pointed, clipped, decisive. All the things Ava wanted her to become.

Ava looked her up and down and a little smile tugged at her mouth. "You're not the one I'm concerned about."

With a quick glance to Ryan, Ava reached around her and slipped out the door.

Jacob followed, advising her to call him if she remembered anything else.

It had been a long day. Promised to be an even longer night.

To HER SURPRISE, Fern slept through the night and awoke refreshed and ready for her session with Ava. Ryan's sister showed up at ten while Ryan was out running errands. Clever of him to arrange his schedule around this.

When Ava left, Fern turned her attention to work.

Somehow she knew her life before "the event," as she thought of her abduction, had been normal. Normal for her, anyway. The laptop before her represented a world of possibilities. A window to what others regarded as ordinary.

After powering it on, she stared at the icons. No one warned her against going on social media, yet she knew it was too dangerous. Hackers infiltrated all the time, could discover her IP address and even trace her back here.

Even the secure VPN was no guarantee. Not when you dealt with men who would do anything to get her back into their clutches. Sell her to the highest bidder.

Fern shivered. She clicked onto the software program for medical coding. Letters, numbers, diagnosis. Felt familiar. Comfortable, like soft slippers instead of walking on gravel. Or Lego pieces.

She needed to attend a meeting, be around others like herself struggling with alcohol. Meetings were forbidden while she remained concealed, so this was a balm to her soul.

Numbers and logic always suited her. In a world with a mother who abandoned her, foster families who mistreated her, Fern found comfort in math and numbers. When she couldn't make sense of why she was ill-treated and no one seemed to love her, the numbers were there. Constant, logical and nonemotional. Numbers made sense. She could create a world where she didn't have to worry about pleasing a foster mother who scolded when she failed to scrub away every spot from a faded linoleum floor or yelled when she spoke too loudly.

Numbers were quiet perfection. She learned to study in silence, marveling over their complex yet simple logic.

People seldom made sense.

Numbers always made sense.

Fern was absorbed in learning about insurance coding a diagnosis for a complex heart problem when the doorbell rang twice, then a third time. Typical signal for Ryan, yet to make sure, she glanced at her phone.

So sweet of him to alert her, instead of walking into the house. After all, it was his house, but his consideration relaxed her.

An hour later, he called out he was going out for a run. She envied his freedom. Despite the comfort of his house, she began to feel a little cooped up.

When he returned, Ryan popped his head in the doorway of the office.

"Hey, don't mean to disturb. Wanted to know if you're ready to take a break. I finished running six miles, and after a shower, I was thinking of relaxing out back with a cold sports drink and great company."

In navy blue sweatpants and a blue hoodie with the Dark Canyon Fire Department logo, he looked cute. The kind of guy she'd give a second look if they passed on the street.

Her smile faded. Ryan wasn't any guy. He saved her, and she had read about the hero complex in one of his books on firefighting. Getting attached was a bad idea.

I can't make things any harder for him. I have to keep him at a distance. Ryan's been terrific, and sooner or later, he'll be out of my life.

Like all the others who'd drifted in and out of it. A revolving door of foster families, friendships, men.

Safer to be alone. Less chance of heartbreak.

"Thanks, but I need to finish this."

Fern sensed his disappointment as she returned her attention to the screen.

The sooner her memories returned, the sooner she could get back to her life.

Even if that life had been filled with loneliness, it was a safe haven.

Chapter Ten

They didn't eat together that night. Ryan told her he was supposed to meet the guys for dinner. Before leaving, he instructed her to make sure she pressed her panic button if anything went wrong.

She refused an offer of takeout, mainly because she wasn't hungry. Plenty of leftovers in the freezer, she told him.

The house seemed so quiet without him.

Two hours later, he texted he would be home soon.

Restless, unable to focus on anything, she put on her coat and went outside into the front yard. The neighborhood was quiet. She had a police officer staying two doors down watching over her.

No reason to feel anxious or worried.

Yet the hypnosis session unlocking those childhood memories made her feel ashamed and exposed. Not her fault. She was a survivor. Life was short, and no way did she want her captors to have any more power over her.

It was about time she stopped thinking of herself as a victim and took charge of her life. Memories or no memories.

Fern looked at the dark sky, the stars glistening overhead, silent witnesses to her trauma. Whispers of a breeze from the distant mountains and canyons strengthened her. The mountains knew secrets and did not judge.

Fern lifted her face to the sky. "You have no power over me," she told her unknown kidnappers. "I am alive and so are my memories. I will recall them, and you will not hurt another woman the way you hurt me."

Feeling alive and energized, she lifted her hands to the sky and twirled, laughing at the feeling of breathing, feeling, simply being alive after months of fear and uncertainty.

"Nothing will hurt me now!" she shouted. "I'm unsinkable."

"Unsinkable in the middle of the desert?" Ryan sounded amused. "Who are you talking to?"

She turned to see him emerging from his truck.

"I didn't hear you pull up," she told him, delighted he was home.

Fern was about to tell him about her revelation when an ominous orange glow flickered in the house across the street. Smoke curled out of the open windows and suddenly gunfire erupted.

Straight at them.

ACTING ON INSTINCT, Ryan shoved Fern downward. He fumbled for his cell, dialing 911.

Fern buried her face into her hands and didn't look up. Chances were those rounds would never reach the street; still, he wasn't taking chances.

The guys responding to the call needed a warning.

"I've got a 10-0 here across from 1900 Maple Avenue. Working fire, house engulfed. Tell the first responders to use extreme caution until the scene can be secured. There must be several rounds of ammo cooking in there."

Other neighbors had come outside to watch the fire. Ryan glanced down. "Stay here and don't move."

Scrambling to his feet, he ran to the street and shouted for them to stay back, yes, the fire department had already been called. Officer Jenkins, the plainclothes police officer watching over the house, ran over.

"Fern okay?" he shouted.

Ryan nodded. "See if you can talk sense into the lookie-loos and get them off this damn street."

Fern peeked upward at him through splayed fingers. "Serves me right for telling the universe nothing can hurt me. Though I didn't think my challenge would end up firing bullets. Still, I knew about the Titanic. You think I'd learn to avoid statements of absolutes, such as 'unsinkable.'"

They watched as smoke poured out of the house and orange flames rose higher and higher. Ryan felt bad for the owner. Guys were trying to get a handle on the beast, but they couldn't risk getting too close.

"Is anyone inside?" Fern asked from behind him.

"Doubt it. My neighbor, Simmons, has been on a business trip for a couple of weeks, and he lives alone."

Lots of people milling around now, with police cordoning off the area for safety. He glanced back at Fern. Orange shadows danced on her troubled expression.

He spotted a police officer headed in his direction. "Stay here. I gotta talk to this guy."

Ryan went to the sidewalk, glancing back at Fern hovering on the stoop. Fern was seemingly torn between going into the house and remaining out here with him.

The officer removed a notepad. "You called it in?"

"I did. Spotted the smoke and heard the gunfire."

The cop asked question after question. How much ammunition was inside, weapons, where were most of them located.

"The house is vacant now. Owner runs a business selling guns, attends a lot of gun shows around the country, so I guess he stashed them in the garage," Ryan told him.

Remaining outside wasn't a good idea, not with all these

neighbors milling around and now... *Oh damn, here comes a news truck.*

Turning, he went to gesture to Fern to get inside. Relief filled him as he saw she'd already left.

Seeing Fern on the late local news would not make Jacob, or Ava, happy. *Hey, we're trying to hide her, and less than a week with you and her photo is all over the television!*

Could be funny if it were not true. Ryan gave the cop a pointed look. "Can I go now? I'm on shift tomorrow and need my z's."

Like firefighters and nurses, cops understood about first responder shifts and the importance of quality sleep. The officer nodded, said he had Ryan's number if he had more questions.

But when Ryan reached the front door and rang the bell for Fern to let him in, she didn't answer.

He tried again. Nothing. Ryan texted her. No response.

Don't panic. Yeah, try telling his accelerated heart rate the same. Fern had to have fled inside the house. Only a few feet had separated them. Why wasn't she answering?

A nasty thought winked on and off like a faulty neon sign: *What if someone snatched her while you were busy talking with the cop?*

He couldn't go there, but like trying to forget the word *elephant*, it remained implanted in his mind, flashing over and over. Cussing, he rang the doorbell again. Nothing.

He called Fern's cell. It went straight to the generic voicemail Ava had set up for her.

Ryan walked around one side of the house and the other. Both gates were locked. He'd taught her the combination. Now he tried it and went into the backyard.

No Fern.

The back door was open. *Whew. I'm overreacting, she probably stepped inside for a moment...*

Minutes later, after a thorough search of the entire house, including the basement, sweat rolled down his back. The April air outside as he ran out the door did little to cool him off.

Fern wasn't anywhere around the house or the yard.

Okay. *Panic now.*

Chapter Eleven

Where could she have gone? Terrible thoughts shot through his mind as he continued searching in front of the house. The crowd had dissipated, thanks to the police officers controlling the scene.

No Fern.

As he was about to admit defeat and ask one of the cops for help, he saw a woman approach the house, hugging herself. Relief mingled with anger.

"Where the hell have you been? You can't disappear like that, Fern. You know how risky that is, being out here in the open!"

"I'm sorry," she burst out. "I wasn't thinking."

"No, you weren't. Do you know how damn worried I was? How I started thinking someone grabbed you again right under my nose? I brought you here to keep you safe and protect you."

Putting his anger on pause, he stopped and looked at her. Fern didn't make any noise, not even a protest.

Moisture swam in her eyes, and he was the reason. Yelling at her. Stupid of him, so stupid, when she needed reassurance. Ryan took a deep breath to apologize when she nodded meekly.

"You're right. Absolutely right. I should have told you

where I was headed, Ryan. Instead, I thought only of myself. Time to stop doing that. You and the others have been wonderful to me, and how do I repay you? It was selfish of me to not let you know what happened."

For the first time he noticed she was trembling inside her coat, her hands shaking slightly.

"Why did you leave?"

"I—I don't know if I should tell you... Please don't be mad anymore."

Ryan gentled his voice. "Fern, I'm not mad. But I need to know why you left the yard and where you went."

"I had to save him from being trampled."

Slowly she opened her coat to reveal a button-like nose. A whimpering dog peeked out at him.

"Everyone was so busy looking at the fire. He was so scared and darted out in front of the cars and no one was helping him. I had to follow him and get him. I think he's hurt."

Ryan peered down at the dog and saw an injured paw. Looked like a burn. "Yeah, he needs a vet."

"He came right to me." She stroked the dog's head. "I was wondering... He has no tag, but the vet can see if he's chipped, and if he's not, instead of putting him in a shelter... Those shelters are so cold and lonely. I totally understand if it's an imposition."

An adorable, injured dog with Fern and her big beseeching eyes. How could he say no?

Ryan sighed. He had no room in his life now for a dog or more complications, but he sensed Fern needed the dog. "Maybe. He needs vet care first and probably a good foster home, but maybe later."

Her expression shuttered. He could almost read her mind. Yet another disappointment.

He gentled his voice. "Let's get him checked out at the

animal hospital first. Good thing you saw him or this little guy might be in real trouble."

She handed over the dog, who snuggled against him as if seeking warmth. "I started calling him Bumper because he kept bumping my hand with his nose."

Bumper. Ryan glanced at the house. With the fire under control and almost extinguished, traffic on the street diminished. He couldn't risk Fern coming with him...

"I know I'm not supposed to leave the house, but if I wear a hat and maybe glasses, no one will recognize me. Can I please come with you? I need to see how he's doing."

More than anyone, he understood the need to follow through with a victim you'd saved from harm. "I'll give you ten minutes."

BY THE TIME they returned from the animal hospital, they were both worn out. Fern admitted her disappointment over Bumper staying with a foster family once he recovered, but she understood.

Ryan almost caved in to having the dog at the house. The little pup had gotten to him as well, licking his nose as he placed him on the exam table for the vet. But with Fern hiding from the criminals who abducted her, trying to regain her memory, and his intense work schedule, he feared he couldn't give Bumper the proper attention and care the pup needed to recover from his time on the streets.

At work the following day, the Dark Canyon fire investigator told Ryan the fire had been deliberate. An empty gas container had been found in the backyard. A broken window at the back indicated someone got inside and started the blaze, setting oil-soaked rags in the kitchen and candles nearby.

They were investigating the homeowner to see if this was a case of insurance fraud, but considering Simmons had thousands' worth of ammo and guns stored in the house, it made no sense. Surely he would have removed them before setting the fire himself.

The puppy had been a stray. Neighbors reported seeing him hanging around Simmons's garage. Poor fellow had probably gotten burned when the fire spread. Investigators found a hole in the garage siding, which explained how the dog had gained access.

And fortunately he escaped the fire, though not without injury.

Ryan had little time to consider it, because he agreed to work back-to-back shifts when one of the guys had a family emergency. When he finally got home after work, all he could do was crash and sleep. There was barely time to exchange greetings with Fern.

Ryan felt bad for her, isolated here in his home. A week after the fire, he sensed her extreme frustration. She was no closer to making gains in her memory. When he returned home from checking on the dog at the veterinary hospital, he found her outside, staring absently at a canvas. Soft yellow light illuminated the patio in the pitch-blackness.

"You'll be happy to know that Bumper is recovering fine. Vet says in another week he can be released to a foster home until he's adopted."

"That's good."

Her voice sounded listless.

"Why are you out here in the dark?" He draped his jacket over her shivering shoulders.

"Guess I lost track of time."

"What are you working on?" he asked, pulling up a chair.

"Nothing special now. I can't get it together."

"I hear creativity is like that. Comes and goes."

"One reason I liked working with numbers and codes. They're stable and I don't have to imagine anything."

Curious, he looked at the palette of colors by her side. "Can I see what you're working on?"

A slight shrug. Ryan went to look at her work. A landscape, with vivid sunset colors. Not vivid. Almost angry.

"Why did you start to paint if you enjoy math so much?"

Fern picked up a paintbrush and stroked the bristles as if petting a cat. "Painting helped save me, in a way. It kept me going through a series of bad foster homes. Oh, it wasn't painting then, but drawings and doodles. I'd sketch out my feelings."

He could only imagine how dark those drawings were. Ryan knew pain, and grief, but nothing like what she'd experienced. He still had a loving, though interfering, family, and caring coworkers. She'd been all alone.

"I can't imagine what that was like. I know what it feels like to lose someone you love, or make a mistake that you always regret, but nothing like what you've been through."

She set down the brush and looked at him, really looked at him, with those huge hazel eyes that seemed to sear through his soul.

"Don't compare my life experiences to yours, Ryan. Everyone is different and everyone experiences grief differently. Some people mourn the loss of a beloved pet more than they do a parent who was never supportive. We don't compete in the pain Olympics."

He managed a crooked smile. "Wise words."

"Partly your sister, partly me." Fern's gaze darted to him. "I should tell you something. I had a toxic childhood. My life was never normal or even close to it. I was bounced around from foster home to foster home when my mother abandoned me when I was ten."

Ryan's steady blue gaze centered on her. He knew this was important to her, and he gave her his full attention.

"My mom was a drunk who wanted her abusive boyfriend

more than me. She left me in the middle of the night. I had a lot of setbacks. And then I started drinking. Heavily. Got into trouble. I was headed down a bad path.

"When I was fifteen, I got into a foster home where I felt loved for the first time in my life. My new parents were reliable, dependable and when they made a promise, they followed through."

Fern sighed. "They were wonderful. Never put up with the trouble I gave them, but they were fair and taught me discipline. Gave me boundaries and respect and made me feel like I could make something of my life."

She looked away, as if ashamed. "I'm an alcoholic, Ryan. The Englehearts, Delia and Joe, didn't lecture me about drinking. They got me into a teenage Alcoholics Anonymous program and stuck by my side the entire time. I could never repay them for their support and belief in me."

"You're a recovering alcoholic." His admiration for her increased. "You manage it well. Is it why you refused pain meds in the hospital?"

Fern nodded. "I'm always afraid of slipping. I've learned to do without. You can do almost anything you set your mind to, Ryan."

"Almost anything," he agreed.

"The Englehearts treated me like their own daughter. They let me stay past my eighteenth birthday, when I aged out, as long as I got a job and paid some rent. Their rent payments were low enough to enable me to use my job to pay for community college. They moved away a couple of years ago, but always kept in touch until they were killed in a car crash."

"I'm sorry," he said gently. "After everything, that must have been devastating."

"It was." She sighed. "Do you ever want to feel happy, feel more than a glimmer of pure joy, but when those glimmers come, you seize them and hold on to them with all your might because you're so afraid the next moment will bring something that hurts to your core?"

His chest tightened. Ryan managed a nod. Yeah, he knew what that was like, and sometimes he felt he didn't deserve the happiness coming his way. Why should he go on with life when the woman he'd tried to save lost hers?

He'd failed at the job, and it seemed like he could never make up for the loss.

Ryan swallowed past the lump in his throat. "I know what that is like, Fern. You're not alone in these feelings. They suck."

Her lower lip wobbled. "They do indeed suck. Big donkey donuts."

Then the spark returned to her eyes and she grinned. "My favorite swear words."

He couldn't help it. He laughed, the sound shattering the grimness in the air. For a moment he regretted losing the intensity and connection, but it was worth seeing her smile. Hell, he'd climb the aerial ladder ten times carrying one hundred pounds of weights for one of Fern's sweet smiles.

Sweet might be the wrong word. Sweet reminded him of a young girl, innocent and carefree. Fern was a woman, an old soul, who had been through a lot.

"You have a sunshine smile," he murmured.

Her smile dropped. "What do you mean?"

Okay, awkward moment. But he needed to be honest. "When you smile, it brings sunshine to dark places."

Pink suffused her cheeks, a becoming shade on her. He felt tempted to reach out, stroke the softness of her skin. Almost subconsciously, he lifted his hand to her face.

Fern didn't flinch or jerk away. She watched him, not with wariness like a frightened animal, but with darkened pupils and anticipation on her face.

He stroked a line down her right cheek, marveling at the satiny smoothness of skin, delighting in the flush, the little sigh she made indicating she enjoyed his touch. Fern leaned forward as he dared to cup her cheek in his palm. Even better.

Whoa, this was great, feeling her soft skin, seeing desire swirl in the darkness of her eyes. Ryan swallowed hard against the urge to push forward, do everything he normally would with a woman responding in kind to the chemistry between them. Lean in closer, brush his lips against hers, gauge her response and maybe go deeper, bonding them together in mutual passion.

But this was Fern, who'd endured plenty of heartache. Slow, even slower, his instincts cautioned. Now wasn't the time to experiment and tease and taste and see how far he could take this.

Ryan dropped his hand. Was she disappointed? He couldn't tell.

Fern turned away. "I have dinner in the Crock-Pot. When you're hungry, help yourself. I already ate."

"I'm starving. Thanks. Don't stay out here too long. Temperature's dropping."

She nodded. "Thanks for your jacket."

Knowing she wanted to be alone, he went inside. As he ate, killing two glasses of tea with the delicious stew she'd made, he thought about how she must feel right now.

Fern had to suffer from cabin fever. Too dangerous for her to go out in public with her abductors still at large.

He consulted a map on his cell phone as he finished dinner. Her apartment was more than an hour's drive from here. Maybe taking her there would trigger a memory. After calling Ava and discussing it with her, he went outside to talk to Fern.

She sat on the patio, staring at the fence like a zoo animal pacing its enclosure, looking for escape.

Ryan pulled up a chair. "How would you like to do something fun? I'm off for the next three days, and I need to get out for a long drive now that winter's over. You could wear your wig and glasses as a disguise and we can visit Oso, drive by your apartment, see if you remember anything."

Paleness on her face and the grip of her fingers on the chair's armrests told him her terror of returning.

"I want to help, Ryan." Fern swallowed hard. "If it's best for me to go back, and that will make me remember so they can prevent this from happening to another woman, then let's do it."

Such courage. New admiration filled him. Fern's strength inspired him. She'd endured so much trauma, and yet instead of thinking of herself, she strove to help others.

"We won't stay in Oso long. We'll continue to Durango. There's a terrific walking trail along the Animas River I think you'd enjoy. It's far enough from here that no one will recognize you."

The hope and dawning excitement on her face was like watching a butterfly emerge from its cocoon. Fern glanced around.

"Drive to Colorado? You'd do this for me? It's your day off, and I'm sure you have errands, things to do with your family and friends. If you change your mind at the last minute, I'll understand…"

Her voice trailed off. Ryan squatted down before her, making sure their gazes were level. "Fern, I know a lot of people have disappointed you in the past. I don't make promises I can't keep."

Not anymore. Not since the day Kate had slipped from his grasp. Couldn't think about that tragedy. Fern came first. She needed this.

Hell, I need this as well.

"The drive will do us both good. We can take my dad's

Jeep. Take the top off as we're going through the mountains. Maybe even do a little exploring and off-roading."

The smile tugging her mouth upward radiated pure joy. "I've never been off-roading but always wanted to try. Didn't know you liked it."

Oh yeah, he liked it. Ryan grinned. "I took the Jeep off-roading a couple of years ago and had a little problem. Dad refused to let me drive it after that."

"Will your dad let you borrow it?"

His grin widened. "I kept an extra set of keys he doesn't know about."

"Why do I get the feeling you were a troublemaker when you were young?"

"Still am."

At his wink, she laughed. Felt good to see her spirits lift and hear her laugh, as clear and enchanting as the distant toll of church bells.

"Tomorrow morning then. Leave around five thirty for my parents' house and get breakfast on the road."

"That early? Won't you wake up your parents?"

"Not if I'm careful."

He grinned as she laughed again. It was going to be a great day tomorrow. He felt it in his bones.

RYAN HAD A mischievous side she liked. Before dawn, they left. He parked his truck in the sweeping driveway of his parents' house. Ryan keyed the code to the garage door and backed the Jeep out as quietly as a thief.

The vehicle was older and smelled like grease and tacos. He grinned at her wrinkled nose.

"Dad uses it for working on odd jobs and off-roading. I think he also sneaks out for his favorite taco truck when Mom's not looking or she'd lecture him on the dangers of raising his cholesterol. I'd have cleaned out the tools from the back but I didn't want to waste time or risk waking them up."

They stopped for gas, and while the vehicle filled up, he gave her a sheepish look. "I'm texting Mom that I took the Jeep and not to worry. Don't want her thinking someone broke in."

"Someone other than her son, you mean."

"Well, if you put it that way."

Soon they were on the road again, heading to Oso. Too cold to take the top off, they opted for the vehicle's heater instead. Bundled into a soft down jacket, a long-sleeved shirt, jeans and pink suede boots with plush lining purchased courtesy of Ava, Fern began to relax. Ryan let her select the music and she used Bluetooth to connect a soothing jazz station to the sound system. Seldom an early riser, Fern felt grumpy, despite the delicious coffee he'd brewed for the road. After a few sips from her insulated tumbler, she began to appreciate the surroundings.

The first light of dawn streaked across the leaden sky, transforming it into a brilliant blush of pink, purple and orange, accented by indigo clouds. Like an artist's brush, the colors stretched out on the horizon. Mountain peaks in the near distance silhouetted with dawn displayed their craggy edges. Fern imagined waking up in the canyons, watching the sun touch the sharp rocks and twists and turns, turning them to fiery orange.

"It must be beautiful to hike in there and see the sunrise," she mused.

Ryan glanced at her. "I've camped before in the canyons. It's fantastic this time of year, before the summer begins and the tourists invade. Feels like you're the only person in the world when the sun climbs over the mountains and shines down on the valley."

"Peaceful. No one around to tell you what to do or how to feel."

He nodded. "It's soothing. You and nature, nothing else. Except you have to be careful because of spring flooding. Those canyons can turn into raging rivers in minutes. I always carry a weather radio to keep up on the rainfall in the mountains."

Fern shivered. "I'm more afraid of fire than water."

Reaching over, he squeezed her hand. "I understand."

Thinking of the cabin as it burned, how she could have perished in the fire if he hadn't pulled her free, twisted her guts into a knot. Couldn't think that way. She was here, alive, and on the road to recovery.

He pulled away and focused on the road leading to Oso.

I understand. Two words meaning a lot to her. No questions or probing, like from Ava or others who only wanted to help, but sometimes she only wanted silence to explore her own thoughts, not pressure from having to answer them. Fern leaned back and cracked the window. Crisp, cool air flowed inside, the delicious balm of sagebrush and pine carried on the wind. The desert seemed to shimmer with life, and she could imagine the creatures hiding in the brush beginning to venture out, looking for food as the sun warmed the land.

Utah had incredible sunrises. Different from the ones she'd experienced while on a vacation in Florida. More dramatic, and in a way, serene.

Ryan hummed along to a tune as he drove. "There's a roadside diner about thirty minutes from here. Sound good?"

Absently she nodded and traced a line on the window. "Did you hear back from your mom yet?"

In answer, he depressed a button on the Jeep's display screen. A text message sounded over the speakers.

"Ryan, your father's going to have a meltdown when he

finds out you took the Jeep. I won't tell him if you don't. Enjoy and please, this time, stick to paved roads."

Fern smiled. What a wonderful mom. "I like your mom. She sounds like fun."

"She's definitely less uptight than my dad, but they're good parents. Dad's stricter and more worried about my future as a firefighter. But once in a while he stops pestering me to join the family business."

"At least you have someone who cares about your future."

The words slipped out before she could catch them and snatch them back. Ryan glanced at her again.

Embarrassed, she asked about the diner and what kind of food they had. Fern busied herself looking up the restaurant and scanning the menu offerings.

By the time he pulled into the parking lot of the Roadside Diner, her stomach was cheerfully announcing breakfast time. The pink neon sign sputtered on and off, but enough cars and trucks out front assured her this was a popular destination.

Smells of frying bacon and rich coffee made her salivate as they walked inside. The counter was filled with men, including some grizzled truckers who barely glanced at them. Ryan asked for a quiet booth in the back and sat watching the door. Fern's gaze darted around. Though no one paid attention to her, it was unnerving being in public like this.

Maybe it wasn't a good idea.

Ryan leaned forward. "I'm not leaving you for a minute, Fern. No one's looking at you. Please, try to relax."

"I'm not nervous."

He gave a pointed look to her hands, gripping the table's edge as if it were a life raft.

"Well, okay, maybe a little. Only because I don't know if this place has good coffee and I need my caffeine fix."

Mischief danced in his blue eyes. "It's a diner. They have to have good coffee or they'd go out of business."

After their food arrived and Ryan dug into his eggs and ham, she was able to lose a little tension and study the restaurant. It had been so long since she'd been around this many people. Most diners seemed intent on their meals. Only one or two men at the counter gave her a second glance.

Ryan slung an arm over the back of the booth. Even relaxed, he remained watchful, as if her bodyguard.

"You're right. No one is paying attention to me," she told him.

"They should. You're the prettiest woman here."

The compliment warmed and unnerved her. Not used to them, Fern rolled her eyes. "I'm the only woman here, besides our waitress, and she's more important than me."

"Because she has the magic juice." He pointed to his now empty mug. "Wish she'd deliver more over here."

Fern waved her hands over their mugs. "I can make her appear. All I need to do is have a mouth full of food and she'll stop by to ask what we need. It's my secret talent."

Barely had she said the words when their waitress appeared with a pot of coffee and filled their mugs. "Where you guys headed?"

As Fern compressed her lips, not wanting to answer, Ryan nodded his thanks. "Going to Cortez, maybe look around Mesa Verde. Tourist stuff."

Relief filled her. Of course he wouldn't talk about their plans.

"Be careful on 491. Heard from Hank—" the woman inclined her head to the counter "—some nutcase in a van speeding like a bat out of Hades nearly ran him off the road an hour ago. Guy was doing at least ninety, as if running from the cops. Some jerks think they own the road and learn too late big rigs like Hank's can't stop or turn on a dime.

Someday someone's gonna smash into that ass and he'll find out too late."

Fern's eyes widened and her breathing hitched. "What... kind of van?"

They exchanged glances. The woman frowned and called out, "Hey, Hank! Got details on that ass who almost ran you off the road?"

Dressed in a leather jacket, his waterfall belly spilling over a belt, Hank ambled over to them. He pushed back a worn ball cap. "Green, I think. It was dark. Guy was driving like a dickwad."

"With windows on the sides instead of panels?" Ryan asked.

Hank frowned. "You know the guy?"

"Doubt it. Want to know what to look for as we get on the road. Don't want an accident."

"Van had dark windows. Not a panel van, I think. Hard to tell because I was too busy controlling my rig." Hank squinted at him. "Hey, I know you."

Sensing Fern's discomfort, Ryan shook his head. "Don't think so."

"I know so. Never forget a face. Three years ago outside Dark Canyon. My rig caught fire after I crashed and you pulled me out. Saved my hide. You're a fireman." Hank grinned and hooked a thumb at him. "Hey, everyone! This guy's a hero. Fireman who saved my sorry ass in that crash."

Hoots and hollers about said ass followed, along with waves and thanks.

Hank stuck out a meaty hand and Ryan shook it. "Thanks, man. Let me buy you and your lady breakfast."

"Just doing my job."

The trucker gave him a serious look. "If it weren't for you, I'd be toast, literally. Never been so scared in my life. Thought I was going to die in there. Because of you pulling me out, I slowed down, learned to appreciate life. Please, let me buy your breakfast."

Fern looked at the sincerity on the man's face, felt the gratitude. Hank wanted to do something in return. She glanced at Ryan. Ryan sighed, and nodded.

"Thank you."

Then his gaze turned speculative. "I could use your eyes and ears. If you or the other truckers you know see that van again, can you call this number? My cousin's looking for it. Guy might have been involved in a hit-and-run."

Fern exhaled a long breath.

Hank copied the number on his cell. "Sure thing. I'll spread the word. Gotta run, but I'll leave money with Sal for your bill."

"Thanks."

"No." Hank looked serious. "Thank you. Stay safe."

They finished their breakfast in silence. Ryan left a generous tip on the table. As they left, a chorus of thanks followed.

On the road, Fern felt introspective. He glanced at her. "You okay? You haven't said a word since Hank mentioned the van."

"I was thinking about Hank and how you saved him." She gave a little laugh. "Being in there, I was so caught up in worry about being in public, would anyone recognize me? It's easy to get wrapped up in your own problems and focused so much on yourself that you fail to see other people have personal issues as well."

"True. But self-care is important, Fern. You have to put yourself first."

"You don't." She shook her head. "You weren't thinking of yourself when you pulled him out of the burning truck."

"Of course I was. Every time I go on a call, I think of myself. Getting on my bunker gear, making sure my head's on straight so I can focus on the job. Oxygen mask on yourself first, remember?"

Traffic began to increase. She thought about the van Hank mentioned. Nothing to worry about, not really. How many vans were on the road? Some people lived in their vans, converting them to campers. Didn't mean anything.

Still, she couldn't quite relax. Ryan gestured to the radio. "Why don't you put on some music you enjoy?"

Fern didn't answer. Movement in the side mirror caught her attention. Acid churned in her stomach and she felt sick.

"Ryan, can you go a little faster?"

"What's wrong?"

"I think we're being followed."

Chapter Twelve

Going on the road with him had seemed like a happy outing, a chance to escape the house and breathe fresh air. Now Fern wondered if it was a huge mistake.

"Which vehicle?" He glanced at the rearview mirror. "The black sedan behind me?"

"Two cars back." Her heart raced. "Blue van. He's been behind us for a few miles now. Right after we left the diner."

A blue van at night could look green. She wondered if this was the same van that nearly ran the trucker off the road... or contained her kidnappers. Anything was possible.

Anything could happen. Tension gripped her.

Dust flew up as he pulled off the roadside and sat, engine running. Ryan's fingers tightened on the steering wheel.

"Let's find out if this guy is following us."

Palms clammy, she waited, watching a line of cars pass, along with a blue van. Panel van, no dark windows. Fern exhaled.

"Guess I'm a little paranoid."

"I wouldn't call it that." He waited for a break in traffic and pulled back onto the road. "Cautious. I'm glad you noticed. Better to be aware than unaware."

Yeah, she'd already been unaware and that had cost her

when they took her captive. Fern scrolled through her phone and changed the music to eighties rock. Ryan laughed.

"Interesting choice."

"I know you like it. Saw your vinyl collection."

A vinyl collection seemed a safer topic than the fear gripping her since the mention of a van nearly running the trucker off the road. That combined with returning to her hometown made her feel as if she were returning to a nightmare.

"Do you think they would still be out there in the same van? Billy and the other guy, I mean."

Ryan shrugged. "I don't know. For all we know, they might have ditched it and stolen another one."

Terrific. So any of the vehicles on the road could be her kidnappers.

"Don't think like that," he said suddenly. "Fear can immobilize you. The best thing you can do for yourself is to recover your memory so we can find these jerks and put them behind bars. Tell me about your job."

Fern consulted her phone and the GPS. Not far from Oso now. She knew a diversionary tactic when confronted with one, but she would play along. Much as she longed for him to turn the Jeep around to the safety of his home, she knew this was best.

She'd been through a lot in her life and would get through this as well. Self-reliance was best.

"I loved my job. It was time-consuming, but I was working on the laptop yesterday on the coding software and remembered how much I loved it. Like Hank, I was so absorbed in my work that I didn't have much of a life."

"Work can get like that," he agreed.

Staring out the window, she remembered numbers and codes and medical terms. "All I ever wanted was to do the best job possible, maybe even to prove I could make up for failing in the past. Coding isn't easy. You have to know the patient's problems as diagnosed by the doctor, and subsequent treatment. The tests ordered by the doctor, and the diagnosis. It means interpreting doc speak, as I call it, plus labs and radiology results, so I can apply the proper codes for insurance. In some cases, I saved patients a lot of money by researching their conditions and knowing the codes so insurance will cover the costs."

Fern sighed. "It's not as action-packed as your career. I don't go racing into fires to rescue people."

"It's not all that," he told her. "A lot of it is training, always trying to keep up so I know the latest tech and methods. Sometimes it's inspections. Some days it means sitting around the station, waiting for calls. On those days I try to work out, read journals. I like to expand my knowledge in case I'm first on scene and have to assess the med sitch."

"Your work is more critical," she said.

"I'd say your job is as lifesaving as mine. I save lives and you save their peace of mind."

"Well, I don't know about that."

He looked intense. "I do. I remember being on a call to a home where the kids, teenagers, were alone and the mom was out working. Their dad had died from cancer and the mom was working two jobs, one to help pay down the medical debt. Mom could barely afford food on the table and a lot of her income went to pay the bills. If you had been there, coding her insurance, I bet she wouldn't have as much debt."

The words gave her a pleasant jolt of warmth. "Most would find my job boring or only be concerned about how much money I make. What happened to the mom? Did you have to call the authorities?"

"Yeah, we did, but we got her into a program with day care, and I worked with the insurance company. Turns out a lot of the procedures were coded wrong, so insurance did end up paying. So see? Your job is critical."

She knew Ryan was one of the good guys, but going the extra mile to help a stranger added another star to his rating. She gave a faint smile.

"Maybe if my mom had someone like you watching her back when I was little, she could have received the help she needed. Maybe if I had direction in my life, I could have avoided some of my problems. Do they make a compass for guiding your life?"

"Would be nice," he agreed.

Fern sighed. "Thanks for helping those kids, Ryan. Probably no one else bothered or cared."

He gave a modest shrug. "I was only doing my job."

No, you were getting involved. Like with me. You always seem to go the extra mile, and other guys wouldn't care, say it wasn't their responsibility. Or bother taking the time.

It seemed too intimate to voice her thoughts, and she sensed he was uncomfortable with praise. Like her, Ryan didn't like the spotlight, but preferred being behind the scenes.

It made her like him even more. Not good, because she couldn't afford to get attached to this man. He had his own life to live.

She glanced at the GPS again. Closer now, the cheery white Welcome to Oso sign making her palms sweat and her heart race. Welcome, yeah, she was welcome. Last time she was here, a horrible man named Billy and his partner pulled her into a nightmare. Seemed like she could never awaken from it, try as hard as she might.

The small town of Oso seemed eerily quiet as Ryan pulled his car onto Main Street. Fern clasped her hands in her lap, the knuckles white. Every face they passed on the sidewalk made her wonder—could they be involved? Did they know something?

She'd lived quietly, seldom interacting socially because life was easier that way. No one needed to know she was an alcoholic. Once an alcoholic, always one. Invitations to parties where people would be drinking were politely turned down. She'd only worked up the strength to date again, looking forward to the date at the Irish bar because she'd heard the food was authentic Irish and the people were unpretentious and the music lively.

Why did this happen to her? She never hurt anyone.

You're a loner. Words Jacob uttered came back to haunt her. Raised in the foster system, no family, few friends.

That's why I became a target.

Ryan suddenly pulled into an empty parking space on Main Street. She stared as he switched off the engine.

"What's going on?"

He pointed to the store out front. "Stay here. I'll only be a minute. Lock the doors."

Though most of the shops were open, she had no idea why he suddenly had an urge to shop. She waited, turning her head from pedestrians passing the Jeep.

A few minutes later, he returned and slid into the driver's seat. His grin seemed infectious.

"Got you a gift." He handed over a small paper bag.

Removing the small circle from the bag, she glanced at him. Then at the storefront that read Camping Supplies.

"I don't understand. What is this for?"

Maybe he wanted to go hiking with her?

"It's a compass. Pocket one, like kids own." Ryan's smile dropped. "So you will always know where north is and you can find your way through life. You're a strong woman, Fern. But even strong, independent women need help to find their direction once in a while, especially after they're given a second chance at life."

He looked away. "Guess that sounds silly."

Impulsively, she threw her arms around him. "Thank you," she choked out, barely able to whisper the words. "It's a wonderful gift. Thank you."

No one had ever been as thoughtful to her as Ryan. The little compass meant more than two dozen roses.

He hugged her back and released her. "Now for the hard part. You ready?"

Fern nodded as he started the Jeep and pulled out of the parking space. After clipping the pocket compass onto the necklace with her GPS tracking pendant, she tucked it back inside her shirt. The two items nestled against her breasts, a reassuring reminder she was not alone.

Still, she couldn't help a shaky breath as Ryan turned off Main Street, following directions to the Oso Care Clinic on Sage Lane. Familiar streets and buildings flashed by, each seeming innocuous, but triggering her fears as if monsters lurked on Sage Lane. She forced herself to focus on Ryan's steady presence beside her.

When he found an empty parking space and pulled in front of the clinic, she could barely breathe. Her hands clenched together as her heart raced. The brick building stood like a sentinel to her nightmares. Pedestrians passed on the street, strangers to her, but perhaps not. Could she have known them? No one gave a second look to the Jeep. A young mother hustled her child inside the clinic.

Such an ordinary day, with ordinary people. But nothing was ordinary in Oso to her anymore.

She swallowed hard. *If I ever get my life back together—no, Ava said don't think that way, you* will *get your life back together—how can I ever return here? Work here without thinking it could happen again?*

A gentle palm covered hers, warm and strong. "Fern, if this is too much for you, we'll leave. Your welfare comes first. You come first."

You come first. Words of conviction. Ryan meant it. She glanced at him, and something in her tight chest eased. No one ever put her first. People had been clamoring for her to remember, remember! You have to do it so you can help other women. Even Ava, as supportive and wonderful as she was, hadn't been this convincing.

Not only had Ryan given up a precious day off to drive her here, but he remained with her through the process. He could have asked his sister or Jacob to make the trip, excused himself with the dozens of chores and errands awaiting him.

She turned in the seat. "Thank you. I—I needed to hear that."

Gently he rubbed his thumb over her trembling palm. "Fern, you need to lean on those wanting to help. You're not alone."

Alone had been all she knew. Alone meant no heartbreak when someone let her down, made promises they couldn't keep. Ryan was a good guy, but after this was all over, he would be gone.

Same as everyone else in her life.

Pulling away her hand, Fern swiveled back to the window, tracing a line on the glass as she stared at the clinic's sign. Familiar, and yet it was only a clinic, a building. Buildings couldn't hurt her. People could and they did, but she felt a grain of hope she could control this. From deep in her core she gathered all her strength and determination. Ryan risked his life every time he went to fight fires.

His courage and convictions fueled her. If he believed in her, then she could do this.

Closing her eyes, she willed the memories to bubble up from the depths.

"I closed that night," she said suddenly. "I asked to stay late to catch up on patient files. I had a key, so no one worried about me working after hours. We had an older man struggling with his insurance and finding the right coding would pay for his procedures, but it meant researching the diagnosis. By the time I left the office, it was dark.

"Billy... I can't remember his face. But the taller guy...a tattoo." Suddenly she could see the details as clearly as the sign on the medical building. "It was a compass on his outside wrist. I remember that because I was walking north and I scratched him, fighting him, and he raised his hand with the ink on it and, and, one of my last thoughts was funny how he was pointing north, like the compass was a real one."

Tears welled in her throat. "I wanted... I wanted so bad to stop them from taking me. I didn't understand, I wasn't anybody, I'm a nobody, and I fought, I really fought, you have to believe me. I tried so hard in the cabin to get free, and Billy hit me so hard I screamed, and it felt like I was going to die there."

As a sob rose up, she squeezed her eyes shut, trying to control the emotions, but it felt like plugging a dam with bubble gum. For months she'd resisted crying, afraid once she did she would never cease. Impossible to stop now. Fern began to cry, big ugly crying she hadn't done since she was younger and everything went to hell.

Two warm arms encircled her as Ryan pulled her against his chest. "It's okay, Fern. Let it out. I know you fought. You're here now, and no one is going to hurt you again."

For a moment she cried as he stroked her hair, murmuring assurances.

Finally she lifted her head. With the edge of a thumb, he wiped tears from her cheek.

"You can't promise I'll stay safe because you can't be there every minute, Ryan." Fern pulled away, scrubbed her eyes with an angry fist. "No one can make that promise."

"Fern, I can promise..." He heaved out a breath. "You're

right. I can't promise that. But I'll try, dammit. I'm not going anywhere."

After finding a tissue in her purse, she blew her nose and wiped her eyes. "I'm such a wreck. I hate crying. Makes me feel weak."

Ryan blinked. "You, weak? You're one of the strongest people I know, Fern. Crying is normal. Everyone cries. Sometimes it's the only way you can deal."

"I bet you never cry. You're a guy."

"Men have emotions, too."

Oh, she knew they did, but big, tough guys had emotions of anger, not tears. At least the tough guys she'd known.

"Men cry. We seldom admit it, though." He rubbed the back of his neck. "I've cried at times after a rescue went south. Do it after the job is over because you become useless if you do it while working. You shove down the emotions and deal with them later in private."

Fern blinked and studied him. "You cried? When?"

Hard to believe he actually cried. But Ryan was different. His compassion and honor were coupled with a wiry strength, both inside and out. He lacked the cruelty of men she'd known who only knew how to make others cry.

He blew out a breath. "Seriously? You need to know?"

"I'd like to know. Maybe I'd feel less of a sobbing mess if you told me."

The interior of the Jeep suddenly seemed like a cocoon, shielding them from the outside world. No one could overhear them, nor did those passing by on the street give them a second glance.

After exposing herself, she needed to know she was normal.

He gave her a grave look. "One time? Well, after you were brought to the hospital and I saw you unconscious for the first time. You were a mess, and they weren't certain you'd make it. They were sure you would die. I found a private room and cried there for a couple of minutes. You were so pretty and fragile lying in that bed, and it killed me inside to think of you taking your last breath, and I hadn't saved you in time."

Fern sucked in a shaky breath. "I didn't know."

Jaw tight, he looked out the window. "Yeah, well, now you do."

Another surprising revelation about him. She forgot about her own distress and looked at him, really looked at him. With his light brown hair cut short and burning blue eyes, he was cute, but Ryan went deeper than looks. Soul deep.

Why had their paths crossed? Oh sure, he'd saved her life, but any of the firefighters could have pulled her from the burning cabin. Yet he was the one who hauled her out of there.

He offered his home as a refuge.

Belle, her sponsor, once told her destiny could really screw you up, but things did happen for a reason. Fern had refused to believe her. The idea of fate mucking up her life was scarier than all the horrors she'd endured. Control was critical. She had to have some control over her life, over something, rather than believe she was a patsy to some mysterious and unknown force.

Yet now she wondered. Something connected her to Ryan, and the feelings she experienced were not gratitude or appreciation. They went deeper.

Scary as hell to think she was starting to care for him. When you cared for someone, anyone, they left. Or did worse.

It was her turn to comfort. Fern put a hand on his arm, resisting the temptation to remain aloof and detached. Maybe aloof was better in the past for avoiding pain, but he'd risked telling her his feelings and opening up to her.

Besides, aloof never got her anywhere. Maybe if she hadn't been so isolated, she could have avoided being kidnapped. *I'll never know.*

"Thanks for telling me. Knowing you cried makes me feel less alone, makes trying to remember those horrid days in the cabin less frightening. I don't feel so much like a freak."

His gaze turned intense as he swiveled toward her. "You're not a freak, Fern. Don't ever think like that. You're a strong woman who suffered a horrible experience thanks to bad guys who think they can do whatever they want and escape the law. Well, they can't. They'll get caught. The more you remember, the closer Jacob and the police will get to capturing them."

"A lot is riding on my messed-up memory. But what if it stays like Swiss cheese and all the pieces remain missing?"

Ryan touched her cheek again, a single caress of his thumb against her wet skin. "You'll remember. I have faith in you."

"You do?"

"Always have, from the moment I brought you out of the cabin. You're pretty, Fern, but you have a fighting spirit, more than anyone I've ever met."

The intimacy of the Jeep, their mingled breaths and this conversation made her heady. For a wild moment, Fern wanted to lean close, seal her mouth against his and kiss him, as if a single kiss could wipe away the past.

She actually leaned forward when he consulted his cell phone, the sweet moment gone, for now at least.

"Damn. So busy talking I forgot to call Jacob. I promised the moment you remembered anything, any other details, I'd call."

Ryan glanced at his cell, frowned. "I can't get a signal here. Soon as we get service, I'll call."

There went the intimacy and connection between them. Back to business. Fern's stomach tightened. Of course he said those things to assure her because the most important thing was recalling her memory to track down Billy and his accomplice.

She wasn't anything more than a witness to her own kidnapping. When all was settled and the men behind bars, she'd return to her fragmented routine. Ryan would return to his. They'd be free to move forward.

Except for the first time in months, she didn't want to move forward. Not if it meant Ryan would vanish from her life. If that was selfish, so be it.

Maybe it was time for a change—to be selfish—and put her own needs first.

Chapter Thirteen

"Where's Fern?"

Ava glanced up from her laptop at her worried mother. "Mom, what are you doing here?"

"Where's Fern?"

Last thing she needed on this hectic day at work, with all her patient concerns piling up in a mountain of paperwork, was her mother to sound like a parrot. Okay, she probably needed reassurance.

"Ryan's taking good care of her. They're together."

"That's why I'm here." Sherry planted herself in front of Ava's desk. "You're her psychologist. You're the one treating her, not your brother. You're the one responsible for her."

Ava sighed. "Mom..."

"I need to know where they are, Ava. I called Ryan's cell, and it went straight to voicemail."

This was more than simple motherly concern. Ava leaned forward. "What is it, Mom? What aren't you telling me?"

"I don't want to worry you..."

"You already are, so tell me."

Sherry stopped pacing. "I was at Jacob's house and overheard something, and Ryan needs to know, especially if Fern is with him."

"Heard what?" She wanted to be patient, but Sherry was stirring up all her emotions.

"I knew it was a mistake for your brother to take her into his home. He's such a good man, and this…"

"Mom! What is it?"

Sherry twisted her wedding ring. Now she knew how worried her mother was.

"She needs to come back to Dark Canyon right away. He—oh dear Lord."

Fear riddled her mother's voice. Ava went over to her, rubbed her shoulders. "Mom, slow down. Tell me what's wrong."

"Jacob… One of his team was investigating Fern's kidnapping and found information on the dark web. He tried to reach Ryan, but Ryan's cell went to voicemail. No one can reach him."

Ava felt her stomach tighten. "What kind of information?"

"It's terrible, so awful."

Patience was usually her strength. Not now. "Mom, what did he find out?"

"It—it was a website for trafficking women. Fern's photo was on it, and she…was listed for sale."

Break it down, bit by bit. "We knew she was kidnapped to be sold because of the sex trafficking ring they're investigating, Mom. This is why Fern had to be kept under guard and her location kept as secret as possible. It's why a plainclothes police officer is staked out in Ryan's neighborhood."

"It's not the same information," Sherry burst out. "Whoever put her photo up there added an update that she is missing and there's a reward for information leading to her return. They're planning to go after her again."

Not unexpected. Still alarming, but with Jacob on the case, Ava felt confident things were under control.

"They want her back, of course, because they counted

on making money from her. It's nothing really new, Mom. I know you're concerned..."

"They had a buyer for her. Jacob's team found out on the dark web. A man overseas was willing to pay a healthy six figures for her, maybe more. But there's a catch. The reward of cryptocurrency is good only if whoever is sheltering her is eradicated."

Blood drained from Sherry's face. "They want to make sure there are no witnesses. Ava, your brother is in danger. Whoever took Fern will kill him to get to her."

Now it was her turn to feel panic. "How much is the reward?"

"Fifty thousand dollars."

Her brother had a price on his head. Many unscrupulous, desperate people would risk killing Ryan to get Fern and the money.

"Jacob said the description of Fern added she can be singled out by a brand on her neck. A black dollar sign on the side of her neck."

Ava's blood ran cold. She'd seen this symbol on Fern's neck, but Fern thought she'd gotten the ink when she was younger. "A dollar sign is a typical tattoo of someone being sold in sex trafficking. Fern must not have remembered getting tattooed."

They needed to reach Ryan. Right now. Every minute counted.

"STILL NO SERVICE." Ryan frowned at his phone. "How did you live here with such crummy reception?"

Fern laughed. Such a normal question made her feel almost ordinary, as if this weren't the town where men had snatched her off the street to become someone's sex slave. "It's a dead zone. A lot of this area of Oso is, which is why I installed a cell phone booster at my apartment. I always had to use a landline when I was at work because the reception isn't great..."

Her voice trailed off. No cell service. No way to call for help.

Her gaze met his grim one. Ryan set his phone down. "They must have known and that was part of their strategy. No time to react, not even dial 911, not that you could even try because it's a dead area."

Dead area. Fern hugged herself. A memory surged. Blood pouring from her nose as she howled in pain, kicked again and again. Billy hovering over her with meaty fists, screaming at her.

"Teach you respect, you little bitch! Next time you do as I say!"

Shivering, she rocked back and forth. "I can't believe this happened to me. I've fought my whole life because no one believed I was worth fighting for. It wasn't until the Englehearts took me in as their foster child that I started to believe in people."

No words from Ryan. No hollow assurances, or murmured condolences. Sitting there, he listened. Really listened, unlike others who couldn't wait to talk after she finished. Few people had that skill set. Ava was one.

Her brother was another.

Fern stared at the building. Voicing this aloud felt almost as painful as those long-buried memories. "It took a long time for me to think I could be loved. Be worthy of love. The Englehearts helped me fight, restored my confidence. But when those...jerks abducted me, it set me back years. Like that children's board game, Chutes and Ladders? I had climbed a ladder to a boring but productive life, and slid down a chute as if I was that ten-year-old girl again."

Still nothing from Ryan. The silence grew too painful. He could think anything of her, including regret he'd offered to drive her here to jog a memory she didn't want returned because it was too painful.

She rubbed her arms. "Say something. Tell me something, anything."

The door to the clinic swung open, and a little girl, about five, perhaps, walked out with her mother. The girl's arm was in a sling.

Ryan gestured to the child, walking past them with her mother. "See that girl? Looks like she broke her arm. Can you imagine the trauma she suffered, getting hurt that badly?"

Unsure of where this was headed, she nodded.

"Kids are resilient. They bounce back. But no one tells you when you're young, or when you grow up, that your mind isn't hardwired to set aside the trauma. Set it aside and believe you deserve to have good things happen to you. That there are people in this world who believe in you and your potential."

His hand rested on her shoulder, giving it a gentle squeeze. "I believe in you, Fern. Several of us do as well. You deserve to have good things happen. Not wait for the next disaster."

She bit her lip. "I want to believe it. I can't move forward until I go back, and it's so scary to go back."

"You're not alone. I'm here with you. So is Ava. Cassidy. Sassy. Mark. Jacob. You have friends and people who want to help, not hurt you. We're with you every step of the way."

Much as she longed to believe him, Fern couldn't. She had to do this herself.

She pulled away. "You're great, Ryan. You have no idea how much I appreciate what you've done, what you're doing. I don't want to drag you into this anymore. You have your own life, your own issues."

"Hey." He gripped her hand in a gentle but firm touch. She knew he wasn't going to let go easily.

"I'm not going anywhere. You're most important now, Fern, and I make up my own mind about my life and my concerns. No one else does that for me." He shook his head. "I've been reading about what happens to victims of sex trafficking. How most victims are drugged with coke or meth or pills and so stoned they can barely say their name. They're farmed out as prostitutes, and if they dare to fight, they're beaten. These vicious men have made it as a business that makes more than 245 billion dollars a year globally from forced labor and sex trafficking. One woman…"

He released her hand and pointed at her. "One young, attractive woman like you can pull in probably around fifteen hundred a day, and that's a low estimate. It's likely they could make more than fifty grand in a month. One month."

The grim figures made her head swim. Fern gave a shaky laugh. "That sure beats my salary at the clinic. I had no idea I was worth that much money."

"It's not funny."

"I wasn't joking."

He looked so damn serious, ready to take on her kidnappers, the world, and she wanted to believe he could champion her. But she was no hero in a storybook.

Only a woman struggling to regain her life and memories, and hopefully, end this nightmare. Or at least prevent another innocent woman from entering it.

"Fern, we have to stop this. *You* have to stop this. I will do whatever I can to help you free yourself." He looked out the window. "Do you remember anything else? What about smells and sounds? You said the man who grabbed you smelled like pot. Anything else? Alcohol or cheap cologne? Maybe something they had to eat? Any sounds like ringtones or the van itself?"

Her temper simmered. She'd already done this with Jacob,

with Ava, and Ryan was the only person who didn't pester her about remembering.

"I thought you weren't going to pressure me on this trip. Thanks, Ryan. Thanks a lot. Let's just go back to Dark Canyon."

"Giving up so easily?"

"I don't give up!"

He gave her a pointed look. Fern's insides knotted. Defense mechanism, she knew, her mind wanting to protect her from trauma. Better to forget than remember.

"We can go back, Fern. If you truly want that, I'll turn the Jeep around and we'll head back now. Might be for the best anyway. Having you out here in the open, I can understand how terrifying it is for you."

She blew out a breath. "I'm not terrified, Ryan."

She knew what he was doing, trying reverse psychology on her. Fern squeezed her hands. "Fine. Keep an eye on the street in case someone wonders what the hell I'm doing, or in case a cop comes along and writes a ticket for loitering. As if cops were around in this crummy town."

For so long, she'd tamped down the anger. Anger led to bad things. Fern bit her lip, closed her eyes and concentrated on her breathing as Ava had taught her. Deep breath. Count to five. Another deep breath.

No cell service, not much of a signal here in Oso. Ringtones? What a joke. The town council talked about erecting a new cell tower near downtown after merchants argued for it, and the weekly paper teased the meeting with a headline about ringtones finally being heard on southern Main Street...

"Ringtones," she breathed, her eyes still closed. "They... The other one, not Billy... When I woke up in the cabin where they held me, his cell phone rang. The ringtone was this..." She frowned. "This high-pitched whistle, and it kept going on and on. I remember thinking it sounded so familiar, from a television show or a movie that was popular."

"That's good. When we get a signal, we can ID it from YouTube. Unless you can imitate it."

Pursing her lips, she blew out a shaky rendition of the ringtone.

"Damn, I know that...that movie, I've seen it a few times. I know! It's from a movie I've seen. A really violent one."

What irony. A movie with violence, just as Fern had experienced violence. The bastards had kidnapped Fern and left her to starve and then burn to death in the little shack.

Quivering, she clenched her fists. "Every time I heard that ringtone, I wanted to scream. But I knew no one would hear me. I heard it recently, and it made me break out into a sweat. I didn't even know why!"

"Now you do."

She wanted to run. Hide. Scream out her frustrations. Her stomach roiled. This was wrong, all wrong, going back to her hometown. After all the work trying to control her reactions to what happened to her, she slid backward.

This isn't about me. I have to remember so no other woman gets hurt.

Fern drew in another shaky breath, the breakfast she'd recently consumed turning sour in her stomach.

"Let's drive the way I was walking home that night. It could trigger another memory. Drive slowly."

Ryan glanced at her as he started the Jeep. "I'm proud of you, Fern."

Proud. She didn't want pride. Nor did she want to be dependent on him. Even if she had feelings about Ryan, she couldn't stay with him for long. It could never work out. This was simply an arrangement of convenience for her, a safe place to stay for now.

Good old self-reliant Fern, too proud to admit you need anyone. Even now when you really do need Ryan.

Absently she rubbed her neck. Remembered how it stung when she got the ink, but the memory of when she got it remained hazy.

Something kept nagging at her. She wasn't merely walking home from work that night, but headed to another destination. But where? Businesses passed by, all familiar and yet strange. A pharmacy and small grocery store weren't far from her apartment as Ryan turned to head down her street.

On the corner was the Irish pub, the restaurant and bar where she'd scheduled a date with that cute pharmacy rep. Ryan barely passed it when she felt her stomach roil. "Ryan, pull over…please, now!"

Barely had he stopped when she flung open the door. Leaning out, she vomited all the contents of her stomach.

She felt two gentle hands pull her hair out of her face and then rub her back. When she finally finished, she took the tissues he handed her and wiped her mouth.

Ryan fished out a bottle of water from the cooler in the back and uncapped it. She drank, the bottle shaking in her hands.

"I hate this." Fern set the water into a cup holder. "I hate not being in control of my life, my memories. Something's at the edge of my memory, and I know it's important and yet I can't remember it. I'm so frustrated with myself!"

"You know what we need right now? I know exactly what will make you feel better."

Fern shut the door. "Please don't tell me another greasy meal."

"Fun. Good, old-fashioned fun. The kind where you don't have to think, only experience."

She rubbed her throbbing head. "Please don't tell me your

kind of fun involves anything requiring exercise or sudden movement. Did I ever tell you I get seasick?"

"We're miles from the sea, Fern."

"Doesn't matter. I can get seasick in a bathtub."

Ryan grinned. "No worries. Trust me, you'll enjoy this."

"That's what you said about the eggs and bacon."

"Ever been zip-lining?"

Moaning, she clutched her stomach. "That's your idea of fun, sailing over a thin line across a steep canyon? No. Big *N*. Big *O*."

"I'm kidding. Nothing risky. We could walk along the Animas River Trail, or go for a long ride on the Durango Silverton steam train—nah, scratch that, that's an overnight stay and a long train ride… Go shopping downtown or hiking in the canyons…"

Silent, she studied her hands. All normal activities for most people, fun things a couple would plan for a day trip. Plenty of people milling around, people who might recognize her.

People like her kidnappers. Automatically she tugged at the black wig covering her hair. It itched.

It was a barrier between herself and the world. A mask to hide behind, yet it provided little refuge. Feeling like she was on autopilot, Fern found herself nodding to all Ryan's suggestions.

No reason to think she wasn't safe. Surely he wouldn't lead her into dangerous territory.

"We'll skip lunch and have an early dinner. There's a bluegrass band playing—" he checked his phone "—at a popular restaurant downtown. The Bluegrass Meltdown isn't for another week, but this restaurant is hosting a few of the lesser known groups lined up for the festival. They also have lighter meals, like soup, that will go down easier than your breakfast did."

His brow furrowed. "Although they are more of a bar than a restaurant. Are you okay with eating in a bar?"

The question startled her a moment. Then she smiled. Few men would be so considerate. Few men knew she was a recovering alcoholic.

"As long as they have iced tea or soda water, I'm good."

Fern looked out the window at the quiet street housing her apartment complex. Such a deceptive scene, with a few shade trees along the sidewalk, and sturdy brick buildings. A good place to call home, with a playground close by. She could see a child swinging now, pushed by a young woman.

Except for those seeing the police work on the street after she'd been discovered, no one would suspect it had been a crime scene where she had been abducted and her life forever changed.

She rubbed the side of her neck and the tattoo. "Funny how the first time I planned to go to a bar in years, on a date, I get kidnapped. It was almost like fate intervening, preventing me from temptation…"

Fern stared out the window, put up a hand as Ryan started to speak. "The bar, the Irish bar, where I was supposed to meet Walter, the salesman I met at the doctor's office. I remember it like it was yesterday. My car had a flat so I walked home from work, but no, I was walking to the bar to meet Walter and listen to this amazing Celtic band. I figured the bar was a safe place to get to know him. And then…they got me."

Ryan's blue eyes widened. "What can you tell me about Walter. Tell me everything you remember." His voice was low and urgent.

This she did remember, seeing his handsome face as if he'd planted himself in front of her. Fern described Walter Landers, down to the blue-and-white-striped tie he'd worn and his gap-toothed smile that she'd found charming.

"Tell me everything you said to him. How well did he know you?"

"We got to talking in the office. Went for coffee together on my break at the café next door. Walter started talking about how he was adopted after being in the foster system for a few years. He was trying to track down his birth mother, one reason he was at the clinic because of a rare medical condition he had. That's one reason I connected with him."

His jaw tightened. "Let me guess. You told him you understood because you grew up in the foster system."

"Yes. He knew I was alone...had few friends, few people to check on me."

"Damn." Ryan exhaled a breath.

Insight struck her. "Ryan, do you think I was set up? It's too much of a coincidence that he asked me to meet him at the pub the same night they kidnapped me."

"I had the same thought," he said grimly.

Ryan glanced at his cell phone. "Signal's still crap. I'll text Jacob."

He fired off a text. Frowned. "It didn't go through. Let's visit this pub as long as we're here, and I can ask the manager about Walter Landers. If he lives in town, if he's ever been there before."

Touching her wig, she hesitated. No telling how long it would take for Jacob to get here to officially interview the manager. Risky to do this. Fern looked at Ryan. Sure, capable and strong. He would never let anything bad happen to her.

Not if he could help it.

"Okay," she said in a small voice.

Minutes later, he pulled into the parking lot of the Irish bar. A Closed sign hung in the window. Relieved, she looked at her cell phone.

"I think they don't open until late afternoon. Maybe we

should leave this to Jacob. I'm having second thoughts about getting out of the car. Someone might recognize me. Even with the wig and sunglasses."

Ryan's fingers tightened on the steering wheel. "I'm such an ass. I was so pumped up about following a lead I never considered how you felt about this. Sorry."

"Don't apologize. Let's go." She looked around. "I'd love to leave this town. Funny how it once felt like home, but no longer does."

He got it. "Want me to take the top of the Jeep off?"

The joy she felt lifted all her previous anxiety. Riding with the top down with a handsome guy. Some women might dismiss it as trivial.

Ryan couldn't have given her a better gift today.

After he put the top into a box in the back seat, Fern pulled off her wig and tucked it into the glove box. "Don't want it to go flying out the window. Someone might see it and think I lost my head. Ha."

He grinned. "More than likely an animal would use it for a nest."

He pulled out of the parking lot. "Time for some relaxation. Durango, here we come."

How long had it been since she'd had a fun outing? Since she'd been outside for a long drive through the twisting curves and canyons leading into Colorado? Fern had to admit she'd been obsessed with work and not her social life. Work was safe and reliable.

Work didn't dump you, or use you the way men could.

Not going to think about that now. I need to move forward. Enjoy the day, while this lasts.

After a while they were headed on 491 going south. "I have to warn you, this is a boring drive."

"As long as the company isn't boring, I'm good."

Wind whipped her hair. She fished in her purse and found

a couple of hair ties and quickly pulled it back, braiding it. Now she could relax.

After a while the scrub, trees and wide open spaces proved soothing.

A few trucks rumbled past them, headed north. Fern's eyes began to close. They opened as Ryan snapped on the radio, singing along to the music he connected through Bluetooth.

A smile touched her mouth. "You have a terrible voice. Remind me to never do karaoke with you."

"Hey, I resent that remark." He puffed out his chest. "I'm in high demand. People pay for my singing."

"You mean pay to stop you from singing." Fern grinned at his scowl. "You know I'm kidding."

He heaved an exaggerated sigh. "And here I thought I could quit my day job."

"Sorry to disappoint."

Fern giggled at his downturned expression. "If you want to change careers, I'll support your decision. Even if it's wrong."

"Well, fine, I'll stick to singing in the car and the road."

"Lucky me," she teased.

The impish glance he gave her quickened her blood. "Be warned. I also sing in the shower."

An image of Ryan in the shower, soaping his body as he sang off tune came to mind. A heated blush ignited her cheeks. She stared out the window to hide it. Last thing she wanted was for her roommate to realize she fantasized about him being naked.

This was a platonic relationship. Ryan had a good heart, and she didn't want impose on him or make him feel uncomfortable.

They stopped at a roadside diner called Bufords. Fern raised her eyebrows as he pulled into the parking lot.

"Coffee stop," he explained. "Thought you'd like a soda as well, maybe a ginger ale, to quell your stomach."

So considerate. Fern's stomach tightened as she considered going into a crowded restaurant, but the thought of a refreshing soda tempted her.

"Soda's good. I'll leave the greasy burgers to you."

Smells of frying hamburgers and something Italian, maybe spaghetti, made her nostrils twitch. Though it was barely lunchtime, the wood tables were crowded with diners. Most of them were men. Judging from the big rigs parked in the lot, truckers as well. Maybe some locals.

Clean and bright, the diner had large windows overlooking the highway and dusty parking lot. A blackboard announced the day's breakfast and lunch specials. In the corner near a window sat a lone pinball machine, almost an afterthought.

The pinball machine looked vintage, perhaps from the 1980s. Fern forgot her anxiety. Oh wow, she hadn't played in months. But you never forgot your first love.

As they sat at a table close to the machine, everyone stared at them. Fern squirmed, wondering if this was a good idea. The place was probably local and everyone knew everyone and strangers...

A man entering the café lumbered over to their table. Tall and intimidating, he had a John Deere cap on his head, gray beard stubble shadowing his face.

"You a union man?" the man rumbled.

Oh dear. Fern's heart raced. She'd never been in a bar fight. Maybe they should leave.

Ryan's expression tightened. "Yeah. Union. I'm a firefighter."

The big man nodded. "Knew it. I'm Norm. Teamsters local 455. My brother is a firefighter, too. Unions always welcome here. Thanks for your service, brother."

As they shook hands, Ryan frowned. "How did you know I was union?"

"Sticker on your Jeep. Welcome to our little roadside stop."

"Thanks, bro." Ryan watched him walk off to the counter. The other diners nodded and returned attention to their meals. "Guess my dad put it there. Or my mom, more likely. She's prouder of me than Dad is, that's for sure."

Tension eased as the waitress came over, took their order. Fern asked for ginger ale, while he ordered a hamburger, fries and an iced tea.

"I envy how you put away so many calories," she told him.

"Don't. I have to work out later to make up for today." He patted his flat stomach.

"I look at a French fry and gain ten pounds."

"You don't need to lose weight."

Compliments made her uncomfortable. So did attention. She glanced at the pinball machine and brightened.

"Hey, I think it works. Do you have any change?"

Ryan fished out several quarters. "Go for it. Do you know how to play?"

The grin she shot him hid her secrets. *Oh yeah, I play.*

She plugged in the money, and the machine lit up, noisy and bright. She began to play, enthralled by this machine. Vintage eighties. The visuals were neon, sharp, and the layout of the machine doomed anyone who dared to stop and think about the next move.

He came over to watch.

"Timing is critical," Fern said as she maneuvered the right flipper to make a shot. "This machine is dope. So eighties and retro."

"It looks like one of my nightmares," he told her.

She laughed, loving this, the noise and the music energizing her. The futuristic music and electronic robotic voice sounded like old sci-fi movies. Flashing lights added to the thrill of play.

Fern crowed with delight as she juggled the flippers on the pinball machine. "I'm an expert. Stand back and pay homage."

By now a crowd gathered around, watching and cheering her on. Giddy with power and her success, she focused on the metal ball, loving the sharp ping of the bells, the points racking up. So much fun. She hadn't experienced this in months.

Ryan's wide grin, the cheers he added, emboldened her. Sure, a lot of bad things had happened to her and some days she fought her way out of the darkness, but having him around shone a beam of hope into her life.

For a moment, she lost focus and the ball slipped between the flippers, vanishing into the machine.

Cries of disappointment echoed. "Hey, you still got the highest score in months," one man told her.

"No one's played this in months," their waitress deadpanned.

She high-fived several guys congratulating her. A heady sense of triumph chased away all her previous trepidation. This place was remote and no one knew her. No history here or bad men lying in wait.

Slipping back into her chair, she drank heavily of the soda he'd ordered for her. Her stomach rumbled.

"I'm hungry. Say, can I get a BLT on rye?" she asked the waitress.

When the woman walked off, Ryan shook his head. "Less than an hour ago you were throwing up and now you want a BLT? You sure?"

"Yeah." She pushed back a lock of hair behind her ear. "It's like I got a second wind. Or my anxiety is gone. Funny, but this is the best place you could have taken me."

"If I'd known that you like pinball, I'd have taken you to

the arcade in Dark Canyon. Used to hang out there growing up."

She beamed. "Something to look forward to."

He tilted his head. "You're a funny thing."

Somehow the remark didn't sound insulting, but rather like a compliment.

"I love playing. Pinball is hands-on, interactive and seems more challenging than video games, for me, at least. Pinball was one of the few things I could count on after my mom left me. You hit certain targets and it creates different fun reactions, depending on the machine. The bells and pings—it's noisy and challenging."

The smile he offered warmed her from the inside out. "Most of the women I've met enjoy shopping or hiking or competitive sports. They're always trying to act and look sophisticated. I've never met anyone as unpretentious as you, Fern. You're different. Refreshing."

Heat crept up from her neck to her cheeks. Ducking her head, she pretended absorption in her soda. "Maybe you haven't been hanging with the right women, Ryan."

"You have a point. Do you know how boring it is to watch someone shop for jeans and try on ten pairs? Enough time to play several vid games on my phone."

The waitress brought over their food. Fern dug into her sandwich with delight. Today turned out to be a great day, maybe the best she'd had in months.

Not because of the pinball, or even getting out of the house. It was all Ryan. She'd felt wrapped in wool, almost suffocated with concern and people worried about her memory and keeping her safe.

His company made her feel alive again.

Barely had he taken two bites of his burger when he groaned. "All this and I forgot to check my phone. Have to have a signal now."

Ryan pulled out his cell. A sheepish look came over him. "Ten missed calls! I turned down the ringer."

As he fiddled with the controls, his phone rang again. "It's Jacob," he told Fern.

"Hey, Jacob, sorry, man, I couldn't get a signal until we got to this café in Lewiston... Wait. What? What?"

Brow furrowing, he looked out the window. She had a sinking feeling again. All the previous joy evaporated like snow under a hot sun.

Ryan stood up and pulled several bills from his wallet. Cradling the phone to his shoulder, he mouthed to Fern, "Take the sandwich. We're leaving."

"I need a box," she began.

"No time."

Fern wrapped the sandwich in a napkin. He herded her to the door as their waitress started toward them. "Money for the check and your tip's on the table," he called out.

"Hey, you don't know how much you owe!" the woman called back.

Ignoring the woman, Ryan hustled her out into the parking lot. When they climbed back into the vehicle, he looked even more grim. "Check and see if anyone is following us."

Fern twisted backward. No traffic in sight. He was headed northeast again, toward Dark Canyon.

"Ryan, talk to me. What happened? Why are we going back?"

Still on the phone with Jacob, he ignored her. Ryan rattled off all the information they'd discovered today, including her description of the ringtone.

They'd been traveling fast for a few miles when he finally hung up. Ryan's expression hardened. Gone was the guy who'd smiled and made her laugh.

He was all business.

"My mom, sister and Jacob have all tried to reach me. There's new information Jacob discovered. It's bad."

With a sinking feeling, she braced herself. "Tell me. Shielding me from it won't help. I need to know."

He swore quietly as he glanced in the mirror. "Where the hell did that come from?"

Out of the corner of her eye, she saw a vehicle in the side mirror. Fern's heart raced. "Ryan, that blue van…"

Barely had the words left her mouth when they were rammed from behind.

Chapter Fourteen

Palms tight on the steering wheel, Ryan focused on driving. He depressed the gas pedal to the floor, but the Jeep was an older model. Speedometer barely registered seventy.

Bam! Hit again from behind, he jerked forward. No one else on the road. If this kept up, they were toast. His mind sped through options. Fern, bless her, wasn't hysterical, but sat calmly, her eyes wide.

"Ryan, what's going on?"

Cursing again, he tried to speed up. "Jacob's team found preliminary info on the dark web. They have to verify it, but there's a reward of fifty thousand dollars—and the reward is also to kill whoever is sheltering you. The men who took you don't want witnesses."

Fern paled. She took out her cell phone and twisted around, taking photos of the rearview mirror.

Her voice quavered. "If that's them, Ryan, and I think it is, stop and let me out. Let them take me. Or try. I won't go down without a fight. You can call for help."

What? Grimacing, he jerked the wheel to one side as the van tried to hit them again. "I'm not letting you out, Fern. Over my dead body."

"Exactly. You're in danger. I won't see you hurt over this. Over me."

Willing to sacrifice herself to save him. Damn. His admiration, and fear for her, doubled.

He looked at the rearview mirror. "I've got to lose these assholes. Or slow them down until we can reach a police station."

No traffic on this road, other than them. Two cars passed them and the van slowed down. Obviously the men in the van didn't want any Good Samaritans following or reporting to the cops what they tried to do.

Then it was open road, no traffic and the van sped up, banging into them once more.

"We have to do something." Fern looked around. "Can we flatten their tires?"

Great idea. "My dad's toolbox is in the back seat. See what's in there."

She unbuckled her seat belt and climbed into the back seat, rummaging in the toolbox. "Ah, got it. Thank the good Lord your dad never cleaned out his stuff."

She uncapped the bottle of screws and unzipped the back window. "Let me know when."

Ryan depressed the gas pedal, putting a little distance between themselves and the pursuing van. "Now!"

Out went the screws onto the roadway. The van swerved to avoid them and sped up.

Fern bit her lip. "I'm sorry. I thought it would work."

He looked at her. "I'm sorry I brought you into this mess. I wasn't thinking. And your wig... You forgot to put it on. They may have recognized you in the café."

He twisted the wheel, going into the opposite lane to avoid the van slamming into them again.

"It's my fault. I got careless. I was enjoying being out with you so much I forgot I can't be like anyone else. Ryan, I never wanted to drag you into this, into danger! Please, let me out and whatever happens, happens."

Fierce anger filled him. Dammit, it wasn't right. Fern was a lovely woman with a selfless attitude. Simply because she'd been alone and lacked family, they had targeted her.

He reached over and quickly squeezed her hand. "You are not alone."

Suddenly they heard the deafening sound of a truck horn. Ryan glanced in his mirror. "We've got more company."

To his amazement, the tractor trailer sped up and rammed the van from behind. The van jerked to the right and ran off the road.

The truck behind them sped up. Sweat poured down his back. Now what? Did Fern's kidnappers work in tandem with this guy, too?

A deafening horn sounded behind him. Fern twisted in her seat. "He's motioning for you to keep going."

After a few miles, Fern watching the truck driver the entire time, she told him to pull over at the next intersection. Ryan did, guiding the Jeep to the dirt road. He parked, but left the engine running. Wary, he glanced in his rearview mirror.

"If this guy is trouble, stay buckled up, just in case."

But he recognized the man running toward them. He recognized the green John Deere cap. Norm, the trucker from the café. Still, he remained ready to run if necessary.

"Hey. It's okay. I called for help," Norm said, holding up his hands. "I'm one of the good guys. We saw you bolt from the café, and then I saw that blue van. Same son of a bitch tried to run my friend off the road, so I climbed into my rig to see what was going on. And then he banged into you and I figured you needed help."

Ryan climbed out of the Jeep, along with Fern. He shook Norm's hand. "Thanks, man. I was afraid we'd end up in a pile of crushed metal."

No reason to explain to this guy, helpful as he'd been, what the real situation was.

But Norm gave him a long look. "When I saw what that van was doing, I got the guy's plates. Called my cousin—he's a deputy in Grand Junction. Had him run the plates, and he told me the van is stolen."

Ryan remained silent. Norm looked at Fern, who kept staring at the ground.

"Not sure what's going on—that's your business. But the way you two tore out of the café, leaving a fifty-dollar tip for Mary, we knew there was trouble. And a brother always helps out another brother in trouble, so I followed you."

"Thank you," Fern whispered.

"They're long gone by now. Probably ditched the van for another stolen vehicle. But at least you're safe."

Understatement.

"There should be a sheriff's deputy here soon," Norm told him.

Ryan looked at Fern, pale and trembling. Talking to a strange police officer was not on the agenda. Trust ran low, especially now that he knew a price was on his head.

"We can't stick around. Have to get back. I need to make a call but..." He palmed his cell phone. "No signal."

"I've got a sat phone. Wife insisted on paying for it for these long hauls across the desert. She always worries." Norm went into the cab of his truck and came out with the phone.

Ryan dialed Jacob and explained the situation.

"If your vehicle isn't disabled, drive to..." Jacob named a gas station on the road back to Dark Canyon. "I'll be there, waiting for you."

After he handed back the sat phone, Fern suddenly disentangled herself from Ryan and ran to Norm, hugging him.

"Thank you. Thank you for reminding me there are good people in this world."

The trucker looked embarrassed, and pleased. "Thanks. It's nothing. We have to look out for each other these days. You guys sure you don't need anything? How's your wheels? That guy sure wanted to run you off the road."

He walked to the back of the Jeep with Ryan, who winced at the dents the van had made. Not going to be easy to explain to his father how his favorite weekend vehicle needed repairs.

"Thank the Lord the spare tire absorbed a lot of those blows." Ryan ran a hand over the tire. "I can drive it, and that's all that matters now. We have to leave."

"I'll wait here for the deputy, tell him what happened." Norm gave him a long look. "I'll tell him it was a case of road rage that popped up and to look out for the van. You had a lady in the car to look after and couldn't stick around because you had to get back home in a hurry. The deputy will probably put out a be on the lookout for the van, and every trucker on the road will watch out for those guys."

Relief filled him. Norm wasn't pressing for details Ryan didn't want to give. "Thanks, man."

After shaking hands again with Norm, he climbed back into the Jeep with Fern. She waved at Norm as they got back on the road again.

WHEN THEY REACHED the gas station near Dark Canyon, Jacob was in the parking lot, leaning against his black Chevy SUV. He wasn't alone. Officer Chayton Benally, the Navajo Nation policeman investigating her case, was there as well. She noticed the tribal police vehicle parked next to the black SUV.

With a grim look, both men came toward them as Ryan switched off the ignition.

She liked Chay. Engaged to Ava, he was brusque at times, but she'd glimpsed his kind heart and heard from Ava how tender he was with the baby they were adopting.

Today he wasn't kind. Chay scowled at them both.

"What were you thinking, going off like that in public where anyone could see you?"

He directed the question at her, but stared at Ryan.

"Fern was restless. She needed to get out of the house, and we stopped at Oso to try to trigger her memory," he told Chay.

Jacob was equally grim. "Fern could have been taken again. You could have been killed, cuz."

Ryan spread out his hands. "How was I supposed to know about all this? We couldn't get a signal on our cell phones."

"Exactly," Chay broke in. "There's many areas of the desert with dead areas. In an emergency, you're stuck."

"And we would call this an emergency," Jacob added. "Leave the investigating to us. You know better, Ryan."

Fern couldn't take this anymore. "Stop blaming Ryan. I'm the one who insisted on leaving. Because of Ryan taking me to Oso, I was able to recall some memories that will aid in your investigation."

Both officers glanced at each other.

"It was too risky." Jacob seemed calmer.

"The risk is already taken," Ryan shot back. "Now, do you want to know what we found out?"

"You tell them, Ryan. Give them my cell phone. I took photos of the van from the side mirror. I need to use the bathroom." Right now she felt like she was going to hurl once more. No amount of sketching, making lists or triangles would soothe her fractured nerves.

"I'll go with you. With what happened, you shouldn't be alone," Chay told her.

Fern sighed. "All right."

Leaving Ryan to tell his cousin Jacob what they'd learned, she trudged toward the gas station entrance. The restrooms were in back. Chay nodded at her.

"I'll be right here in the hallway."

Inside, she waited for the nausea to abide or resolve. Fern gripped the sides of the sink, staring into the dusty mirror. Pale, oh so pale, the face staring back at her. But she did it. She'd returned to Oso and, with Ryan's patient help, recalled important details of her abduction.

The time spent on the pinball machine seemed like years ago. She ran water into the sink, splashed her face and dried it with a paper towel.

By the time she emerged, the nausea was under control. So was she.

Chay escorted her out into the convenience store. "Need any food? Chips? Snacks? Water? Soda?"

"A ginger ale would be great." Thoughts of the uneaten BLT left in the Jeep sent her stomach roiling all over again.

The soda he bought her felt fantastic on her parched tongue. When they rejoined Jacob and Ryan outside, she felt somewhat normal again.

Bright sunshine and a cloudless sky greeted them. Such a gorgeous day, the kind you anticipated going for a long hike or even a simple walk along a scenic river like the Animas in Durango.

Not being chased down by evil men who wanted to take her prisoner and kill Ryan. The last thought almost made the nausea return.

Chay put a gentle hand on her shoulder. The contact settled her a little as she took a deep breath and looked at Jacob.

"Do you need anything from me?" she asked him.

"Ryan told us everything. I need you, and him, to be safe and stay home. Unfortunately the photos you took are blurry. No way to run a facial recognition." Jacob handed back her cell phone. "But the information he provided from your recalled memories helps. We'll check out this Walter Landers."

"He was short, about five feet, six inches, with sandy hair thinning in front, a little scar here." She pointed to her chin. "Gap-toothed in front, and he liked expensive suits. Italian silk, I believe. Dark colors. Oh, and he wore lifts in his shoes because one day he came in without them and was about my height."

As the men stared at her, she added, "He also liked wearing socks with golf clubs on them. So I believe he enjoyed playing golf."

Chay shook his head. "That's a tremendous help, Fern. Great description. I'll get going on this."

With a nod, he climbed into his patrol vehicle.

Fidgeting, Ryan looked impatient to be off. She understood. After the frantic rush on the road to escape the van running them off, nowhere on the road seemed safe. Only the walls of his house provided any security.

With a price on his head, though, was his home truly safe? What kind of desperation forced these men into offering to kill a man in order to get Fern back into their clutches?

Chapter Fifteen

The good news was the information Jacob's team discovered on the dark web was incorrect. The reward offer had been vague, and after following up, Jacob's team discovered it was a dead end.

His mother, as usual, had taken everything to the extreme and thought Ryan truly had a price on his head. She'd never been a helicopter parent, but Sherry could turn overprotective if she thought one of her children was endangered.

The other good news was details Fern provided to the police could prove useful in tracking them down, including the cell phone ringtone and a description of Walter.

The bad news was the men were actively searching for Fern. Jacob had grimly informed him the van trying to ram them off the road fit the description of the same one used to abduct Fern.

The sheriff's deputies found it by the roadside, abandoned, and took it into evidence. But it looked stripped down, and they doubted they'd find anything useful, such as fingerprints or DNA evidence.

He wasn't happy about leaving Fern to go to work, so the next day he used his considerable sick time to take a day off.

Ryan began questioning his life choices. Not for the first

time, he wondered if he should have agreed to quit the fire department and follow his dad into business.

Safer, for sure. More money. Oh yeah. No adrenaline rush like he had now. No saving lives. At least his family would quit worrying about him.

Fern came into the living room, where he was reading an online article about new hazmat equipment.

"Cassidy Garner texted me and would like to see how I'm doing. Is it okay if she visits?"

Since the whole world probably knows where you live now, why not? But he clamped down that thought and offered a brief smile. "Sure. Does she want to have lunch here?"

"I don't think so. A quick visit."

Sure, a quick visit. Cassidy, Fern's nurse at the hospital, probably worried about her former patient, since Ryan had taken her out on a drive that could have sent her back to the hospital.

Or worse, to the morgue.

He set aside his tablet. "What's wrong?"

Oh, he knew her expressions by now. Fern was an open book when it came to showing her feelings, much as she tried to hide it.

"I spent a little time with Google, finding out what you do for a living, Ryan." Fern perched on the edge of a chair. "I don't know anything about fighting fires. So I thought I'd learn a little. I thought maybe it was dying from a fire or smoke inhalation, but it seems cancer is a biggie. I mean, who would think? But you come into contact with all those chemicals in smoke, and maybe even asbestos, and your chances of contracting cancer are significantly higher than most people."

Ryan said nothing, but he watched her, wondering where this was going.

"You keep saying you're just a guy doing his job. That's

where you're wrong. You and the other guys are heroes, every time you rush off to fight another fire and put your lives on the line.

"But I have to be honest, Ryan. I'm starting to get feelings for you. You're incredible, and I owe you so much."

"You don't owe me anything." Damn, he didn't want her feeling as if he ran a bed-and-breakfast.

"Yet I can't help worry about you every time you go to work."

"Okay."

You don't want to get involved with a guy like me who may never come home after a shift. Because you've had enough men in your life who never came home.

She glanced down at her hands, as if unable to voice her thoughts. Finally she looked at him.

"I was only being honest."

"I get it. No worries." He'd heard plenty of the same from his last girlfriend, Kim March. She broke up with him when he almost bought it during a three-alarm fire at a local warehouse. He'd been on the stairs, starting upward, when he got blown down. Fortunately the hose crew doused him and got him out.

But Kim freaked out and declared she couldn't deal with the possibility of losing him. He'd appreciated it and tried to talk to her, but her mind was made up.

A couple of weeks later, he discovered she was more concerned about not having a date the night he worked that fire. There'd been an art gallery showing with many high-profile people there, and Kim was irritated he had to work and couldn't escort her.

Ryan knew he was better off alone.

Maybe Fern felt the same way.

He returned to his reading, and Fern vanished down the hallway, probably to work on her laptop.

An hour later, Cassidy showed up. With her blue eyes, strawberry blonde hair cut into a shag, and friendly air, she was attractive. Nice as well, but he wasn't in the mood to make friends.

She and Fern hugged.

"I'll be in my office, let you two catch up," he told them.

Before Fern started to protest, he went down the hall.

Seemed like only a short time later when Cassidy popped her head into his office. "I wanted to let you know I'm leaving. Fern seems better."

Better? He could have killed her. "I guess."

"She does. In the hospital, she was isolated, and though her body healed, her spirit was low." Her smile dropped. "You okay, Ryan?"

"I'll be fine. Thanks for checking on her."

"Don't be hard on yourself, Ryan, for taking her out of the house. She needed it. Fern is tougher than everyone realizes. And she seems happy here," she said gently.

"I know how tough she is. But tough doesn't count when there's a killer out there and her kidnappers still running loose." He stopped short from saying, *and they almost got her.*

Thanks to his recklessness in thinking everything was cool, it was like an ordinary day out with a pretty woman. Not a kidnapping victim who had to disguise her appearance.

A victim who was recognized. That itself made him wonder.

How did they find Fern? Was he followed from Oso? Or worse, Dark Canyon itself?

With a scrutinizing look, she nodded and then left. He went into the kitchen to find Fern making sandwiches. "Turkey on whole wheat sound good?"

"Not really hungry," he admitted.

Fern gave him almost the same look as Cassidy. "You

have to eat, Ryan. Please, don't blame yourself for what happened yesterday."

Was there anyone else to blame? But to keep the peace and make her happy, he helped himself to a turkey sandwich, managing to eat most of it and kill a bottle of water as well. Much as he longed for a beer, he hadn't kept any alcohol in the house because of Fern.

His desire for a cold brew mattered less than her comfort.

Fern pointed to the stairs. "I promised Cassidy I'd keep up with my exercises. I'll be downstairs, working out."

Nodding, Ryan began to clean up. His cell dinged a message. Jacob, with an update.

He called Jacob, and the news was mixed. The kidnappers had not followed him from the house. The plainclothes police officer monitoring the house ensured they were safe there.

Only some guys at the fire station, like Bob, along with Cassidy and Ryan's family knew where she stayed.

He wondered about that. "What if someone ran the plates on the Jeep? Is that how we were found?"

"More likely someone was tracking your truck because they had the license plate and saw you pull into your parents' driveway and then drive off in the Jeep. That's more probable. Once they had the Jeep's license, it was a matter of following you to Oso and the roadside diner," Jacob told him.

The idea of someone watching him at all times gave him the creeps. Worse, the kidnappers knew where Fern now lived. Her safety came first.

"Be cautious, Ryan. Don't trust anyone except family."

He hung up, deeply disturbed. Then he texted Mark, asking his cousin to come over and check on the security system.

Glad for the reprieve from his dark thoughts, Ryan met him outside a few minutes later.

Ryan clapped his cousin on the shoulder. "Come on in. If

you're hungry, Fern made sandwiches and there's extra. No beer, but plenty of iced tea and water and even lemonade."

"Iced tea sounds great." Mark checked the cameras out front, and then they went inside. Mark made sure to lock the door.

After checking over the interior cameras upstairs and the DVR system, Mark seemed reassured. "Everything okay with the system?"

"System is fine. I'm the one who needs fixing."

"Talk to me."

"Let's go outside. Fern's downstairs, doing her PT. You just missed Cassidy. She came over to see how Fern's doing with her workouts."

His cousin's expression tightened. Ryan glanced at him. "You used to date Cassidy."

Saying nothing, Mark followed him outside, onto the patio. Ryan got it. A man had a personal life, and judging from his cousin's stiffness, Cassidy was real personal.

They sat at the patio table with two tall glasses of iced tea. A chill hung in the air, the weather at the fickle point of trying to decide to usher in spring or announcing winter still hung around, get used to it.

He updated Mark on the sitch with his truck being tailed, and the Jeep. "I'm thinking of renting a car."

"Might be a good idea, until they catch whoever did this."

Mark sipped his tea. "I had a feeling everything wasn't right with you. By the way, everyone in the family knows about your joy ride with Fern."

Damn. "Word travels fast."

"It's family." Mark shrugged. "They worry all the time."

Oh yeah, he knew it. "Speaking of family, I heard your dad is dating Susan Baylor. You okay with that?"

"I'm okay. Even if he married again, yeah. Dad deserves

to be happy. Hope her pain in the butt ex won't be an issue, but he could."

"In what way?"

"Ken Baylor is harassing Susan. Forget about the fact they've been divorced for a few years." Mark scowled. "Never liked that guy after he moved into my neighborhood."

"Ken is a royal jerk," he agreed. "Maybe he'll lay off Susan."

"Doubt it." Mark sipped more tea. "So what about this joy ride with Fern?"

"I screwed up."

"Hard to imagine you doing something that risky, especially with someone else's life at stake, without taking precautions."

At least his cousin gave him that much credit, unlike his parents, who lectured him with texts all morning. "I did, but it didn't do much good in the end. And yeah, I'm feeling like I let Fern down, but it's more than that. Has to do with my career. Second thoughts. Maybe my family is right. It's too dangerous."

His cousin looked surprised. "That's out of left field. Never heard you talk like this, Ryan. Yeah, your job is risky, but you have training. You don't rush into a burning building without gear."

Ryan laughed. "Not without PPE and our PASS."

"What's that?"

"Personal Alert Safety System, which alerts if we're immobile for more than thirty seconds."

"Yeah, I remember the Twin Towers attacks..." Mark's voice drifted off.

They both fell silent for a moment, remembering the 343 firefighters killed in the September 11 attacks, and the devices that kept beeping in the rubble.

So many good lives lost that day.

Ryan cleared his throat. "My dad keeps thinking I should change careers. But how can I? This is my life."

"He worries about you being in a fire you can't escape."

Fires were living, breathing creatures. They provided heat and comfort during an icy winter, and could kill indiscriminately. It wasn't the flames that got people most times. People breathed in smoke, smoke mixed with godawful chemicals.

"Tell me about your work." Mark stretched out his legs. "What do you do when you get to a burning building?"

"Lots. Something most people don't understand is why we break windows if a building is on fire. It's to vent the building. Smash windows, let the smoke and gases escape. Increases someone's chances for survival, and by reducing the smoke, we can see easier."

"Most people think firefighters spray water and then enter," Mark said.

Ryan laughed. "Like in the movies? It's science, man. Water hits fire and heat and what do you get? Steam. It's not only the fire, but the heat and smoke, and all the smoke drops down, which is why they tell you to drop to the ground to avoid the smoke in a fire. It's black inside once you hit those flames with water. Like pitch-black until we vent the room or the building. We bring in hoses to work along the way, but it's a hell of a lot easier to enter and search before the hose is turned on."

He named a few other procedures he knew, and practiced, by heart.

Mark nodded. "So you know what to do if there's a fire. You've trained…"

"Always. We're always training, like you did in the army."

His cousin studied the back fence. "Let me ask you this— not why you want to quit. Why did you choose this job as a career? Don't give me the canned response—you wanted to be a hero, save lives, help humanity."

His cousin sounded a little bitter. Ryan drew in a breath. Most times he didn't want to talk about this, but Mark got it. After being in the army, his cousin showed little emotion. Mark asking him these questions could open his cousin up to talking about what happened, and why he came home.

"Yeah, I did, but it was more. Fires always fascinated me. I know some choose firefighting as a career for the adrenaline rush. For me, it's something more. Fire is beautiful and yet deadly. A beautiful killer, if that makes sense. I wanted to conquer it, defeat the enemy and beat it. Control it so it couldn't hurt anyone."

"Sounds like a military reasoning."

Not surprising, since many police and fire rescue personnel were ex-military. "There's times when I knew it was hopeless. You go into a burning house to rescue a kid, grab him out of bed and go for the other rooms, but the hall is burning. It's pure hell. No entry. You know whoever's in those back bedrooms is dead. The worst is a kid who was too little to save himself…"

Throat tightening, he managed to say, "It's a hard reality and you have to live with it.

"Then there are the saves you'll never forget because those are the ones worth holding on to when you're trying to sleep, wondering if it's worth it. Worth the risks, the women who want to date you because you're a firefighter and they love the glam, the excitement, but won't take a relationship to the next level. What's the point when there's a chance I'll go into a burning building and never come out? A lot of women can't deal with that risk of heartache.

"The saves where you see a kid's face covered in black soot and he starts coughing through the O2 mask and you find out later he made it and he's gonna be fine. His parents don't have to fund a funeral instead of a college fund."

Mark nodded. "I understand."

Mark didn't offer any information about why he understood, and Ryan didn't press him. Sometimes the work they did led them on a lonely path. Ordinary civilians usually couldn't comprehend the grueling work, hours and the emotional battles facing soldiers and firefighters.

"But all the training in the world—the gear, the hoses, the backup, the team who has your six—can't make up for the ones you lose, who are there so close and slip through your fingers. The ones who make you lose sleep at night."

Mark braced his elbows on his thighs. "The enemy within," he mused.

"A hard enemy to fight and control. I've been to fires where you know it's a lost cause, no matter how much water you use, how fast you arrive. The fire wins. Those are the bad days. When the bad days overtake the good, maybe it's time to reconsider."

"Like I did with my military career?"

His cousin sounded bitter. He knew Mark wouldn't talk now about why he quit the army and didn't want to pressure him.

"Maybe. If I quit, my mom will finally calm down, Dad will be happy and Ava less worried."

"What about you? Will it make you happy? Or miserable?"

Ryan thought for a minute. "I honestly don't know. Hard to say when this is all I've known."

"Your enemy within sounds easier to defeat," Mark mused.

He didn't want to walk down that road of self-examination, vanish into the darkness of his own thoughts. This was too serious, especially with Mark, who had his own demons to battle.

"Want to check out the bird feeder? Fern loves it."

Not batting an eye at the sudden change of topic, Mark accompanied him over to the bird feeder containing the camera.

He examined the feeder. "The solar panel should keep the battery charged, but if it gets low, use a charger."

"Fern's been taking care of it, makes sure to keep it full. She enjoys seeing the birds feed every morning and dusk."

"It's her, huh? Making you rethink your job."

Startled, he shook his head. "No, not really. I've been considering it..."

But the knowing look his cousin gave him made Ryan give up the excuses. "Maybe, in a way. I keep blaming myself for what happened yesterday, and what if they'd grabbed her?"

"They didn't." Mark glanced at his cell phone. "I have to run. Stop the self-blame. Won't do any good."

He wanted to tell his cousin to do the same, knowing that Mark had been through hell and back. Instead, he nodded. "Thanks, man."

When Mark left, Ryan leaned against the door and closed his eyes. His own demons were pretty damn nasty at times. But instead of seeing the face of Kate, the woman who literally slipped through his fingers last year and fell to her death, he saw another face.

Fern, terrified, as her kidnappers dragged her away once more, never to be seen again.

Chapter Sixteen

That night, leaving his truck in the garage after giving Fern strict instructions to call Jacob if anything appeared out of the ordinary at the house, he took an Uber to the rental car agency. Ryan rented a compact vehicle and made arrangements to park it at the house where the plainclothes police officer kept watch.

With the car parked away from the house, he felt safer but still apprehensive about being watched. So when Cap asked him to cover a shift the following day when he was still off duty, he almost turned him down.

Yet he knew Cap wanted to discuss something serious when his boss said he didn't want to use a floater from the pool.

Ryan suspected Tom had other ideas in mind, such as lecturing him on his career flashing a warning sign.

When he got to the Dark Canyon station at seven the following morning, Cap was there waiting with a mug of coffee. Ryan accepted the brew and followed him into the glass-paned office.

Here it comes...

To his surprise, Cap handed him an envelope. "Got this yesterday. Congratulations. You've been awarded the city's Fire Service Recognition Award in honor of the work you did on the Pinyon Canyon Avenue fire last year."

Confused, he stared at the words on the page. "Cap, that wasn't anything much. I was doing my job. Like every other day."

"The mayor doesn't think so. Neither do your colleagues. Everyone at the house was asked to nominate someone, and they chose you."

Guilt flashed through him quickly as an out-of-control burn. Lately he hadn't been there for his team, his mind elsewhere. "I don't deserve this. There are others who've done much more."

"You're a good smoke eater, Ryan. You're courageous without being reckless, and you're a team player, through and through."

He heard the hesitation. "But…"

"We're worried about you."

We. Not merely Cap. "Why? What have I done? I pull my weight. I pitch in."

Ryan already knew the answer before his boss opened his mouth.

"It's this business with Fern Hensley. Having her move in with you. Ever since she did, you've been off."

Cap picked up a clipboard. "You showed up late for shift. Forgot to clean the hoses before you rolled them on your last run. There's other incidents, minor. I could go on."

"My personal business is mine. If I'm off, tell me. But don't you dare blame Fern or my personal life."

"I'm not blaming her. I feel bad for what she went through. But she's an outsider, Ryan. An outsider who carries risks to anyone sheltering her, like what happened to both of you yesterday."

Cap leaned forward. "I don't want to lose one of my best firefighters."

So that was the real issue. He wondered if Sherry had a

talk with his captain and her worry trickled down, like a leaky dam.

He wasn't mad. Not yet. But getting there. The men and women of Dark Canyon Fire Department needed to butt out.

"I mean it, Cap. I'll stay focused. But Fern isn't the only victim here, and people seem to forget it. Ever think about that? There's a killer out there, and kidnappers taking women to be sold into sex trafficking."

Lowering his voice, he locked gazes with Tom. "There's evil walking among us. Any innocent woman could be next. What if it was your wife, or your sister, or even your daughter? What would you do?"

"Anything I could to get them back," Cap said evenly. "I understand."

No, you don't. Tom was a good man, a hell of a firefighter and a good captain who cared about the men and women at the station, but he was loyal to the town and its people. Fern was an outsider. Cap stated as much.

For the first time, he realized how alone Fern must have felt even before the kidnappers took her. No one to lean upon, or close friends to call during times of trouble.

His heart beat faster as he remembered how she'd been lying on the cabin floor, overcome by smoke, nearly a victim. No one to even bury her.

Saying anything more to Tom would jeopardize his houseguest. Mark warned him. *Don't trust anyone but family.*

He stood, nodded. "I won't let you down again, Cap. No more mistakes."

"Good. Get to work. You're on cooking detail today."

Ryan started to head for the kitchen when a woman walked into the fire station and called out.

"Hello? I'm looking for Ryan Colton."

Recognizing her as the woman who'd taken the dog to the vet after the house fire, he walked toward her. "I'm Ryan."

"Carrie Armstrong." She reached out her hand. "I've been meaning to track you down, but I've been so busy with the spring hiking season in full swing."

"How's the dog? And the little girl?"

Carrie smiled. "Both are fine, thanks to you. But that's not why I'm here. I wanted to tell you something about Kate McIntyre. I didn't have a chance the other day because I had to rush Wobbles to the vet."

Ryan's chest tightened. He gave an indifferent shrug. "I tried to rescue her. I'm sorry for your loss."

Carrie's steady gaze met his. "It was a tragic loss, true, but that's not why I'm here. I wanted to tell you about Kate and how she shouldn't have been on the cliff that day. She was a beginner, and we never send beginners to that section of canyon. Also, Kate shouldn't have been alone, but with a guide."

This was news. Ryan frowned. "What are you saying, Ms. Armstrong?"

"I'm saying neither you nor I are at fault for her death. Especially you." The woman sighed. "I keep going over and over in my head why she was on the rock wall that day. Kate was depressed and thought rock climbing would help. She should never have gone by herself. We always make students sign waivers, but eventually, everyone has to take responsibility for their own actions."

He began to understand. "Thanks for letting me know."

Carrie nodded. "Well, I have to get back to work. I only wanted to let you know—in case you feel you should have, could have, done more."

For a moment, a haunted look came over her. "Sometimes I wonder if I could have."

"You didn't put her on the rock wall," he said gently.

She nodded. "And you did everything you could to save her. Goodbye, Mr. Colton."

He watched her walk out of the station, his thoughts jumbled.

Of all the mistakes he'd made as a firefighter, and most were minor, Kate was the one he regretted the most.

You have to move on.

As he headed for the kitchen, his mind wasn't on the mistakes he'd made on shift. It was how alone Fern had been.

Same as the other women who'd been taken.

There was a connection there. He knew it. Being in Oso, hearing how she had few friends, led a fairly solitary life, made him suspicious.

Fern had been targeted because she had no family. Few friends. No one would miss her.

As he watched the spaghetti sauce cook in the stainless steel pot, he called Jacob for an update on the case. Nothing new.

Extremely concerned, he called Fern. Phone went straight to voicemail. He texted instead, then called Officer Jenkins, the plainclothes police officer guarding the house today.

Jenkins promised to check on Fern.

The sauce began to bubble and boil. Ryan turned down the gas and tried not to worry. Impossible now.

Now more than ever, it was critical for Fern to recover her full memory so they could nail these guys.

NONE OF THE usual activities she'd undertaken since moving in with Ryan soothed her fractured nerves lately. Fern tried working on the computer, doing the lists Ava had recommended. Physical therapy, painting, reading, even her sessions with Ava here in Ryan's home proved ineffective.

Ava had suggested relaxation might help trigger important memories in the cabin. The pressure on her to remember had doubled since another woman had been kidnapped.

She needed to move forward. Ryan's generous offer to

stay with him had been a step in the right direction. Now she'd fallen backward and wondered if she could recover.

Numbers made sense. Coding was numbers and logic. Fern itched to get back to work and scanned for medical coding jobs. But the terror and grief clawed at her, and she knew work was impossible.

Trapped in fear, she wanted to escape the pit. She wanted her old life back, the solitary, reliable Fern who paid her bills on time and worked to the point of obsession. The Fern who enjoyed seeing bright smiles on patients when she explained how their illness would be paid through insurance.

The horrific experience of being taken against her will, bound up with zip ties, her body left on the rough wood floor, then the acrid stench of smoke stinging her eyes and nostrils...

Rebuilding her life would take time. She understood that. Yet until she recalled all her memories, Fern knew she'd never become whole and happy again.

She felt like a mosaic with missing parts. Every time she felt a little joyful, like riding with Ryan in the vehicle, something happened to smash it once more.

Tomorrow night was dinner with Ryan's parents. She wondered if it was a good idea. Would they scrutinize her over what had happened? Be worried their only son was endangered by sheltering Fern?

Fuss over Ryan while blaming her? She got it. Ryan had a caring family. A slew of Coltons, from cousins to aunts and uncles, who loved him.

I'm alone.

Maybe I'm better off staying here alone.

How could she entertain stepping outside the house when her kidnappers were roaming free? Yet inside Ryan's house she felt trapped, except when he was present.

With Ryan around, she not only felt safe, but energized and alive. However, Fern knew her presence meant a threat.

The kidnappers wouldn't hesitate to kill him, and her, together. Maybe even set another fire, hoping they'd both perish.

You don't have any money, not enough to leave. You have no place to go. What are you going to do? Until you become whole again, and stable with your memories intact, you're stuck.

Folding her laundry as she sat on the guest bed while Ryan worked a shift, she made triangle patterns with her socks. The patterns soothed her. Repetition of familiar shapes.

Shapes helped clear her mind. They made sense in a way the world did not. Shapes were reliable. Predictable, unlike people and their motives.

A faint memory pricked her mind. She'd never done this as a child when feeling threatened or scared. Hiding in the closet, clutching her favorite, worn stuffed bunny, she learned to be quiet and still, lest she invoke her mother's rage.

Or worse, William's anger.

Fern went still. Why were triangles so important and what drove her to create these shapes? Much as she liked numbers and her job of coding, geometry had never been her best subject.

She closed her eyes, trying to evoke memories. Shapes were important. Stop signs were red octagons. Yellow railroad signs were circular. Brown trapezoid signs indicated a national recreation area.

Yellow pendant signs warned motorists not to pass.

Her eyes flew open. *This is ridiculous. I'm trying to remember triangles and all I can recall is my driver's ed class.*

But as she returned to folding socks, she kept making

triangle shapes. Fern stared at the white ankle sock she'd formed into a triangle.

This had to mean something and wasn't merely self soothing.

Her conscious mind might have forgotten plenty, but her subconscious kept repeating the pattern.

Ava told her during a session how tricky the subconscious was, and how your mind would never make everything crystal clear in dreams. Fern admitted to having dreams of being naked. Ava explained it had nothing to do with actually being naked, but feeling vulnerable.

If anyone has a right to be vulnerable, it's me.

Maybe the triangle represented something from her kidnapping. Abandoning the laundry, she went downstairs to the basement and her sketch pad. Fern took the charcoal pencil and began drawing triangles.

Nothing.

After returning upstairs, she went into Ryan's office and switched on her laptop and began surfing the web. Triangles, triangles. What did they represent?

Absorbed in the deep dive she'd undertaken, she was surprised to hear her stomach grumble. Fern glanced at her cell phone.

Almost two thirty! She'd forgotten to have lunch. Time for a break, maybe mix up a green salad with chicken to make up for the tacos Ryan had brought home yesterday.

In the kitchen she set about making her lunch, shaking her head in amusement at the junk food in the refrigerator. Ryan was equally bad at snacking. Forget about nutrition. *We've got our own food pyramid. Mexican food at the bottom, followed by sugar and snacks and...*

The bowl she held slipped from her loosened fingers and crashed on the tile floor, shattering. Fern barely noticed. Her mind kept screaming a warning.

Not a triangle. A pyramid.

Not a pyramid such as those in ancient Egypt or the Mayan ruins. A corporate kind of triangle/pyramid.

"Hierarchy," she said aloud, staring out the kitchen window. "Who's at the top of the food chain?"

Willing herself to remember, she gripped the sides of the sink and closed her eyes, forcing herself to think about the terrible little shack where she'd been imprisoned. Smells of male body odor, grease and the oil lamp that burned because there hadn't been electricity. Drugged and feeling as if she were hallucinating, everything had been a daze, but shortly after they'd taken her to the shack, Billy and his partner had talked when she wasn't quite so out of it.

Before all the drugs had infused her system and she could barely think straight.

Oh, they'd been clever not to mention names in front of her, but not so clever to leave out all the details. She had been lying on the floor, eyes closed, pretending to be unconscious but listening all the while.

"Billy, how the hell are we gonna hide this one from the boss? He'll skin us alive if he finds out we took her on our own."

"If he finds out. He ain't gonna find out. He thinks he can order us around because we're at the bottom of the food chain, but we'll show him. This one ain't going to Mexico. I've got a bead on a buyer in California who wants her for some wealthy guy overseas. Gotta up the price."

"Yeah, well, the guy at the top of the food chain won't like it. Selling this one won't get us that much money, not as much as his cut, dammit."

"Maybe we can recruit others to do it for us. Make our own secret pyramid scheme." A rough laugh, grating on her nerves.

Fern's eyes opened. That was why she made triangles. Her

conscious mind had wanted to forget everything to protect her, but her subconscious knew the importance of the symbol.

"The triangle is a pyramid, a central power structure, and Billy and his friend violated that system. They were at the bottom, grabbing women to abduct and sell in Mexico, but the real power was at the top of the food chain. Someone in authority, the real leader with decision-making ability. I was never meant to be part of the regular shipment of women out of the country. Billy and the other guy took me to sell on their own," she said aloud.

Excited and hopeful for the first time in days, she picked up the broken bowl, dumped it into the trash and danced around the kitchen.

"I remembered, I remembered!"

Fern scrolled through her cell phone to call Jacob and hesitated. Instead, she called Ryan. The call went straight to voicemail.

Without leaving a message, she hung up.

Though she knew Jacob needed to know, she felt more comfortable telling Ryan first. He was the reason why she recalled these important details. Ryan gave her a place to feel safe and relaxed.

If only she could recall the other man's name, that would help even more. Billy had been more bossy and the leader of the pair. The other man had been physically stronger, intimidating. He growled a lot, sometimes snarled like a big predatory cat.

A tiger. No, more like a lion. Lion... She closed her eyes. "Horoscopes," she muttered aloud.

Her eyes flew open again. "Leo. His name is Leo!"

Immensely pleased with herself, she did not hesitate and dialed Jacob's number. His phone also went to voicemail.

After leaving a detailed message of what she remembered, Fern hung up.

Next she called Ryan again and told him that she remembered.

He whistled. "That's terrific news. Do you remember everything?"

Phone gripped in her palm, she recalled details of the kidnapping, the whispered voices, the hateful sting of the needle when they drugged her.

"Everything," she told him.

"Excellent. Hey, I have to run, but we'll talk later. Jacob will want to debrief you. You okay with that?"

"I can handle it. No worries," she told him.

After Ryan hung up, Fern thought about it. If Jacob wanted to come over and question her with ruthlessness, she could take it. *I'm strong enough now.*

Strong enough to leave Ryan's house. I can't be a burden to him any longer.

After tomorrow night's dinner, she'd tell him.

Chapter Seventeen

The last time she'd been at this house, Ryan had "borrowed" his father's vehicle and they'd snuck away. How happy she'd been to get out on the road, free with no worries!

Plenty of worries now. Fern smoothed down her navy-blue skirt as she climbed out of the rental car. Paired with a sensible powder blue blouse with long sleeves and low-slung heels, her hair worn loose around her shoulders, she knew she looked good.

This dinner wasn't about looking good, however. She wanted to assure his family there would not be any trouble from her.

She was determined to enjoy herself and this dinner. It had been so long since she'd socialized with others, she worried she would not fit in.

As if reading her mind, he glanced at her. Whistled. "You look terrific, Fern. Really pretty."

"Thanks." She grinned. "You're pretty as well, especially with that tie."

Laughing, he fingered the tie she'd bought him online, a blue tie with fire hydrants. It provided a whimsical contrast to his plain white shirt and dress pants.

With Ryan at her side, confidence returned.

"Mom is informal, but Dad, well, he's a hyper businessman." Ryan shrugged.

She understood. The dress code provided a cushion against parental scrutiny and criticism.

As they walked up the driveway to the imposing house, he clutched her hand. Simple human contact that felt reassuring. Fern sensed the occupants inside noticed her through the floor-to-ceiling living room windows that afforded stunning views of the distant purple mountains.

"My father can be hypercritical as well, though deep down, he is a good man. Parents, you know?"

Time for a little self-reflection. "Actually, I don't know," she confessed as they reached the front door. "My mother was great at criticizing, but far from a good parent. Fortunately my foster parents made up for her neglect."

He stopped, turned and rubbed her shoulders. "Are you nervous about this dinner?"

"No." She studied his brilliant blue gaze and sighed. "Yes, a little."

"We don't have to do this. If you want, we'll go home right now. I'll make an excuse to my parents and Ava."

"No." She looked at the frosted glass doors etched with the Colton monogram. "This will be good for me, Ryan. And I don't want you giving up time with your family over me."

It took all her courage to walk through the double doors into the entryway. Her low heels clicked on the black-and-white-marbled tile. Wealth and luxury radiated in the sweeping staircase, polished furniture as elegant as pictures she'd seen in magazines, and a crystal chandelier hanging above their heads.

Fern remembered the two-room squalid apartment where she'd lived with her mother, with its peeling wallpaper and scuffed linoleum flooring.

You're out of your league, kiddo. Try not to gawk.

Ryan's warm hand in hers loaned her strength. He wasn't his parents. Dedicated to saving lives, he lived in a house with secondhand furniture and enjoyed it.

Tension slipped from her as he led her inside to the living room.

Ava sat on the white-and-blue-striped sofa, smiling at an older man with bushy gray hair as he cooed to a baby in his arms. The older man resembled Ryan. She recognized Chay next to Ava. Another man she didn't recognize lingered near the marble fireplace. Tall, with a muscular build and short light brown hair that looked windblown, he had an intense air.

Must be a Colton, she thought. Ryan had the same dynamic intensity.

Sure enough, Ryan brightened as he spotted the man. "Noah. I thought you were working."

"For a chance at your mom's prime rib, I can take a break," the man shot back, grinning.

"My cousin Noah," he murmured to Fern. His voice dropped. "Noah does search and rescue with his dog, Dancer. He's the one who alerted me to your presence in the cabin."

Another Colton to thank for saving her life. Their gazes met, and Noah gave a brief, friendly nod.

I owe him my life as much as I owe Ryan.

Comforted by the presence of these two stalwart, protective men, Fern relaxed a little. She nodded back at Noah.

"Where's Sabrina?" Ryan asked.

"She was busy, but sends her love."

An older woman came into the hallway, wiping her hands on a dish towel. Ryan hugged her, and she hugged him back in obvious affection that made Fern wistful.

"Ryan. You finally made it. You must be Fern."

The woman smiled, holding out her hand. "I'm Sherry Colton. Welcome to our home."

Her handshake was firm, but not overbearing. "Please, make yourself comfortable. Ryan, you know where the bar is. Can you serve Fern?"

Sherry's smile was warm. "We have wine, prosecco, bourbon, vodka, scotch, whatever you like."

"Thank you. I don't drink."

No surprise on Sherry's face. "Ryan, we have soda in the minifridge under the bar and cold water. Excuse me, but I have to get back to dinner."

They watched his mother scurry down the hallway and vanish into the kitchen.

A blonde woman in a simple but expensive black sheath and heels Fern knew were designer sat in a chair away from the rest of the group. She had a shrill voice, mentioning a newly opened Asian fusion restaurant in town. With her thin face, model-good looks and long blond hair, she commanded attention.

So many people, more people than she'd encountered in months. Fern drew in a calming breath. Ava noticed her, and her beaming smile fed her confidence.

"Fern! You look amazing. So glad you made it." Ava waved.

Chay nodded at her with a brief smile. Fern was glad of his company. Chay was quiet and reassuring.

Introductions were made. The blonde was Kim March, the Coltons' neighbor who had grown up living next to Ryan and Ava.

Ryan's father seemed friendly enough in his greeting as he handed the baby to Chay, who handled her like a pro. He came over, shook hands with his son and smiled at Fern.

"Nice to meet you, Fern. Welcome to our home. I'm James Colton."

Ryan gave his father a level look. "Dad, I thought this was a family dinner."

His father shrugged. "You know your mother. She loves company. She saw Kim earlier today, and Kim asked about you. Your mother figured one additional place setting wouldn't hurt. You haven't seen Kim in months."

Ryan's expression tightened. Fern swallowed hard against the emotions rising in her throat. She saw the way Kim looked at Ryan, as if he were dessert and she craved sugar.

A woman noticed these things.

I should have stayed home.

"I haven't seen her in months on purpose, Dad," he murmured with a furious edge in his tone.

But he put a hand at the small of Fern's back and guided her forward with a proprietary smile.

"Everyone, this is Fern. She's living with me."

Making it sound like they were lovers instead of introducing her as his houseguest was intentional. She glanced at the blonde again, who frowned.

Unsure of what Ryan's endgame was, Fern decided to play along for now. She squeezed his arm and stepped closer to him.

Everyone acted friendly enough, but Kim eyed her like something she'd stepped into with her designer heels. Then she offered a wide smile, which never met her dark eyes.

Fern had dealt enough with women like Kim. They were constantly sizing up anyone thought to be competition, and angling how to get rid of them.

I'm not the competition, Kim. And I've already had people try to get rid of me, in ways that would make you scream endlessly.

Fern automatically moved her gaze elsewhere, not wanting to give her any more attention than she deserved.

Ava and Chay stood. "We're going to put Ella Grace down

for a nap," she explained. "Ryan, why don't you and Fern catch up with Dad and Noah?"

They took the seats vacated by the couple. Noah remained by the fireplace, sipping a drink. Ryan turned to her.

"How about a ginger ale?"

"Sounds good. With ice, please."

"I'll get it." Noah headed to the elegant hand-carved bar in the corner. "Beer for you, cuz?"

"Cola is fine. On the rocks."

Noah blinked, but left and returned with two drinks. Kim kept smiling at them both, but the facial gesture seemed strained.

"It's good to see you, Ryan. Your mom tells me you've been quite busy," Kim said.

"I have."

Though polite, the edge in his voice told her Ryan hadn't expected this visit, nor did he welcome it.

"Kim and I used to date," he told Fern. "A long time ago."

"Not that long ago," Kim said, with a laugh as fake as her long eyelashes. "We had good times. Ryan and I used to hike a lot in the canyon. Remember Rye?"

Kim spoke with the proprietary tone of an ex who knew Ryan well.

"Yeah, we did some hiking." Ryan turned to her. "Speaking of hiking, weather's supposed to be great next week. You up to a short exploration of Dark Canyon wilderness? Won't be a long walk. Only a short one to stretch your legs."

"Maybe. I wouldn't want to hold you back."

On a hike or anything else.

"You won't. It'll be fun, and I know an easy stretch of the canyon. I won't let you overdo it."

His look was warm, as if they were boyfriend and girlfriend.

"Have you done a lot of hiking, Fern?"

This from his father, who looked at her as if Ryan had brought home a stray cat and the man couldn't decide if the cat was going to claw him or purr.

"A little, before..." Her voice trailed off. Oh damn, this was all wrong. She did not want any of them to think her weak. Find a chink in the armor she'd worn to protect herself, and jab deep inside.

She sipped the ginger ale to soothe her throat and continued.

"I've done some rock climbing, when I had time. In my hometown there's an indoor sporting center with rock climbing, and I'd practice there when I could. Nothing too steep, but enough to train myself for the real thing."

"Rock climbing is dangerous..." his father began.

"Training is important," Noah cut in. "Those canyons can be tricky. Smart of you to know that."

She held back what she truly wanted to tell Ryan's dad. Life is risky. You never know from one day to the next what will happen. No matter how much you plan, bad things happen. Make the best of each day you're above ground.

But maybe his father, with all his money and responsibility, couldn't understand that. Still, she did appreciate his desire to protect his children. His family.

I have no family.

Usually the realization made her sad. Tonight, for some odd reason, it strengthened her. As Ava always told her, she'd survived many horrid experiences and come out the other side with her spirit and her strength intact.

I am a survivor. I have taken what life threw at me and emerged from the grinder as myself.

Kim turned to her with another wide, fake smile. "Fern, how did you and Ryan meet?"

Panic rose up. Struggling for answers, she glanced at Ryan. But to her surprise, Noah spoke up.

"You might say I found her first and introduced Fern to Ryan."

Grateful for the save, she nodded at Noah. "Noah brought us together," Fern told Kim.

No details necessary.

Ryan covered her icy palm with his warm one. "Fern's amazing. She's a terrific cook, and we enjoy being together. She also copes well with my long absences when I'm on duty."

"Well." The long-drawn-out word sounded flat. "Being a firefighter's girlfriend was challenging, Fern. I hope it doesn't bother you as it bothered me. I constantly worried about Ryan never coming home."

The woman gave a long sigh. "I never understood why you choose firefighting instead of working in your father's business, Ryan."

"Neither did I," his father commented. "The offer is still there when you're ready to get a real job."

Beside her, she felt Ryan tense. Noah's frown was directed at Kim, but she sensed this was a long-standing family argument.

"Ryan has a real job, Uncle James. Same as me," Noah said.

"There's no future in it and certainly limitations when it comes to income," Kim interjected.

Enough of this criticism. Didn't anyone recognize Ryan's bravery and the importance of what he had chosen as a career?

Fern locked gazes with Kim, ready to go to battle.

"Ryan's work is critical," she told Kim. "He's essential to Dark Canyon. The town is fortunate to have men like him, and Noah, to keep people safe. Some people choose careers that give other people a chance at life, at their own futures, and that means more than making money."

Kim recoiled as if Fern had slapped her. Ryan squeezed her hand.

"I see your new girlfriend likes your lifestyle, Ryan," his father said diplomatically.

But the truth would come out, eventually. Tired of the games, Fern leaned forward. "I'm not his girlfriend. Ryan was kind enough to reach out to me when I didn't have a place to live, and I accepted his offer to stay with him."

"How long have you been staying with Ryan, Fern?" Kim drank her wine.

"A while," he interjected. "Fern's settled in quite nicely."

She flashed him a grateful look.

On the other hand, the hostility on Kim's face warned the woman was not over the breakup with Ryan.

"I've never seen you around town, and I know a lot of people. Ryan is a generous person. It's good you don't have to pay rent and he lets you stay there."

Kim made it sound like she sponged off the man. Fern's temper rose. Before she could speak, Ryan did.

"For someone who was never interested in my life when we broke up, Kim, you certainly are interested now."

Relief filled her. He'd swiftly turned the convo around. Kim shrugged. "Only an observation. It is your life. I was merely curious. I'm glad you moved on, Ryan. I have. Did you know I'm seeing Chet Powell? He's the new chef at Fusion Up. We're talking about moving in together."

"Good for you," he said evenly.

"Perhaps you and Fern can join us for dinner sometime. Chet is an excellent host."

Not in my lifetime. Ryan acknowledged the offer with a slight shrug, indicating his indifference.

This certainly had turned from a friendly family gathering into awkward city.

Relieved when Sherry came into the room to announce

dinner was ready, she accompanied Ryan to a dining table that seemed larger than her childhood home. Fern swallowed her anxiety. Determined to see this through, she joined Ryan at the table.

The appetizer of shrimp cocktail was excellent. Fern made an effort to taste every dish. By the time they started on the prime rib, Kim was still chattering about her past relationship with Ryan and asking pointed questions about Fern.

Fern made noncommittal answers but sensed Ryan's growing fury.

Across the table, Ava's worried gaze met Fern's. With the smoothness of a man accustomed to commanding conversations, Ryan turned to his sister. "Ava, tell me how Ella Grace is doing. I can't wait to hold her after dinner."

Talk turned to the baby, turning attention away from Fern. She managed to focus on her dinner, smiling now and then, but feeling tongue-tied. This was all so normal for them. Her? She never had family dinners around the table. Arguments had always turned violent. Fern learned to never speak up.

Until she lived with the Englehearts, Fern barely knew how to act at the dinner table. Sometimes she'd hidden underneath it to escape the flying cutlery her mother threw at William.

The fights and the loud voices…

The prime rib was tender and rare, the new potatoes excellent. Fern helped herself to a small piece. She drank heavily from her water glass. Others, except for Ryan, sipped red wine.

Though stressed, she wasn't tempted by the wine or the expansive liquor collection. Fern felt firmly in control.

"Kim, how is your new job at Colton Holdings?" Sherry asked. "James tells me you're not only managing the office, but you've been handling a few new clients."

With animation, Kim began chatting about the properties she'd signed on to sell through the business. James said little, focusing on his meal.

So that was why Sherry invited Kim. Not that it made Fern feel any more relaxed. Ryan's ex-girlfriend had direct ties to the family business.

Sherry steered the conversation, asking Noah about Sabrina as well as his work, and chattering about baby Ella Grace. Fern ate as she listened. Her throat tightened as Sherry explained to her that Annie Ross, Ella Grace's birth mother, had been found dead in the Dark Canyon Wilderness. Her friend and roommate Lori had been helping Annie raise the baby in Wilson, but after Annie's suspicious death, Lori wanted Ella Grace to be safe, so she left the baby at the fire station.

Lori had told them some details of Ella Grace's background. Ava and Chay planned to legally adopt the baby and the name Ella Grace honored Annie.

Fern remained quiet, glad no one shot any more questions at her.

Only when James directed his attention at his son did she grow tense once more.

"Ryan, it's never too late to quit the fire department and join me at Colton Holdings. I could use your help. I'm not getting younger, and it will take you a while to learn the business."

"You're too young to retire, Uncle James," Noah said lightly.

"I'm not looking at retirement. I am looking forward to the future of this company and our family." James gave Ryan a level look.

Suddenly Ryan seemed fascinated by cutting his prime rib into tiny pieces.

"You'd love working at Colton Holdings, Ryan. Your father is right. You can make much more money in real estate. A career at a firehouse?" Kim gave a dramatic sigh. "It's unlike being a sous chef, where you can work your way up to exclusive restaurants."

"James, now is not the time," Sherry chided.

"When is it the time, Sher? We barely see him anymore because he's always working, and when he isn't working, he's never around."

James talked around his son as if Ryan were invisible. She sensed Ryan struggling to hold back his temper for the sake of the family dinner.

Turning back to Ryan, who remained quiet, James raised his fork and jabbed it in his direction.

"I accepted your choice when you graduated from the fire academy. You needed action and excitement. Now you're getting older, Ryan. It's time to think of your future. Turn to a career where you use your brains, not brawn."

Fern's grip on her fork tightened as she carefully set it down.

She hated being the center of attention. Always had. Better to stay quiet and demure instead of drawing people to her. Fern knew she was a product of her disturbed childhood. She'd worked hard to overcome shyness and learn to assert herself.

In crowds, though, and parties, she still struggled to make her needs known and socialize with strangers.

Ryan's family gathering sounded like a perfect way to slide back into the ordinary world once more. Unfortunately, this wasn't a typical gathering, not with his ex-girlfriend there.

If this makes you uncomfortable, think of how Ryan must feel.

She wanted to put her arms around Ryan and shield him from past hurt and his father's criticisms. Sherry seemed adoring and eloquent and devoted, loving with James and her children.

His father, on the other hand, was a strong patriarchal type who liked to control things. Understandable, for a businessman like James Colton who headed probably a multimillion-dollar company. But the man's attitude about Ryan's career made her bristle.

Fern knew she had to say something in Ryan's defense. Dedicated and courageous, Ryan had done much for not only her, but the entire town of Dark Canyon.

Galvanized into action by her feelings for Ryan, though she had a habit of shunning any confrontations, Fern lifted her chin and faced James Colton.

"You should be proud of your son for the lives he's saved. Ryan is a selfless, dedicated firefighter. It takes brains, quick thinking as well as physical strength to be a first responder. His integrity and compassion for others, putting their needs before his own, should be lauded. Not condemned."

Silence filled the air. Even Kim blinked in apparent surprise. Noah, with a wide grin, clapped.

"Well done, Fern. About time someone took up our cause."

James turned to his nephew. "Your cause?"

"I'm in search and rescue. Ryan and I are colleagues in keeping this town's citizens safe."

Kim gave her long hair a graceful flip. "That may be true, but I agree with James. Ryan, when we were together we barely had time to share meals. If you weren't working you were training."

Enough of this dogpile. Fern gave a wide smile to Kim, as fake as the woman's nails. "Training is imperative. You should see him sweat as he works out in the basement. All those muscles."

The purr in her voice sounded almost foreign to her. Ryan looked amused. Distress pinched Kim's thin cheeks. She looked stricken, like a child given the opportunity to choose rum raisin but picked plain vanilla and regretted the choice.

With diplomatic grace, Sherry interjected. "You and Ryan are excellent at your jobs, Noah. By the way, how is Sabrina? Please invite her over. I have a new piano composition I've learned, and I'm planning a recital."

"Bring the earplugs," Ryan advised with a grin.

Sherry gave him a withering look while Ava joined in. "Ryan, stop teasing."

"I'm not. Love you, Mom, and you're amazing on the piano, but your choice of music and mine don't agree."

Lively discussion began on music choices. Fern ate her green beans, marveling at how Ryan's mother did her own rescue—a skillful turn of topics to save the family dinner.

When the dishes were cleared, Fern and Ava helping while Kim kept discussing the *mar-ve-lous* dishes her new boyfriend created, Sherry invited everyone into the living room for coffee, tea and dessert. Chay took Ryan to the nursery to spend time with his new niece.

Noah bid everyone goodbye. Sabrina had texted him she was home, and he was anxious to see her.

When Noah left, Fern politely excused herself to go outside for fresh air. As she stepped onto the back porch, a cool breeze washed over her, drying the sweat trickling down her back. Bracing her hands on the railing, she stared up into the starry night.

Here, she could breathe again. Ryan's parents clearly loved him. But the tension between Ryan and his father triggered old memories about her own childhood.

Not that William was a father, or even a father figure. Her mother's drunken boyfriend had been too self-centered to care about Fern, except when he got mean and needed a target for his sarcasm and cruelty.

The French doors behind her opened. Fern stiffened as James joined her by the railing.

"There you are. I need to explain myself to you."

"No, you don't. It's your family."

His father gave a wry smile. "Can't have you walking out of here, thinking I'm a terrible parent. I'm not, Fern. I love my son. Both my children. I am proud of them."

James stared into the darkness. "I worry about Ryan. Every time sirens scream down the street, I'm afraid one day he may not return. It's one reason why I want him to join me in the business."

Fern touched his sleeve. "You're devoted to your company. Can't you see Ryan feels the same about his firefighting career? You have to trust he's making the right decisions when facing a fire. If not for him, I'd be dead. I owe him my eternal gratitude. Men and women like Ryan, and Noah, and all first responders who put the needs of others before themselves, deserve our thanks."

James nodded. "I understand and appreciate your taking his side."

"I appreciate you not mentioning to Kim the circumstances of how Ryan and I really met." There. She stated it.

"It's none of her business, though I can't say I'm surprised she sided with me. Most of Ryan's previous girlfriends did as well. Not you."

"I'm not his girlfriend."

Another wan smile. "Could've fooled me. Excuse me a moment."

After James went inside, Ryan joined her. Fern smiled. "How's Ella Grace?"

A wide smile touched his face. "So tiny and cute. Holding her is like holding a piece of heaven. Ava and Chay are great parents."

Ella Grace is fortunate. Fern shivered, as she remembered her own childhood.

"Cold?" he asked softly.

She shook her head. "I had an interesting talk with your dad."

"Yeah? I bet. I apologize for Mom inviting Kim. She didn't think it would be like this. I had no idea she was working for the old man."

"It's been an interesting evening," she agreed, emphasizing interesting. Like interesting such as the old curse – May you live in interesting times.

"Dad hiring Kim puts even more pressure on me." Ryan jammed a hand through his neatly combed hair. "Mom told me he had to hire her because he's shorthanded. He'll never stop reminding me of obligations I have to the family business."

He snorted, his blue eyes, so much like his father's, filled with turmoil. "I'm tired of fighting him, Fern. He's never accepted my lifestyle choice."

Compelled to defend him, Fern gripped his hand. "It's a lifestyle choice any parent would be proud of, Ryan, while stressing them out each time you respond to a fire. But it's your life. I can't see you settling into a desk job and barking out orders to subordinates."

The intensity he radiated seemed to fill the air. His fingers curled around her as if he cherished her support. "I'm not a desk jockey, Fern. Never have been. You understand. Why can't my father?"

"Because he's your dad." Her voice gentled. "As much as it bothers you, you're blessed to have a father who loves you enough to care about what happens to you."

As the words came out of her mouth, James came outside once more. Heat suffused her face. Before she could stammer an apology, Ryan's father held up a hand.

"I came outside to let you know Sherry's crème brûlée is worth every calorie and you should both enjoy it. Thank you for defending me, Fern. She's right, son. I do care and I do love you, and every time I hear sirens, it sends my heart racing because that could be you headed into danger. Never coming home."

Shadows danced on Ryan's face, showcasing his tight jaw. "Dad, we constantly train, all the time. I'm a professional, and yeah, there's always a risk, but teamwork and training reduce the risk."

James put a fatherly hand on Ryan's shoulder. "I understand. That won't keep me from worrying, or stop me from keeping the door open in case you change your mind and want to join me at Colton Holdings."

Sensing this was an opportune time for Ryan to privately talk with his dad, Fern murmured excuses about stepping inside to help Sherry with dessert.

Ever the hostess, Ryan's mother told Fern she had everything under control and did Fern want to try it? Fern agreed and sampled a small piece at the kitchen table. When she finished, Sherry insisted on cleaning up.

Her eyes lit up as Fern told her how delicious the dessert had been.

Next, Fern headed to the living room. But Kim was there, talking with Chay and Ava.

Making polite small talk was too difficult right now, especially with Kim trying to one-up her. Maybe she could give it a go, for Ryan's sake.

Seeing her, Kim got up and motioned to the hallway. "Fern, may I have a word?"

When they were out of earshot of the others, Kim faced her. Gone was the superior smirk. Kim looked stricken.

"I'm not one to gossip, but I thought you should know something. I was in the kitchen, and Sherry and Ava were talking about you." Kim pushed a lock of hair behind her ear, exposing a perfect round diamond stud.

So tasteful. Pretty, unlike the words Kim told her.

"Sherry said she hoped you would move out soon and take the offer of the rental house she and James set up for you. It's an expensive home with a view of the mountains, with 24/7 security, and if the contract isn't signed soon, they'll lose the offer. They still had to discuss it with Ryan."

Fern's heart sank.

Kim didn't look spiteful or filled with glee. In fact she seemed apologetic. "I'm sorry, but I thought you should know... I see you didn't. Not that I was eavesdropping. I simply happened to be nearby."

Her voice trailed off. "I'm sorry to be the bearer of bad news."

Sorry? You should be dancing. Yet Kim did truly look contrite. At least Ryan's ex didn't know the full story or why his family wanted her out. For that she felt a pinch of gratitude.

So that was how they really felt about her. Nothing personal. No. They only wanted Fern to leave Ryan's home and stay at the luxurious, impersonal house James and Sherry would rent, along with 24-7 security.

"Thanks for telling me."

Kim nodded and went toward the living room.

Dryness coated her throat. Fern didn't know whether to leave, slamming the door behind her, or maintain a polite attitude and stay.

Leaving would upset Ryan. She couldn't do that to him. Not in front of his family. Later, when they were alone, they could talk in private.

Fern headed down the hallway to the guest bathroom to splash water on her flushed face.

Instead, she heard a faint cry from a darkened room. Fern

went toward it. The nursery Sherry and James had set up for baby Ella Grace.

On a white dresser, a duck-shaped lamp glowed softly in the darkness. The new grandparents had gone to great lengths to make the bedroom welcome for Ella Grace. From the white changing table, to a comfortable rocker by the window, to the baby-safe crib.

In the crib, the baby whimpered.

Years of caring for younger foster siblings had taught her well. She checked the baby's diaper. Dry. Ella Grace continued to fuss, so Fern picked her up and cooed.

Ella Grace felt so tiny and fragile in her arms. Fern shifted her weight, humming a nursery rhyme as she rocked from side to side.

"You're so blessed, Ella Grace," she told her in the darkened nursery, only the light of the whimsical yellow duck lamp casting cheerful shadows across the room. "Your mom left you when you're too little to remember. Instead you have Ava and Chay, good people who cherish you. Your Uncle Ryan thinks the world of you. Your grandparents love you, all the Coltons will love you. You'll grow up happy and protected, and you'll never know the heartache of watching your mom walk out the door, screaming for her to come back and waiting in the dark for hours, crying and wishing she would return."

Comforted by the rocking motion, the baby yawned and closed her eyes. Asleep.

Setting Ella Grace carefully in her crib, she tucked the pink blanket around her. "Sleep well, sweet baby."

As she turned away, Fern caught sight of a silhouette in the doorway. She stiffened, recognizing Sherry.

"I heard her fussing and wanted to set her back to sleep. I only wanted to help." Hard to keep the defensive note from her voice.

But as she stepped out into the well-lit hall and partly closed the door, she noticed the wetness on Sherry's cheeks.

Ryan's mother wrapped her arms around Fern. "I'm sorry all those things happened to you, Fern. I didn't know."

Uncomfortable and yet feeling as if she'd crossed an important threshold, Fern briefly hugged her back. "It's not something I tell people."

Not even your son.

Sherry stepped back, wiping her eyes with her hands. "I didn't mean to eavesdrop. I was only going to kiss her good-night."

Funny how eavesdropping was a common activity tonight in the Colton home. Fern managed to gather her lost composure. Ryan's parents would never know how much it hurt to realize they wanted her out of his home.

"I'm glad Ella Grace has you as a grandmother, and family who cares." Fern meant it.

"How old were you?"

"Ten. It was a long time ago." Fern started down the hallway, hoping Sherry would stop asking her about her childhood.

Sherry made sympathetic sounds. "How can a mother abandon her child like that sweet baby? It's so horribly unfair."

Sensing this was more about her than Ella Grace, Fern stopped short. She looked at Sherry. "Life isn't fair. The pain, well, you learn to live with it and survive. You become clever at wringing out each little bit of joy, like a dishrag, thirsty for each drop. I was fortunate to have good foster parents who cared. They helped me get through it. You never get over the hurt. But you do move past it, and it makes you grateful for all the blessings sent your way."

Ryan's mother didn't ask more questions, but she squeezed

Fern's hand before releasing it. "I understand what Ryan sees in you. You're quite special, Fern."

"He's the one who's special. I'm blessed he came into my life."

Because it was a good time to introduce the subject and Sherry could tell her in person about the rental house, she added, "I'll always be grateful for everything he, and Ava, have done for me. But I think it is time I should look for lodgings elsewhere."

"Nothing could prepare us for what happened the other day when you both were out in James's Jeep. I will admit, I was terrified when I thought my son was in danger." Sherry studied an elegant nail. "I also discussed with my family about lodgings for you elsewhere, where you would be safe."

Fern's stomach roiled at the admission. Hearing it from Kim was one thing. Confirmation from his mother was something else. A definite admission that his family didn't want her around. She got it. Who would want a woman with a target on her back that extended to their only son?

"But I see how Ryan looks at you, Fern. How he acts around you, in a way he never did around Kim."

Sherry made a dismissive wave. "Kim may be an ambitious career woman, but she was all wrong for Ryan, and they both knew it."

"I don't think I'm right for him," Fern said softly. "I won't impose on him anymore. He's been wonderful to me."

They'd reached the hallway's end, blocked from going farther by Ryan. He'd overheard.

"Let's get one thing straight, Fern. You're not an imposition."

"I've been your guest far too long, Ryan."

"I'll be the one to decide if you're overstaying your welcome." He spoke in his clipped, commanding voice she sensed he used while fighting fires. "Not my family or anyone else. You're staying, Fern. Even if you don't like it, Mom."

Beneath her expertly applied makeup, Sherry flushed. "Don't be rude, Ryan."

"It's not rude to state the facts and how I feel. Fern is my guest in my house, and I won't have her pressured to move out."

The hardness of his voice, the protective way he bristled, made her glad he was on her side. But she'd seen how much his family loved him and couldn't be a burden any longer.

If something happened to Ryan because of her, Fern would never forgive herself.

"I can't do this, Ryan. I'm endangering you."

Turning, he cupped her cheek with a tenderness that nearly made her weep. "I can take care of any threats, Fern. You're not moving out on my account."

His gaze narrowed as he eyed his mother. "Or anyone else's."

"I agree," Sherry said softly. "It's between the both of you. I'll talk with your father, Ryan, and assure him."

Anxious to take the focus off herself, Fern gestured to the nursery. "Ella Grace is adorable. I picked her up when she was crying and she went straight back to sleep."

Talk turned once more to the baby. Ironic how such a small, innocent child could defuse tension.

A little while later, Ryan announced he had an early day and they said their goodbyes. Fern thanked Sherry again for the delicious dinner.

It wasn't until they were driving away in the rental car that she could relax a little. However, there remained the predicament of her presence in Ryan's house.

Streetlights showcased downtown businesses, where pedestrians shopped the stores on Main Street. Soon they were headed to the other side of town, away from the upscale homes where Ryan had spent his childhood.

Fern found her voice as they neared his neighborhood.

"I won't be a wedge between your parents, or anyone in your family, Ryan."

Her protests were met with a wave of his hand. "Listen to me, Fern. I know the Coltons can be intimidating. Dad can steamroller over anyone interfering with his family, and Mom, well, she can lose all social graces if she believes any of us are threatened. But it's my life. My choice. I want you to stay with me.

"If you choose to move out because you're tired of me, that's different."

Tired of him? "Never," she said fiercely. "On the contrary, you make me feel alive again, Ryan. In a way I've never felt, even before the kidnapping. My life was ordinary. Safe and dull. You woke me up and helped me to step outside my shell and the barriers I put around myself, ones I didn't even realize were there."

He pulled into the driveway of the house where the plainclothes officer stayed. Ryan shut off the engine and turned to her.

Making a humming sound deep in his throat, he cupped her cheek. "You've done the same for me. You're so different from the superficial women I've had relationships with in the past. You never take anything for granted. I adore the way you seize each day and are so grateful for it."

Fern closed her eyes against the gentle brush of his thumb on her flushed skin.

"I mean it, Fern. You championed me in front of my family, and that takes tremendous courage. My father can be intimidating."

Her eyes flew open. "Intimidating, perhaps. He loves you,

though. You have a family who cares about your welfare, Ryan."

Not wanting to say any more, her throat tight, she slipped out of the car.

When they were inside his house, the dead bolt securing the door, Ryan headed into the living room. He patted a spot beside him on the faded sofa, nothing like the silk-covered one in his parents' house.

"I can't stay here anymore, Ryan," Fern told him, refusing to hold his hand, much as she longed for the comfort of his warm touch. She folded her hands into her lap, staring at them, willing herself to say the words.

"I'm a complication in your life. I don't belong here. I appreciate—oh how I do! I appreciate all you've done for me, giving me a place to stay, but I've decided to accept your family's offer of a rental home, with security, until the kidnappers are caught."

Ryan shifted closer to her on the sofa, the springs creaking beneath him. "You're not complicating anything. How the hell did you find out about the rental home?"

"Kim told me she overheard your family discussing it."

His expression turned dark with fury. "It's a family matter and none of Kim's business."

Hastening to reassure him, she looked up. "I'm no cheerleader for Kim, but she wasn't being mean about it. I think she wanted to warn me. But it doesn't matter. I was already considering moving back to my old apartment in Oso. Maybe not getting my job back, but there's remote work I can do…"

Slashing the air with his hand, Ryan scowled. "No. You're not going anywhere. Not unless you feel uncomfortable being here with me, Fern. No one is going to make you leave. Your old apartment? That's a stupid idea."

Now her temper began to rise. "Stupid idea? What's stupid is staying here, where everyone in your family scrutinizes me, where I'm a guest and keeping you from living your life. No privacy, and worse, my presence means you're a target as much as I am!"

Tears rose in her throat, much as she tried to fight them. This was so wrong, so difficult. She'd started to fall for Ryan, and she needed to bolt. Couching it in other reasons was safer.

Whenever she cared for someone, they always left.

Shadows in the living room seemed to deepen as the night darkened the windows. Ryan went over and drew the blinds. Grateful they were no longer showcased to anyone outside, like a painting hung on a wall, Fern continued.

"I won't see you get hurt on my behalf, Ryan."

There, it sounded noble, neatly tied up like a Christmas package, with a shiny red bow and paper. Even though inside the box remained empty.

"You're lying, Fern."

Moving closer, he reached out and took a strand of her hair between his fingers. "I can tell. I know you well enough by now. That little nervous tic in your cheek, the way you can't look at me."

Oh, he knew her well. Ironic. The one man she desperately needed to leave before she did something stupid like fall in love with him knew the hollowness of her words.

Too late. *I'm already falling in love with you.*

She had to convince him. "I'm not your responsibility, Ryan. Your responsibility ended the moment they put me into an ambulance."

"I know."

"Then let me go." Fern's voice cracked. "Before you get hurt, too."

Gently, he tugged her hair. "No."

The memory of smoke filling her lungs, ties biting into

her wrists as flames devoured the weathered walls of that cabin, flashed through Fern's mind. She shuddered.

"Please." Her voice dropped to a whisper. "I'd die if anything happened to you. You have others who love you, care about what happens to you."

"No, Fern." The word was said in a swarthy growl of command, brooking no argument.

This time he released her hair and drew her into his arms, a shelter she desperately wanted. "You have someone who deeply cares about you. Me."

Hot tears stung her eyes. He became a blurry visage. "I'm all wrong for you."

"You're right for me in ways I don't quite understand myself. All I know is the thought of you leaving is killing me. All the other women I've had relationships with, well, when they walked out the door, it hurt only my pride. Not my heart."

With a happy skip, her heart beat faster. "Ryan..."

Gently, he pressed a finger against her wobbling mouth. "I care about you, Fern Hensley, and it has nothing to do with your past or saving your life. If you tell me you don't feel the same about me, I'll help you pack your bags and arrange for you to stay elsewhere with armed security guards. But God help me, I'm falling in love with you."

Though her mind argued this was a horrible idea and she needed to leave, her heart thrilled at his words. Always in the past, logic and reason won over silly emotions.

Not tonight. For the first time, she wanted to leap into the unknown and damn the consequences. Tomorrow she might have regrets. They both might. But tonight she deserved this closeness, this tender intimacy.

Lonely for too long, starved for affection, she craved his touch. Only Ryan's touch. It filled her with wonder as his stunning blue gaze met hers.

"What's your answer? Do you want to leave?" he asked softly.

Fern slid her arms around his strong neck as if saving herself from drowning. "No."

Fern's heart pounded against her ribs as his fingers tangled in her hair. A tantalizing scent of his cologne, the brush of his night beard against her warm cheeks filled her senses as their mouths met. A small voice in the back of her head screamed this was not right, she had to stop it now, but she silenced it. Ryan capturing her in his arms, his strong body against hers, felt right.

His mouth moved subtly against hers, inquiring, hesitant as if he feared pushing her too hard. Fern responded with an open mouth, her tongue darting inside the cavern of his. The kiss, deep and moving, sealed their fates.

When they finally broke apart, breathless, Fern's eyes remained closed for a moment longer, her lips slightly parted. When she opened them, the vulnerability she felt remained, but the passion and sheer want in Ryan's eyes soothed it.

"I've wanted to do that for so long," she whispered, her voice trembling slightly. "I was afraid you didn't feel the same way."

Ryan traced the curve of her cheek with his thumb. "How could I not?" The words came out in a hoarse voice, as if he struggled with his own emotions.

They fell into another kiss, deeper this time, unspoken longing pouring out between them. Sofa springs moaned beneath them as Ryan pulled her closer, his heart's frantic hammering echoing her own. Books, magazines and a coffee mug scattered on the table before them spilled to the floor as she kicked out her feet to lie supine against his firm weight.

The noise broke them apart. Amusement danced on his face. "Oops. Forgot how small this couch is. Not exactly room to maneuver here."

Fern sat up, managed to stand and grabbed his hand. "I know a better place."

Following her down the hall, he balked at her bedroom door. "No. Mine is bigger."

With an urgency meeting her own, he tugged her toward his bedroom. Fingers trembling, Fern stripped off her stockings, shoes and clothing, stopping at her panties. She gave him an uncertain look.

He stopped unbuckling his trousers. "What's wrong?"

"Are you sure you want this?"

Ryan gave a rueful look downward. "Oh yeah. With you, absolutely."

He blinked. "Birth control?"

"Condoms?"

A sheepish grin as he opened the nightstand drawer. "Take your pick."

Charmed by his adorable confession, and emboldened by the heat in his eyes, she chose one.

Fingering the foil packet, she hesitated. "Ryan, it's been a long time for me. I don't want to disappoint you."

Stripped down to black boxers, he came forward and took the condom from her hand. Ryan dropped it on the nightstand. "If you feel uncertain or need to stop at any time, tell me."

Gently he pushed a lock of hair from her face. "I want you, damn, I want you so much I can barely breathe. But I get it if you're not ready or you get scared."

His understanding, twined with the desire in his eyes, took her own breath away. She trusted him, and knowing he would follow her wishes, even if she needed to stop, made her pick up the condom and tear off the foil.

"I'm more than ready, Ryan. Now, get naked."

A wide grin touched his mouth. He shrugged out of his boxers and her breath hitched. What a body.

Lean, like a finely tempered steel cord, with muscles roping his arms and legs, his flat abdomen showing the results of all those workouts in the basement. But it wasn't his body, or his impressive erection, that made her step toward him.

The emotion on his face told her he not only desired her, he cherished her. Ryan was willing to let her make the moves. Empower her.

Release control to her.

After being abducted and treated like a commodity, her kidnappers thinking only of using her for someone's sex slave, his consideration edged aside the hesitation and fear. Emboldened, she dropped to her knees with the condom in hand.

First, though, a small taste...

Ryan's eyes closed. He fisted a hand in her hair and groaned, the sound music to her delight.

She kept doing it, but in the back of her mind a little voice taunted her. Fern stopped, drew back.

He glanced down. "You okay?"

She gave a small nod. Nothing was going to ruin this moment. Not her fears, nothing.

Ryan reached down, helped her to her feet. The tremor running through her couldn't be disguised.

To her amazement, his arms wrapped around her and he held her. Not tightly, but close enough. It was such a warm, comforting gesture, Fern melted into him. For a few moments, they stood in each other's arms, enjoying simple human contact.

She wanted this.

She wanted him.

Encouraged, Fern broke away and palmed the birth control. Her fingers stroked his erection, and then she bent down and rolled on the condom. He was willing to concede to her every need.

Now she had to show him what those needs were.

Ryan was a good soul who cared. His courage and willingness to help others fueled her passion for him. He helped her to believe in people once more, and fed her hope the world could be a good place.

As he cupped her face, his expression filled with tender concern, she tunneled her fingers through his hair. "Every time I'm afraid or think bad things will happen, I push back those thoughts remembering you. You make me brave, Ryan. God help me, I think I'm in love with you."

A small smile touched his face. "Me, too. You make me out to be better than I am. I'm only a guy who happens to be crazy about you, Fern Hensley."

"You're so much more." She caressed his jaw. "So much more. Same way I am not a delicate, fragile woman. I've been through a lot, true, but I'm not made of glass."

Ryan touched his mouth to her cheek. "Far from it, sweetheart. You're a diamond that can cut the thickest glass, and I'm damn lucky to have you in my life."

The mere touch of his lips against her skin sent ripples of need shuddering through her. "Then let's stop talking and get to it," she whispered.

"There's only one thing standing between us, sweetheart."

"What?"

"Your panties."

Fern glanced down and groaned. He laughed, pulled them off and gently pushed her back onto the bed.

Their lips met in the briefest of kisses. Then they touched again, and, oh God, it felt truly like a miracle. Fern felt alive, more alive than she'd been over the past few months. His mouth was firm and warm, a promise of more than mere sex.

His kiss felt like a pledge of love.

As he grazed the side of her throat, dropping a kiss and lingering over the hateful tattoo there, she felt absolution. For what? Fern didn't know. But with every sweep of his mouth, gone was her trepidation, replaced with burning desire.

Ryan made her feel whole.

Ryan made her feel treasured.

Not as a prize to be sold, but a woman he adored.

As they kissed, she felt a deep connection to this man. Not simply because he pulled her out of a raging fire, but because their bonds ran deeper. Fern couldn't explain it. She only knew to follow her heart for once, instead of listening to her head.

Fern looked up at him, sliding her arms around his neck. "Don't hold back, Ryan. I need you. I need everything you have to give to me."

A brief smile touched his mouth, then Ryan covered her naked body with kisses, his hands fisting in her hair. A shiver born of sexual awareness seized her as she tested the granite-hard muscles of his shoulders with her fingers. The spark between them caught and flared. She turned her face to where his shoulder met neck, put her mouth on the flesh there and tasted the tangy salt of his skin. Smelled the musky spice of him.

Ryan kissed the tiny hollow of her throat, the movement of his mouth increasing the hot throbbing between her legs. She twisted beneath him. His hand drifted to the curve of her hip, then dipped between her thighs.

Fern jerked upright in shocked pleasure. He quieted her with a soft murmur, pushing her down, and she felt his finger slide between her feminine folds. Smooth as silk, he glided back and forth, creating tendrils of coiled tension.

She was soon a wound spring, ready to release the fires he stoked with each caress, ready to feel the full burn with erotic pleasure.

This was what she'd hoped for, searched for, in a lover. A man willing to give her pleasure before his own and fulfill her needs first. A man who truly cared for her, not only for sex.

Still, it meant losing control. Letting go.

"Shhh," he murmured. "Just let go. Surrender to it."

"Yes," she whispered.

She did just that. All tension within her exploded, and she wailed as it burst from her center and from her throat, shattering her consciousness as if it were glass. And when her eyes fluttered open, she saw Ryan looking down at her with deep satisfaction, and with a hint of male pride.

"Now," he murmured, and pushed open her trembling thighs.

This wasn't merely sex, this was something more, and they both felt it.

She sensed him holding back, and yet he quivered with need.

Time to let him know she wasn't fragile glass. Fern wrapped her legs around his hips and coaxed him farther. Ryan caged her with his body and wrapped his arms around her, holding her tight as his mouth met hers. The kiss was a maelstrom of unleashed lust. He took her mouth with fury, his tongue plunging inside with masterful strokes. Tasting her, taking all and leaving nothing, building her fervent and growing ardor.

Pausing, he glanced down to gauge her reaction. Any fear or hesitation, she knew he'd stop.

Assuring him, she opened her legs wider and arched her hips upward.

"Do it," she told him in a breathless whisper. "Please. I've wanted you for a long time."

He nudged his lean hips between hers. The breath caught in her throat. She arched upward. A promise lingered in his passion-darkened eyes.

Ryan lifted the long mass of her dark hair and kissed her

neck. He ran his tongue over her skin. "Don't be afraid," he murmured. "I promise, I'll take good care of you."

Fern opened her legs wider, the ache between them exquisitely sharp, demanding to be filled. Wide-eyed, she watched Ryan settle closer. The silky hair on his muscled chest rubbed against the sensitive, hardened crests of her nipples. He rose above her, gaze fierce, his shoulders blocking out the view of the ceiling. She felt the demand of his erection.

Ryan slipped forward, beginning to penetrate. Then, with a soft murmur and a powerful movement, he surged forward. Fern gasped, and then lifted her hips as they began the dance.

The delicious friction twined with the smoky heat of his gaze. Fern ran her nails across his back as he pumped furiously inside her.

She wanted more. Fern wriggled and arched impatiently, wanting all of him, wanting him gasping in need as much as she. He smiled, and his hips began to piston, his sex sliding in and out until his breath became rapid pants. Then he stiffened above her, and Ryan threw back his head and shouted her name, the cords in his neck strained.

Ryan collapsed with a heavy sigh, burying his face in the pillow beside her. She stroked the sweating, quivering muscles of his back, and her legs cradled him tenderly. When he shifted his weight off of her, Fern instinctively curled next to him, putting her head on his shoulder. Her eyes slowly closed, and her breathing deepened. She felt sleepy and oddly comforted by Ryan's arm about her waist.

She, whom men had abducted to be used as a commodity, marveled at the feelings flaring between them.

If only it would last. Tomorrow might look different. But for tonight, she'd cherish lying naked in his arms, feeling loved for the first time in years.

Chapter Eighteen

When Fern woke the next morning, sun streamed into the bedroom. Yawning, she rolled over and touched an empty pillow.

Blinking, she forced herself to wake up. Fern sat up. Ryan was gone. Joy over last night faded into disappointment.

A cream-colored note sat on the pillow. She picked it up.

Good morning, sleepyhead. Much as I wanted to stay here, I had to work. Didn't have the heart to wake you up. Text me later. Love you. Ryan.

Well, as love notes went, it wasn't literature, but the PS made her smile.

PS. I'll carry the memory of being in your arms, such perfection, and this time I *mean* perfection, through the day. Hope you don't have trouble walking, sweetheart, after the workout I put you through.

The PS was accompanied with the drawing of a grinning figure surrounded by flames and holding a fire hose. The figure had devil horns. Fern laughed. Typical Ryan. Well, they had awakened during the night to make love two more times, each time leaving them breathless once more.

She quickly showered and dressed. When the coffee was brewing—was it really after ten o'clock?—she fired off a quick text with hearts and fire.

He texted back several smiley faces and added he had to rush out to a call.

Always working, always rushing into danger. Fern set down her phone and poured coffee. Sitting at the kitchen table, she couldn't help her secretive smile.

The sex had been amazing, emotional and everything she'd ever hoped for in a lover.

So perfect it scared her.

Her smile faded.

Her pragmatic mind warned this relationship with Ryan couldn't last. He'd leave her, like everyone else eventually did. She was struggling to get her life back together, always looking over her shoulder because her abductors wanted her dead. Who could maintain a relationship, faced with that?

Knowing it was fear talking, Fern thought about calling Ava. Normally such a dramatic event, having sex for the first time in months, after the trauma of being kidnapped, would be an event to discuss with one's therapist.

But when the therapist was the brother of your new lover? Fern laughed.

What a conundrum.

Best to discuss her feelings with Ryan. She didn't need a third party.

What she truly needed was an update from Jacob on the case's progression. Had the clues she provided, when she regained part of her memory, advanced anything?

She dialed his number, only to get his voicemail. After leaving a message, Fern hung up.

Dressing in comfortable yoga pants, a loose T-shirt and sneakers, she went downstairs to work out.

Though she hated that Ryan had to work today, perhaps

it was best they both had their time apart to deal with the turbulent emotions of last night. Maybe Ryan didn't feel the same way, but Fern doubted it because it had been so real, so raw and passionate.

Ryan was honest and not the kind of guy who would sweet-talk a woman into having sex. He lived life to the fullest.

The rest of the day passed quickly as she showered, then did laundry, putting fresh sheets on both beds, cleaned up the house and worked on the laptop. Medical coding was coming back to her, and she felt confident she could get another job, probably a remote one, with a new doctor's office. Or even a local hospital.

She typed up a new résumé and began looking for jobs online.

A new life. New hope and possibilities. But would Ryan be part of it?

Fern took a break finally around dinner. She made a light chicken casserole, reasoning it could be frozen for Ryan when he returned home. He didn't care if it wasn't pretty enough for a cooking show or some influencer's Insta.

Fern stopped cutting up vegetables. Knife hovering in the air, she stared out the kitchen window.

Ryan lived every day with a vibrancy and vitality few men she'd known ever demonstrated. Ryan didn't care about her looking perfect with makeup, or what clothing she chose to wear. He cared about her, her feelings, who she was, including her past.

Her phone rang as she popped the casserole into the oven. Jacob, judging by the ringtone.

The news was not good. They had no leads on the case, despite the clues she'd given them. But Ryan's cousin had questions, as well as some information.

"Your date you were going to meet the night you got taken—Walter. You didn't know him well?"

"No. I'd met him at Dr. Sonder's office the previous day when he came there to sell something, maybe medical equipment, no, I think it was drugs. Did you find him?"

"He doesn't exist."

Knees weak, she sat on a kitchen chair. "He sure did exist when he asked me to meet him for drinks."

"There's no trace of him." Jacob's deep voice sounded almost like a growl. "He's gone. No one in Oso recalls seeing him. Not even your former employer. The receptionist said he arrived one morning, the morning you had the day off, and asked when you'd return because he wanted to discuss something with you. Tell me everything that happened."

Her stomach roiled. "He came into the office, and we struck up the convo about Irish history because I was reading a book about Ireland. He asked me to meet him at the Irish bar that night to hear this terrific band from Ireland. Only to meet him for drinks... I thought it was safe."

Jacob's next words sent a chill down her spine.

"There's no history of a Walter Landers. The man doesn't exist. Looks like everything was a ruse. He was targeting you, Fern."

"Are you saying he set me up?"

"I believe so. We figure Billy and his partner went rogue on the top guy organizing this sex trafficking ring and wanted a woman they could sell on their own to make quick cash. But they needed help. So they found you through the foster system, did some checking and then had Walter lure you to the bar so they could gauge a time when to take you."

Sweat broke out on her forehead. Stupid. So stupid of her, and trusting. The one time she agreed to meet a stranger, look what happened.

"I always took my car to work. Parked in the lot out back, and if he was watching me, he must have known which one was my car. Maybe even followed me home," she said slowly. "But that morning I had a flat so I walked. It wasn't far. Walter texted that the bar was a short walk from the office as well and parking was limited. He said he would meet me there but to text him when I left the office so he didn't have to wait alone."

Jacob snorted. "And he suggested it was such a brisk, cold night out and you had been working inside all day, that you also walk."

Fern covered her face with one hand. "Yes. How stupid of me. He must have been the one to flatten my tire."

"You're not stupid," he said in a gentler tone. "You were deceived by a pro, and meeting him there was a hell of a lot safer than him picking you up in his car. You did the right thing, Fern."

"At the wrong time." She couldn't help her bitter laugh.

"It is what it is. If there are other important details you recall, call me. If I'm not around, leave a voicemail and I'll get back to you right away."

"Thanks." She hung up.

His pragmatic words reassured her.

She settled into the living room to watch television. YouTube had several videos on Ireland, and the green, lush landscape and lilting music soothed her ragged nerves.

Halfway into a video, she heard a noise at the front door. Not a knock, but something that banged against the wood.

A bird? Thinking of the birds out back flocking to the feeders, knowing birds sometimes crashed into windows and doors, Fern went to the front door. If it was a bird, perhaps she could save it.

She opened the front door.

No stunned bird on the doormat that read Welcome.

As she went to close the door, she saw a note taped to the wood. Words painted in blood red.

Fear skidded down her spine. Fern struggled to calm herself. She counted to five, took a deep breath. A whispered scream came out.

She knew enough not to touch the menacing note, much as she wanted to rip it off the door and ball it up. Burn it in the fire pit.

Instead, she dialed the number of the officer staying a few doors down.

Paul Jenkins immediately answered, and when he heard the problem, he announced in a clipped tone he would be there immediately.

Barely had she hung up the phone when it texted a message Officer Jenkins was outside.

Fern opened the door. Brown hair cut military short, square-jawed, Officer Jenkins wore jeans and a T-shirt, but the pistol on his belt meant business.

She pointed to the note. Even though he was there with her, she couldn't bring herself to read the words. They were burned into her brain.

LEAVE BEFORE SOMETHING HAPPENS TO YOU FERN.

He frowned. "Why did you open the door?"

"I thought I heard a bird. There wasn't much noise, and if a bird was lying there, stunned, I wanted to save it."

As reasons went, it sounded lame, but the rugged police officer actually smiled.

"My wife does the same thing. She loves the little birds that visit the feeders in our yard."

He turned his attention to the note. Fern hugged herself against the night's chill as Jenkins studied the front stoop and the note. Cradling his cell phone, he gestured for her to go inside. He joined her a few minutes later, closing and locking the front door behind him.

"A unit will be here shortly to dust for evidence and take the note. They'll take care of it. With your permission, I'll check the security footage on the DVR."

She escorted him to Ryan's office. He opened the cabinet, plugged in the code she found in the drawer and began reviewing the footage. Fern hovered in the doorway.

"Is someone threatening me? Could it be the kidnappers?"

"Maybe. But criminals like that rarely announce threats. They only act on them. Don't worry. Might be neighborhood kids pranking around."

"The note doesn't seem like a prank, but a threat."

"We're treating it as such. Because of what happened with you and Ryan on the road, knowing the kidnappers are still at large, we're taking precautions."

Jenkins had a kind, fatherly air, and his even voice took the edge off her fear.

"Would you like me to stay the night, until Ryan gets home from his shift? Does he return tomorrow morning?"

Fern managed a nod. Dead tired on her feet, yet unable to relax because of the threat outside, she knew sleep would be fleeting.

"Thank you, Officer Jenkins." Fern waved in the direction of the kitchen. "The fridge is fully stocked, and there's snacks and some leftover casserole I froze if you get hungry."

"I already ate, thank you."

"I'm headed to bed."

An hour later, nestled in Ryan's big bed, she couldn't sleep. Snug in her flannel pajamas, she clicked on the remote to watch television. Much as she hated seeing the news, Fern felt she had to find out what happened in the outside world.

The local news was grim. She sat up, sheets twisting in her hands.

Another woman had been reported missing, and this one, like her, had been formerly in the foster system. No witnesses to her abduction, but grainy footage from a traffic cam showed her struggles as two men took her off the street and shoved her in the back of a light-colored van.

Billy and his mysterious accomplice had a new vehicle and new victim.

Fern switched off the television. Another woman. What would happen to her? Would she also be left to die inside a burning building? Or shipped off to another country to be sold?

I can't sit here and let this happen. I have to do something to help.

The euphoria felt last night making love with Ryan had vanished. Back to reality. Fern stared at the dark television screen.

She pulled on a soft flannel robe and went to find Officer Jenkins. He sat on the living room sofa, working on a laptop. Looking at the sofa, remembering how she and Ryan had kissed there, made her throat close tight.

Such a sweet memory. *I hope I never lose that one.*

Jenkins glanced up. "What's wrong?"

Fern perched on the edge of a chair. "I watched the news and heard another woman was kidnapped."

"Yes." Jenkins closed the laptop. "We released the news to the media in hopes someone saw something."

Her hands tightened on her lap. "Do you think it's the same men who took me?"

"Could be. Unless the operation has expanded."

Fern saw her life stretching before her like a ribbon. In the not distant past was the love and desire Ryan expressed for her. The future was filled with threads unraveling. Until these men were caught, more women would suffer.

She would never get her life back, have a chance for the happiness she deserved, until they were caught. Sometimes you had to leap out in faith to do the right thing.

Even when you put your life on the line.

Ryan risked his life each time he went on a call. He'd made it his career. Knowing this fed her courage.

Fern looked up, letting her hands relax. "I want to propose something to the police, to Jacob and the other investigators on this case."

Expression neutral, Jenkins told her, "Go on."

Here we go. "I'd like to offer myself as bait in an operation to lure these bastards and finally catch them. Before another woman is kidnapped."

Chapter Nineteen

Ryan was not happy when he got home the next morning and discovered what Fern planned.

Officer Jenkins had left, telling Ryan about the note. Unfortunately there were no fingerprints. The excellent security cameras outside had shown images of a person dressed in shapeless black taping the note to the front door and then running down the street. The figure wore a black hat and a mask, hiding his features from the camera.

"No." Ryan shook his head. "Listen, I've had a rough shift. Calls all day and night, no time to sleep. With some of our guys sent to fight the wildfire at the edge of the reservation, we were shorthanded all night. All I've had is two granola bars eaten in the truck on the way to accidents. We'll talk about your idea later, Fern."

Knowing he was tired and needed sleep, Fern didn't want to push it at first. But time slipped away and she had to take action, before more innocent lives were ruined.

"I can't talk later, Ryan. I'm angry. Furious."

Unable to sit, she paced the living room, wearing out his Berber rug. "Before they took me, I was living a normal, maybe solitary existence. Never bothering anyone, never breaking the law. Hells bells, I didn't even have a traffic ticket!"

He blinked at her use of curse words. Of course as curse words went, they were mild. Seldom had she ever cursed. Always trying to be the good girl, please everyone else.

Fern tired of putting others' needs before her own. She needed to do this, had to do something instead of hiding in his house.

"What gives these jerks the right to take women and sell them like merchandise? As if our only value comes from our bodies? Stripping away all our identities and everything we've ever loved?"

Knowing it would be impossible to stop, she raged on. It was as if all the pent-up fury from the time she was little until her kidnapping boiled to the surface, a volcanic eruption of emotion too long suppressed.

"My whole life has been about being meek and quiet, afraid to speak up, fearing either I'd get chastised or no one would love me. Well, you know what?"

Fern took a deep breath. Ryan sat quietly on the sofa, listening. Not saying a word, not rebuking her the way some men might or rolling his eyes or trying to interrupt.

He kept looking at her, his expression encouraging her to continue. So she did.

"I'm worthy of love. I have a voice, opinions, and I matter! I deserve better than the fate those, those, those…"

"Assholes?" he offered.

A tremulous smile touched her mouth. "Yes. Better than what they tried to force out of me. I deserve better than what William and my mother gave me. I deserve to be happy."

Knowing she had to convince him, Fern went to Ryan and sat beside him and took his warm hand into her trembling one.

"I can't be happy here, hiding out like a prisoner, knowing there's something I can do to help, Ryan. I won't be happy until those men are caught and I can finally get my life back. Until I know other women will be safe as well. The only way I can help is to offer myself as bait to trap them, with the police waiting nearby."

At his frown, she rushed on. "I have to do this because I'm the only victim who's still alive and they're after me. They want me, Ryan. The police will ensure I'm safe. Can't you see? This is my one chance to make everything right. My chance to do more than hide away as if I'm the one who did something criminal."

Fern took another deep breath. "My chance to help prevent this from happening again. Regaining my memory about Billy and Leo didn't help the police. This will."

He looked tired and worn-out. Part of her hated doing this to him when the man clearly needed rest. But if she didn't speak now, Fern knew she'd lose her nerve.

He gave a longing glance at the hallway, where his bed and much-needed sleep awaited.

"Well?" she asked.

"It's about time you got angry." He squeezed her hand. "With everything you've endured, your anger is more than justified. I'm proud of you, Fern."

No one had ever expressed pride in her. Warmth spread through her at his praise.

Then he shook his head. "Despite that, I don't want you to offer yourself as a sacrificial lamb to catch the kidnappers. Can't you see that? It's way too dangerous. You have no police training. Let an undercover policewoman do it."

Sliding her hand out of his, she bristled. "An undercover policewoman isn't who they're after. I'm the one they want. I have value to them."

Ryan's jaw tightened. "You talk about value? You have value more than as enticement for two desperate criminals, Fern. I won't let you do this."

"You won't let me?"

The words came out slowly as she digested their meaning. Everything in the past came rushing back.

Her mother, refusing to allow her to go to school.

William, laughing at her powerlessness over his occasional slaps.

The foster parents who wouldn't let her save her money to buy a pretty backpack, but took every cent she made from babysitting.

I've survived a hard childhood, abuse, alcoholism and a kidnapping. I'm not going to take it anymore.

Fern stood up. "You can't stop me, Ryan. I love you, and I'll always love you, but you have no claim over me."

Rubbing a hand over his face, he sighed. "It's been a bitch of a shift, Fern. I'm going to bed, and we'll discuss this further when I get up. Please, make sure to stay inside and keep the doors locked. You hear anything or see anything threatening, wake me up immediately."

"You need your sleep."

"I need you to be safe."

He headed toward his bedroom.

Staring after him, she felt her entire body tense, her throat close up. She loved Ryan. Loved how he cherished her.

Cherishing her didn't mean he had the right to tell her what to do.

For too many years, she'd lived according to other peoples' rules and standards. No longer.

It felt freeing, acknowledging her independence. Fern knew Ava would be happy to see her finally stand on her feet.

Even at the expense of defying her brother.

She had to do this to help Jacob and the investigators catch Billy and Leo. No matter how much it might cost her with Ryan.

AFTER MANAGING TO catch only four hours of sleep, Ryan woke up groggy and still tired. Too agitated to try to rest, he showered and dressed in blue sweatpants and a Dark Canyon Fire Department T-shirt.

Fern wasn't in the kitchen but sitting outside on the patio, watching the little birds fly in and out of the feeders. Though he'd asked her to remain inside, he couldn't blame her for being out on this beautiful spring day.

Reassured she was okay, he made fresh coffee and sat at the table, rubbing a hand over his weary eyes.

Offering herself as bait to the police to catch the kidnappers sounded like an excellent idea on paper. Yet he knew everything could go south in a heartbeat.

Much as he trusted his cousin Jacob and the other police, he couldn't trust them with Fern's life. The note deeply worried him. Someone threatened her, and he wanted to find the person and rip them apart for that threat.

The greater threat was Fern herself, wanting to put her life on the line.

As he took a bracing sip of caffeine, he thought about how much she meant to him. How horrible it would be to lose her. He wasn't a poet, hell, he had trouble writing a fire report, but she stirred something inside him. Something deep and permanent. Never one for hearts and flowers and mush, Ryan finally understood why some guys fell hard and deep in love.

I'm headed there myself.

Taking his coffee, he went outside to join her.

She glanced up as he sat at the table. "Good morning. I can make you lunch, or breakfast, if you're hungry. I thought you'd get more sleep, though, so I don't have anything ready."

He sighed. "Honey, I told you when you first moved in, you're not here to cook. Or clean. I don't want you to feel obligated."

Fern gave him a long look from those incredible hazel eyes. In the sunlight, he could see flecks of green and caramel among the brown.

"I don't feel obligated. It's my pleasure, Ryan. I like taking care of you and making sure you're comfortable."

Normally he'd bask in her assurance. Not today.

"I'd feel more comfortable if you'd drop this idea of offering yourself as sacrificial bait."

"I would argue, but you only woke up and it's cruel to debate before your first cup of coffee."

Ryan scowled. "It could be my second cup."

"Doubt it. Your shirt is on inside out."

He glanced down and groaned. Then looked up to see her impish smile. Ryan set down the cup, pulled the shirt over his head. He paused, seeing the glow of interest on her face as she stared at his chest.

"Like the view? I can leave the shirt off," he teased.

Amused, he watched a delicate flush tint her cheeks. Fern swallowed. "Um, wouldn't want you to catch a chill."

Before he could respond, she added, "Though I'd be happy to keep you warm."

Warm? He was heating up now, and it had nothing to do with the shirt he put back on. Ryan's hand covered hers. For a moment they sat in companionable silence, the sweet intensity between them building. So hot, like arcs of electricity shooting into the air.

Much as he longed to take her hand, lead her back inside, march her down the hallway to the bedroom and make love to her again, Ryan knew they had to talk.

He withdrew his hand, swigged the rest of his coffee, prepared to gird his loins in a different interaction with Fern— convincing her to drop the idea of being bait.

A loud ringtone with a man singing about a fiery love sounded inside. Fern glanced at the house.

"Is that your phone?"

Ryan raced inside to grab his cell on the kitchen table. Seeing the name on the screen, he groaned again. Damn.

"Colton," he answered. "I'm off shift."

"Not anymore." The smooth voice of his captain dashed all his plans. "We've got a level one hazmat at Mountainview Avenue, potentially turning to level two."

He rubbed a hand over his face. As senior hazmat technician at the Dark Canyon Fire Department, he had to respond. "What's the situation?"

"House fire, one-level single-family residence, pool chemicals inside. Lots of chlorine. Guy ran a business on the side."

Ryan blew out a breath. Pool chemicals were especially dangerous in a fire and, ignited, could release toxic gas. Chlorine alone was corrosive and could damage skin and eyes.

He needed as much information as possible.

Most household fires were deadlier than the average public realized. Plastics and normal household chemicals all could release dangerous vapors. Bleach mixed with ammonia made chloramine gas, which could be fatal.

Pool chemicals, with their high levels of chlorine, ah man...

"Police on scene now," his lieutenant told him. "We're on our way."

The truck was already responding. Dark Canyon had its own special hazmat response truck, outfitted with gas meters, suits, boots and everything they needed in case of a chemical spill.

Or worse.

He gauged the distance from his home to the station and realized he'd never make it in time. "Pick me up on the way."

Now he had to tell Fern, delay their discussion. Work came first. Saving lives came first.

As he headed outside once more, Ryan had a fleeting wish that for once his needs and hers came first.

Chapter Twenty

Gone again. *Better get used to it if he's going to be in your life.* Much as she wanted that, Fern wasn't certain about any kind of permanent relationship with Ryan.

Discussing her idea of being bait in a sting operation had to be put off. How could they talk if Ryan was off saving lives?

Listless, she ambled about the kitchen, debating on making dinner. The fire was riskier than usual, he'd told her, with chemicals mixed in. He might be gone for hours.

Maybe she'd bake something. Cookies or brownies. Comfort food. No, she needed veggies. A nice salad. And then she'd bake something sweet for Ryan.

She had promised Ryan she would not do anything rash, such as embark on this mission to offer herself as bait. Not until they could sit down and have a heart-to-heart.

It was going to be a rough talk. But she had to convince him she'd be fine.

Fern went into the kitchen, took a paring knife and began cutting vegetables.

A knock came at the door. With Jenkins gone, Fern felt wary about answering. Maybe it was Jenkins, checking on her. She glanced at her phone. No messages.

Knife in hand, she paused.

"Police. Miss Hensley, we're here to check on you."

Huh. She peered out the peephole. An officer in a uniform framed the round hole.

"Badge, please."

A gold shield was held up.

"Just a minute."

As a precaution, Fern called Jenkins. No answer.

Then a text came from Jenkins. Have to leave. Fire near my family. Worried for my pregnant wife. Told the department to send a replacement.

Sympathy filled her. She glanced at the peephole again. Maybe this was the replacement officer. The man did have a gold shield and a uniform.

As she unlocked and opened the door, a ringtone sounded. Fern froze.

The whistling theme from the movie *she remembered well.*

"Oh God," she whispered. "No. Please, no."

With all her might, she tried to shut the door, but the man on the outside pushed it in, sending her toppling to the floor. Screaming, she scissor kicked, trying to get away.

"Hello, Fern. Remember us?"

Never could she forget that deep voice with the cruel laugh.

No, not again, not again. Please. Fern's scream died in her throat as she clawed at the floor, trying to find purchase, kicking her legs, willing them to move, move, move!

Like her nightmare, she was immobilized. Fern gasped for breath and tried to crawl away, her heart in her throat, her pulse hammering, but someone grabbed her legs and pulled her.

Outside. Where she'd have no control.

She'd read about this—never let the criminals take you

to a second location because they'd have more control over you there. Do everything you can to fight them.

The knife! She rolled and swiped at her attacker, who dodged the blow and laughed again. Fern got a good look at his face.

His craggy face with the scar on his chin, the beady, bright blue eyes that looked soulless.

Billy. She tried to swipe at him again, but he dodged.

Then he stomped on her hand. Pain exploded, bright and sharp. She whimpered and released the knife.

"You're coming with us."

As they dragged her out onto the stoop, she managed to fumble for the knife. Fern sliced her hand, leaving blood on the concrete.

A sign for Ryan to find.

Then the knife was wrested from her hand. She felt a painful, hateful prick of a needle and everything went dark once more.

UPON ARRIVING AT the scene, Ryan realized an incident command post had already been set up. He was the senior hazmat tech.

Ryan shrugged into his breathing equipment and gear, donned his orange boots and duct-taped the suit to the boots so nothing could get inside.

Along with the two other hazmat techs, he trudged to the porch. Orange flames shot out of the garage, where most people stored chemicals. Radio chatter and static blared as he assessed the situation. Clutching the specialized gas meters, they went inside.

Upon entering, he swept the gas meter over the area. The meter could detect Cl2 in parts per million. But it showed nothing.

Fire had caught at the back end of the house. Ryan and the others emerged.

"Gas meter is negative," he radioed to the incident commander. "We'll check the back and the side."

They did so, seeing piles of junk, auto parts, but no pool chemical containers. Something was off. He reported their findings to the incident commander. No hazardous chemicals.

Ryan used protocol to decontaminate, just in case. As he shed the hazmat suit, he watched his team train water on the flames.

This call was different. Ryan felt it in his bones. His mom used to say he had good instincts about danger. She'd called it his "sixth sense."

He'd used it to his advantage on the job. It tingled now, like a feather stroking his spine.

Fire engulfed the home's back. At any time, the fire could jump to the front rooms.

House was an older wooden structure. Damn, he hated these kind of fires, hazmat or no hazmat. Wood went up like kindling in a hot campfire. The burning structure could also collapse.

No self-evacuation, which could mean no one at home. Or worse—someone trapped inside.

"Who called it in?" he demanded of the incident commander.

"Guy who lives here. Pete Sanders."

After donning his fire gear and boots and helmet, Ryan whipped his head around. Definitely needed to talk with the homeowner.

Neighbors had gathered around to watch. One woman screamed out, "Old Pete Sanders is still inside! He lives alone."

He had a sinking feeling about this one.

"Does he own a pool cleaning company?" Ryan asked. "Store chemicals?"

The woman shook her head. "He's retired and hoards car parts and other stuff."

Lieutenant Sims ordered Ryan, Mike and Bob inside. Ryan gripped an axe.

"Mask up," Sims ordered, and led the way.

"Fully engulfed," the lieutenant announced into his radio.

"Fire department, Mr. Sanders, call out," Ryan yelled through his mask as he entered the house.

To his relief, the hoarding was limited to piles of old newspapers and they could navigate through the room. But old newspapers were a firetrap.

Flames had already caught on the ceiling and advanced down the hallway, a tunnel of hot orange. The home was a tinderbox. Other firefighters had already vented the roof to let the heat and smoke escape.

They broke open doors, could see little through the acrid smoke.

"In here," someone screamed from behind a closed door. "Help me."

The door was jammed. He struck the wood with his axe and broke through. A man was on the floor, trapped by a fallen dresser.

Ryan reached him, pulled him free.

"Rye, what's your twenty?" the lieutenant's voice crackled over the radio.

"I'm okay," he radioed back. "One victim, coming out."

Ryan scooped the man over one shoulder and struggled out into the hallway.

The guys already had a hose on the flames, battling the fire inside as he ran out with the victim. As he went to place him on the ground, the man grabbed his coat.

"Who—who are you?" he asked, coughing.

"Try not to talk," Ryan said gently. "I'm Ryan Colton, the firefighter who rescued you."

"Colton...you're the one. My wife...still inside, basement," the man rasped. "Cathy. Help her. Please."

The other firefighters helped him place the man on a stretcher. Guy had burns, had inhaled a lot of smoke.

Ryan called out to his lieutenant. "Lieutenant, I'm going back in. Wife's in the basement."

"Not without backup."

"I'm right behind you," Bob yelled.

Breathing equipment in place, axe and heat detector in hand, he was already racing inside as the guys trained water on the flames. He tugged open the basement door, and he and Bob ran down the rickety stairs. Tremendous smoke filled the air. No sign of the wife, not even a sig from the heat camera.

Glancing up, he saw the ceiling ready to go.

"Rye, get out of here," Bob radioed as he ran for the stairs.

"One last sweep," he radioed back.

Just as Bob made it up, the ceiling collapsed near the stairs. With the stairs gone, Ryan ran to a basement window. Now the basement was on fire, reaching the piles of newspapers stacked neatly throughout. The papers caught, smoldered and burned.

Ryan tried to open the window. Painted shut.

Now he knew why his sixth sense tingled.

I'm not going to die in here. It's not my time.

Using his axe, he smashed the basement window and cleaned out the glass. Narrow, it would be a tight fit. Already he felt heat at his back reaching for him.

He radioed for help. He tossed his axe and thermal camera outside. Mike and Bob were there as he hauled himself up, and they pulled him through the window.

"Rye, you okay?" Bob asked.

Tearing off his mask, he nodded, breathing in fresh air.

Lieutenant Sims came over, led him to Nick, who handed him an O2 mask as Ryan sat on the back of the truck.

The sinking feeling overcame him. Lost another person. He tried but, damn, almost bought it himself.

"Couldn't find her."

The lieutenant clapped his shoulder. "Damn good thing you're fit. If you were Bob, you'd never have cleared that window."

"Hey, I resent that remark." Bob grinned, his face crinkling with concern. "I thought you were right behind me, Rye. Damn, I'm sorry."

"I'm good," he assured him, coughing.

Nick checked his vitals. Ryan tried to remove the O2 mask, but Nick replaced it.

"No dice. You may have breathed smoke."

Ryan removed the mask again. "I'm fine. Need to check on your patient."

The man lay on the stretcher, barely conscious. "Mr. Sanders, your wife, Cathy, are you certain she was in the basement?"

Eyelids fluttered. Sanders looked at him, removed the oxygen mask and rasped, "I'm sorry. I needed the money. He promised a lot of money to get you here. Said you were the hero type who would go after her."

"Who is he?" Ryan demanded.

But Sanders fell unconscious.

Ryan's guts tightened as he glanced at Nick, who gestured to the ambulance. "Gotta go."

As the ambulance growled away, he looked around. It didn't make sense. He'd searched the basement, no signs of life. Only newspapers and boxes and piles of clothing.

Seeing the wide-eyed neighbors, he went over to them. "You said Sanders lived here. Where's his wife?"

"Wife?" One woman shook her head. "His wife left him fifteen years ago. He's lived alone ever since."

His heart raced in a panic as he walked back to the truck, feeling as if his head were going to explode. He took his personal phone, dialed Fern's number.

No answer.

The bad feeling increased. Ryan radioed his lieutenant. "Lieutenant, I have to get home. Something's wrong."

"Go," he ordered. "Take our command vehicle. I'll clear it with the incident commander."

Not needing a second authorization, Ryan sped off toward the SUV. He raced homeward. When he reached the neighborhood, all seemed quiet. Ryan parked at the house where Officer Jenkins stayed.

Exhausted and yet running on adrenaline, Ryan looked for Jenkins. Usually he sat on the porch, reading a book and drinking coffee.

No one there.

Though it wasn't a reason to be alarmed, combined with the circumstances of the fire he'd fought, the absence raised the hairs on his nape. Maybe Jenkins had to leave. But the police officer would have called for backup.

Something wasn't right.

The man might be at the house, like last night, staying there to guard Fern. Yet Fern would have told him.

Warned him to give the officer a heads-up when Ryan walked through the door, lest he get a gun in his face.

An older model black sedan pulled up to the driveway and Officer Jenkins parked and got out. The worry etched on his face echoed Ryan's.

Then it clicked. He'd been so busy with the scene, securing everything, the man on the sidelines looking familiar, and yet he'd ignored him because he had a job to do...

"You were at the fire," Ryan told him.

Jenkins nodded. "Had to go. Got a call there was a hazmat sitch in my neighborhood, and I needed to evacuate my family. I texted Fern what happened and told her the department would send someone else here to take my place."

No one had. There was no plainclothes officer guarding his house. Guarding Fern.

Like him, Jenkins had been lured away from keeping Fern safe.

He walked quickly, his boot heels clicking on the sidewalk, echoing the beat of his rapid heartbeat. Fern had to be inside—she was okay and promised she wouldn't leave. Promised she'd wait for him to come home. No way could she change her mind and not tell him.

Jenkins was running behind him.

Please be there. Please. Words became a frantic chant, the way he'd used to wish away the monster in his dark closet at night.

Before he grew into an adult and discovered life's real monsters hid in plain sight and not in your closet.

Ryan was running now, pummeled by adrenaline, all exhaustion gone, his arms and legs pumping. Breath coming in and out in little gasps, he finally reached his home. Fern's sanctuary.

"No, no, no," he moaned.

The front door stood ajar. Blood smeared the front stoop, tiny droplets as if Fern had cut her hand. Or worse.

Ryan ran through the house, screaming her name.

No answer. Nothing but the frantic beat of his heart and his own harsh breaths.

Fern had vanished.

Chapter Twenty-One

Panic squeezed his throat. Ryan stared at the blood on the stoop. Fern was hurt.

Jennings reached the house and squatted down, studying the blood. Calm and collected, the officer was pragmatic.

The love of his life was missing. Ryan took a deep breath and counted to five, took another deep breath to calm the hell down. He was useless like this.

Fighting fires took professionalism and stuffing your emotions way down inside. He had to do the same now to help Fern.

"Fern's smart." The police officer pointed to the blood droplets. "She left a clue."

Puzzled, he looked down. "How is that a clue?"

"Tells you she was forced. She didn't walk off on her own. There was a struggle."

Suddenly he realized with all her talk about leaving the house, striking out on her own, this clue was quite important.

"I could have come home and assumed she left because she wanted to leave," he said. "Because she'd been talking about it."

Jenkins nodded. "Who else knew Fern talked about leaving?"

"My family. They found a rental for her. Mom, dad, my sister, her fiancé, Chay, and you..."

His voice trailed off as he stared at Jenkins.

The man stood up, nodding. "Let me call this in. Don't touch anything. Go into the house and pull up the security footage."

As he headed to the office, Ryan texted his cousin Jacob, telling him what happened. Jenkins didn't seem as trustworthy now.

He scrolled through the footage and was dismayed to find the front door cameras had been blacked out. Jenkins joined him in the office.

"Spray-painted over to hide their faces and the abduction," the officer explained.

Anger wouldn't help Fern now. Answers would. He narrowed his eyes at Jenkins.

"Fern was under your protection. You were supposed to watch her, and only you knew she'd been talking about leaving the house and living elsewhere. In my book, that makes you a suspect."

The older man met his gaze with a level look. "I know it looks bad. But I was set up, same as you. We both were called to a fire to get us away from Fern."

Now Pete Sanders's words made sense. He called Nick for a report on the fire victim.

Nick answered immediately. "I was going to call you, Ryan. Sanders is on a vent. Guy kept apologizing before they vented him about taking money to lure you to the fire."

Ryan thanked him and hung up. He didn't have time for understanding or convos. Ryan kept scrolling through the security footage, hoping and praying something, anything, would show up.

Hearing Jacob call out, he ran to the front door. His cousin looked grim.

"Fern's gone." Ryan relayed what happened and cursed the fact he'd been lured away from protecting her. He should have known something like this could happen.

"Hey." Jacob put a hand on his shoulder. "Easy, cuz. It's not your fault. Let's focus on what happened, how we can get her back."

Giving a brusque nod, he jerked his head at the door. "You heard about the threatening note. I'll show you the security footage."

As Ryan came to the footage of whoever left the note, Jacob frowned.

"This person... Whoever left the note is left-handed. The way he tossed his head, combined with the slim physique. This isn't a man, and I highly doubt it's the one who took Fern."

Ryan studied the footage closely. The head toss, pert and sassy, a person, no, a woman accustomed to turning her head, displaying long, silky blonde hair.

"Left-handed." Ryan clenched his fists. "Son of a... I think I know this woman. It's my ex-girlfriend, Kim, who lives next door to my parents."

Jacob's jaw tightened. "I'll have her brought in for questioning."

"No time. We'll go visit her right now."

Every minute counted. The more time wasted, the farther away the kidnappers took Fern.

A patrol unit took them there, lights and sirens blaring to speed to the quiet neighborhood. Ryan was out the door, barely giving the officer time to park. Jacob caught up to him as Ryan was about to pound on the door. Anger shot through him, a vicious, deep anger that made him want to kick the door down, demand answers.

"Let me handle this."

Ryan nodded, stepped back. When Kim answered the door, he could see the surprise and panic flare on her pretty face.

"You know why we're here?"

"No, I..." Kim stepped back and bristled. "It's an odd time for a social visit, Ryan."

Typical Kim, turning a situation around as if she were the one offended.

"This is far from social," he snapped.

Her eyes went wide as Jacob once more put a restraining hand around his arm. Good thing he did, because Ryan was ready to charge into the room.

Jacob pushed forward, blocking Ryan. "Fern Hensley has been abducted. We're here about the note you left on my cousin's front door."

Managing to sidestep Jacob, Ryan watched her carefully. He knew Kim well enough to know when she lied. Guilt and then fear crossed her face.

"You left the note." How he managed to speak calmly was a damn miracle.

"I—I—"

"That's right, Kim. It's always about you. Always has been. Ever wonder why I broke up with you?" He gave a derisive snort. "She doesn't care about Fern, Jacob. Only her own hide."

Jacob's gaze glinted, as if he'd digested Ryan's information and gleaned valuable information. "It's best if you're honest with me now, Miss March. You're facing trespassing charges and more, and this is your chance to mitigate any further damage."

"I didn't hurt her. I didn't know she'd been kidnapped, I swear it!" Kim clenched her hands in her lap. "It was only a joke..."

"A joke?" This time Ryan couldn't remain quiet. "You left a note threatening Fern on my front door and you call it a joke?"

She didn't meet his furious gaze. "I—I was jealous. When

I saw her with you at the dinner, how close you both were, and I heard your parents wanted her out, well, they wanted her gone, too!"

Incredulous, he stared at her, wondering how the hell he'd ever become involved with Kim. "You were jealous? You have a boyfriend."

"He's not like you! No one is like you, Ryan. I miss you, and when I saw Fern was with you, living with you, I thought the note would scare her into leaving. I didn't mean any real harm."

Tears filled her eyes, but they weren't tears of regret or sorrow. No, not over Fern. Kim only cried for herself, because she was scared of the consequences. Such privilege. Her entitlement was a sharp contrast to gentle Fern, who cared for others and had a good heart.

They were wasting time here. Ryan glanced at Jacob. "She had nothing to do with Fern's disappearance. She doesn't know anything. I can tell."

Jacob nodded. He looked at Kim with disgust. "Ryan, do you want to press charges against her for trespassing?"

"Not now." He turned back to his ex. "If I ever see you around my property again, I will have you arrested. In the meantime, I suggest you look for another job. When my father discovers what you did, he won't want you around, either."

"But Ryan…"

Kim's beseeching look didn't pull weight on him anymore. Disgusted, he stormed away.

When they returned to the house, Ryan got a call. Tempted to ignore it, he knew he couldn't.

Jacob, talking to the police officers dusting and securing the crime scene, saw his distress. "What's wrong?"

"Brush fire. Dark Canyon Wilderness. Have to report to the incident commander. They need me to help create a fire line. They're already doing back-burns to keep it from spreading."

Never had he felt this helpless, not even when Kate McIntyre slipped through his gloved fingers. Back then, he'd been too much in shock. With the disappearance of Fern, the woman he loved, and aw, hell, he could admit it now, he felt out of control.

He wanted to help, rush out and try to find her. And when he found the sons of bitches who took her, there would be hell to pay.

Jacob nodded. "Go. Do what you do best, Ryan. Your job, keeping people safe. I'll deal with this."

"Promise you'll call or radio dispatch with any news, and I mean any news, about Fern?"

"I promise."

As Ryan headed to his car, he knew Jacob would keep that promise. Coltons always kept their word. They were family, and families counted on each other when times were rough.

This was one of the roughest times he knew, and he needed his family support as much as the public needed him to deal with this brush fire.

FERN ROUSED FROM unconsciousness to a smoke-filled inferno burning nearby.

Blinking hard, gasping for air, she struggled out of the narcotic-filled daze to look at her surroundings.

No weather-beaten shack this time. No flames consuming dry wood walls, coming closer. Looking around, her eyes watering, she realized she lay on rocky earth. Canyon walls surrounded her. Smoke filled the air, acrid and harsh. Close by, a wildfire burned.

She struggled to sit up and realized her wrists and ankles were restrained once more by zip ties. Billy and Leo had dumped her here near the wildfire, probably to let her burn. Finish what they had started and failed back at the cabin.

At least this time they hadn't broken her leg or beaten

her. Maybe they were in a hurry, or thought her too weak to fight for her life.

I am not going to die here.

They'd tried to kill her once, and a brave, commanding firefighter had rescued her. No rescue for her now. Fern knew she was on her own.

Coughing, she peered into the smoke-filled air. The wildfire encroached on the canyon, shutting off access. Though she'd pressed the GPS locator on her necklace so police and Jacob could track her position, Fern wasn't certain it would work. The distance might be too far.

She had to find a way out, and if no help was coming, she'd do it alone.

You're not alone.

Ryan's voice echoed in her memories. He'd been there time and again for her, steadying her when she felt ready to falter, reminding her she had courage and strength.

He admired her.

Respected her.

Loved her.

I'm not going to die here. Not when I have so much to live for and I was given a second chance.

Love was worth fighting for—hells bells, she was worth the fight.

A tiny stream trickled nearby. Leo and Billy were in such a hurry to dump her, they'd failed to check out all the surroundings. On her hands and knees, ignoring the pain from stones cutting into her legs, she crawled over to it. She found a sharp stone sticking out from the ground.

With some effort, she sawed back and forth with her wrists, grimacing as the stone cut her skin. She did not stop.

I need a little help here. Fern glanced skyward.

Her luck turned. The zip ties Billy and Leo used were old

and they snapped. Fern pulled her wrists free, then tore off her blouse and wet it, tying it around her mouth and nose like a mask.

The shirt would act as a filter from the smoke. Ash would not get through the fabric, clogging her lungs. At least for now.

Ryan had told her most fire victims died from smoke inhalation.

Next she went to work on her ankles, using another stone to saw through them. Finally her ankles were freed.

Fern wet the shirt again and coughed, then retied it around her face. She thought of the sign she'd left Ryan at the house, managing to cut herself to leave blood on the stoop so he'd know something was wrong. He would not assume she left him and went elsewhere.

Wind blew, carrying arcs of sparks and more smoke. Then it shifted, showing a tall structure in the distance.

A fire tower.

If she made it there, she might have a chance. Ryan told her the towers were stocked with water, food and firefighting equipment. It looked out of the range of the wildfire.

He'd given her the little pocket compass as a gift to find her direction in life. Now it would guide her to the tower, hopefully, toward survival.

After removing it from the necklace, she held it steady. The fire tower was north. North like the North Star, the only star in the sky that never moved.

Steady and true, like Ryan.

If I get out of this, I'm making a fresh start. With Ryan, if he'll have me. Stop thinking like that. You will get out of this.

Fern stood on shaky legs, willing herself to walk forward. Willing herself to climb over rocks and navigate the canyon, toward safety.

Toward life.

THE DARK CANYON WILDERNESS was about forty-five thousand acres of prime Utah backcountry. People came from across the country to navigate the desert and forest, take in the ancient cliff dwelling ruins. The canyons and mesas were quiet, peaceful, and the topography shifted from forest to desert. You could lose yourself out here, or as Ryan found at times, find your purpose.

One of the most popular hikes was the forty-mile loop, beginning at the rimrocks of Cedar Mesa sandstone, where hikers moved downward more than two thousand feet to a dry streambed. It was a challenging hike, and he'd done it plenty of times.

Always wary of flash flooding, Ryan knew the trouble times were the summer and fall thunderstorms, but since the canyons were broad, the danger wasn't as severe. Still, it helped to be alert and aware, especially when spring brought occasional flooding. So far, they hadn't had to rescue any hikers inside the fire line, and he was immensely grateful for that.

In summer, temperatures could reach over a hundred degrees. Now, in April, they were tolerable, that is, if one embarked on a hike.

Outfitted in firefighting equipment, pounding the soil, Ryan sweated as if the temperatures were summer.

Working a fire line called for different skills than a house fire. Ryan's shoulders ached from digging a trench down to the bare soil to remove brush and other vegetation that could feed fuel to the fire. They'd created an anchor point, where the fire was the coldest. Smoke swirled around them, but at his vantage point, he could easily see.

If they contained the fire, it wouldn't advance to homes on the edge of the wilderness.

A spring rain sure would come in handy now, but though clouds scudded overhead, they weren't counting on it.

Without words, he worked with his team, his mind focused on the job, trying not to worry about Fern. With relentless determination, he kept at it until he heard a call from dispatch that had nothing to do with the fire.

"Ryan. We got a ping on Fern's necklace. Over," Jacob's voice crackled over the radio.

Ryan whipped his head around. "Where?"

"Edge of the Dark Canyon Wilderness." Jacob gave the GPS coordinates. "We're going to send a team in there."

As he plugged in the coordinates to his cell, his flare of hope turned to a sinking feeling. *At least we found her. There's a chance.*

Memorizing the coordinates, Ryan went to the mobile command set up nearby. He consulted the satellite tracking app the incident commander used to give orders to those fighting the blaze.

A chill raced down his spine. Sons of bitches had dumped Fern at the edge of the fire. Right where the flames were racing.

She didn't have a chance.

By the time rescue reached her, she'd be dead.

He spoke into his shoulder mike. "Jacob, I'm only about two miles from that location. I'm going in."

"No."

"No choice. I'm here. You're not. No one else is. You don't know the terrain like I do."

The slick rock and the sand would make hiking to her a bitch, and minutes counted.

"I'll radio you when I find her. Colton out."

The incident commander lifted up his helmet and studied him. "Colton you do this, it's against orders."

"Have to, Chief."

The man, burly and rugged, gave a brief smile, outlined in his soot-stained faced. "Not my orders. Someone's orders."

His captain gazed at him. "Not my orders, either, Ryan.

Go get her. Radio if you need help. We need to stay here. But we've got your back."

Ryan struggled against the emotion clogging his throat. These men and women were his family as much as Jacob and the other Coltons. He nodded. "Thanks."

"But you're not going in alone." Tom shook his head.

On this he would not compromise. "Look, I'm not asking anyone else to risk it to retrieve Fern. You're needed here."

Tom grumbled, but lifted a bulky item off the folding table. "Here. Take this. It's all we can spare, but it will help. Use it to track her and then radio back your coordinates. Battery's running low. Keep the drone turned off until you get closer to her last known location. We'll keep in touch with you and radio back hot spots and the advancing fire line."

Ryan took the drone and the remote. He'd trained with this drone for wildfire fighting and knew it was an older model. It didn't have infrared for sighting hot spots, but it would help to scout ahead for Fern's location. "Thanks."

It was a lot to carry, but the drone was critical.

After consulting with the GPS and making sure his sat phone worked, he checked his gear. Emergency pack with medical kit, navigation guide, headlamp, communications radio, rogue hoe. His hardhat and Nomex flame-resistant shirts and pants, gloves and boots would protect him. Ryan grabbed two additional NIOSH-approved N95 masks.

Fern had nothing to protect her.

He marched into the wilderness, toward Fern.

He only hoped he wasn't too late.

Chapter Twenty-Two

Fern had doused all her clothing and hair in the little creek and struggled to walk to the fire tower. But the rugged terrain and the soft sand made hiking difficult. Stopping to rest, she looked around, wondering if she was walking directly into the fire. Hard to gauge from the smoke and the wind blowing in her direction.

Well, if I burn to death this time, at least I'll have tried to save myself.

She wiped tears from her eyes, telling herself it was from the acrid smoke, not thoughts of her life ending.

Think of Ryan. He risks his life all the time to save people, rushes into burning buildings without a thought for his own safety...

Ryan also has training and wears protective clothing, her cynical self added.

Fern laughed and coughed. She could almost hear Ryan's voice in her head, agreeing.

Then his deep, stern tone urging her forward, to keep moving. *Don't stand still. Don't give up.*

An odd whirring noise sounded overhead. Blinking back tears, she looked up.

A black drone flew overhead, zipping along the canyon. Her heart leaped with joy. Ryan had shown her a vid of such drones and how firefighters used them to scout out the fire's location, fight the flames themselves and even locate stranded hikers.

"Hey!" Fern waved her arms, coughed and screamed again, trying to get the machine's attention and whoever operated it. "Help! I'm here!"

Suddenly the drone dropped from the sky a few feet away, crashing on the soft sand.

Despair nudged her. Maybe the smoke got to it, or the battery died. But surely whoever operated the remote would have seen her.

Unless the remote's battery died as well.

"Please," she whispered. "Please, someone come. I don't want to die here."

She began the bargaining stage so familiar to her after dropping to rock bottom during her drinking days, before her foster parents brought her to Alcoholics Anonymous. *If you get me out of here, God, I promise I'll be good. I promise I'll make something of my life. I promise to help others.*

"I promise I won't run away again like before, and I'll stick with Ryan and see where we go," she said aloud, and then coughed.

Smoke swirled, a grayish fog, and cleared. Out of the clearing walked a figure in soot-stained yellow, with dark trousers, a white hardhat. An N95 mask covered his face.

Fern blinked, not wanting this to be a hallucination caused by the drugs Billy and Leo had given her.

She waved her arms again. "Hello! I'm here. Help!"

"Fern?" the figure asked.

Stunned, she stood in disbelief as he raced forward. The figure tore off his mask, revealing the features of someone she knew well.

Someone who had saved her from the hell in the cabin, and once more reached her side.

"Ryan?" A sob rose in her throat.

"Fern. Thank God."

Never had she hugged anyone so tight. Then, brisk and professional, he looked around. "Got to get out of here. Fire's advancing and the wind is shifting."

He fished two more N95 masks out of his pack. "Here, put this on. It will help filter the smoke."

She pointed to the distant fire tower. "I was headed there, thinking maybe someone was up there."

"Not now, but good call."

He consulted the tablet-sized remote in his hands. "Drone battery is dead. We'll have to hoof it to the fire tower and use the radio to keep abreast of the fire line."

Ryan spoke into his shoulder mike and received a transmission of crackling noise that reported the fire's position.

"Colton out." He looked at Fern. "Fire's blowing to the west, away from the tower. If we can make it to the tower, there's equipment there. Oxygen masks, water and, best of all, a radio that has a more powerful signal."

"Thank you." She coughed, her eyes watering from smoke, and emotion as well.

He set the remote down on the ground. "Have to leave this and the drone here. Too much to carry."

He gazed at her. "Can you walk?"

Fern nodded. The drugs they'd injected into her had mostly worn off, though her legs felt like rubber. But she'd run out of here if necessary.

"Let's go."

Brisk, professional, the air of command in his voice. She'd never seen him at work, not like this. Taking charge, compelling her forward, focused on getting them out.

The sand beneath their feet made it difficult to walk, her shoes sinking into it like quicksand. Every few minutes Ryan's radio crackled, giving him updates on the fire line and the battle being waged to contain it.

Thigh muscles bunching and burning, she began to wheeze. Maybe the narcotics hadn't left her system after all.

Ryan hooked an arm around her waist and helped her walk through the sand and navigate the boulders in their way. Finally they reached the tower. She looked up at the steep ladder. Though it was a series of switchbacks, allowing one to rest at landings, it was a long way up.

"Can you make it or do you want me to pull you up?"

Fern shook her head. She was making it on her own.

"I'll be right behind you."

Slow going, dragging herself up, one step at a time. At each landing, she stopped, struggling to breathe. Ryan let her rest, not pushing her, but she knew, judging from the dizzying feeling, she needed oxygen.

Finally she reached the top. Ryan pushed past her and helped pull her upward to the walkway ringing the tower office.

Arm around her waist, he helped her inside. Huge windows allowed excellent views of the entire Dark Canyon Wilderness. There was a cot, binoculars, extinguisher, propane stove, radio with a headset, even a mini refrigerator. Best of all, a small cabinet, from which he pulled out a portable oxygen bottle. After she pulled off the N95 mask, Ryan slipped the plastic oxygen mask over her face and opened the canister.

He set about calling on the radio, giving the incident commander their position.

Finally he returned to her side, after securing two bottles of water from the supplies.

Fern breathed in the oxygen, her head clearing. She blinked, her eyes still watering.

Springs creaked as he sat on the cot with her.

"Now we wait."

She removed the mask. "What are our chances?"

"Good. They'll get to us." He didn't look at her. Jaw rigid, he stared at the windows before them.

"The tower's not manned these days, except when they can find someone willing to work for very low pay. Not necessary, anyway, not with the tech these days like the drones flying overhead to spot fires. It's mainly used to aid stranded backpackers who get lost or injured," he said.

"Will you get into trouble for leaving that drone?"

His mouth twitched in a faint smile. "Trust you to worry about me, after all you've been through. Nah. I'm good."

The smile vanished. "As long as you're safe, and okay."

"Thanks to you."

His jaw went taut. "When I thought of those bastards taking you, leaving you to burn to death again…"

He looked away.

Fern touched his arm, needing this connection and reassurance, for both of them. "I'm here. I'm not going to die, Ryan."

Glancing at her, he gave that faint, almost haunted smile again. "No. You're a tough one, Fern Hensley. Strong, resilient. I counted on that when I heard you were missing again. Put the mask back on, honey. You need that O2."

Ryan stood and paced the tower's small interior as she put the oxygen mask on again. "Soon as you feel strong enough, and they have a safe area overhead for the helo, we can leave. Smoke's too thick right now."

Bracing his hands on the desk, he stared out the window. "I hate this canyon. Too easy to get caught here."

Something else bothered him. Her intuition warned it wasn't her or their precarious situation.

Fern removed the mask. "You've been here before."

He didn't seem to hear her, as if lost in his own thoughts. "I let a woman die out here."

She felt a gut punch at the words. "Tell me."

Maybe it was her voice, raspy from the smoke, or he simply needed to unload. Whatever the reason, Ryan began to talk.

"It was about a year ago, in the spring. I'm a rock jock, you know? Loved to climb, always did it when I could. The challenge, it's great and keeps me going."

He snorted. "Something Dad never understood—the physical need to get out and get moving in nature."

Fern put the mask back on and listened.

"Cap always liked having a rock jock on the team, came in handy for rope rescues when the park rangers in Dark Canyon got overloaded or couldn't get a rescue in time. Well, last spring, I got a call. We got a call. Stranded hiker rock climbing on the Sundance Trail."

He pointed out the window. "The trail is amazing to hike. You descend about twelve hundred feet into the canyon. Then you're surrounded by these terrific rock walls, just pressing against you, with a stream in the middle. Done it many, many times. Thought it would be a piece of cake."

Shaking his head, he gave a grudging laugh. "Me and my assumptions. Well, we got there, with all our equipment, ropes, harness, you name it. I put on my equipment and climbed up to rescue her. She was dangling from a rope that wasn't secured right."

Fern watched him.

"Her name was Kate. Kate McIntyre. Terrified. Frozen in place, couldn't go up, couldn't go down. Her anchor was coming loose, and I knew it wouldn't hold. Only one anchor. Should have used at least two. Dammit, I secured three anchors to get to her!

"I reached out to her, secured her to the line. I told her

not to move, I would do all the work. I told her everything was going to be okay."

Fern didn't need to guess the ending. The haunted look on his face told her everything.

Ryan checked the oxygen canister. "She was twenty-four."

She removed the mask. "A year younger than me," Fern mused. "Was she an experienced climber?"

He blinked, as if the question startled him, then motioned for her to put the mask on again. "No. I found out a few days ago from her instructor that Kate was a beginner. She wasn't experienced enough for that climb. Her parents said the same thing at her funeral, but it doesn't matter."

"Do they blame you?"

As he shook his head, she breathed in more oxygen, then removed the mask.

"Why do you blame yourself if her family doesn't, either? You did your job. You tried to rescue her. You didn't push her off the cliff."

"I didn't save her!"

Fern looked at him calmly. "I never took you for a martyr, Ryan Colton."

His gaze narrowed. "I'm not."

"Then let it go." She spoke softly, coughed. Took in more oxygen. He needed to hear this, needed her words. Months ago, this brave man risked his life to save hers.

Now she needed to save his—from any more guilt.

"You rushed into a burning cabin to save me. What if you were too late? Would it have been your fault?"

Ryan looked away. "No. The wood was weathered, shack was nearly engulfed when I arrived. It was timing. Luck."

"Would you have blamed yourself if I died in there?"

He rubbed a hand over his face. "Fern, the comparison isn't the same..."

"Of course it is. Different scenarios, different outcomes,

but you acted the same in both. You did your job to the best of your ability. So what makes mine different from Kate's?"

"I..." Ryan looked away. "You were nearly unconscious. Restrained. I saw you tried to crawl away. Tried to save yourself."

"And Kate? I'm sure she tried to save herself as well. Or did she?"

Silence hung in the air for a minute, broken only by the wind rushing outside the windows, the crackle of the radio. Ryan finally met her gaze.

"I was on the ropes, and I had the carabineer and harness ready to secure her. I told her to remain still. I could see if she moved, she'd fall."

He spoke slowly, reciting the memory as if they were back there in the canyon, his equipment prepared to save the stranded Kate.

"She clung to the rock wall. Didn't even scream. Just looked at me as if she'd already given up. I begged her not to give up, I was almost there, so damn close.

"Kate told me it didn't matter anymore. I couldn't help her. I begged her to hang on. I reached for her, tried to pull the harness around her, kept telling her she was going to be okay."

Ryan swore softly. "She told me it would never be okay. Never told anyone what she said. Not even my captain. Or the chaplain when we talked."

"You held it all inside, because that's what guys like you do. Never show your emotions." Fern understood.

"She struggled and started to slip. I grabbed her hand, told her to hang on."

Fern held his hand, giving him her support, her love. "Kate did not."

Gripping her hand, Ryan didn't say anything for a moment, as if digesting her words.

"She let go."

"And you didn't."

Slowly her words seemed to permeate through to his mind. Ryan squeezed her hand.

"I didn't."

"You did everything in your power, everything you'd trained for, to save Kate."

Finally he looked up. The sorrow lingered in his gaze, but the haunted look vanished. "I did everything."

Fern slid her free hand over his soot-stained cheek, her heart swelling with emotion. "Ryan, something I've learned over the years, when I struggled with drinking, when I remembered how vicious my mom's boyfriend was to me, how my mom walked out with him instead of staying to care for me, her only child. We're all responsible for our lives. You can try to save someone with all you've got, but all the wishes and equipment in the world won't rescue someone who doesn't want to be saved."

"Kate did," he said slowly, closing his eyes. "She wanted to live."

"How can you know that for certain? You tried your best." Fern caressed his cheek. "You reached out to her in her moment of need. You said and did everything right."

His eyes opened, and she saw the pain in them. "Then why couldn't she hold on?"

"Because she couldn't. It's time for you to let go as well. You can't save everyone."

He gave a short, bitter laugh. "That's what Cap says. We can't save everyone."

Fern put his hand over her heart. "But those of us you can and do save, they make it worthwhile. We're the ones you have to keep fighting for, Ryan."

For a moment he closed his eyes again, as if relishing her

touch, her understanding. Maybe as if he sought forgiveness, but for what? There was nothing to forgive.

Knowing he needed her support, Fern clasped his hand. "You did everything, Ryan. You did what you could. What you're trained to do."

Noise crackled from the radio. Ryan squeezed her hand, went to the microphone. He listened.

"Colton out."

Finally. Relieved, he motioned to Fern. "We can leave now."

The smoothness of his expression assured her Ryan finally made peace with his past. She knew the feeling. Life sometimes handed you a heap of trouble, but with the right people along the way, you could free yourself.

She only hoped they could get out of here the same way and move forward.

Chapter Twenty-Three

Ryan wasn't happy with Fern descending the ladder, even taking it slow. The helo would be here soon, and the smoke might blow in their direction, making rescue difficult, if not impossible.

With the drugs still in her system, he knew she couldn't hike out. Even with the right equipment, she might not survive. Wildfires were tricky and, with a shift of the wind, could send flames in their direction.

The helo would safely airlift her to the hospital.

"I'll go first down the ladder and help you," he ordered.

"No, I'll go first before I lose my nerve. I'll be okay with you behind me."

Much as he disliked the idea, he recognized the stubborn lines on her forehead. Part of him wanted to lift her over one shoulder and jog downward.

Part of him was damn proud of her for surviving once more.

But if she insisted on doing it her way, well, there were precautions.

Ryan removed rope carabiners and climbing rope from his pack, then put a safety harness around her waist and a rope. With one of the carabiners, he secured it to his belt.

Next he wound a length of rope around one of the sturdiest poles at the top and attached a strong climbing carabiner.

They went outside, onto the walkway, and began to descend the ladder. Fern was directly in front of him, easing her way down, one rung at a time.

Going too slow, but they still had time. In the distance, he could hear the helo's whirling motor.

"We're gonna make it, honey. You can do this," he encouraged.

Leaning heavily on the railing, she was too unstable. The railing was only a support and rickety...

Suddenly her feet slipped and the railing snapped. Fern screamed and dropped. The rope securing them pulled hard, nearly spilling him as well.

Dangling hundreds of feet in the air, Fern grappled for purchase. Ryan clung to the ladder. He tugged off his glove and reached out a hand. "Grab my hand," he yelled.

"I can't reach!"

"You can!"

Fingers wriggling, she managed to clasp his hand. He couldn't let go. Not going to let go, not going to watch her fall to her death.

Like Kate had. No. Not going to lose her. Not now, not ever. Not after all this.

"Don't you dare let go," Fern screamed at him. "I'm counting on you, Ryan Colton."

Something in his chest eased. Guilt? Relief? He wasn't sure. Didn't matter. "Never," he yelled back.

Ryan swung her around so she directly faced the ladder. "Hook a foot around the railing."

Working with her, talking softly, he got her to steady herself. Fern's eyes squeezed shut.

His mind raced over solutions. In the past, he'd used a Munter hitch on a belay system to lower stranded climbers to safety. The adjustable knot was easy to tie, and self-regulating. Best bet to get Fern down. Her legs couldn't take the strain of climbing the stairs.

Fern was secure for the moment. He opened his pack and began setting up the belay system.

"I'm going to lower you down."

He prayed this would work. Dimly he remembered the rope training Cap scheduled for him.

This has to work.

Ryan glanced overhead. The helo hovered, lowering down a basket. Knew they couldn't hold that position long. Slowly he lowered Fern down. To his relief, she didn't scream or kick or struggle.

Her trust in him was absolute.

Fern's feet touched ground. Relief flooded him. He quickly released her, then rappelled downward. Soon as he reached the bottom, he released the ropes and slung her over one shoulder.

Her lack of protests worried him. He jogged over to the basket, motioning for them to lower it farther. Then he strapped Fern in, making sure she was secure, and gave the thumbs-up to the rescue personnel waiting above.

Not until she was inside the helo did he relax a little. They lowered the safety harness for him. He strapped himself in, and they raised him up.

Smoke swirled around them. "Gotta go," one of the medical technicians yelled above the roar of the chopper. "Wind's shifting."

"I'm in. Let's roll," Ryan yelled back.

He gave a worried glance at Fern, lying so pale and still as oxygen was administered.

Then they were off, flying out of the canyon, in the direction of the hospital.

Toward medical help. He prayed they weren't too late.

Waiting had never been his strength. He knew he lacked patience, even though he'd acquired more of it after years on the job.

Firefighting patience was one matter. Family matters were another.

He'd paced these hospital corridors before. Usually for family, like when they were kids and he'd roughhoused with Jacob and Noah. That one time when Jacob ended up here in the emergency room. All because Ryan had been a little too rough as captain of the pirate ship and made Jacob walk the plank. When Jacob resisted, Ryan gave him a little shove and Jacob landed on the ground. Sprained wrist, not the broken bone they all feared.

He'd caught pure hell for that later, but the waiting to hear if Jacob was okay was worse than the tanning on his bottom.

Waiting to hear if Fern was okay was much, much worse.

Gathered in the hallway with him were a few firefighters and his friend Nick Malone. Nick had gone to the cafeteria to fetch him a much-needed coffee. Ryan had shrugged off medical treatment. Running on fumes and little sleep, exhausted beyond belief, he cared only about Fern's condition. She seemed so fragile, lying on the stretcher as they airlifted her to the hospital and rushed her to emergency treatment.

Nick came toward him, holding a small cup of coffee. Expression grim, he handed it to Ryan.

His stomach roiled. "What's wrong?"

"Not sure if I should tell you this...but one of the guys told me there was a bad wreck on the highway. Two men in a van going fast. They crashed. One died on impact. The other is here, at the hospital."

Ryan uncapped the lukewarm brew, took a bracing sip. At least it was strong, even if it tasted like old socks. "Anyone we know?"

He honestly couldn't take any more bad news today.

"Not really, but someone Fern knows well, unfortunately," Nick said evenly.

It didn't hit him at first. He was so tired, Ryan couldn't make the connection. Then he looked at the anger on his friend's face and knew.

The coffee cup fell from his shaking hand to the floor, spilling liquid over his trousers, boots and the floor.

Ryan stared at him. "Who is it? Which one of her kidnappers?"

"Billy. Leo's dead."

Billy. The man who thought to end Fern's life, left her to burn to death first in the cabin and now in the wildfire. The man who broke her leg. Tormented her. Wanted to sell her as a sex slave.

He managed to speak calmly. "Here, in this hospital?"

Nick nodded. "I did a little snooping. He's conscious, but not speaking to anyone. Clammed up tight. Knows he's in trouble. Right now he's in ICU under heavy guard."

Not heavy enough. Ryan turned to head to the elevators when he spotted his cousin Jacob headed in his direction.

Always intuitive, Jacob stopped him, caught his arm as if he sensed where Ryan was headed.

"Let go." Ryan scowled.

"You heard."

"Yeah, and I owe him a visit for what he did to Fern."

"Easy. Billy's not going anywhere. There's several officers making sure of that."

"Let them stop me."

He wanted to march into Billy's room, punch him, maybe break a few bones and worse, for what Billy had done. Make him pay. Let him know Fern was not alone, never alone, and when you hurt someone loved by a Colton man, you had better make peace with your maker, fast.

"Don't. You're needed here. Fern needs you."

The words calmed him a little. "Has the bastard said anything?"

"No. He's refusing to say anything."

"I could get him to talk." Ryan raised his fists.

"I get it. I do." Jacob placed himself square in front of Ryan. "You have to let the system do its work, Ryan. Concentrate on Fern. She needs you. Please. For her sake."

He tried to control his raging temper,nodded. Ryan managed to speak in a controlled tone. "Nick told me they crashed."

"Courtesy of myself and others. We forced them off the road."

The news made him calmer. Jacob was in control.

"How is Fern?" Jacob asked.

"Don't know. Doc's in with her now. She suffered a lot of smoke inhalation, again, and the drug in her system left her weak and might have caused more damage than we realized."

Anger boiled up, bright and fierce, all over again. "They injected her with ketamine. Not enough to knock her out, only enough to make her disoriented and woozy. But it adversely affected her respiration, and combined with the wildfire smoke…"

Words died in his throat. He couldn't continue, couldn't face the possibility of Fern not recovering from this.

Not after everything she'd endured. *Please, let her live. Let her be okay.*

Jacob looked as if he'd like to deal Billy a little justice of his own. "I'm familiar with the effects. Ketamine is used as a date rape drug. Enough of it can kill."

He felt sick, thinking about how close Fern had come to both.

Jacob studied him. "You okay now? Promise you'll leave Billy to us?"

Ryan nodded. "As long as you promise you'll do everything you can to give Fern and the other victims justice."

"Trust me on this. I want justice for Fern and the other women as much as you do." Jacob's voice carried a deadly edge.

Still, he couldn't relax. Not until Fern was fully recovered and out of this hospital. That reminded him...

"Pete Sanders, the victim in the hazmat fire I saved—got any updates?" he asked Jacob.

His cousin's eyes narrowed. "Burn unit thinks he is not going to make it."

"Sanders apologized, said he got money to lure me there," Ryan told him.

"We believe he started the fire and called it in as a chemical fire to get you there, but it got out of control. Whoever targeted his house and gave him money knew Officer Jenkins lived only two doors down and worried about his pregnant wife."

"And they knew I was the senior hazmat technician and would be there. A chemical fire that posed a real threat to the neighborhood would also tear Jenkins away from guarding Fern," Ryan mused. "Who would know Jenkins lived there?"

"Another cop, maybe. Jenkins knows a lot of police from many departments all over. He used to work in Provo and then Moab before moving here."

Damn. "Fern said Billy dressed like a cop and showed what looked like a police badge at the door, which is why she opened it. Could Billy have gotten both from a cop?"

Jacob shrugged. "Easy enough to fake both these days. You can buy cop outfits and fake shields online. Still..."

His cousin's tight expression echoed the worry in Ryan.

The doctor came out of Fern's room. Judging from the cautious smile, it was good news, but Ryan couldn't relax until he knew Fern would be all right.

"She's young and strong. Smoke inhalation is serious. It

can weaken the heart and cause cardiac arrest, but she was smart in tying the shirt around her mouth to mitigate it."

The doctor gave him a stern look. "Now that you know she's going to be all right, you get yourself checked out. Can't have something happening to you."

Ryan promised he would, soon as he checked on Fern.

Before anyone could stop him, he went into the emergency room bay where she was lying. Fern was awake, looking pale, but her face broke into a smile upon seeing him.

He took her hand, glad for the feel of it beneath his own.

She removed the oxygen mask. "Is it over?" she asked, her voice hoarse and thick.

Gently he replaced it. "It's over, sweetheart. No worries anymore. You're safe now. For good."

If he spent the rest of his life insuring that would happen, he'd be a happy man.

Chapter Twenty-Four

Two days later, Fern was released from the hospital into Ryan's care. Being free from the antiseptic atmosphere wasn't her only concern. Knowing one of her kidnappers had been in the same hospital had been upsetting. She'd found out by accident after overhearing a nurse.

Fern trusted the justice system would take care of Billy. As Ryan kept telling her, she had to focus on herself now.

Officer Jenkins had stopped by the hospital to check on her and apologize for abandoning his post. Fern told him no apology was necessary. If she had a family and they were threatened by a hazardous fire, she'd have done the same.

While in the hospital, Jacob had updated her on the case. The house across the street from Ryan's home had been arson. Investigators found the gas can used in the fire had been purchased from a hardware store in Oso by a man who looked like Billy.

"We believe Billy and Leo set the fire to lure Ryan out of the house so they could grab you. They didn't count on the ammo going off, or the large police presence. Got scared off," Jacob had told her.

The good news was Jacob and his team had finally tracked down Walter, thanks to matching prints the man had left at Dr. Sonder's office. His real name was Timothy Simpson, who had a record for larceny. However, when police went to his apartment in Oso to arrest him, Simpson was dead.

Suicide, Jacob informed her grimly.

Now, as Ryan escorted her into the house, he gave her a questioning look as she stepped inside. Fern braced herself to feel anxiety—for this was the place where she'd been abducted.

Instead, all she felt was comfort. She gave him a reassuring smile as he closed and locked the door behind them.

"It feels good to be here again, with you." She meant it.

The familiar scent of his home—coffee, the tang of spices they both enjoyed, and Ryan himself—embraced her. A weight lifted off her as she headed for the living room.

The sofa where they had first started making love. Fern took a deep breath. Such joyful memories pushing aside the bad ones.

As she sat on the sofa, stroking a hand over the fabric, indulging in those memories, Ryan stood before her. His eyes lit up when he gazed at her, and his smile was welcoming and warm.

"Hey," he said softly, taking a step toward her. "You okay?"

Fern nodded, her eyes not leaving him. She felt a surge of emotion, something tender and almost overwhelming. "Yeah. I… I'm good," she said, her voice trembling just a little.

The house was quiet, but it felt full. Full of peace and security and love, love Ryan brought with him in his big, commanding presence.

She gazed at the walls, worn sofa, bookshelves crammed with reading material, the big-screen television. Everything felt right.

Ryan's house felt more like home than her apartment. More like home than anyplace she'd ever called home.

For a moment she remained still, soaking up the peace and quiet, letting it fill her up. She'd been to so many places in her life—places that never truly felt like home. The hospital had been sterile and cold, and her apartment was merely a place to sleep at night. But this felt like it was made for her.

Ryan sat down beside her, close but not too close, giving her space to breathe but offering quiet comfort all the same.

"Found a good ink shop in town, if you still want to remove this?" He gently touched the dollar sign tattoo on her neck.

Throat tight, she nodded. "I was thinking a good artist could turn it into something pretty, so it wouldn't leave a scar."

The scars inside would take longer to heal, but time would help. Belle, her sponsor, assured her of this. She'd phoned Belle in the hospital and told her everything, including the news she had yet to share with Ryan.

"I have a surprise for you," Ryan said.

He'd heaped gifts upon her at the hospital. A warm blanket his mother gave him for Fern. A favorite mug. A stuffed animal to hug.

"Another one?"

"This one you can't unwrap. I'll go get it."

He vanished down the hallway and returned with a box, placing it in her arms.

A soft whimper came from inside the carton. Fern peeked inside. "Bumper!"

"His foster parents agreed you saved him, so you should be his new owner," Ryan told her as she lifted out the puppy and discarded the box.

The puppy licked her nose, and she laughed. Ryan's wide grin echoed her own feelings.

"Smart dog. He's already worming his way into your heart," he teased.

She set Bumper down, watching him explore his new territory. "I hope he's housebroken. I wouldn't want him ruining your carpeting."

"I'm told that was the first thing they taught him." Ryan rubbed the back of his neck. "Been meaning to tell you, but wanted to wait until you were stronger. Noah, Mark, Ava and I went to your apartment. You lost the lease, so we moved your stuff into storage. Sorry."

Fern shrugged, feeling oddly lighter at the news. "No great loss."

"We can help you find a new, pet-friendly rental in Oso, if you want. If you planned to try to get your job back or another one there."

Ryan looked away. "Although I was hoping…"

His voice trailed off. Then he studied Bumper, sniffing the carpet. "Better put him outside."

They went outside, watching Bumper lope across the grass and bark enthusiastically at the birds at the feeder.

"I know it's not your home, but I wanted to formally ask you if you'd move in with me. I'll understand if you're not ready."

So much like Ryan. Honest and direct. No games, no manipulation.

Time to level with Ryan. "I've been studying medical coding again to refresh my skills. I've been applying all over, and I have an offer of full-time remote work with a large medical practice near Salt Lake. It would mean in-person meetings there, but only for two days a month."

"Salt Lake. Wow. That's quite a distance."

"But worth it. My old job gave me a high recommendation. The human resources director told me they wanted me to start next month. Remote work means I don't have to live in Oso anymore. I can live wherever I wish."

"And what do you wish?" he asked softly.

"I always thought I was supposed to be looking for something…something out there—" she gestured at the mountains "—something I had to find. But I think I was just looking for this. For somewhere I could feel like I belonged."

Fern removed the paper from her jeans pocket. The list was the most important one she'd ever jotted down. "I made a list of things I'm looking forward to. Your sister suggested this when I was in the hospital. A list for my future. So I could find my new direction in life."

Ryan's deep blue gaze remained steady. "Am I on the list?"

She handed it over, her heart thudding hard. "You're at the top."

Barely scanning the paper, he set it down on the nearby table. Ryan reached out, his hand brushing against hers lightly. His voice was low, steady. "You don't have to look anymore, Fern."

Fern's heart skipped a beat. The words settled inside her, filling that empty space. She felt something in her chest shift—a quiet, contented warmth that had been missing for too long.

Barely able to speak for the tightness in her throat, Fern nodded. "I don't need to search for direction anymore, Ryan. I've finally found my way home. It's right here with you."

The joyful smile on his face assured her of that future. Fern went into his open arms. His kiss was deep, soulful and promised passion.

She no longer needed his compass or any kind of GPS.

Fern knew she was exactly where she was meant to be—here with Ryan Colton, the love she'd searched for her entire life.

* * * * *

COMING SOON!

We really hope you enjoyed reading this book. If you're looking for more romance be sure to head to the shops when new books are available on

Thursday 21st May

To see which titles are coming soon, please visit
millsandboon.co.uk/nextmonth

MILLS & BOON

FOUR BRAND NEW BOOKS FROM
MILLS & BOON MODERN

Indulge in desire, drama, and breathtaking romance – where passion knows no bounds!

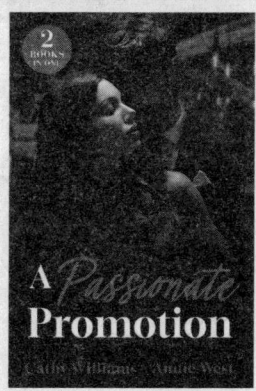

OUT NOW

Eight Modern stories published every month, find them all at:

millsandboon.co.uk

LET'S TALK
Romance

For exclusive extracts, competitions and special offers, find us online:

- **f** MillsandBoon
- **X** @MillsandBoon
- **◎** @MillsandBoonUK
- **♪** @MillsandBoonUK

Get in touch on 01413 063 232

For all the latest titles coming soon, visit
millsandboon.co.uk/nextmonth